# JEFFERSON PARKER

## *California Girl*

D0533162

HarperCollins*Publishers*

HarperCollins*Publishers*
77–85 Fulham Palace Road,
Hammersmith
London W6 8JB

The HarperCollins website address is:
www.harpercollins.co.uk

This paperback edition 2005
1

First published in Great Britain by
HarperCollins*Publishers* in 2004

Copyright © T. Jefferson Parker 2004

The author asserts the moral right to be identified as the
author of this work

ISBN 0 00 714938 7

Set in Meridien by Palimpsest Book Production Limited,
Polmont, Stirlingshire

Printed and bound in Great Britain by
Clays Ltd, St Ives plc

This novel is entirely a work of fiction. The names,
characters and incidents portrayed in it are the work of the
author's imagination. Any resemblance to actual persons,
living or dead, events or localities is entirely coincidental.

*For Tyler and Thomas*
*Long may you run*

# Acknowledgments

Many thanks to Richard Lewis for his fascinating accounts of the Brotherhood of Eternal Love in Laguna Beach. He handed me a wonderful piece of history, and his generosity of spirit and time are both very much appreciated.

Heartfelt thanks to Larry and Nina Ragle, who read an early version of this book and offered me scores of questions, corrections, illuminations, and improvements.

Donald A. Stanwood gave me an incisive and invaluable reading at an early stage.

Many thanks to Chris Evans, director of the Surfrider Foundation. I hope you like the Mexico sequence.

Thanks to Richard Shaner for his insights into religion and the religion business.

For their stories and memories of Laguna Beach and Tustin in the 1960s, many thanks to Mike Schwaner, Randy Hicks, Greg Nichols, and Dionne Wright.

For his comments on the medical aspects of miracles, thanks to Dr Kurt Popke.

Sherry Merryman, Investigative Sleuth for Authors, unearthed a million little things for me, and some big ones, too.

At the FBI, I thank Rex Tomb, Deak DeLoach, and Howard Teten.

I thank Steve Bagley for Corvair Spyders.

Sincere thanks to Robert Gottlieb and everyone at Trident Media Group. You are terrific allies.

Last, but really first, thanks to Rita for everything.

# 1

## *Here and Now*

I drove past the old SunBlesst packinghouse today. Nothing left of it. Not one stick. Now there's a bedroom store, a pet emporium, and a supermarket. Big and new. Moms and dads and kids everywhere. Pretty people, especially the moms. Young, with time to dream, wake up, and dream again.

I still have a piece of the flooring I tore off the SunBlesst packing-house back in sixty-eight. When I was young. When I thought that what had happened there shouldn't ever happen anywhere. When I thought it was up to me to put things right.

I'm made of that place – of the old wood and the rusted conveyors and the pigeons in the eaves and the sunlight slanting through the cracks. Of Janelle Vonn. Of everything that went down, there in October, 1968. Even made of the wind that blew that month, dry and hot off the desert, huffing across Orange County to the sea.

I have a piece of the picket fence from the grassy knoll at Dealey Plaza, too. And a piece of rock that came not far from where *Mercury 1* lifted off. And one of Charlie Manson's guitar picks.

But those are different stories.

Later I met my brother Andy at the Fisherman's Restaurant down in San Clemente. Late August. The day was bright as a brushfire, no clouds, sun flashing off the waves and tabletops. Andy looked at me like someone had hit him in the stomach.

'It's about Janelle,' he said.

Janelle Vonn in the SunBlesst orange packinghouse in Tustin.

Thirty-six years ago, two brothers who didn't look much alike, staring down at her and across at each other while the pigeons cooed and the wind blew through the old slats.

A different world then, different world now.

Same brothers. Andy stayed thin and wiry. Tough as a boiled owl. Me, I've filled out some, though I can still shiver the heavy bag in the sheriff's gym.

San Clemente, and you have to think Nixon. The western White House, right up the road. I picture him walking down the beach with the Secret Service guys ahead and behind. Too many secrets and nobody but the seagulls to tell them to. Andy's newspaper ran a cartoon of him once, after he'd been chased out of office, and the cartoon showed him walking the beach with a

2

metal detector, looking for coins. Thought that was a funny one. I kind of liked Dick Nixon. Grew up just over the hill from us. He was tight with my old man and his Bircher friends for a while, used to come to the house back in the fifties when he was vice president and in the early sixties when he'd lost for governor. They'd sit around, drink scotch, make plans. Nixon had a way of making you feel important. It's an old pol's trick, I know. I even knew it then. In fifty-six I graduated from the L.A. Sheriff's Academy and Dick Nixon sent me a note. The vice president. Nice handwriting. It's still in my collection of things.

But that's a different story, too.

'You don't look so good, Andy,' I said.

Brothers and we still don't look much alike. An old cop and an old reporter. There used to be four of us Becker boys. Raised some hell. Just three now.

I looked at Andy and I could see something different in his face.

'What gives?' I asked.

'Listen to me, Nick. Everything we thought about Janelle Vonn was wrong.'

# 2

## *1954*

'Because the Vonns are direct descendants of murderers, that's why,' said David Becker. 'One of their relatives got hung in Texas. And I saw Lenny Vonn bust a brick with his bare hands once. One chop. That's exactly what he'll do to Nick's head. The Vonns are crazy.'

The Becker brothers. Four of them, walking down Holt Avenue in Tustin for a rumble. June and still light out, the sun stalled high above the groves like it didn't want to come down. Air sweet and clean with the smell of oranges.

Nick was second oldest. He imagined Lenny Vonn's hand crashing into his skull. Wondered how a skull compared to a brick. Nick was sixteen and strong, had played Tustin varsity football as a sophomore, started both ways. Not a talker.

Andy was the baby. Twelve, skinny, buck-toothed. He wasn't officially a part of the rumble but figured there was no way Lenny Vonn could crush Nick's skull. Nick was God.

David, the one who had seen Lenny Vonn break the brick with his hand, was eighteen. He was the oldest and smart but graceless and unformed.

'I'll yank Casey Vonn's head off and piss down his neck.' This from Clay, fifteen. He smiled at each of his brothers in turn, a clean, straight-toothed grin that was both knowing and mean.

Clay had gotten them into this. Grabbed dumb Casey Vonn's new baseball cap and tossed it over the fence to the German shepherd that snarled and snapped and threw himself at the chain link every time the school kids came past. Clay laughed while the dog tore it to shreds. Told Casey he'd throw *him* over next time. Casey so dumb he believed it.

The next day at school Casey's big brother Lenny shoved David hard against the lockers and said it was rumble time for what happened to Casey's cap. Lenny was large and chinless, with an enormous Adam's apple and sideburns like Elvis. Brothers, said Lenny, three-on-three, the packinghouse, no weapons. On David's face, breath like coffee and cavities. David asked Lenny to forgive Clay, said he'd pay for a new hat. Lenny spit in David's face.

The Becker brothers angled into one of the grove rows, walking along the irrigation ditch, clods of earth throwing them off-balance and doves whisking through the sky above them. Nick led the way.

'The Vonns got two sisters,' said Clay.

'Can they fight?' asked Andy.

'Maybe I'll *make out* with them when we're done beating up their brothers,' said Clay.

'They're seven and five,' said David. He knew right from wrong and wrong angered him. He was going off to college in September. He stopped and shook out a Lucky Strike and tapped it on the side of his lighter. Nick saw his hands shaking.

'Gimme a cigarette,' said Clay.

David gave Clay the pack and lighter. He lit one and put another behind his ear.

'Me, too,' said Andy.

'No,' said Nick.

'I don't want to do this,' said David. He coughed. He'd spent hours the night before praying for courage.

'Fine,' said Nick. 'It'll be me and Clay.'

'I can fight,' said Andy.

'No,' Nick and David both said.

Clay's cigarette looked good so Nick plucked it out of his mouth and took a puff.

Nick saw by the look on his face that David didn't want his baby brother to see him get his ass kicked.

'Keep your hands high,' Nick said. 'If we stay back-to-back we'll be all right.' Like there was a science to this kind of thing.

The SunBlesst packinghouse sat behind the railroad tracks in the middle of the grove. The tracks marked the city limits but everyone thought of the packinghouse as being in Tustin. It was a big wooden building with a metal roof and twenty-foot-high metal sliding doors that let the conveyors swing out to the freight cars. The wood was black with creosote. On one of the doors was a giant painting of one of the Sun-Blesst orange box labels. It showed a raven-haired beauty holding out a perfect navel orange and smiling. Behind her were rows of orange trees. The sky above the trees was indigo blue and the words *California Girl* charged out of it in bright yellow letters. Once someone had left a flatcar of labels outside and the Becker boys threw them into a Santa Ana wind that blew them all over town, onto the lawns and streets and school yards, and everywhere he went for a week Nick saw that pretty woman offering him an orange.

The Vonns were waiting for them by the railroad tracks. Lenny had his T-shirt tucked in tight and his cigarettes rolled into his right shirt-sleeve, Levi's cuffs rolled into two-inchers, work boots. His brothers more or less the same. Black hair and big round ears. Lenny flicked his smoke into the gravel and stared at Nick.

Nick figured it was him against Lenny, Clay against Casey, and David the oldest against the middle Vonn kid, Ethan. 'What do you say, Lenny?' he called out.

'I say fuck you.'

'That's all?'

'And your whole ugly family.'

Casey Vonn laughed. Then Ethan.

Nick stopped at the bottom of the railroad berm, where the gravel led up to the ties and tracks. David and Clay came up beside him. Sweat rolled down David's cheek. Nick turned to see young Andy hanging back in the orange grove.

'You know, Lenny, we could just apologize to you and not fight.'

'It's too late for apologies. The dog ate the hat. It was new.'

'Then you apologize to us,' said Clay. 'How about that?'

'For what?' asked Lenny.

'For being so dumb,' said Clay. 'Look at you dumb shitheels trying to be cool.'

War screams, then, and gravel chattering and dust rising as the Vonns hurled themselves down the berm.

Nick figured on a left from Lenny because of where Lenny kept his cigarettes. Lenny flew toward him and Nick stepped away and got him with a left hook. Lenny wheeled and came back at him and Nick drove a straight right into his nose. Felt the crack. Lenny went to one knee, wiped the blood off his face, and looked at it. Pouring like a faucet thrown on.

'Gung fuggin kiw you.'

The blood unnerved him and Nick let Lenny

8

stand up. Knew it was a mistake but let him up anyway. He caught Lenny coming in with a big left haymaker that landed high above the ear and sent a bullet of pain up his hand.

Then someone clobbered Nick from behind and he was down before he felt or heard it. Looking back, he saw Clay pummeling Casey, David down and looking his way but no opponent in sight, Andy still watching from the trees. Then a shadow falling above him and Nick understood someone was about to club him again.

This time he heard it. Ethan behind him with something big and heavy. Felt the jolt, then the loud whine in his ears. Lenny kicked him in the face. Kicked him again in the ribs. Nick felt the fight huff out of him.

Clay slugged Casey one more time and climbed off. Saw Ethan Vonn swing the short thick branch at Nick and his brother crumple like something dead and Lenny kicking him hard.

Clay covered the distance fast and jumped Ethan the clubber from behind. They fell onto Nick and rolled off. Clay came up with the club and caught Lenny low. Lenny stumbled back, two disbelieving eyes wide open through the blood as Andy rocketed through the air and knocked him to the ground.

Ethan struggled to his feet, turned, and labored up the berm.

Nick got himself upright as Lenny shrugged off

Andy and sidled away, half crawling and half falling after his brother.

Clay kicked at him but missed.

Andy, on hands and knees, breathed fast and hard.

'Yer fuggin dead,' said Lenny.

'Yeah, yeah,' said Nick.

'Dumb shitheels,' said Clay.

Nick picked up the club, then took a knee like they did in football. His head hurt and he felt the vomit stirring inside. He watched two Lennys make the top of the berm, faces and sideburns and shirts soaked in blood. Twin Caseys clambered up next, both blubbering, eyes swollen and lips cut. He felt a hand on his shoulder and he knew without turning it was David.

Nick looked up to see four girls looking down at him from the tracks. Then just two. The bigger one had brown braids and wore a dirty pink blouse. The younger one was dark-haired and dimpled and had an inquisitive look on her face.

The older one stepped down the berm a few feet toward the Becker brothers and launched a white rock that flew wild. Then another. She scurried back up and ran away.

The younger one followed her sister's footsteps almost exactly. She had a faded blue dress and a red ribbon in her hair and a pair of scuffed brown cowboy boots. An orange in each hand. The SunBlesst girl's baby sister, thought Nick. Looked about five.

'I am Janelle Vonn and those are my brothers,' she said.

She dropped the oranges and scrambled back up the gravel and out of sight.

# 3

That night Max and Monika Becker loaded their four sons into the Studebaker and drove across town to the Vonns' house. The Studebaker was a green fifty-one Champion with the big conical nose for a front end and an oddly sloping rear. They called it the Submarine. They cruised along Holt Avenue through the groves, Max erect behind the wheel and Monika's straight yellow hair lifting in the window breeze.

Nick sat on the scratchy backseat, felt his knuckles throbbing all the way up into his ears. Still seeing double sometimes, his neck thick with pain and a big lump risen on the back of his head. Didn't say anything to his parents about the vision trouble because he hated doctors.

David sat up front beside his mom, thinking he'd be glad to get to State, out of this stupid small-town stuff, into something more than oranges and fistfights.

Clay sat in the back, pummeling Casey Vonn

12

again between thoughts of this Dorothy girl in his homeroom. Wished he could smoke like his dad was doing. The Vonns were shitheels.

Between Clay and Nick, young Andy sat with the pride of the new warrior, his heart beating hard and true. He had fought alongside Nick, and they had won. The world outside the windows of the Studebaker now seemed not only larger but more attainable.

The Vonns' house was old but it sat right around the corner from a new tract freshly cut from an orange grove. The house was wood – not stucco like the new ones – and the white paint was peeling and the roof sagged and two of the windows were plywood. The lawn was just dead weeds. The new tract had streetlights but they stopped short of the Vonn place.

'We're staying here, boys,' said Monika Becker, turning her pretty face to the backseat.

'I'm not going to apologize,' said Clay.

'You'll do exactly what your father told you to.'

'I won't mean it.'

'That's another topic, Clay. For now, keep a civil tongue in your head and mind your manners.'

Nick watched his father flick his cigarette butt into the curb and start up the dark driveway. Khaki trousers and a white shirt tucked in with the sleeves rolled up. Irish Setter boots and a belt the same color. Nick had always liked the old man's walk: loose and casual but his head always up and steady. His father didn't miss much. He could tell what was wrong with an orange grove by looking at one leaf from it, tell a grower how to up the yield without running down the sugars or ruining the soil. Hardly needed his lab over at the SunBlesst corporate building for things like that. He could see his wife's depressions coming days before they hit, would rearrange his work hours to be there for her. Or, if they stood in the corner of an orange grove in early September with their Remington pumps, it was always his father who saw the birds way out in the blue, his father who could tell a dove from a nighthawk through a hundred yards of twilight. And of course he'd knock it down before you were really sure you saw it.

A porch light went on and the door opened. Nick saw a small woman, then a tall man with overalls and no shirt. The woman's hair was dark and pulled back tight. She looked older than his mom, but Nick figured they must be about the same age. Mr Vonn had long, active muscles that bunched when he shook Nick's father's hand. A dark triangular face, small chin. He looked to Nick like a man from another country.

Nick listened to their voices through the open window of the Studebaker, but he couldn't make out much. His father gestured back to the car, canting his head inquisitively. Then Mr Vonn disappeared and Mrs Vonn turned and watched. She brought her hand to her collar. A minute later the three Vonn boys came single file onto the porch – Lenny, then Casey, then Ethan. Casey's eyebrows and cheeks were covered by white tape.

'Oh my gosh, boys – what did you do to that poor Ethan?'

'That's Casey,' said Clay.

'Don't confuse the issue, Clay.'

'They started it, Mom,' he said.

She snapped around and caught his face in her big hand. When she was angry her voice went to a throaty hiss and her lips pulled back around her big straight teeth and Nick thought she was scarier than his dad. *You started it, Clay. You started it with the baseball cap and your arrogant attitude. Don't you lie to me.*

'No, ma'am, no.'

'Someday someone's going to rain on your parade in a big way, Clay. That, I guarantee. And when it happens we'll see how tough you are.'

Then Max Becker turned to wave them out of the car.

Monika locked eyes with each of them in turn. 'Do not disappoint me, boys. Do exactly what we talked about.'

They stood behind their father on the porch, spread in the pool of light. The Vonn boys faced them from a few feet away. Nick saw that Casey's face was swollen badly and Lenny's nose was huge and red. Their big ears were backlit pink by the porch light. He saw that Mrs Vonn's knuckles were big where she held her collar and stared at him with shiny black eyes.

Clay apologized unconvincingly but handed Casey a dollar to cover the baseball cap. Said to give him the change at school.

Max Becker cleared his throat.

David and Andy said they were sorry.

When it was Nick's turn he was looking not at the Vonns but beyond them, into the living room behind the open door, at the peeling walls and sagging brown sofa and the floor lamp with the dented shade and the fraying braided rug and the cheap lighted china hutch with nothing inside it but a few coffee mugs and votive candles and a collector's plate with the face of the Virgin Mary on it displayed upright in the flickering light.

He had never seen such failure before. And he understood in one instant that it could be his someday.

'I'm sorry,' he said. He meant it for Lenny but couldn't take his eyes off the room.

The Vonn boys didn't say a word. Nick figured they were thinking revenge.

Just then the Vonn daughters hustled into his vision, the older one still in her dirty pink blouse, holding a cob of corn and glaring at him. Then Janelle Vonn, changed into a white dancer's tutu that hung almost to her knees, clunked across the floor in her cowboy boots with a small guitar slung over one shoulder. She had the same inquisitive look she'd had out in the orange grove, and one eye swollen shut and blackening.

'I'm sorry,' Nick said again.

Mrs Vonn turned back into the house and the girls scattered away like chicks. The door slammed.

His parents said nothing on the drive back home. Nick could tell that a new worry had taken ahold of them. Not the rumble. That was over now. Their dad had locked their shotguns in the gun cabinet and told them there'd be no bird hunting this year. Said that boys who couldn't control their fists couldn't be trusted with firearms. Pretty goddamned simple. Backhanded Clay hard above one ear, sent him spinning. Would have taken a belt to them like the old days, but even Andy was too big for that now.

No, the new worry was Janelle, and how she'd gotten her eye closed. Nick was pretty sure it was connected to him hitting Lenny. And Clay hitting Casey. And Ethan hitting David. Maybe even his father hitting Clay. Each hit causing the next one until there was no one left to hit but a little girl with a tutu and a guitar.

# 4

## *1960*

Andy steered the submarine up Red Hill Avenue, into Lemon Heights. Meredith sat close beside him, her hand on his knee. Through his jeans he could feel the exact shape of her palm and thumb and each finger. He tried to open his leg a little, invite her hand to go farther up, but he had an accelerator to work and she'd never moved much north of his knee anyway. Wasn't going to in the middle of the day, heading home from school. That was for sure.

'Lots of homework?' he asked.

'Not really.' She wore a pleated skirt and a sleeveless white blouse. It was almost Thanksgiving, sunny and warm.

'I'll come by after work if you want. We can go to Oscar's.'

'Okay,' said Meredith.

'After that, there's a meteor shower,' said Andy. 'We can watch it from our spot.'

'Sounds fun.'

Andy downshifted and made the left onto Skyline. Meredith had removed her hand from his leg but he could still feel it there, warm and soft and a little damp. He was preposterously aroused now, as he was every time he drove her home. Every time he sat in a car with her. Held her hand. Thought about her. Dreamed about her. Smelled the sweater she had let him borrow – Heaven Sent perfume mixed with Meredith. She was sweet and bright and the most beautiful girl Andy had ever seen.

Lemon Heights was where the rich people lived. The heights were rolling foothills with eucalyptus and avocado and sycamores, even a few lemon trees from the old days. The houses were big and each one was different, not like the tracts expanding below, where two or three floor plans repeated themselves up one street and down the next. Some had swimming pools and tennis courts. There were horse stables and garages big enough for two cars. A color television set in every house, and Andy had heard that the Boardmans had two.

He pulled into the Thorntons' driveway. It was a large semicircle lined with sycamore trees that were just starting to turn yellow with fall. The house was brick, low and large, with white trim and the window glass darkened for the Southern California sun. The driveway circled around a knoll of deep green dichondra. In the center stood a thirty-foot flagpole. Dr Thornton flew the stars and stripes every day except when it rained.

'No one's home,' she said. 'Would you like to come in?'

They stood in the cool shadowed kitchen and kissed. The swimming pool threw wobbling crescents of light through the sliding glass door to the walls.

He grasped her wrist and tried to pull her hand down but she broke it loose with a soft laugh and put her arm back around his neck.

'No,' she said. 'I more than like you but I'm not ready.'

'I know. I understand.'

Andy did understand, and the decision was hers. They kissed for a few more minutes. She pulled her lips away from him just as the warm slick issued into his briefs.

'I have to use the bathroom,' he said.


The *Tustin Times* office was back across town, by the high school. Andy sat at the editor's desk and used the big black Royal to write the obits for the week.

*Joe Cannon, Former Engineer and School District Trustee Dead at 77*

*Early Tustin Needlepoint Artist Remembered – Lacemaker Commissioned by Eleanor Roosevelt*

*Dr Richard Riley Healed Congolese Every Easter*

Beth Stevens sat at the Arts and Culture editor's desk across from Andy. She stared at the paper in her machine, tapping her fingers on the keys but not hard enough to engage them. Like him, she was a high school senior hired for eight hours a week, after school was out. She was tall and freckled and moved quickly.

'What's another word for blue?' she asked.

'What shade?' he asked back.

'No, blue as in unhappy.'

'Melancholy.'

'I already thought of that.'

'Sad,' he said.

'I already thought of that, too.'

'I'm trying to write, Beth.'

'But all you can think about is *Meredith*.'

He looked up. Beth's unpredictable and direct assaults always caught him off guard.

'I don't care if you don't like her,' he said.

'Name one intelligent thing she ever said.'

The Linotype roared into action in the basement. Andy felt the vibrations and heard the rattle of the Royal's ribbon spool.

'She read *Les Misérables* in French and wrote a paper on it.'

'And the paper was in *French*, too?'

'Yes. It was good.'

Beth was quiet for a while. She typed furiously, stopped, then typed furiously again. Andy was always amazed at how fast she could type with hardly any strikeovers.

Beth ripped the paper and carbon from the platen, straight up so it would make lots of noise but not tear. From the corner of his eye he saw her place the original in one tray and the copy in another.

'She'll be fat someday, like her mother.'

'I don't care.'

'You're sickening, Andy. When it comes to her.'

He shrugged, felt the cool spot down in his pants, but didn't look up. Thought of Carol Thornton's calves, the alarming bigness with which they disappeared into her skirts. And her arms above the elbows. Meredith looked nothing like that.

Andy found Gunnar downstairs working the Blue Streak, setting the week's editorial. The room smelled of hot metal and machine oil. Gunnar was a small, pointy-toothed Swede with fingers blackened by decades of typesetting and printing the *Tustin Times*. Andy thought that Gunnar looked old and somehow permanent sitting before the big machine. He'd seen Gunnar, sitting right here, almost every week since getting a paperboy's route five years ago. When he had just turned thirteen.

Andy watched him touch the keyboard, then saw the brass letter molds drop from the magazine to the travel belt on their way to the holder. Then the spacebands falling into place at Gunnar's deft, strong strokes.

Gunnar swiveled out of his chair, crouched across the room, and locked the door. Then to his desk where he removed a bottle of vodka and two small glasses. He poured them half full and gave one to Andy.

They clicked the bottoms and sipped. 'Andy, I liked the Garcia story,' he said. 'He was a mean old man but you made him tolerable.'

'Thanks,' said Andy. He'd been worried about the Garcia obit, wondering if he'd gotten enough truth into it. 'Maybe a little heavy on the creative writing.'

'You know, he advertised with us for twenty years, always paid his bills. We can afford to let you polish him up.'

Andy nodded and sipped more vodka. His father and mother were liberal drinkers and Andy felt at ease with the stuff, like it was natural for him to drink it. Actually liked the flavor. Never felt thick or out of control. Just stabilized. With a slightly lower center of gravity. Sometimes a little goofy. Though J.J. Overholt, the *Times* publisher, would fire them both in a heartbeat if he walked in on this. Overholt didn't drink.

'Nixon was in again yesterday, talking with J.J.,' said Gunnar.

'Amazing that the vice president of the United States has time for the *Tustin Times*,' said Andy.

'He wants to be president. Badly. He'll do anything.'

'Stoltz with him?' Andy asked. 'Stoltz is the guy who's going to be president.'

'No, no. Stoltz just wants to make money and fight Communists.'

'Stoltz got Nixon this far,' Andy said with conviction.

Andy wanted to know things. He read the *Los Angeles Times* and the *Santa Ana Register* and every magazine he could get his hands on. Listened to the L.A. radio news while he did his homework. Liked the politics. Thought he was getting to know the way things worked.

'No, no he didn't,' said Gunnar. He smiled his pointed smile. 'He just wrote some speeches for him during Ike's campaign. Nixon will court the extreme right wing privately, but he can't afford to be seen with them. If you know what I mean.'

Andy thought about this, sipped more vodka. The Linotype machine cycled through, fresh slugs cooling in the bin. Andy looked at the hard lines of type, wondered again how Gunnar could read so well backwards. Gunnar would catch mistakes the editors didn't see. Things even Overholt missed. Collected a quarter each for them, which kept his secret bottle full. The amazing part was that when he was done with all the physical and mental effort of setting type, Gunnar ran the press, too.

Upstairs Beth pounded on her Royal. Sounded like a machine gun. Gunnar looked up, shook his head, and smiled.

Then his smile subsided and he locked his cool gray eyes on Andy. 'You haven't heard about Alma Vonn?'

Andy waited.

'Killed herself with gin and rat poison. Dead when the girls came home from school today.'

Andy thought of flying through the air and into Lenny Vonn six years ago. Of the blood running down Casey's face, of the girls on the tracks by the packinghouse. He remembered how shabby the Vonn house had been and he remembered his father saying later that trouble had chased the Vonns to California and trouble would probably find them here again. He could still picture how tightly Alma Vonn's hair was pulled back that night. He'd seen her since then, peddling his J. C. Higgins past their house on his paper route. The Vonns had never subscribed. And Alma Vonn had looked at him plenty of times but never once shown him any recognition.

'I've never written a suicide obit,' Andy said.

'Some papers admit the suicide, and some cover it up,' said Gunnar. 'J.J. decides for us. If the person wasn't noteworthy, J.J.'ll usually just leave out the suicide part.'

'Yeah, I know.'

Andy raised his glass and finished off the vodka. Wondered if J.J. Overholt and the Vonn girls might have different ideas about who was noteworthy.

Gunnar finished his, too, and collected Andy's glass. 'Did you like *The Dwarf*?' He'd loaned Andy the book a month ago.

Andy had grown up believing that written words were to be respected. That some were even sacred. An enthusiasm for words was in his blood but he didn't know how it got there. The Beckers had a big bookshelf in the living room but his mother and father had never talked directly about writing. It was just something natural, like his taste for alcohol or his limitless desire for Meredith Thornton.

'It was great, Gunnar.'

Gunnar smiled, pointed teeth in a lined and somewhat wicked old face. 'I knew you would like it.'

After burgers Andy parked on the street and took Meredith into the little orange grove not far from her house. The night had cooled sharply and she wore her long red overcoat. They came to their clearing and Andy spread the blanket. He lay down first, then Meredith arranged herself next to him with a kind of gentle formality. They could see the house lights of Tustin scattered below, and the black acres of the groves.

'I really like you, Andy.'

'I like you, too.'

'It's nice to be up here with you.'

A meteor with a tail sailed across the sky, left to right, the tail dissolving behind it. Then another, in the opposite direction. Some were just short flashes, like sparks.

Andy watched the meteors drop and skate through the darkness, thought of Alma Vonn and her daughters. Wondered how it had happened, who had walked into the bedroom, had she knocked? Or maybe Mrs Vonn was in the bathroom or the garage. How old were those girls – ten, twelve? He wondered what type of rat poison it was, where she'd gotten it, how much of it she'd taken. When did she decide to do it? What was she wearing? Anything playing on the radio? Was it painful? Did she turn a color? Did she regret it? What finally made her do it? Did a vision or some review of her life take place?

He was looking forward to writing this obit more than he'd looked forward to writing anything in his life. Alma Vonn was a door to the world, and he could push through it with questions and words. He would be closer to understanding. Closer to wisdom. The power and strangeness of this made his heart flutter, then gallop.

'What are you thinking about?' asked Meredith.

'I don't like it when you ask me that.'

'I know you don't. But if we're together I have a right to know.'

Andy wondered why thoughts weren't private. Weren't you just a prisoner if you had to surrender your thoughts on demand? 'Alma Vonn killed herself today.'

Meredith pushed up on one elbow. 'That's so terrible! Absolutely terrible, Andy. I feel so bad for those little girls.'

He watched two meteors fall side by side like

27

sparks from the same firework. She settled one arm across his stomach and her head on his chest. She began crying.

Andy watched the meteors race and fall. Eighteen. Nineteen. He listened to Meredith's sobs and wondered at her capacity for joy and sorrow and empathy. He wasn't sure if it was larger than his or if she just had more noticeable ways of expression. He felt the wholeness of her. Thirty-five. Thirty-six. So what if he'd written most of her paper on *Les Misérables*? Meredith had labored through every word of the novel in French, and language didn't come easy to her. Like it did to him. Or his brother Clay. Fifty. Fifty-one. But she had understood it. Her emotions had been genuine and exactly what the author had intended her to feel, in his opinion.

A dry cool breeze picked up from the east and the meteors were everywhere now, crisscrossing the darkness in sudden arcs, boring into the sky.

'It's almost scary how many of them there are,' she said.

'I lost track.'

'I wonder what would make her do that,' said Meredith. 'They seemed like a nice enough family.'

'Dad said trouble would find them anywhere.'

'Like Jean Valjean.'

'The Vonns are more complicated than a novel.'

'Oh.'

She stood and looked down at him. Her long

red coat showed up clearly in the dark and Andy would never forget that color. Like there was some special light on it. Behind her the sky was dizzy with silent meteors.

'Don't hold it against me,' she said.

'Hold what?'

'That I'm not ready and you are.'

'I know it's different for you.'

'How?'

'You lose something.'

She nodded almost imperceptibly and the breeze lifted her fine golden hair. One wing of her red overcoat collar had come up and stayed up, which gave her a slightly disorganized look. Her hair shined more brightly than it should have. More of that special light. Andy felt his breath catch in his throat.

'Then don't bully me, Andy.'

'I'm sorry. I won't.'

'I love the falling stars. I made a wish on every one. A whole lot of them for us.'

'I made some for us, too.'

# 5

The Becker brothers all made it home the day before Thanksgiving. David flew into L.A. from San Anselmo's School of Divinity near San Francisco. Nick and Katy drove over from their place in Santa Ana near the jail, where Nick worked. Clay and a new friend, Eileen, came down from the Army Language School in Monterey.

David had the idea to invite the Vonns to Thanksgiving dinner. Because it was the Christian thing to do, he said. Because he had visited and ministered to them and they were in shock and pain. David had changed since San Anselmo's. A new confidence in himself and his calling, a neat new mustache.

Clay said with a smile that Alma Vonn was lucky she'd never have to see the rest of her family and he didn't want to, either.

Monika Becker said Clay had the face of a movie star and the soul of a devil and Clay smiled.

Nick said why not – the Vonn brothers had all moved out. It was just the girls and the dad.

Andy thought it was a great idea but he didn't say why.

'Decided,' said Mr Becker. 'David, you make the call. Do it in person, not over the phone.'

Half an hour later the Studebaker rolled back into the Becker driveway. David strode into the house to say that Karl Vonn and he had prayed together. To David's great relief and surprise Mr Vonn had then accepted the invitation to Thanksgiving dinner tomorrow. He and the girls would come early afternoon, because the Beckers liked their turkey early.

'Don't you say one word,' Mrs Becker said to Clay.


Andy was thrilled to silence at being seated across from Karl Vonn. Andy could feel the heat of life and death and heartbreak and suicide coming off the man. Like he'd just come back from a spectacular battle. But Andy couldn't think of anything to say that wouldn't seem impolite or just dumb, so he studied Karl Vonn's ears and outdated clothing while Meredith made easy conversation with him. Karl told her about the 'seemingly never-endin'' ride on the Sunset Limited that had brought his family of seven across the state of Texas to California.

'I love Union Station in Los Angeles,' said Meredith.

'Oh, the tile on that floor's nice,' said Karl Vonn.

Andy drank another glass of wine while Nick talked a little about the Orange County jail, where he worked days. Nick still wasn't much of a talker, but he said the jail was getting too small. The way the county was growing they'd need a bigger one soon. Either that or you let inmates out early to make room for new ones, which wasn't exactly what the people expected when they sent somebody to jail. To Andy, Nick wasn't God anymore, but Andy still liked his big brother's good face and muscles and the calm sarcasm of his mind.

Nick's wife, Katy, blue-eyed and blond and eight months pregnant with their first, watched her husband with what looked like reverence. Andy couldn't figure if she was rationally impressed by Nick or maybe a little simple.

'I'm so happy to see him walk in from work and put that gun away,' said Katy. 'I know for the rest of the day nothing bad can happen to him.'

Andy saw Karl Vonn go extra quiet when Nick spoke, figured that Karl had seen some of that jail stuff from the other side.

After a brief but elegant prayer of thanks, David leaned his tall thin body back in the chair and looked at the Vonns with a bright-eyed eagerness. Like everything he was about to hear would be interesting. Like he really cared. He sat across from Janelle and Lynette Vonn and listened to their stories from sixth and eighth grades, respectively. Heard about friends, snobs, boys, the plan to get a horse someday. Andy liked the strength in David. The strength it took to care about people. Thought his oldest brother had a kind of glow on him. Andy heard him tell the girls to start diaries as a way of understanding their lives.

'And a diary is always a good place to keep a secret,' David said with a pleasant smile.

'Do you young ladies have secrets already?' asked Katy.

'When they *develop* secrets,' said David.

'Janelle's got a secret boyfriend,' said Lynette.

'And you don't,' said Janelle.

'Girls,' said Karl. 'Let's not talk about all that right now.'

Janelle smiled at David without embarrassment and Lynette looked down at her plate.

'I know a secret,' said Clay. He looked at Karl Vonn. 'Have you heard about the international Communist conspiracy to establish a one-world Soviet government?'

'Some, in the papers,' said Karl Vonn. 'I'm not really clear on how it works.'

'Oh, it works,' said Clay. 'Look at Latvia and Lithuania and Estonia. The Congo. French Indochina. Cuba. The pieces of the puzzle keep falling into place, just like Lenin said they would. It's a war on two fronts – at home and abroad. Khrushchev said America will fall like overripe fruit into their hands. Have you read *Das Kapital*?'

'Too busy at the tire shop,' said Karl.

'Some of us work for a living,' said Nick.

Clay shook his head as if he'd anticipated this answer. He turned to Eileen, his new friend from the language institute.

'Clay's gotten passionate about the Communist conspiracy,' she said. 'He's certainly informed. And I think there's something to it.'

'I do, too,' said Max Becker. 'What language do you study, Eileen?'

'I have French, German, and Spanish now,' she said. 'What the government wants most is Russian and Arabic. I'm good at pronunciation and vocabulary but the rules of grammar throw me because they change by the language. Clay's the one with a mind for lingual structures.'

'And a tin ear for the music of them.'

'No,' she said. 'Really, Clay – your French and German are superb and your Russian is coming along beautifully.'

'Russian for you, too, Clay?' asked Katy.

Clay nodded, sipped his wine. 'Mandatory.'

'What will you do with it?' asked Meredith.

'The government,' said Eileen. 'You know – State Department, Foreign Service, Diplomatic Corps – even military. Wherever they might need you.'

Andy knew that Clay was already being paid by the government to finish his studies at the language institute. The whole family knew, and it had been a day of quiet celebration when news of Clay's acceptance to the institute arrived by special delivery. Roger Stoltz had helped expedite the application through his friendship with Dick Nixon.

Later Clay had told Andy it was a CIA 'scholarship.' He had no way of proving it but Andy believed him. Clay had told him he had applied to the agency. Wanted to do some undercover work, maybe fuck up the Communists without having to go to war or drop the big one on them. But first he had to finish school, and the agency was paying for it because he picked up languages like a dog picked up dirt. And because his grades for two years at UCLA were straight A's, though he never studied more than fifteen minutes a week, tops. He'd taken some firearms training from this old marine instructor, and could outshoot Deputy Nick with both eyes closed. And learned some hand-to-hand stuff that would shrink your sphincter. And if Andy said one thing about it Clay would never tell him another secret as long as he lived.

Andy had kept these secrets because he believed in secrets. They came naturally to him, like taking written words seriously or drinking alcohol or wanting Meredith Thornton, who now, out of sight under the tablecloth, placed a warm hand on his thigh.

Then looked at him with the most puzzling and beautiful expression he'd ever seen.

And though he'd looked into those dark brown eyes for what seemed like weeks at a time, he saw something new in them now, something delighted and determined and full of joy.

'Meredith,' said Clay. 'What are you thinking about over there?'

'I hate it when Andy asks me that,' she said with a laugh. Max and Monika Becker laughed, too. Meredith's face reddened and her hand eased off Andy's leg.

'You're a lovely young lady,' said Clay. 'You're what, a senior now?'

'Thank you. Yes.'

She looked at Andy again. Bloomed into a smile that made his heart stumble.

Then pumpkin pies.

Max Becker talked more about the international Communist conspiracy, and this new organization called the John Birch Society. He'd heard about it from Roger Stoltz, who was starting up a local chapter. It was a group of conservative men and women who wanted to expose the Communists for what they were – subversives, atheists, and murderers intent on ruining the United States of America by undermining the freedoms that made it great.

Monika added that she thought Roger Stoltz was a good man and a patriot and he had promised to come over later in the evening.

Karl nodded agreeably but drifted off into a memory so clear and painful that Andy thought he saw Alma Vonn's tiny image flickering in his black eyes.

Nick put his arm around his pregnant wife and set a hand on her very large bulge.

Clay and Eileen left the table early and changed shoes in the mudroom to take a walk around the property because Eileen was from Maine and had never been in an orange grove.

David smiled through his mustache and helped his mother with the dishes.

The Vonn girls helped Max and Meredith clear the table.

Andy watched Meredith with a vague ache in his heart and a very specific and painful one in each of his nuts.

'She's a beautiful girl,' said Katy. 'You're lucky.'

'I know.'


After the feast Andy asked Karl Vonn if he could talk to him a second on the front porch.

Vonn didn't even hesitate. 'Sure,' he said.

Without asking, Andy poured Karl a glass of wine, then one for himself. They sat on rattan chairs with a round rattan table between them. It wasn't quite dark yet but the porch light was already on. Andy wondered if Karl Vonn's agreeability came from years in prison or jail.

'I . . . I'm very sorry about your wife,' Andy managed.

'Oh?'

'Yes, um-hm. Very.' He felt his words failing him. It was an entirely new experience, and terrifying.

'I still can't believe it,' said Mr Vonn. He took a sip of the wine, but from the way he held the rim of the glass Andy could tell he wasn't used to a wine goblet.

'I'm supposed to write the obit.'

'Obit? Well.'

'May I?'

Andy set his glass on the porch rail and brought a small notebook out of a back trouser pocket. Then a ballpoint from his jacket. He felt a gush of sweat break onto his face and back, and an odd tightness of vision.

'I'm just going to—' He stood and freed himself from the sport coat. He took a deep breath, then sat down, gathered up his pad and pen, took another large gulp of wine. 'Tell me about her, will you?'

'Well, gosh,' said Karl Vonn. He shook his head and looked down, then back directly at Andy. 'That I can't really do, just sitting here with a boy and a notebook.'

'Why not, sir?'

'I think the words would burn your fingers.'

'All I want is a little truth.'

'That's what truth does.'

Andy wrote the sentence, pen sliding off the edge of the little pad in his hurry.

'When was she born, Mr Vonn? What year were you married? Was she happy then?'

He looked long and hard at Andy. Andy looked down from the black eyes to the tight lips and the big pores of the nose and the slightly receding and unhandsome chin of Karl Vonn.

'Born nineteen-seventeen. She wasn't a happy woman. Never was, except for maybe our first year.'

'Why was that?' Andy asked. His heart was slowing down. He was getting a rhythm. Thought of J.J. Overholt always reminding him to get the *why*. The who and what and when and where, but don't forget the *why*.

Vonn studied him again and Andy looked away again. 'Andy, I'm not going to do this. Someday, you want to know about Alma, then you can come by and we can talk some. I know you want something for the paper so I'll write it up when I get home and send it to you at the *Times*. Facts about her. All right?'

'All right, sir.' Andy felt hugely relieved but he knew that he had failed. He took a large gulp of wine for courage and consolation, set the glass back on the porch rail.

Karl Vonn stood and offered his hand and Andy slipped his pen into his pocket and shook it. 'Shaking hands reminds me of something Alma told me,' said Vonn. 'It was after I came back from the Pacific. We were talking about death because I'd seen some. She said she'd be ready to go when she couldn't count her dead loved ones on two hands.'

Andy rolled the words around in his mind. Made sure he had them straight. Eleven seemed like an odd number to come up with but he couldn't help but ask the obvious. 'Did she lose someone recently?'

'Yeah, Irene. A sister back in Brownsville.'

Janelle let the screen door slam shut behind her. She looked at Andy, then at her father. Climbed into one of the porch chairs. Pulled a foot-stool into place, crossed her bobby-socked ankles over the rattan.

'Except Mom didn't love Irene,' she said. 'Didn't love anybody, including herself. That's why she killed herself. Put that in the newspaper if you want.'

'That's disrespectful and untrue,' said Karl Vonn. 'He won't print something like that.'

'No sir, I won't.'

Janelle Vonn stared at Andy. Her nose was upturned and her cheeks lightly freckled and full. She was rounded. Not sharp. Antithetical to her father. Andy was convinced that in some illogical and maybe even miraculous way, Janelle's face was never going to become the drawn, hopeless face of her mother.

'It's better to love everybody,' she said. 'You can't love too much. You can only not love enough. Says right in the Bible. Somewhere. I'm sure of it.'

With this she hopped onto the footstool. Shook her curls for one blurred moment, spread her arms. Then fixed Andy with an unfathomable eye-to-eye look. She tried to make her voice rough and grown-up as she sang:

40

Baby, time will pass you by
But you can catch up if you try
So be whatever you want to be
And, baby, you can count on me.

She jumped off and ran back into the house laughing, colliding with Meredith on her way in.

Karl Vonn watched her go, then settled his black eyes back onto Andy. He sipped the wine with difficulty, still holding the glass by the rim.

'So, you saw a lot of death in the Pacific, Mr Vonn?'

'I killed fourteen up close. That isn't for the paper, boy.'

'I understand.'

'You absolutely do.'

Roger Stoltz and his tiny pretty wife, Marie, came by later that afternoon. Everyone followed them to the living room with their wine and after-dinner drinks and cigarettes. The Stoltzes got the seats of honor, Andy noted – the nice leather recliners his father and mother usually sat in. Max's was blue, Monika's white. His parents and the others arranged themselves in a circle of respect. Karl Vonn and his two daughters were introduced to them. Stoltz smiled at the girls, hugged each one, and touched their arms consolingly. Marie looked into each girl's eyes while she spoke to them.

Andy noted David's obeisance to Stoltz. Stoltz was eight years older than David. Stoltz had helped to arrange a position for David when he was finished with his Presbyterian education. David would be attached to First Presbyterian in Anaheim. This was no mean feat for a young minister. The presbytery in Southern California had too many young ministers as it was, David had told him. Something like three *thousand* too many.

The room swam with voices and faces and the flames from the big fireplace. Andy couldn't get Karl Vonn's words out of his mind, or Alma's words, or the expression on Meredith's face earlier. His shirt-sleeves were rolled up and his tie loosened but he was still sweltering in a room that was apparently fine for everyone else.

He stood next to Meredith and listened to Roger Stoltz hold forth about the Communist threat, how it was so obvious what the Bolsheviks had in mind with the United Nations, and watch Cuba he said, with Fidel and Raúl and Che Guevara down from the Sierra Maestra you're going to have Russian puppets running a country ninety miles off our shore. Khrushchev will try to bring in all kinds of menace, he said – machine guns to missiles – you watch, you'll see.

Andy had heard Roger Stoltz use that sentence before: *You watch, you'll see.* Stoltz's voice was clear and not loud but the timbre of it cut through other voices and bored straight into Andy's brain.

Marie looked ten years older than her husband. Something preserved about her, thought Andy – something halted, like a photograph.

Meredith led him outside for some fresh air.

He followed her off the porch, away from the light and windows. In the darkness of the grove they kissed. Andy felt a determination he'd never felt from her before, the same thing he'd seen in the look she gave him before Clay had tried to claim her attention by embarrassing her.

'Ready to do all this again?' she asked, breaking away, almost breathless.

'Yeah, sure.'

The agreement was they'd do the Becker family get-together early and the Thornton family dinner later.

'I love you, Andy. I realized it, just sitting there watching you and your family.'

She'd never said 'I love you' to him and he knew that these words made all the difference in the world. For the second time that night Andy's words failed him. He was aware that his mouth was partly open and something hard was lodged between his chest and his throat.

'I'm ready now,' she said.

'*Where?*'

'The Serenade. Nobody'll know if we park the Submarine in back.'

'I'll get a bottle of wine.'

'Fantastic. I'll say my goodbyes. I'll hurry.'

*   *   *

While Meredith waited in the Submarine Andy signed the register as Mr and Mrs Neal Cassady. He hoped the name would mean nothing to the middle-aged Mexican woman at the desk. He had placed his Tustin High School class ring on his left hand and spun the black face of it inward so it looked like a wedding band. She did not meet his eyes as she handed him the registration card or handed him the pen or took his cash.

A few minutes later Andrew James Becker pushed open the door to paradise: four walls, a painting of a Mexican casita in a desert, a bath-room, and a bed.

To be kissing Meredith while standing next to that bed was almost too much for him. He went very slowly, helping her with her clothes and letting her help with his, all while his penis seemed to be bellowing at him to hurry up. When she held it for the first time Andy bit his lip and shot immediately. Almost cried with embarrass-ment but she held on to the shocking thing and laughed in a way that made him feel better. He kissed her everywhere while she shivered and shook. He had never imagined such wonderful, powerful tastes and smells. Like he'd wandered into a secret garden.

A little later when she took him inside Andy could tell she was tense and afraid. But she was wet and eager too as she pulled him in hard and got it over with with a faint yelp. She cried in his arms so Andy cried, too, then they found themselves laughing. They held each other and made love again.

Later Andy got his watch off the floor and gave Meredith the bad news.

'I don't want to go,' she said. 'We didn't even open the wine.'

'Let's have a glass,' he said.

'There's no time. But please come here, Andy. There's time for you to hold me.'

# 6

## *1963*

David stood on the crumbling asphalt of the old Grove Drive-In Theater in Orange and looked up at the movie screen. It was early summer and the screen shimmered down at him with white heat.

'What would your church *do* with this property, Reverend?' asked the realtor. His name was Bob. He was sweating hard. A small American flag was pinned on his lapel.

'We have some ideas,' said David.

Bob smiled uncertainly. Wiped his forehead with his jacket sleeve and looked up at the screen again. 'It's been sitting empty for five years. Ten acres. Speakers and speaker stands, playground for the kids, snack bar and kitchen, projection room, everything. The property taxes killed it and the walk-in theaters ended up with most of the business. A management group owns it now.'

The last movie David had seen on that screen was ten years ago, when he was seventeen. Burt Lancaster in *From Here to Eternity*. He and some buddies had climbed the wall just after dusk, run to one of the empty parking spaces and set up their beach chairs, turned the speakers around them all up high, and sat in the chill night while the bullets flew. The theater manager found them half an hour later. Let them stay because most of the spaces were empty anyway.

'You wouldn't have to sweat the taxes if it was church property,' said Bob.

'No, I wouldn't.'

'How large is your congregation?'

'Measure not faith by the bushel,' David said flatly. It sounded biblical and he figured Bob would get the gist of it. The fact of the matter was he had no real congregation of his own. Except for the inmates he ministered to at the county jail. Nick had helped him get that gig.

David had been driving past the old drive-in theater almost every day for the past three years, on his way up to First Presbyterian in Anaheim. First Presbyterian kept him busy with the youth group, let him do some weddings and funerals, but that was about it. David felt the minister was threatened by him. He hardly ever got to preach. Felt like he was wasting his time.

But when he drove past this old theater he always wondered. The speaker stands like rows of neglected crops. Three of the four original screens destroyed by weather and neglect. Nothing but the skeletons of the frames. The one big blank screen still standing, a pointless miracle. Pigeons along the top. The snack bar with the windows broken out. And the sign out front with the GROVE DRIVE-IN THEATER letters busted down through the years to GROVE DRI -IN  HEATER, to G OVE DRI N EATER, then finally to nothing at all.

And the blank marquee over the entrance. Something about that blank marquee got to David, more than the empty screen. It was what he saw when he considered his future as a Presbyterian.

'It's on city sewer?'

'Oh yes.'

'And the hundred-year floodplain ends just south of here, right?'

'That's true – no extra flood insurance to pay.'

And the zoning was right, thought David, and the seismic activity was negligible and the orange groves to the north were going under for tract homes next month, and so were the orchards to the east, and busy Beach Boulevard was one block away and the population of Orange County would double in the next ten years.

And he had the capital commitment from Roger Stoltz's people.

'I'll have an offer on your desk by noon Friday,' he said.

'That was easy,' said Bob.

'It won't be what you're hoping for.'

'The owner in Pasadena is motivated.'

'So is God in heaven.'

\*   \*   \*

Eight weeks later the Reverend David Becker broadcast his first sermon from the leased podium in the Grove Drive-In Church of God. Four worshipers sat on folding chairs in the chapel proper – the former snack bar – to see the first 'drive-in sermon' in person. More important to David were the thirteen automobiles parked outside on the pleasant August Sunday, speakers hooked over their side windows to carry his voice into each vehicle.

'My dear friends,' he began. 'I thank you all for attending this first service of the Grove Drive-In Church of God. God loves you. This is my primary message and it will always be the primary message of this ministry. Please, wherever you are – here in the chapel or out in your station wagon or sedan or maybe in that beautiful Corvette I saw just a minute ago – bow your heads and pray with me. Dear God in heaven . . .'

David had accepted the counteroffer on a Tuesday, arranged his financing the next day through Stoltz's friends at Orange Savings & Loan, resigned from the ministry of the Presbyterian Church (U.S.A.) on Thursday, and spent the next seven weeks scraping, painting, carpeting, slurrying the lot, tearing down the old movie-screen frames, repairing and replacing faulty speakers and wiring, hiring an organist with her own portable instrument, erecting offering boxes accessible through the windows of exiting cars, and creating a series of marquee announcements designed to bring them in by the carload.

When he was finished with his first sermon David stood out by the exit to watch the cars go by. He gave each driver an open and sincere smile. He didn't mean to pressure them into offerings, but if they took it that way, fine. Sometimes that's what it took to coax a little faith from a tight wallet. Dressed in khaki trousers and loafers, with an open-collared dress shirt under a sky blue sweater, David felt more genuine than he'd ever felt inside the Presbyterian robe. And he felt somehow closer to his congregation, too.

All twenty-seven of them, he counted, while he waved and the cars drove away.

When they were all gone he paid the organist. Then he sat on one of the folding chairs in the former snack bar and said a long prayer of thanks. David now suspected that he would not waste his life. He understood that he had answered a risky and unusual calling. He felt that he had just barely, by the grace of God, gotten away with something. It was the happiest day of his life. He heard a car engine growl to a stop next to the snack bar.

After amen he reached down to the offering boxes, which he'd made portable by way of two-piece stanchions and removable hinge plates welded to the uprights outside. He opened them and with one hand removed all of the bills.

'That was a very good message,' she said.

He recognized her immediately. She was petite, with dark red hair cut short. Mid-thirties. Capri pants and big sunglasses and a snug red sweater.

'Funny to see a minister with a big handful of cash,' she said with a canny smile.

'In a drive-in snack bar chapel,' said David. 'But you're not exactly dressed for the Resurrection.'

'The whole point of drive-in worship, correct?'

He smiled and nodded and looked at her. No ring.

'But your message was still good, Reverend. The sermon is everything. If you can't deliver on that, they'll just go to the next place. I'm Barbara Brewer.'

David dropped the bills back into one of the boxes. Stood and smiled. 'David Becker.'

'There's hardly enough there to buy a week of groceries with,' she said. 'For one.'

David studied her. Rested a finger on his mustache and pursed his lips. Furrowed his brow but his eyes were bright with humor and faith. 'I'm very content and thankful right now,' he said. 'It's hard to explain.'

'It shows. And you should be. You just left the Presbyterian Church of America in the dust and nobody knows it but you and me.'

'True. How about breakfast? The Sambo's up on Beach has good pancakes.'

'We'll go dutch. I was the one in the new Corvette.'

'I know.'

* * *

51

After a breakfast that lasted nearly two hours and a frighteningly revealing walk on the beach in Laguna, David took Barbara to the old family house on Holt Avenue.

He pulled the Corvette into the driveway and parked. The house had turned old suddenly, like a once-pretty aunt, as the tract homes grew up around it. The porch looked out of style and the slat construction seemed old-fashioned next to the stucco walls of the subdivision. A year ago groves of Valencias and a walnut orchard had surrounded the old house. Now Barrington Woods.

David made no move to get out. Even the Submarine – waxed and polished as always – had become an eyesore amid the snappy new Ford wagons and Chevy sedans parked in driveways off the freshly poured streets. Barrington Woods smelled of cooling asphalt and sawdust and new-lawn fertilizer. He thought of the way all those years ago the Vonns' house had seemed ugly and futureless to him.

'We don't have to do this now,' she said.

'I want you to meet them.'

'I believe I should.'

Monika smiled when she opened the door and saw them on her porch. It wasn't the big care-free smile that David had grown up with, but a controlled one. In the last year David had sensed in her a new conservation of energy.

While Max, as if siphoning his wife's fuel, got

more expansive and adamant by the month. Max spread his arms and hugged them both. He was wiry and strong as always. David smelled the usual gin and Canoe and Lucky Strikes. Heavy on the gin today.

Monika cut her son a look when he introduced Barbara Brewer as his fiancée.

'Fiancée?'

'Yes.'

'I'll be damned!' said his father.

'I'm happy for you both,' Monika said with another measured smile. 'But David, you should have given me a chance to get ready for this. I mean—'

'It happened quickly,' said David.

'When? This morning?' she asked with pleasant sarcasm.

'It was one-twenty this afternoon,' Barbara said cheerfully.

A brief hesitation while his parents waited for him to say something and David wondered exactly what.

'The greatest of these is love,' he said.

'I'm just awfully goddamned happy for you two, son.'

'Thanks, Dad.'

Max spread his arms and hugged them both again.

# 7

Janelle Vonn showed up for David's service on a drizzly Sunday in mid-November. She slouched in a chair at the back of the snack bar chapel. He recognized her immediately but still couldn't quite believe it was the smart little eleven-year-old he'd invited to Thanksgiving dinner almost three years ago. He'd seen her a few times since then, around town. Each time a little older, bigger, a little more sure of herself. He'd always thought of her as unfortunate.

She was dirty and poorly dressed – jeans with holes in them and a T-shirt dyed in competing colors. Barefoot even in the chill. Hair long, no style. Same black eye that had been swollen nine years ago when he stood on her porch and apologized for his brothers beating up hers. She looked worse than the inmates he counseled at the jail. At least they were clean. In spite of everything she was startlingly pretty and obviously drunk.

After the service was over Janelle wobbled up

to him and plunked herself down in one of the folding chairs. She almost missed.

'I need to talk to you,' she said.

'What's wrong, Janelle?'

'I took some reds and don't feel too good.'

'Red whats?'

'Pills. Downers.'

'Stand up and come with me.'

David helped her up but she folded into him. He got an arm around her and towed her back to the office. The girl smelled strange – human body odor undercut with something green and pitchy and new to him. Her feet were dirty and she wore a toe ring.

Barbara was at the desk making phone calls. She hung up hard and stood. 'What's this?'

David explained as best he could and lowered Janelle onto the big green Naugahyde couch where he napped and wrote his sermons. Got a pillow under her head.

'Can you drink some coffee?' asked Barbara.

Janelle shook her head no. David saw her pupils were large and he smelled the funny green smell again.

'She's high on marijuana,' said Barbara. 'I can smell it.'

'That's what I thought,' said David. He'd read about the stuff, knew it led to heroin addiction, but had never once seen or smelled it.

He put a blanket over her. Barbara stood beside the sofa with her hands on her hips, looking down.

'God, that feels good,' said Janelle. She shivered once and looked up at the ceiling.

David snugged the blanket around her feet, then sat and felt her forehead. It felt cool. 'When did you take the pills?'

'This morning early.'

'Why?'

'Just for fun.'

'When did you smoke the marijuana?' asked Barbara.

'On the way here.'

'You drove?'

'Hitchhiked. He had some. A cool guy. The thing about these kind of ceilings is all the shapes. I can see an octopus on roller skates and a flower growing out of a clown's head.'

David glanced up at the old acoustic ceiling, two decades of shapes and stains.

'What happened to your eye?' asked Barbara.

'What do you mean?'

'It's black.'

'Oh, that. Casey came over.'

David looked at Janelle's dreamy expression, then up to Barbara's sharp, assessing face. Barbara had turned out to be six years older than him and wiser.

'Why hit you?' she asked. 'What did he want?'

David had never heard a silence say so much.

'Nothing,' Janelle finally said.

'But you said no,' said Barbara.

'Yeah. That's all I did.'

David looked at Barbara but she was focused on Janelle.

'Was your father there?' Barbara asked.

'Casey wouldn't a tried that with Dad there.'

'Tried what?' David asked.

Barbara glanced at him quickly but said nothing.

'Just the old thing. No big deal.'

'Does your father know what Casey does to you?' asked Barbara.

'He beat up Casey and Lenny for it. A long time ago.'

'Lenny, too?' asked David.

'He started it.'

David felt a great anger rise up in his chest. He thought of that day by the packinghouse, how he'd ended up on the ground covering up against the blows. How he'd let his man get away to bash Nick with the branch. Wished he could go back, beat the living shit out of Lenny and Casey all by himself. He thought of the long prayers he'd said the night before that rumble, for the courage and strength to fight. Wondered why the Lord had not given him those things.

'We should call the Albert Sitton Home,' he said.

'No,' said Barbara. 'You should call Nick.'

'No cops,' said Janelle. She slapped one hand onto the sofa back to pull herself up. Barbara removed it.

'Make the call, David,' she said.

\* \* \*

When Nick got there half an hour later Janelle was snoring loudly. David and Barbara looked like a thousand other parents he'd talked to in the last year or two. Just dawning on them that young kids were prone to dope and sex. Though from what David had told him this was quite a bit worse.

Goddamned brothers and who knew about the old man. No wonder the mother had done what she did.

David woke Janelle and sat her up. She took one look at Nick and shook her head.

'Tell me what happened,' he said.

'Nick the cop.'

She flopped back to the sofa and pulled the blanket over her face. She moaned.

'That black eye didn't just grow there,' said Nick. He sat down a couple of feet from her. 'Come on, Janelle. Sit up and act like the young lady you are.'

She struggled back up and pulled away the blanket. Her long dark hair washed over her face. She blew a part in it, looked out at Nick. Then she shook her head and the thick hair fell back over her face. 'I kinda dig it like this,' she said. 'Here, in my secret cave.'

'Nice, isn't it?' asked Nick. 'No creeps.'

Janelle nodded.

'No brothers,' said Nick.

'I hate my brothers,' she said. 'It was neat when you guys beat them all up. Ethan's all the way in Florida now.'

Nick smiled and shook his head. 'That was a long time ago.'

'I had the biggest crush on you guys. All four of you, but most on Clay. Where is Clay?'

'Vietnam.'

'Doing what?'

'Advising the government.'

'How old is he now?'

'Twenty-four. A year younger than me,' he said.

'Far away,' said Janelle. 'That's too bad.'

'He'll be back for Christmas. Maybe we could get the families together.'

'Have eggnog with lots of rum?'

Nick looked at David, then Barbara, then at the hair-shrouded fourteen-year-old. 'Janelle, are you going to tell me what happened or sit there and act like a child?'

Janelle was still for a long moment. Then blew another opening in her hair. 'It's no big deal. It's a small deal.'

David said, 'You wouldn't have hitchhiked all the way here for a small deal, would you?'

'True,' said Barbara. 'And a black eye on a pretty girl, that's not a small deal.'

Janelle sighed. She was very still for a long time. When she spoke again her voice was just a whisper.

'I wasn't strong enough. I didn't understand. I . . . *Those pigs.*'

59

# 8

Nick found Casey Vonn at Foothill Rents. Sundays were busy, men bringing back Rototillers and lawn seed broadcasters and backhoes. Casey was in the yard wrestling a trencher back into place. Dirty T-shirt, cutoff sleeves. Oily jeans with a knife on his belt, muscles and tattoos.

Nick had seen him around, mostly on a black Harley hog ripping up and down the Tustin streets like he'd just held up a bank. Big ears and a thatch of black hair.

The warrant check had Casey with drunk in public and an assault that got him ninety days in County. The assault was a while back, just after Nick made patrol. But he remembered it had to do with Casey's motorcycle gang, the Hessians, and Casey had put the guy in the hospital. It figured.

'Hey, Casey Vonn,' Nick said, crunching across the oil-stained gravel. He came from the sunshine into the shade of a big metal port.

Casey didn't look at him. Just rammed the heavy trencher forward. Then yanked it backward, lining it up straight.

'Still a little crooked,' said Nick.

Casey picked a big crescent wrench off the table, flinched, and Nick saw the wrench flying at his face. Turned and took it high on his shoulder. In a flash Casey was over the back fence, running alongside the flood control channel. Nick got over the chain link easy and hit the ground running. Saw Casey up ahead in his clunky boots, figured he'd catch him in less than thirty seconds. Thought: knife. Nick had run down plenty of creeps in the last seven years and it was one of his favorite things about the job, kind of like being on the football field for the Tillers, knowing you had a step on everyone. Or a couple of steps. What a good feeling, to close the distance, see the guy in front of you look back and his eyes get big. Then take him down according to what he'd tried to do to you. This big-eared sisterfucker Hessian with a crescent-wrench greeting card, he was going down hard.

Nick took him low, ramming his shoulder into the small of Casey Vonn's back. Nick held on tight while they fell, then he let go and scrambled quick to get a handful of Casey's black hair and his .45 against the back of Casey's head. When Casey was compliant Nick reached down, flipped open the knife case, and tossed the heavy weapon into a green tumbleweed.

'You're slow as shit, Casey.'

'You're the goddamned football star.'

'Get your hands behind your back.'

Casey was breathing hard and fast. His cigarette box had come out of his pocket and gotten torn up in the fall. There was a trail of broken up smokes and shredded tobacco.

Nick watched Casey's skinned, bloody, grease-stained hands cross submissively on his back. He got the cuffs tight but not too tight, then stood. For a second, looking down, he saw two of Casey. Felt his balance go out of whack for just a second. Ever since the rumble and the branch they used on him.

'You could have hurt me with that wrench, Casey.'

'It got your attention.'

'Janelle is what got my attention.'

'What about her?'

'She told us everything you and Lenny did. She's got a black eye to prove it. You're looking at serious charges, so there's no use bullshitting me.'

'I never did nothing to her and I'm never changing that story. You do what you want, pig.'

'I hate that word for cops.'

'What charges?'

'I know guys who'd kick your teeth out right now,' said Nick. He looked down at Casey. Too easy.

Casey didn't say anything right away. Just lay

with his face in the dirt getting his breath back now. 'What charges, Becker?'

'That's what I need to talk to you about.'

'I never did nothing to her. Whatever she said she's lying. Fuckin' girl drinks, you know? I've seen her put away half a bottle of schnapps, no problem. Lies all the time. Do anything for money.'

Nick put both hands on one of Vonn's shoulders, rolled him over, and sat him up. Cuts on his cheek and lower lip, nothing serious. Casey sat cross-legged and hunched.

'Maybe we can work a deal,' said Nick.

'I'm listening.'

'You tell me everything you and Lenny and Janelle used to do, and I'll make sure you don't get charged for any of it.'

Sirens wailed and Nick thought the timing was great. Stupid confusion crossed Casey's face. Nick could tell he was guilty just by the set of his lips.

'Most of it's probably not a crime anyhow,' Nick said. He surprised himself with the idea. Then went with it. 'It's never been a crime to touch your brother or sister. It's just everyday brother and sister stuff. I know. I got little sisters, too.'

Vonn eyed him. 'What are you talking about?'

'It's just touching, is what I'm talking about. Tell me about the Foot Tickle, Casey. And the Leg Tickle and the Bun Bunny and the Front Bunny.'

'Those are all lies.'

'I told you it's no big deal. It's not even a crime.'

'Then why'd you chase me down?'

'And after that, I want to know about the black eye and the dope.'

'What dope?'

Sirens louder now. More good timing, Nick thought.

'The reds, Casey. Don't tell me you didn't give her the reds.'

'Wasn't me,' he said quietly, looking down at the dirt.

'Lenny?'

Casey spit. 'Ask Lenny about Lenny.'

'I already did and he said you gave Janelle the reds. And Janelle said you gave her the reds. Lots of fingers pointed at you, my friend.'

'They're fuckin' liars, man.'

'That's why I chased you down, Casey. That's how bad I wanted somebody to tell the truth. So just start off with that kid stuff, the Bun Bunny and all that. Just start with one thing and then go to the next.'

'What if I don't? What if I just get my lawyer?'

'That's fine, but I've got to arrest you before they'll appoint one. And lawyers are for creeps like Lenny. So suit yourself.'

Two uniforms came jangling down the flood canal road but Nick told them to wait back by the rental yard.

For the next half hour Nick listened and asked questions. He almost brought out his notepad and pen but he figured that would be enough to spook

Casey Vonn back into the slime he came from.

When Nick was sure he had enough he got the knife from the tumbleweed and put it in his pocket. Walked Casey back toward the rental yard. Nick switched the cuffs to the front and the deputies helped him get Casey over the fence.

Nick told Casey to sit in the back of his unmarked and he'd get him a cigarette. He told the rental yard customers gathered around the car to beat it and they did.

When he'd finished lighting one of his smokes for Vonn, he told him he was under arrest for statutory rape, assault, and narcotics violations.

'You behave yourself, I'll forget about the wrench,' he said.

'You said the tickle and bunny stuff isn't a crime because she's family.'

'Let's ask a jury.'

'You never said nothing about a jury.'

An hour later Nick and two deputies arrested Lenny at his home out in Modjeska Canyon. Took all three of them to pry Lenny out of the bathtub. Skinny as a scorpion and he smelled bad and his eyes had a terrible wattage in them. In the garage Lenny had a nice chopped Harley Panhead with a Fat Bob gas tank done up in flame orange and red. And maybe ten thousand little white pills that looked and smelled like Benzedrine hidden down in some old fishing gear under the workbench.

\* \* \*

On his way home that evening Nick stopped off at Millie's for a couple of drinks. He liked the quiet before returning to the happy, deafening chaos of the Becker family. Willie was almost three. Katherine one and a half. Stevie two months. Katy was big and beautiful and often exhausted.

He opened the door to find Willie screaming and chasing Katherine around the living room. Katherine wailed happily. Katy right behind them hollering for them to be quiet while the baby in her arms screamed in sheer excitement.

Nick reached down and ran his hand through Katherine's hair. He hugged Willie against his leg, brushed his hip holster to make sure Willie didn't have a hand on it again. Leaned into a kiss from Katy.

'How'd it go?' asked Katy.

'Popped 'em both.'

'My hero!'

'My hero!' screamed Willie.

'*My hero!*' screamed Katherine.

The baby wailed and kicked.

'It's nice to be home,' Nick said.

'Got our Sunday—'

'*MY HERO!*'

'*MY HERO!*'

'*WILLIE AND KATHERINE, BE QUIET! I'VE GOT THE SUNDAY PORK CHOPS ABOUT READY, HONEY! THE PORK CHOPS ARE ALMOST READY!*'

She was flushed and pretty. A couple of vodka

tonics into the evening, thought Nick. He liked her that way. Loose and easy and a little goofy. She'd gained a fair amount of weight after three children but Nick liked that, too. Her flesh was firm and cool and it always smelled sweet.

After pork chops they watched *Walt Disney's Wonderful World of Color* in black and white. Nick wondered when the new color sets would get down into the three-hundred range so they could afford one. Five hundred bucks would get you a nice RCA Victor with Vista Color, but they didn't have that kind of money.

They put the children to bed and Nick made fresh drinks and brought Katy one in the small bathroom where she was brushing her straight blond hair. Nick left the bathroom door cracked, lay on the bed, and watched her. He liked to see this, liked the way the just-combed hair stood out before settling back into place. Katy had on her slinky floral night slip, didn't cover much. A loose robe over it. She sat on the counter with her head turned slightly toward the medicine chest mirror, one leg crossed over the other, one foot on the floor flexed to keep her balance.

Nick watched her turn off the light and come toward him. He felt surrounded by complex and contradictory emotions, like bats at dusk, swooping down from different directions.

She got under the covers and turned her back to him. 'I'm tired tonight, honey. Is that okay?'

'Sure. I understand.'

'You, too?' she asked.

'Not tired, really. Lend a guy a helping hand?'

'I really am tired, Nick. Why don't you believe me?'

'I do. I know how it is all day with the monsters.'

'Rain check?'

'Rain check.'

'I love you, Nick.'

'I love you.'

He kissed the back of her head and flipped on the reading light. Picked up an Ian Fleming paperback. Bond got laid every night or so. Nick got laid – had last gotten genuinely laid – thirty-four nights ago. Before that, twenty-eight. A hand job here and there. Nick suspected there was something out of whack with this, but it wasn't the kind of thing you just talked about. Before the children, a whole different story. It had gone out the window when Willie was born and never come back.

Better to just not think about it. Bond wouldn't let him not think about it. Bond pissed him off.

Last night he'd had another dream about the secretary in the district attorney's office. Sharon. Second time in a month. In the dreams he always said something funny to her. In real life he'd never said a word to her except for a hi or two.

He offed the light and got into his robe and slippers. Sat in the rocker in Steven's room and watched the baby sleep awhile. Liked the smells in here. Wondered what an eight-week-old human being dreamed about. Wondered how Clay was doing over there in the jungle. Just one letter, four months back. An advisor. Nick got up and made another drink.

Out in the garage were two of Nick's favorite things. One was a wooden cabinet he had built. It was eight feet high, with double doors and shelves that slid out on ball-bearing runners. He'd painted it red to match one of his other favorite things, their Ford Country Squire station wagon with the wood-look siding. The family called the big cabinet the Odd Box and the wagon they called the Red Rocket. The car was red outside and red inside, too, with red vinyl seats and plenty of chrome on the dash. Nick kept the car inside against the weather and the box locked against the children, though the things inside it were essentially valueless.

He dialed open the padlock and swung out the Odd Box doors. The lower shelves held the dirt collection and the older things. The higher the shelf, the more recent. The top three shelves were still empty.

He glanced at the bottles of dirt from important places. The grave he and his brothers had dug for Jake the collie. The lake where he'd caught his first fish. Soil from Northrup Field, where he'd scored his first touchdown. From Prentice Park, where Katy first told him she loved him. Maui beach sand from their honeymoon. Earth from the Sheriff's Academy range. Soil from the hospital grounds where his children were born. Each bottle was labeled with the date and the location.

And oddities: the toy panda he'd gotten for his second birthday and treasured well into third grade. The first baseball mitt his father had given him, old and shapeless and dark with oil. A pastel drawing he'd won a magazine contest with. A luminous dial pocket watch he'd gotten one year for Christmas. A hummingbird's nest. Fossilized branches he'd smuggled out of the Petrified Forest in Arizona.

And so on. Up through his marriage and his children and his Sheriff's Academy training and his career.

Nick pulled out the shelves one at a time, looking them over for nothing in particular. Just getting the feel of time passing. Of his life going by. A rock from near the *Mercury 1* liftoff. Cool, big daddy. He'd been collecting things longer than he could remember. His mother said she'd never know what his pockets would be full of by the end of the day. She found a baby king snake in his pocket once. A field mouse. A cherry bomb. A handful of live ammunition he'd found out in one of the groves when he was five. Pack of cards with pictures of naked women on them – another orange grove treasure. Nick could never pass up a good souvenir.

He closed up the cabinet, spun the lock dial, and pulled on it once.

Back inside he sat in the living room a minute, listened to the sounds of the house. The Hotpoint was noisy but it sure froze those ice cubes in a hurry. He moved the drapes and looked outside to the houses across from theirs, the driveways and the sidewalks and the streetlights dampened by a light autumn fog. Grape stake fences. Trash cans at the curb. A white Country Squire station wagon and a blue Kingswood Estate and a brown Vista Cruiser and a yellow Colony Park and two green Mercury Commuters. Backboards and hoops above the garage doors. Kitchen lights on at the Fortners'. Off at the Sloans'. Kids in their rooms with baseball cards and Beatles cards and dolls and plastic dinosaurs. Or, one town over, two brothers molesting their sister, mom a suicide and dad not home. Poor girl drugged to the gills, trying to forget about it. Bright girl. Pretty. Dimples. Goddamned tutu and a guitar. A real shame. Nothing will happen to her tonight, anyway. Maybe I did some good.

# 9

Andy read the Vonn arrest reports early Monday morning. He sat in the Sheriff's Department pressroom with Sunday's Contact Log and a paper cup of coffee on the table in front of him. The *Los Angeles Times* and *Santa Ana Register* and the *Orange County Journal* police reporters would be in by eight, so Andy beat them by an hour every day. Scooped them once in a while, too. Almost impossible for a weekly. Like anybody knew it. Like anybody read the weekly *Tustin Times*.

He would have appreciated a call from Nick on this one, even though the *Tustin Times* had a policy against incest stories. Unless teetotaling J.J. Overholt broke his own rule. He had similar policies against rape stories, suicide stories – unless it was a public figure – and sex crime stories. Against almost anything negative relating to churches or ministers. The press club wags said that the *Tustin Times* was allergic to anything alcoholic or interesting.

Andy flipped through the log. The usual public disturbances, suspected prowlers, domestic quarrels, bar fights, false alarms. And drunken driving. Overholt's bread and butter, he thought. Suspected drunken drivers were identified in the *Tustin Times* Law Enforcement Logbook by full name, age, and city of residence in boldface Helvetica twelve-point type. The press club line on that was, death to drunken drivers unless the driver was one of Overholt's friends, but Overholt didn't have any friends.

Andy poked away on his Royal portable. Got four little stories they might use, mainly to fill space around last-minute ads. Made notes on the Vonn arrests.

Later that day, after doing his interviewing, Andy tried to write the Vonn story. 'Brothers Arrested on Morals, Drug Charges.' Top of the pyramid he stated the facts. Made it clear that Casey and Lenny Vonn, twenty-four and twenty-seven, of Tustin, were arrested on *suspicion* of morals and drug crimes.

From David he had gotten Janelle's black eye and intoxicated appearance at the Grove Drive-In Church of God. Barbara told him that Janelle had been barefoot in the chill morning and that the church had had sixty-two worshipers that day, best ever.

From Nick he'd gotten some chase details and the crescent wrench and where the little white pills were found. He included the fact that vice investigator Nick Becker was all-county for Tustin High, 1955–56. Nick told him to be careful with the sex stuff. It was Janelle's word against her brothers'. There was no way the crime lab could perform tests for forced oral cop done months ago, which is what Janelle was alleging. When she wasn't looking at ceilings and having marijuana-induced visions.

The Vonn brothers had refused to talk to him. Their public defenders had no comment.

He had talked to Janelle briefly by phone. She said the whole thing was just a scary mess, what had Andy heard from Clay over in the jungle? He told her what he knew – next to nothing – and thanked her. He couldn't use her name in the piece. Could not state that the victim of the sex allegations was the Vonn brothers' own sister. Janelle was the center of it but she couldn't be seen. Like wind in a windstorm. It was Overholt policy not to name minors as victims or perpetrators of crimes. One of the few of the old man's editorial policies that Andy thought was good.

Sharon in the DA's office had told him they'd review the arrests by late afternoon and file, or not, tomorrow. She asked Andy to say hi to his cute detective brother.

Andy had talked to Karl Vonn again, for the first time since that Thanksgiving dinner when he and Meredith had gone to the Serenade and made love. Karl wouldn't comment on the arrests except to say that his boys were just like everyone else, innocent until proven guilty. In the silence between questions Andy still had trouble meeting the great black eyes of Karl Vonn, widower, father of five, killer of fourteen up close.

But Andy couldn't get more than two paragraphs. It was too big and too raw. No focus. No hook.

He ripped it out of the typewriter, mashed the paper and carbons into a ball, and bounced it off the wall into his wastebasket.

Press club officers and invited members met Thursdays for dinner, drinks, and alleged business. This week it was at a new steak house, Lorenzo's, up in the hills in Anaheim. Some of the *Orange County Journal* execs were part owners so the reporters figured on a deal at bill time. Recording secretary Becker got there early like most of them did, had a couple of cocktails in the bar with the other reporters.

'So Andy, when you going to leave that crummy little paper?' asked Phil Liades. He was an editorial writer for the *Journal*. To Andy an old fart – forty, maybe even forty-five. He'd come out strong for Nixon in sixty and was already gearing up against Kennedy for sixty-four. The *Journal* had blamed the president for the Bay of Pigs failure. And said the Missile Crisis didn't prove Kennedy was tough on Communists, just desperate for respect. Liades wore a little enamel U.S. flag pin on his lapel.

'When you leave your crummy big one,' said Andy. 'Maybe I'll take your place. But then I'd have to write all that glowing crap about Dick Nixon and Roger Stoltz.'

'Pays the bills,' said Phil.

'So can blow jobs,' said Andy.

Phil laughed and Andy nudged him with an elbow. At twenty-one Andy was the youngster. Dropped out of Fullerton after two years but a full general-assignment reporter already. Even if it was just the *Tustin Times*. Andy liked popping off and making waves and seeing what he could get away with. He thought of Janelle Vonn just after this last comment. Of her being forced into things. That wasn't funny. But he told himself that was different. There was real life and there was newspapers. In newspapers this was the way you talked.

'What are you guys laughing about?' asked Teresa Dessinger, squeezing up to the bar beside Andy. She didn't take a stool.

'Jobs,' said Andy. 'Phil wants me to take his. I told him I could write crap for a living but not *right-wing* crap.'

'Lies from the drunk-driving monitor,' said Phil.

'But the *Journal* is changing,' said Teresa brightly.

The Dessingers had founded and still published the *Orange County Journal*. Teresa was a great-granddaughter of the founding couple and daughter of the current publisher. She was tall, auburn-haired, peach-skinned. One year back from Stanford with some fancy business degree, Andy had heard. Barely a year older than him and already editing the daily 'Beach Cities' editions of the *Journal*. She made him nervous and eager to impress.

'When you get to be publisher it'll be perfect,' Andy said. 'Until then, you guys should cover the crooks on the board of supervisors and leave Jack Kennedy alone.'

Teresa Dessinger looked down at Andy. 'I agree.'

'To the new *Journal*,' said Phil Liades, raising his glass.

Andy touched his drink to Teresa's and nodded.

'Would you sit with me at dinner?' she asked Andy. 'I'd like to hear more.'

'Don't give my job away,' said Phil.

'Already told you I don't want it,' said Andy. 'Another drink, Teresa?'

Then back to the bar after dinner. Phil and two others left early. The press club corresponding secretary staggered to the bathroom sick on scotch and sodas. The treasurer drove her home.

By eleven it was Andy, Teresa, and two *Los Angeles Times* reporters in a booth arguing whether a newspaper should print what people want to read or what they need to read. Whether Nixon shaved twice or three times a day. Whether

Castro had been morally right for publicly executing half a thousand Batista thugs or was just another Latin American cutthroat. Whether to put fluoride into California's drinking water and, if so, what next?

Andy gave as good as he got, maybe better. As Andy saw it, he had an advantage: he wasn't really a newspaperman. Wasn't going to be doing this very long. The last thing on earth he wanted was to end up old and drunk and bitter like half the reporters he saw. Sad. Humiliating.

No, he was going to find a way to write that wasn't for some paper that was in the litter box the next day. Some way to get it down fully and with some insight. Some understanding of what was going on under the surface of things. Maybe a book like *The Grapes of Wrath*, or *Catch-22* or *All the King's Men*. Or a movie like *Citizen Kane* or *From Here to Eternity*. Wouldn't it be great to write something beautiful someday?

All of which he spouted off to Teresa Dessinger as he walked her to her car around midnight.

She stood next to her new Comet convertible, a red jewel twinkling in the parking lot light.

'It would be great,' she said. 'But not everybody has the talent to write like that.'

'I'm going to try.'

She put her key in the door and the lock snapped up. 'Come to work for me while you write your book. I can use you on the "Beach Cities" editions. You can have Laguna Beach. It would be all yours. And I can pay you better than Overholt by quite a bit.'

'I disagree with your editorial policy.'

'Fine. You disagree with Overholt's, too. Just write me some news and some features. I'm a liberal editor. Laguna is an interesting town. More going on than in Tustin.'

Andy felt as if someone had thrown open a window. Hell, knocked out a whole wall. More money. More liberty. Better beat. See *Teresa Dessinger* every day instead of J.J. Overholt?

'Give me a few days to think about it,' he said.

'The offer's good until the middle of December. My writer is going to be leaving.'

She dug a business card from her purse, scribbled something on the back, and handed it to him.

'By the way, Andy, I know what kind of jobs you and Phil were talking about when I walked up. You guys aren't as cool as you think.'

'I never wanted to be cool,' he said, wondering exactly what he meant. Trying to show her how determined he was? How cool?

Meredith was not waiting for him in his bed, as he expected. It was one of her nights to stay at his place but the only trace of her he found in his darkened apartment was a note on the neatly made bed:

Dear Andy,

I decided to go home. Fourth or fifth night you've not come home by midnight, just in the last month. I know you need to do your job and experience life to write about, so I'm not upset with you at all. Just feel a little wrong here with no you, and no real commitment. I know how much you hate that word. Maybe we're just wrong for each other. Maybe we just want different things. I told you once not long ago that I had picked out four names for our four beautiful children. I really didn't mean it to be funny or to scare you. But you can't talk to me about maybe settling down, even though you stopped with college. You're out in the world doing what you want and I'm still learning how to teach *other people's* children to read and write. I don't want to bother or upset you but I think my heart is breaking.
XOXOXOXOXOXOXOXOXOXOXOXOXO
XOXOXOXOXOXOXO

M.

Andy stripped down and got into the bed. Looked up at the ceiling. Felt his heart racing inside his ribs.

Meredith Thornton had left him.

He wasn't surprised but it still felt strange. He knew it was coming but not when or how.

Thought it might involve that Alan teacher she worked with.

He went out to the kitchen and sat by the phone. Picked up the ear-piece, then put it back in its cradle. Looked at the manuscript piling up by the typewriter.

He imagined Meredith in her apartment. Figured she'd be awake. Probably awake all night for this one. It puzzled him how much he could have loved her just three years ago. And how much less he loved her now. Back then she was all he could think about. All he wanted. She was everything good and desirable.

Now she felt heavy to him. Stifling, unhappy, impatient. It hurt him to see the disappointment he caused. It angered him, too, because he thought he was doing what was right. A writer lives. A writer experiences. A writer doesn't settle down with his high school sweetheart in the town they grew up in, raise four children named in advance, and end up with a damn thing worth writing about. James, Joseph, Jennifer, and Jacqueline? How could he support them on a reporter's wages? A writer rises above these things. A writer goes to New York. Or the jungle, like Clay.

He picked up the phone, heard the dial tone, put it back down.

Still, it worried him. How his love had just gotten used up. Was love finite? Were the poets and songwriters in some kind of conspiracy to make love sound longer-lasting than it was? Or was there something missing inside him, some part that wasn't there? Look at his mom and dad. Both sets of grandparents. Almost all the aunts and uncles. Nick and Katy. The Thorntons. J.J. and Mae Overholt. Those ancient Dessingers.

He slid the manuscript over in front of him. Grabbed it and riffled the pages with his thumb. Three hundred and four pages. He'd stopped right in the middle of the scene where Tracy from California boards the train from Orly to Bordeaux. She steps over a pool of red wine from an old lady's dropped bottle. Tracy's boyfriend, Robert, waits for her in a little village, uncertain whether he really wants her to come or not. Because of Anne-Marie. And because he needs freedom to write. What neither knows is that in less than three hours the train will derail and Tracy will be decapitated.

Andy had spent a summer in Europe after his freshman year of college and had lived every moment of this story. Kind of. He'd written Meredith a letter every day. Sometimes two. When she'd volunteered to quit her good summer job and come join him, he encouraged her to stay in Tustin.

Last month, after she'd told him the four children's names, he'd asked her to read the manuscript. She didn't really like it. Said she liked the style. And the California part, where they were happy. But mostly it just made her quiet.

82

Andy read the spilled wine section. Borrowed it from *A Tale of Two Cities*. He found Dickens sentimental but the wine was great symbolism. He pushed the manuscript away.

*Fall Wine*, by Andrew James Becker.

He picked up the phone and dialed Teresa Dessinger's home phone off the back of the card she'd given him.

'I'll take the job,' he said.

'Give me two weeks to get the reporter out.'

'You said he was quitting.'

'I said he was leaving. Good night, Andy. And good decision.'

He lay in bed for a little while. Just before sleep he felt a very small smile trying to get onto his lips. Too tired to move. Thought about what had happened. Felt free. Unweighted. Ready to live. Smithy of his soul and all that.

He slept better than he'd slept for weeks.

The next morning Andy got to the sheriff's station an hour later than usual. Slight hangover. No promising stories. He stayed late to jawbone with the other reporters, fill them in on all the important press club business of the night before.

Back in Tustin, he found J.J. Overholt in his office. Roger Stoltz was with him so Andy went to his desk and thought about last night.

Stoltz came by a few minutes later on his way out. He was a man who never seemed to age. Same suntanned face and crisp mustache and cheerful brown eyes Andy remembered from nearly ten years ago. Same thick black hair, unruly like a boy's. Andy instinctively disliked him.

Stoltz asked about Clay. When Andy said he hadn't heard from his brother in months, Stoltz said he was doing an important and dangerous thing over in Vietnam.

'I'll be glad when he's back,' said Andy.

'Me, too. I'll be glad when all our men are back.'

'You really think those Commies are a danger to us?' Andy asked.

'They want this country, Andy.'

Andy looked for zeal or imbalance in Stoltz's eyes. Saw what looked like good cheer and conviction.

'Your father's really doing some fine things with the Tustin Birch Society chapter,' said Stoltz.

Andy had seen the cars parked in front of the Becker home on meeting nights. And the Santa Ana Police Department motorcycles lined up at the curb because Max had managed to recruit some motor patrol officers over to the society.

Andy had lingered for a few minutes at a couple of the meetings. Listened to the JBS party lines: 'Get the U.S. out of the UN,' 'Support Your Local Police,' 'Goldwater in '64,' 'No on Fluoridation,' 'Better Dead Than Red.' They showed films documenting Communist takeovers and atrocities, some of them gory and disturbing. Something about black-and-white film, Andy had thought, the way it captured body bloat and bullet-riddled corpses and blood. And films on the growing use of drugs – how to spot a heroin addict, what marijuana cigarettes looked like, how to tell if your teenager was under the influence of drugs.

The Birch Society members were local men and women – small business owners, a savings and loan officer, a pharmacist, some defense engineers, a teacher, a dentist, a pilot. They were serious about the Communist conspiracy and seemed happy to have a newspaperman around. Roger and Marie Stoltz were there both times. They owned a small chemical company, RoMar Industries. Solvents and industrial cleaners.

Max Becker had given a speech one night. Andy had never seen him speak before. It surprised him how passionate and eloquent his father was. His topic was the way the Communist conspiracy worked inside a free country. How they used drugs and music and subversive textbooks and ignorant politicians to brainwash the youth. The youth were the most valuable members of a free republic, Max said, and the most vulnerable.

'Mom buys that JBS stuff, too,' said Andy. Though she'd remarked to him once that Roger Stoltz and the JBS were taking over Max Becker's life.

'She's very well informed,' said Stoltz. 'Well, say hello to them for me.'

\* \* \*

Andy thanked Old Man Overholt for six years of employment and gave his two-week notice. The publisher talked for a while about writing and papers and marriage and self-control but Andy hardly heard a word of it. He sat in Overholt's office, nodding occasionally.

Then he went back to his desk and wrote the Vonn brothers arrest story.

It came fast and he put in a lot. It wasn't really straight reporting. Not really an editorial or think piece, either. Just a story about a family and it was true. He got Karl's cold black stare, and Alma's saying she'd die when she couldn't count her dead loved ones on two hands anymore, and Janelle's guitar and Lenny's shining flame orange and red chopped Harley Panhead. And the notion that these poor people had come halfway across the country to find a better life and had instead found ugliness, misery, ruined innocence, and death. That we owed them respect for trying. That they had borne a specific burden so that we would not have to bear it. This last idea was something Andy had talked about with David. Wasn't sure how to write it but felt it very strongly in his heart. Andy changed all the names and places and some smaller things so nobody would know who it was about. Wrote it the best he could.

He knew Overholt would kill the story. But he dropped his two carbon copies into the publisher's in-box anyhow. Put the original in his briefcase.

Three years ago today that Alma Vonn had killed herself, Andy thought.

This one is for you.

Meredith burst into the *Tustin Times* office a little after noon, her makeup running and her eyes swimming with tears. She fell into Andy's arms and hugged him harder than she'd ever hugged him in her life.

He couldn't get her to stop crying. He guided her outside and they stood by a sycamore tree, leaves mostly gone, branches forking into a pale blue sky. A dry wind chattered the big dead leaves across the sidewalk. He tried to hold her close but she pushed him away.

'I'm not going to see you again,' she said. 'It's over, Andy. I can't live like this anymore.'

Her face was a mask of defeat and hopelessness.

'I understand.'

'Why aren't you crying?'

'I'm trying to be strong, Meredith. I still love you. I want you to know I'll always love you.'

She sobbed and hugged herself and looked up at him with the most abject sadness that Andy had ever seen.

'You don't know, do you?' she asked.

'I know that I love you. I do, but I think it would be better if—'

'They shot John Kennedy.'

\*   \*   \*

87

Max Becker brought his three available sons home that evening. David came with Barbara. Nick came alone. So did Andy, walking into the hushed kitchen and wondering why they had been called here. Max had been abrupt on the phone.

Andy noted the paleness of Monika. Her eyes were red and she couldn't look at him.

They came together in a loose circle in the old kitchen, the TV droning on from the den, speculation about the president and one Lee Harvey Oswald and a murdered officer Tippett.

Max asked them to hold hands. His voice trembled.

'Sons and daughter,' he said. 'This is the darkest day of our lives. Your brother Clay has been killed in Vietnam. I'm uncertain of the specifics. David, say a prayer.'

# 10

## *1968*

The wind blew hard that day, the first strong Santa
Ana wind of the season. October second, hot and
dry. The kind of wind that got you a static shock
every time you touched something that would
conduct. Touch a metal doorknob, you got a little
blue zap. Kiss your sweetheart, same thing, a
sharp little arc cracked from lip to lip.

Nick got the possible 187 at 4:48 that afternoon and was rolling by 5:09. The delay was
thanks to his partner, Al 'Lucky' Lobdell, who was
talking to his wife on the phone about their son.
Kevin was seventeen, having troubles. Lucky's
voice had been soft and grave.

Nick drove. Lucky sat across from him in the
Fairlane. Chewing gum, staring out at the wind-
bent trees as if seeing them for the first time.

'Two murders in two days,' said Lobdell. 'The
Laguna thing had to be queers.'

'Laguna PD's playing it pretty tight,' said Nick.
The Sheriff's Department had gotten the statewide

bulletin from Laguna Beach PD that morning. Fatal stabbing at the Boom Boom Bungalow, a beachfront motel that catered to men. No suspect, no witnesses. Dead victim was Adrian Stalling, age twenty, of Bakersfield.

'A stiff at the Boom Boom,' said Lobdell. 'Ours is at the old packinghouse near Tustin?'

'That's right, Al.'

'Should have torn it down years ago. City Council tried to, but it's just outside the city limits.'

'Yeah. It's been empty awhile.'

'Bums and rats. Kids doing the wrong things. That was Shirley on the phone. Kevin got suspended from school today for cussing a teacher. Like he does his mom. Three days of suspension.'

'Sorry to hear that, Lucky.'

'Not as sorry as me.'

'What were you doing when you were seventeen?'

Lobdell looked at Nick, then back through the window. Lucky was a big man, barrel chest and small feet. He seemed preoccupied at times, like his back was up against a wall that Nick couldn't see.

'I graduated early with job credits,' said Lobdell. 'Joined the army.'

Nick steered off Fourth Street to Newport, then drove the service road along the railroad tracks. Still a few groves around the packing-house. Gravel popped under the chassis and the orange leaves shifted in the wind. Silver and green and silver again. Sun bright and low in the west.

Nick thought of himself and his brothers tossing the SunBlesst packinghouse crate labels in the air on a day like this. That dark-haired beauty and her big orange raining out of the sky for days. Remembered the rumble. The crack of Lenny Vonn's nose. The terrific pain when they clubbed his head with the tree branch. And Andy flying out of the trees to spear Lenny Vonn. Clay. All because of Clay. Be five years next month since he died. November 22. And the war getting worse and worse.

Nick parked the Ford by the railroad tracks. Tustin PD had a couple of units there, and the Sheriff's had two more.

And Andy's convertible Corvair Spyder. Custom rims and an ice blue paint job. White top, turbocharged. Press card taped to the inside of the windshield. Andy was a hotshot reporter now for the *Journal*. Won Orange County Press Club awards left and right. Had a police band radio in his car, another in his house, another on his desk at the *Journal* building in Costa Mesa. Said he never turned them off, which was probably true. Made half the crime scenes faster than the detectives. Middle of the night on some dismal 187 down in the bad section of Santa Ana there was Andy with his ice blue Corvair and his notebook.

Nick got his case from the trunk. Brand new. Bought his own, the kind with the lock. Organized exactly how he wanted it. Good feeling, to have the tools you need and know how to use them.

He climbed up the rotting old steps of the packinghouse. Smelled the creosote. Felt the boards giving under his feet as he walked across the platform toward the big sliding doors. Heard the metal roof shimmying in the wind. Saw the stains on the roof where the nails had rusted through. He could still see the faint image of the SunBlesst girl and her orange. Faded with age. Her face alone as big as he was.

Inside, the sunlight came through the wall slats in slanting beams. Dust rose in the shafts and a feather zigzagged lazily down. Nick heard the flapping and cooing above him. Didn't bother to look.

It was pretty much just one huge room. Rafters high up. Big industrial light housings still hanging, dented up from kids heaving rocks at them. Bulbs long shattered. Mullioned windows along all four sides, glass busted out years ago. Some of the safety screen still twisting from the frames. A row of desks, drawers gone, along one wall. Floor covered with crate labels and old newspapers that shifted in the drafts. Little circles of rocks where the bums had lit fires. Probably burned the labels to stay warm, Nick thought.

'Some kids found her,' said one of the Tustin officers. He led Nick and Lobdell toward the far northwest corner of the building. 'There was no lock on the door.'

Nick stepped over a fire ring made of concrete

blocks. Reached down for a sheet of newspaper. The *Santa Ana Register*. May 23, 1968. Date kind of blurred on him for a second. Still saw double once in a while. Still had a little trouble with his balance. Nothing big. Damned Vonns. Damn Clay. Damned mean beautiful Clay Becker. Back when Clay died Nick thought his heart was going to explode because he couldn't do anything about it. Not one goddamned thing.

The wind slammed into the building and the metal roof shimmied again. Paper skidded across the floor. The pigeons flapped and circled and receded back into the dark of the ceiling. Feathers floating in reeds of light.

'Old buildings always smell the same,' said Lobdell. 'Always smell like old rat piss. No matter if they got rats in them or not.'

'That's human piss.'

'You're a piss expert?'

'I guess.'

Nick wondered if Lobdell was thick or just acted that way. Maybe it was a way to deflect things or to sneak up on them. They'd been partners two days. This was Nick's first murder as a lead detective in the homicide detail. Lucky Lobdell had already told him that Nicky boy was going to call the shots. He was going to swim hard or sink fast. When he'd said it, Nick had seen nothing but stubborn challenge in Lobdell's small gray eyes.

The uniforms stood in a wide semicircle. Andy was a part of it. He had his pen in his right hand

and his notepad up. A camera around his neck. Stopped writing when Nick and Lobdell got there. Nick had not seen an expression like that on Andy's face since they'd stood holding hands in the old Becker house five Novembers ago.

They were standing around a bunch of old mattresses. Half a dozen of them strewn about. Stained and flattened. Mixed in with the newspapers and crate labels and some filthy blankets.

The body lay on one of them. On her front. A powder blue turtleneck sweater and underwear. Arms out, legs together. Skin blue-white in the packinghouse gloom. Neck of the sweater empty, collapsed, black-red. Her head lay ten feet away, over on its side like someone had kicked it there. Some blood on the mattresses and floorboards. Purple-black on the old brown wood. Not as much as Nick would have thought.

Nick moved past the officers and Andy got up closer. Knelt down and looked across the dirty floorboards at the head.

'Unholy shit,' he said quietly.

'Goddamn,' said Lobdell. 'It's the beauty queen, isn't it? The one they took her crown back?'

Nick heard him light a cigarette. Saw the match trail a wisp of smoke down the far periphery of his vision. Saw Andy on the edge of his vision, too. But he couldn't move. Couldn't take his eyes off the sleepy-eyed, composed, and once beautiful face.

'Janelle Vonn,' Nick whispered. 'Unholy shit.'

'Maybe your brother here can write you up some better lines,' said Lobdell.

Nick finally stood. Trembled for just a second. First case and you know her.

*I am Janelle Vonn and those are my brothers.*

'Deputies, seal off this scene,' he said. 'Set up an entry log by the sliding door. Everybody signs in. Everybody signs out. Don't leave the door unattended. Andy, you gotta stay back and out of the way. Soon as another reporter gets here, you'll have to leave.'

'Got it.'

Nick sketched the scene into his new clean notebook. He paced off approximate measurements and made a note to get exact ones later. *Vonn Crime Scene – 10/02/68*. He used his compass to get the orientation right. Asked the Identification Bureau deputy to start the photography, black-and-white, then color. Start with Janelle. He watched the deputy coroner place a gloved hand on the bottom of Janelle Vonn's foot to guess body temp and help estimate time of death.

*There was no lock on the door.*

He was interrupted by the assistant coroner, an assistant prosecutor, chief and assistant chief of the Tustin PD, a ranking OCSD lieutenant, and a reporter from the *Los Angeles Times*. A crowd had formed along the tracks. Nick felt like a greeter, then a host, then a bouncer. Andy didn't have to be told to leave.

He and Lobdell made a pass with flashlights. It was hard to see, the way the sunlight slanted through the wallboards and all the debris.

Nick watched the ID men collect. He missed this part of it, the physical gathering of evidence. Flashlights and tweezers and paper bags. They started about ten yards away from Janelle Vonn and worked closer in a big circle. Came up with an empty matchbook from a local bar called the Epicure. An empty matchbook with a plain white cover. A wadded Juicy Fruit wrapper that didn't look old. Empty pack of Camels, six feet from the body, cellophane wrap could hold latents. A ballpoint pen that was out of ink.

About fifty inches away from Janelle's body, underneath a section of newspaper, one of the ID men found a St Christopher medal on a chain. A circular gold frame with an inset purple enamel bust of the saint. No stains. No rust. Looked new. Knocked off in a struggle?

Lobdell snorted, walking fast and toeing things out of the way around the ID men. Flashlight beam zigging and zagging. Nick watched him for a second. Wondered how you could spot anything moving that fast.

Then Lobdell stopped and stared down. Held his flashlight in both hands like a baseball bat. Took a slo-mo swing. Good hip rotation. Watched the ball sail out of the packinghouse. The pigeons cooed and fluttered. Nick thought if it was up to him he'd put Lobdell in Traffic or behind a desk where he could do a lousy job of less important things than murder.

'Lobdell connects. Hey, Nicky boy, I just homered. Check this.'

He was way off on his own, almost in the northeast corner. Over a hundred feet from Janelle Vonn, easy.

When Nick came up Lobdell stopped chewing his gum and aimed his flashlight beam onto a handsaw covered in blood. Right there on one of the old crate labels. A pruning saw, the kind with the blade that folds back into a wooden handle. For trees and shrubs. No blade, just the bloody handle with the wood ripped where the bolt and blade had broken away. And under it the SunBlesst girl still trying to give away that orange.

'Let's get some pictures of this thing,' said Lobdell. 'What do you think, Nicky? Look around, maybe you can find the blade.'

Nick knelt and held his flashlight while Dale Rainor, the assistant coroner, ran a magnifying glass over Janelle Vonn. Marks on her throat, he could see them through the blood. Some hairs and fibers. Nick thought the stiff, shiny slicks on her underpants might be semen. Good, he thought: blood types. Good old ABO. Best thing they could get besides an eyewitness. When they were done with Janelle's back side Nick put on rubber gloves and helped Rainor arrange the body bag. Helped turn her over into it. Her neck was a black stump and her arms and legs were stiff with rigor and Nick was suddenly sickened and furious.

'I'll get him,' he said.

'What they all say,' said Lobdell, blowing smoke.

'This is personal.'

'Everything in this job's personal for about six months.'


'Investigator Becker, sir? You may want to see this.'

Nick joined the deputy in the great doorway of the packinghouse. In the blustery twilight two Tustin PD uniforms marched a man down the tracks toward their unit. The man was a tangle of hair and beard. Weird eyes. Red-faced, filthy jeans and a black T-shirt. A denim jacket lined with dirty fleece. Boots with no laces. Cuffed and struggling but no match for the big men holding each arm. His mouth a black hole in the beard. He was snarling at the officers but the wind snatched the sounds and scattered them into the air.

Nick clomped across the old wood, went down the wobbly steps. Hustled down the tracks toward the Tustin car. Could smell the guy from ten feet away. The officers pulled him to a stop when Nick got close.

'Found Wolfman here snoring out in the grove,' said Officer Huber. 'Won't give us his name. Why don't you show him your arm, Wolfie?'

The man growled.

'Show him your arm,' said Huber. Huber tried to turn him around but the man twisted a lace-less boot into the ground and resisted.

'Didn't do it,' he mumbled.

Nick shot a look at Huber and the big man shrugged.

'You didn't do what?' asked Nick.

'The girl in there.' Wolfman fixed Nick with his very pale tan eyes. He really did look like a wolf. The eyes held no emotion that Nick could identify.

'Did you see what happened?' Nick asked.

'I didn't touch her.'

'Of course you didn't. Let's go sit in the back of that car over there. Get comfortable. Have a talk.'

'Look at this,' Huber said, twisting the man around by one arm.

Huber clamped his hand on the man's wrist, just above the cuff. Yanked up the sleeve of the filthy fleece-lined jacket, all the way up past the elbow.

Get ready for needle tracks by the hundred, thought Nick. The hypodermic highway.

Instead, he saw a black patch of hair, thick as a dog's, running from the man's knuckles almost to his elbow. The whole top half of his forearm. Like a patch of Labrador retriever grafted onto a man.

Wolfman growled and snapped at Nick and Nick flinched.

Huber and Graff laughed. Nick laughed, too. That or piss his pants.

He helped the officers get Wolfman into the back of the PD cruiser. The book told him to leave the cuffs on but it didn't seem right so he took them off. Then he shut the door and got into the front seat, passenger side. Left the door open because of the smell.

'Smoke?' asked Nick, offering a cigarette through the mesh divider.

'Okay.'

'Stick the end back through.'

Nick flipped open his Zippo with one hand, torched the Tareyton. 'What's your name?'

Wolfman sat back and took a deep lungful of smoke.

'Terry Neemal.'

'Spell that?'

Neemal did and Nick wrote it down.

'I'm Nick Becker. You going to tell me the truth, Terry? Or give me a bunch of crazy Wolfman shit?'

'Those guys started the Wolfman shit. I can't help the arm.'

'I'll treat you like a man if you'll treat me like one.'

'I didn't touch that girl.'

'See her go in?'

'No. But I saw a guy go in. It was dark so I didn't see too good. Saw him go up the steps.

After that, all I could do was hear. But not so good, because of the wind.'

'Where were you?'

'Out in the trees. I can't sleep where it stinks.'

'When did you go in?'

'This morning. To see if anyone left anything good. I used the door because I heard them slide it open last night. Sometimes it's got a lock on it. Then someone smashes it off. Then they put on another one. So I use a window. But one time I cut my leg climbing in and it got infected bad. I went in and looked around and there she was.'

'How come you didn't call us?'

'None of my business. Didn't have a dime, either.'

'Are you kidding me, Terry? A girl gets her head cut off and it's not your business?'

Terry shrugged and looked down. Nick looked at the deep lines in the weathered face. The miles-away indifference in the pale brown eyes. Drugs, maybe. Insanity. Both. Guessed him early thirties. Close to his own age.

'But you didn't split, either,' said Nick. 'How come?'

'I thought when the cops came I'd sneak off into the trees.'

'But you were snoring, so they found you.'

Neemal nodded.

Nick thought about taking the guy downtown right now. He'd take him there later, anyhow. For sure. But he thought he could engage the man more easily now, and he seemed ready to talk. The nutcases he'd seen, they'd talk a blue streak for half an hour when they felt like it, then not say a word for six months. Or go completely batty. Or kill themselves.

'Got another smoke?'

Nick pushed another one through the mesh. 'Terry, I'm going to tape-record this, if you don't mind. It's better for both of us.'

Neemal shrugged again and Nick wondered how much time he had.

'Don't go anywhere,' Nick said.

'Funny.'

'Get your ID out if you got one.'

'They took it away at Atascadero. That was a long time ago.'

Nick hustled into the packinghouse, got his new case, and trotted through the wind back to Terry Neemal.

At one that morning Nick was still at his desk. The wind was still howling through the county, rattling the black windowpanes of the Sheriff's Department building. Tape recorder and a legal pad in front of him. A bag of Carl's Jr fast food, too, stains working into the paper. Food cold by now and barely touched.

Terry Neemal was in custody.

A padlock had been found in the grove not far from the SunBlesst packinghouse. It was a good Schlage.

Janelle Vonn's purse had been found not far from the lock. It was a loose leather bag with fringe on the bottom and a drawstring on the top. Sold by Neck Deep Leather, Laguna Beach. What a lousy name for a store, thought Nick. Wallet with a California driver's license and eighty-five in cash. House and car keys. A Mercury Savings & Loan checking account with a balance of just over two grand. An address and phone book. A date book. Personal items, including a diaphragm and spermicidal gel, hairbrush, lipstick, nail files, ballpoint pens, scraps of paper with phone numbers and notes scribbled on them.

In the date book box for Tuesday, the day she died, Nick had read: *Red & Ho 7.*

They'd found a black miniskirt and a pair of boots thrown into a far dark corner of the packing-house.

They'd not found the saw blade.

Now Nick's own voice came from the tape recorder and he checked his handwritten transcription. The inside of his first knuckle, middle finger, right hand, had a shiny divot in it that had started to bleed.

Chase bad guys all day, Nick thought. See a young woman with her head sawed off, interview a psycho, and you get bloody making notes.

Q: Describe him again.
A: Regular-sized guy. Hard shoes the way they sounded on the wood. A jacket maybe.

Something bulky around him. It was dark and cool by then. I told you all this. I couldn't see that good.

Q: What time did you say?

A: Midnight. I don't got a watch but I know what time it is usually. Remember I told you that?

Q: Bulky, like a coat or a sweater?

A: Maybe bigger. Longer.

Q: Like what, a blanket or an overcoat?

A: Maybe like that. (Yawn) I'm getting tired, Nick.

Q: Just a few more questions.

A: When I was little I always thought there was ghosts in wind like that out there. You know, like the wind was so strong it would gather the ghosts up, pull them right off of things. Scared me. I'd hide under the bed. And these balls of cat hair would come rolling along the floor in the draft. Right at me. Thought they were the ghosts coming to get me.

Q: Interesting. Did you kill her, Terry?

A: Not me. I'm still telling the truth.

Q: Tell me what you did after you found her.

A: Seems like about the twentieth time you asked me that.

Q: It's the seventh.

A: I'm really getting sleepy now.

Q: Come on, Terry. Just once more, from the time you found her. Look, if you killed her, that's okay. I understand and you can just say so, then we can get this over with and move along to the next thing.

A: I didn't kill her. Even if I had an opportunity I could not have been the one that killed her.

Q: And why is that?

A: Because I never hurt anybody in my life.

Q: People here say different, Terry. Your old juvenile investigator works burg-theft now. He gave me a nice little rundown of the people you hurt and fires you set and things you stole.

A: That was my family.

Q: You set your brother on fire when you were eight. He was four. He almost died.

A: I already told you that doesn't count.

Q: I'm not seeing any logic there, Terry. But I'll take your word for it. Okay? Now tell me what happened after you found the girl in there. You sure her head was off, or did that maybe happen later?

A: No. It was off, Nick. I wouldn't forget something like that.


It was 3 A.M. when Nick parked along the tracks outside the SunBlesst packinghouse. Didn't mean to slam the Fairlane door but the wind came up just as he pushed. Just about took the door handle out of his hand.

He followed his flashlight beam up the steps and across the platform. The crime scene tape slapped against the wallboards. There was a new combination lock on the door and nobody had told him the numbers. He stood in front of the SunBlesst woman's big faded smile, listened to the crime scene tape rippling on the old wood.

Nick walked around back, picked an empty window, climbed up and over. Smell of creosote again, and pee and old fires. And the faint sweet smell of citrus, blown through the cracks by the wind.

The beam danced through the trash as Nick moved toward where the body had been. Pigeons shifting above.

He held the light steady on the blood. Still surprised there wasn't more.

Knelt. Thought.

*Janelle. Freckle-faced little girl with an orange in her hands. Tutu and a guitar. Molested by her brothers. Dope and booze by fourteen. Then Andy's article, different names but some people figured it out. David's church took her in. Miss Tustin till she did a* Playboy *magazine cover. All that a year ago but pretty quiet since. Heard she'd quit the dope and booze. Going to college, wasn't she? Nineteen and all that behind her and her head sawed off in a filthy packing-house.*

Nick listened to the wind outside, let his light beam roam the big wooden cavern. Stood up and started out. Saw one of the floorboards by the window was busted. Reached down and yanked. *Going to get this fucker.* The nails shrieked in the wood and the pigeons blasted into flight, frantic wings in the dark. The board broke off in Nick's hand. Nails still in it. Nick threw it through the window and climbed out.

# 11

Nine the next morning. Three hours of sleep. Day warm and breezy, sun cutting the ocean into silver bevels where Nick lifted a thin curtain and looked out a window.

'How's a nineteen-year-old chick afford this?' asked Lucky Lobdell.

'And two thousand in the bank,' said Nick.

Janelle Vonn's place was downtown Laguna, a cheery yellow cottage on a bluff above the beach at St Ann's. Out a highway-side window Nick saw a market, a realtor's office, and Rainbow Connections – a shop selling hippie dresses.

'I smell maryjane,' said Lobdell.

'I smell incense.'

'Like the piss thing yesterday. You got the nose but look who found the saw.'

'It's hard to miss patchouli, Lucky. But good work on the saw.'

'It wasn't work, it was luck.'

'Good either way.'

Lobdell stood in the hallway. Leaned forward and touched a picture frame. He made the cottage around him look toylike.

'The dopers use patchouli incense to hide the pot smoke, don't they?' he asked.

'So I've heard.'

Nick took the living room and kitchen. Lucky Lobdell took the bedroom and bath.

To Nick's eye the place was rented furnished. Blue fabric sofa ten years out of style. Same with the glass-topped coffee table in front of it. Thought he remembered the style of rocking chair from a high school friend's house, a Sears product with a beige background and a brown oak-leaf and acorn pattern. A big dust apron around the bottom. A scuffed-up pine floor with a braided oval rug in the middle, blue and gray.

Easy to spot Janelle Vonn's stuff. A Beatles *Revolver* album cover and a peace sign poster on one wall. A WHAT TO DO IN CASE OF NUCLEAR ATTACK poster on another wall, with a photo of a guy kissing his ass goodbye. Some framed black-and-white photos of a guitar player onstage. Nick didn't recognize him. The pictures looked amateurish, with the microphone making a big round shadow on the guy's face. There was an elaborate macramé plant holder hooked into one corner of the ceiling, creeping charlies spilling out from the pots. The curtains were just bedsheets thumbtacked to the window frames. White sheets with little pink roses that the sun had faded.

The kitchen was small and had a yellow and chrome dinette. The table had been last set for three. Yellow straw place mats, three wineglasses with a little dried red left at the bottoms. Lipstick on one. Water glasses – two almost full and one with lipstick almost empty. A large faint circular red stain in the middle. Plates and silverware in the sink rinsed but not washed.

Yellow walls and cabinets. White refrigerator. Yellow counter tile. Nick opened the refrigerator. Orange juice, relish, three eggs, three packets of soy sauce. On top of the fridge was a large jug of Bali Hai wine. And a small ceramic mushroom with two sticks of patchouli incense in it, one of them half burned. A quarter of the wine was left. Nick figured the bottle bottom matched the red stain on the dinette table and made a note to have the bottle dusted for prints.

A wastebasket under the sink solved the dinner mystery. Mexican takeout from Pepito's on Ocean Avenue here in Laguna. Nick fished out the receipt. *Red and Ho at seven o'clock*? Enough food for three – $7.45.

There was a bay window with a bench seat. Most of the seat was taken up with textbooks. *An Introduction to Economics. The Norton Anthology of English Literature Revised, Volume 1. The Art of Sound: Appreciating Music* was open to page 114, with a postcard of Watts Towers holding the place. The postmark was eight days ago.

Hello Sweet Lady,

    Hadn't seen these since the riots.
Wondered if God made different colors of
people so we'd fight, to keep us from
building heaven on earth. Think of you
every second. Got a song this morning,
going straight to the demo.

    Love,

    J.B.

A red telephone on a pile of paper an inch
high. Nick set the phone aside and glanced
through the pile. There were three pads of lined
notebook paper with most of the sheets gone.
Crowded with numbers and doodles. Corners
bent, pieces torn out. Even the cardboard back-
ings were covered with ink. Loose sheets of typing
paper, covered, too. The girl was a chronic
doodler: mostly flower petals and clouds with
tightly detailed cross-hatchings. Like those old
woodcuts, Nick thought. Horses. Waves. Not bad.
And pages torn from phone books, some with
circled numbers, but the circles were so big you
couldn't tell which number she meant.

There was a worship program from David's
Grove Drive-In Church of God, too. No surprise
there. Nick was about to flip past it when he
caught the date – October 6, 1968. This coming
Sunday, he thought. How'd she come up with
that? Do they mail them in advance or something? A reminder? David would know. The

sermon was 'Keeping Your Heart Young Through God's Love.'

Next to the pile was a shoe box half full of bar and restaurant napkins with names and numbers on them. Business cards. Pens and pencils. Matchbooks: Frank Cavalier Bail Bonds – Get Out Fast! The Sandpiper Nightclub. Lorenzo's – Fine Steaks & Cocktails.

Hadn't the *Journal* just given Lorenzo's a glowing review? Yes, thought Nick, four out of five forks. And the *Register* had said it stunk. He flipped the cover open to a tiny map and the phone number. Dropped it back into the shoe box.

Nick smelled Lobdell's cigarette smoke wafting into the kitchen. A moment later Lobdell walked in holding a pretty golden crown with orange-colored jewels on it, and a handful of newspapers.

'She was Miss Tustin,' said Lobdell. 'The one they took the title away from. You remember.'

'Sure. It was only a year ago.'

'Look – they let her keep this chintzy crown, but they stripped her title away. Must have broke her heart. All these newspaper clips are the fun stuff she did. She saved them in a drawer.'

Lobdell held out the little crown and the papers, looking from one to the other. Then at Nick. Cigarette in the crown hand. He shook both the crown and the newspapers like he had just presented compelling evidence, then lumbered back into the bedroom.

Nick figured that Janelle had come here to start over. Came to Laguna to get away from Miss Tustin and the *Playboy* cover and all that.

Nick picked through the papers and shoe box. Janelle Vonn's handwriting was relaxed and innocent – big loops, not much slant, *i*'s dotted with small circles. He flipped the pages, noting that some of the names and numbers were repeated. Too lazy to look through the stack? Why not put them in the phone and address book she carried?

On a loose sheet of paper near the top:

B. Beat
Dr T/O Sun
Jesse B.
CB
UCI $

He dialed the first one and got Blue Beat music in Laguna. Craig the owner said they weren't open for business yet but were working on the building. Sure, he knew Janelle, couldn't believe what happened. Great girl. Full of wonder and feeling. Into music. Into experience. Beautiful laugh and smile.

Craig wanted to know if they caught the stabber from the Boom Boom Bungalow.

Nick said he hadn't heard of an arrest, but the Laguna cops were handling it.

Peace, said Craig.

The second was a Laguna number – no answer.

The third was a Los Angeles area code – J.B. again – but it just rang, too.

A stoned-sounding man picked up at the CB number. Nick identified himself and the guy said 'kiss my butt' and hung up. Nick called right back but got no answer.

The University of California, Irvine, admissions office confirmed that Janelle Vonn was receiving Pell grants and loans totaling one hundred and fifty-six dollars for this, the fall quarter. And an annual two-hundred-dollar scholarship award for the next four years, from the Tustin Chamber of Commerce. This award had been rescinded by the chamber last November. Nick could tell by her tone of voice that the UCI clerk knew what had happened.

'Check this,' said Lobdell. He stood in the little hallway holding a coat hanger by one big finger. On the hanger was a black leather jacket with silver studs on it. Elegant pleats on the sides, with red leather showing through. Kind of motorcy-cle-looking but kind of European-looking, too, thought Nick. He knew nothing about fashion. 'It was hanging on the closet door. Not *in* the closet, but on the door of it.'

'What's the label say?'

'Neck Deep, Laguna Beach,' said Lobdell. 'Made me think of her neck.'

'Same outfit that made her purse,' said Nick. 'I don't like that name. Made me think of her neck, too.'

\*    \*    \*

113

The spare bedroom had a mattress on the floor, covered with bright Mexican serapes and big pillows in a batik print with gold tassels. Three SunBlesst orange boxes with the dark-haired beauty on the label. *California Girl*. Someone had drawn a mustache on one of them. Nick wondered if the label model reminded Janelle of herself.

One of the crates held paperback books and fashion magazines. One was filled with record albums. *Disraeli Gears* out front. The third had a folder with Janelle Vonn's birth certificate and high school diploma, a Tustin High School year-book for 1967, and two large envelopes of Vonn family pictures. There was a handful of pay stubs from the Five Crowns Restaurant in a bag with a smiling dog on it. She made a dollar five an hour. The most recent stub was almost six months old. Two pay stubs from the Gleason/Marx Agency in Hollywood for a total of seven hundred and fifteen dollars.

'And check this, too,' said Lobdell, darkening the doorway again. A handful of odd-sized letters and envelopes clutched in one hand. 'Our honey had a honey. "Until I touch your body with my fire . . . your two perfect mirrors of skin and soul . . . the city lights and the naked trees and the different yous who live in me . . . brush my lips across your crying eyes." Fucking poetry, I guess. It's written that way, little short lines. No periods or commas. Guy's name is Jesse Black.'

'Those are song lyrics,' said Nick. 'He was up in Los Angeles eight days ago, making a demonstration tape.'

Lobdell lowered the letter. 'You know him?'

'Postcard in her college book.'

'Here's one: "The outline of your back is still fresh upon my hand and all the colors of your heartbreak stain the floor. I misjudged your beauty and the contour of your love like a wave that never made it quite to shore."'

Nick saw a fist hit the back of a pale woman. Saw her dark curls shiver and shake. And red-black blood on the packinghouse floorboards.

'A demonstration tape for what?' asked Lobdell. 'This guy wants to be the next Ringo or something?'

'Read another one.'

'Like this stuff, huh? "High heels clickin' down the avenue, sweet new baby off to try the old soft-shoe." What, she's gonna be a dancer?'

'Then what happens?'

'"But the neon fades with sunrise and your face looks like the dead, you should be at home new baby in your very own bed. Come back baby to your very own bed." Hubba-hubba. See, Nicky, she stays out too late dancing. Makes her look old and ugly.'

Dancing with other guys, thought Nick.

'Here,' said Lobdell. He looked around the room like an unimpressed buyer. Dropped the letters onto a yellow and black serape on the guest

115

bed. 'I never understand this fancy stuff. I only read for facts.'

*Yeah, yeah, yeah.* Nick read them over. Didn't find anything else that reminded him of Janelle's body in the packinghouse. But that one . . .

He read it again. All about this guy who lets his lover go then changes his mind. Then it's too late and he goes nuts with regret. Ends up 'talking to the shadows on the walls.'

He went back to the kitchen and called the Blue Beat record store again. Craig told him sure he knew Jesse Black. Local guy, great song-writer. Great singer. All of twenty years old, if that. Janelle Vonn hung out with him some. The girls really dig him.

Nick looked across the living room to the framed pictures next to the kiss-your-ass-good-bye poster. Described them over the phone.

'Yeah,' said Craig. 'That's him. Shiny brown hair and kind of pale-looking. Strong jaw. If I remember right, Janelle carried around a camera. Shot some of his gigs at the Sandpiper, stuff like that.'

Craig told him that Jesse had left Laguna to live in Los Angeles a few months ago. Going to make it in the music business. Didn't know how to get ahold of him, though you'd figure he'd come back after what happened. Might look at Big Red in Bluebird Canyon, a crash pad for the music scene, Craig said. Probably no phones up there. Or try Jesse's mom and dad. Local family, up on Temple Hills. In the phone book, probably. If not, the dad was a music teacher at UCI.

'You any relation to the reporter Becker? Andy?'

'We're brothers.'

'He came by here about ten minutes ago, asking about Janelle.'

Nick thanked him again, went into the bedroom. More music posters and a James Bond *Thunderball* poster, too. More plants. More makeshift, thumbtacked curtains. A dresser with bottles of perfume on top, made the room smell feminine. Nick felt odd being in a young woman's room. Unmade bed. Dirty clothes in an open hamper. Like he should have permission from her. Didn't seem right he got to see her stuff and she never would again.

The bedsheets had galloping horses on them.

There was a collection of Troll dolls in a basket in one corner.

And hundreds of Beatle cards in a Thom McAn shoe box.

A girl, thought Nick. Just a girl.

Nick Hovered and watched the ID men as they photographed and dusted for prints. Wished he could just pitch in and do it himself. Missed his days on the ID Bureau, the way it was all physical, the stuff that ended up convicting in court. He especially liked the dusting, liked the finger-print brushes and the vials of powder, the way you chose a color that would contrast best with the surface. Liked the names of the powders. Dragon's Blood and Midnight Black and Ice White. Liked the way you'd brush the dust on something that looked clean and come up with a fat thumb or a big piece of a finger. Like his dad pulling a big fish out of a little stream.

Lobdell thought Nick was wasting their time. They weren't going to find the answers in this cottage. What, he said, she made dinner for two guys, then went to Tustin with them so they could saw off her head? Lobdell told Nick it's always sex with pretty girls like Janelle. The guy wasn't getting any. Or the guy was getting too much, couldn't keep her happy. Or the guy just ripped off a piece for himself and the rest of it was to cover his tracks. Head and everything. If you can figure out the guys in her life, you figure out everything, said Lobdell. And don't forget the Wolfman. You get a nutcase in the works, anything can happen. But it was Nick's case. Nick was going to swim hard or sink fast. Nick wished Lucky would shut the fuck up.

Nick watched the guys writing out the tag numbers and dates, taping them next to everything they were going to print: wine and water glasses, silverware, tabletop, doorknobs, light switches, you name it.

The hard work was comparing the lifts to the cards at headquarters. Thank God for good criminalists. They'd start with guys who had a record of similar crimes. You could go blind and crazy doing that, trying to see if a whorl was a match or a bust, trying to see if you had a good identifying bifurcation or just a blood bridge. Could take hours. Days even, if you had enough suspects. Not that they'd have a lot of prints of guys who did stuff like this.

There was talk of this big computer up in Sacramento getting all the prints together and comparing prints automatically someday. Just plug in your lift and a second later your bad guy came out. Nick figured he'd believe that when he saw it. Next they'll say they can ID a guy from one drop of blood.

Back at Headquarters he called the National Crime Information Center in Washington, D.C., and was passed along to Special Agent Alan Creasen. Creasen took down the particulars surrounding the murder of Janelle Vonn and coded them for entry into the new NCIC computer.

'Beheaded with a pruning saw?'

'Correct.'

'Post or ante?'

'Post, we think. The autopsy is later today.'

'I'll need that information. And the rape analysis, too. Detective Becker, this might take a while. We're only a year old. The computer here is hot, slow, and temperamental.'

Nick called the Gleason/Marx Agency of Hollywood. They were a modeling agency and had found work for Janelle three times. Once in a magazine car stereo ad. Once in a newspaper shampoo ad. And once for the *Playboy* cover that had gotten her uncrowned as Miss Tustin. Janelle's net on the *Playboy* shot was six hundred because she was one of several models used on that month's cover in a spread called 'California Girls.' Nick remembered seeing it then and thinking Janelle was the most beautiful. But she ended up paying a high price for such a low wage when they took her crown away because of it.

Nick found Lenny Vonn that afternoon. Same house out in Modjeska Canyon. Brother Casey and father Karl were there, too, the three of them sitting in the garage drinking beers while Lenny cleaned out the carb on his yellow and orange Panhead. Casey had a Hessians vest on. His hair was almost to his shoulders and matted. Full beard, dark sunglasses even in the cool shade of the garage.

The three of them stopped talking and watched Nick come up the driveway.

'Vonns,' he said.

'Beat it, pissface,' said Lenny. 'Private property.'

Casey shifted the cooler he was sitting on so Nick could only see the back of his filthy vest and filthy hair. Under the influence of God knows what, thought Nick. Probably holding. Probably carrying, too.

Nick now pointedly regretted that Lucky had

a meeting with Kevin's principal this afternoon. Lucky couldn't very well miss it with the boy having been suspended. But Nick knew he should have waited to come here. He hadn't figured on a hive of Vonns, either, and that was stupid of him.

''Lo,' said Karl. 'We already talked to Andy about it.'

'I'm sorry,' said Nick. 'I thought she was a sweet girl.'

'Get out of here, you fascist pig,' said Lenny. 'I'm not kidding.'

Nick sighed and looked at Karl. 'Talk some sense into your stupid son, will you? I'm in charge of Janelle's case. If anybody's going to get this guy, it's going to be me.'

'Like that makes you a—'

'Shuttup, son,' said Karl. 'Let him talk.'

'Just a few questions,' said Nick.

For the next half hour Nick held his pen in his right hand and his notebook in the left. Kept them both low so the meat of his right fore-arm never left the handle of his .45 ACP, snugged against his hip under the tweed sport coat. Hardly wrote a note. Hardly took his eyes off Casey's back. Casey turned a second and just stared at him, eyes hidden behind the dark glasses.

Nick found out that Janelle had lived in the old Tustin house until she was fifteen, then moved in with 'friends.' Nobody could come up with a full name for any one 'friend,' but it might have been a family named Lawson or Langton off of Seventeenth Street. Karl was pretty sure Langton. Nick wondered if it was the Langtons from Tustin High School. Howard a coach and the daughters about Janelle's age.

Nick found out that after he'd arrested Lenny and Casey, Janelle had started drinking more and taking more pills. When that *Tustin Times* story came out about the arrests, the names were all changed but some people still figured out who was who. Tustin was small enough for that. Janelle had to give statements and that was hard. She got really sad and withdrawn. When the charges against Lenny and Casey got knocked down to one assault for Casey and possession of illegal substances for Lenny, Janelle got almost suicidal. Then, David and the Drive-In Church congregation got her some doctors and gave her a place to live and some money and cleaned her up and got her back in school. Grades went up and one of the Chamber of Commerce guys saw her after class one day when he was picking up his daughter and thought Janelle should enter for Miss Tustin because she would be exceptionally beautiful if she was cleaned up and dressed right. And she'd come through a living hell with her mom and the rat poison and those brothers of hers. And if she was Miss Tustin, she'd get a good college scholarship and some cash and lots of opportunity, and the Vonns weren't exactly rolling in it. He talked her into it and sponsored her.

Janelle liked being Miss Tustin. Thought it was kind of funny, but harmless. Enjoyed people. Enjoyed the attention. No pills or booze. Made a run down to Baja with three truckloads of clothes from the Drive-In Church, gave them to people poorer than she ever was. Got her picture taken a lot. Tustin people thought she looked like the old SunBlesst girl, so they did up a poster of her with oranges, an old-fashioned kind of picture that made her look really pretty and made it seem like Tustin still had orange groves.

But all that only lasted two or three months. Then she got on the cover of *Playboy*. Wore almost as much clothing as she did for the SunBlesst girl poster, but the Tustin City Council demanded a new queen. She split Tustin for Laguna and started UCI same month. Didn't talk to any of them after that. Didn't want to see a Tustin face or hear a Tustin name. Felt like that part of her was dead. Said she wouldn't go back to that town if you gave her a million dollars.

But she did, thought Nick. One last time.

It was mostly Karl and Lenny who talked. Casey just sat there on the cooler with his back to Nick. Getting more and more tense the more he heard, Nick could see. Shoulders moving in. Head hunching down a little. Hands in front of him. Moving now. Nick eased his hand under his coat and popped the holster snap. Casey caught the sound. Big dirty head turning Nick's way.

'Just to keep things fun and fast, I'm going to

need alibis from you, Lenny, and you, Casey. What were you two princes doing two nights ago? Tuesday.'

'We got drunk and watched TV,' said Lenny. 'Right here. Right, bro?'

'Right.'

'What shows?' asked Nick.

'Fuckin' *Mod Squad*,' said Lenny.

'*It Takes a Thief*,' said Casey.

'Fuckin' *Twilight Zone*,' said Lenny.

'Then *Alfred Hitchcock* and we fell asleep,' said Casey. He didn't turn but his hands were still moving in front of him. Like they were doing something small.

'Now get off my property,' said Lenny. 'You got what you need.'

'You know Red and Ho?'

Casey turned. Blank stares. Like three empty glasses on a shelf.

'You should probably go, Nick,' said Karl. 'They were here. I was, too. The kitchen faucet was dripping bad and I'm a fair plumber. The *Twilight Zone* was the one where the world ends and the guy's in the library with all those books and he breaks his glasses.'

'That's a good one,' said Nick.

'Yes, it is,' said Karl Vonn.

Nick heard something click and saw Casey's shoulders move.

He took two steps forward, held one foot over the Hessians emblem on the back of Casey's vest.

Pushed hard. The cooler tipped up and Casey went over and rolled onto his back. He lay there for a moment, looking up the barrel of Nick's gun. Sunglasses still on. Roller in one hand with the paper already in it, a bag of tobacco in the other. Yellow-brown flakes and strings spilled onto his stomach.

He aimed the roller at Nick, pulled a trigger.

'Someday,' he said.

'Never,' said Nick.

'Lunatic pig,' said Lenny.

That evening Nick watched part of the autopsy. It was performed by Dr Warren Gershon at the Meak Brothers Funeral Home in Santa Ana because the Coroner's Department had no autopsy room. Certain county funeral homes allowed the autopsies to be performed on-site, no charge. But Nick knew they pressured the next of kin to have the embalming and funeral arrangements done there, too. Wives and husbands crazy with grief. Made some good money that way. Meak Brothers was located downwind of a Kentucky Fried Chicken restaurant and Nick went from the smell of deep-fried thighs to formaldehyde as he walked in the embalming room door.

Nick watched the doctor and his assistants make the big Y incision with the scalpel. Cut the ribs with loppers and pull apart the cage. Tijuana Brass playing quiet on a radio, a perky little number Nick would detest for the rest of his life.

The crack of bones loud above the music.

Watched them cut out her organs. Cut out her heart. Examine and weigh and record.

Tutu and a guitar.

He noted Janelle Vonn's head, partially wrapped in a white towel and placed faceup in a plastic cooler of dry ice. Skin blue-white. Vapor wafting over the top, then down to the floor like horror-movie fog.

They got scrapings from under three fingernails and the right thumbnail.

When Gershon was done with that Nick asked them to amputate the thumbs and three fingers that had had flesh and blood under the nails. Bag and label them separately. Freeze them for evidence.

'That's very unusual,' said the doctor.

Nick left the room without excusing himself and drove to Angel's Lawn cemetery to be near Clay. Shivered and heard the traffic blasting by on I-5 while he thought about his brother.

Then to Sharon's place in Orange.

She let him in and they talked awhile in the near dark. His eyes burned as he felt the awful collapse of his will. His will to ignore. His will to put aside. His will to call it a job and leave it at the office. He just couldn't make himself do it. Maybe homicide wasn't his thing, he said.

It would pass, she said.

Nick said he'd be all right. Don't worry. Said

this is what homicide detail was about.

Sharon understood all of this. Her dad a cop and her ex a cop and she took Nick into her room and talked to him and held him and did the things that made him forget and feel better.

When he was finished, he left for Millie's bar.

Two doubles and two bowls of pretzels later he was ready to go home.


'Dad's home! Dad's home!'

*'Be quiet, kids. QUIET!'*

Nick could hear their voices on the other side of the door. Katy unlocked the deadbolt from inside and Nick fell into the deafening family he loved with such frustration.

'WILLIE SLUGGED ME IN THE STOMACH!' screamed Katherine.

'SHE BIT MY LEG!' Willie screamed back.

Steven racked his plastic Thompson submachine gun with spring-loaded noisemaker, then lowered the barrel into his family with a gleeful smile. Pure Clay, thought Nick.

*Klat-a-klat-a-klat-a-klat-a-klat-a-klat!*

Katy hugged Nick and smiled hugely. She was large and beautiful and Nick felt the crack in his heart get bigger. Sometimes pictured it going across his whole heart at once, breaking it in two. Did his own heart even count after what Janelle had gone through?

'My hero,' she said.

'MY HERO!'

*'MY HERO!'*
*Klat-a-klat-a-klat-a-klat-a-klat!*

'I love you guys,' Nick said quietly. He touched them one at a time. Katy on the arm and Willie on the head and Katherine on the cheek. Perfect precious parts. All in place.

Except for Steven, who saw his father's hand coming toward him. Stevie let the old man eat some hot lead from the Thompson and ran yelling down the hall.

# 12

Andy sat in the *Journal* newsroom and looked out the darkened windows. Seven o'clock, Thursday, one day after seeing Janelle Vonn in the SunBlesst packinghouse. The lights of Costa Mesa twinkled in the cool breezy night outside.

The presses downstairs were silent for now. The AP and UPI teletype machines were quiet while the night editor dozed in his office. The city desk guys were off in the cafeteria shooting the bull. Associate publisher Jonas Dessinger was long gone, execs on the fifth floor long gone, too.

Andy took another big gulp of cool coffee, wondered why he wasn't hungry. Hadn't really slept since late Tuesday night. Heard about the Boom Boom Bungalow stabbing and didn't put that story to bed until three in the morning. Guy was an elementary schoolteacher from Bakersfield. Eleven stab wounds. Looked horrible, the way the skin swelled up to close the slits. No way the *Journal* would print stuff like that.

Perp still at large. Then Wednesday and Janelle. Twenty-six straight hours. And still counting, because Andy's source at the County had a hot tip for him but she wouldn't give it to him over the phone.

He never could sleep with stuff like this going down. Teresa could sleep through an atomic explosion, so long as she got herself relaxed first.

He'd scooped the *Los Angeles Times* today. Waxed 'em. Just like he'd waxed them on the Boom Boom stabbing. Great to beat the big boys. The *Times* reporter who did the main Janelle Vonn story had Janelle still living in Texas when she was eight. Said Karl had worked as an electrician when he was a plumber. And they went to press too soon to even know about Terry Neemal.

Clobbered the *Santa Ana Register*, too. They got Neemal but none of his mental hospital stuff or his criminal jacket. Nick had helped him with that because Neemal's juvenile record was sealed. Not the first time Nick had come to the rescue.

But the clincher was Andy's sidebar photograph. He'd snapped it through the window of the Tustin PD cruiser when his brother ran back into the packinghouse for his tape recorder. Neemal even bared his teeth for the shot. Growled, gave Andy the full Wolfman act. The front-page picture showed this hairy, weird-looking guy glaring at his handcuffs, one sleeve pulled back to show a wrist like something out of a horror flick. Hands dirty. Eyes crazed.

‘WOLFMAN’ QUESTIONED IN BEAUTY QUEEN
DECAPITATION
*Story and photos by Andy Becker*

The *New York Times* had even picked it up.

A million phone calls to the *Journal* to say Andy's article and pictures were great.

A hearty handshake of congratulations from *Journal* publisher Jonathan Dessinger.

An indifferent handshake of congratulations from *Journal* associate publisher Jonas Dessinger.

A telegram from newly elected Republican congressman Roger Stoltz, all the way from Washington.

Andy's guess was that Terry Neemal was a severe nutcase who had the bad luck to be found near a murder scene. Nick had corroborated that idea in his blunt, almost wordless way. But it was hard to completely dismiss a guy who as an eight-year-old set his brother on fire, walked out, locked the door, and had a bowl of Wheaties.

At eight-thirty Andy locked up his desk. Got his briefcase, stopped by the supply cabinet for some more typing paper, and headed out.

Put the top down and took the Corvair down Coast Highway to Laguna, ocean rippling off to his right and a fat moon low over Catalina Island.

A Wolfman moon, he thought. Good title for a paperback crime novel except Neemal probably didn't do it. But Neemal was still a great newspaper story. And the picture was press club award material, no doubt. *Story and photos by Andy Becker*. Turned the police band radio loud. Hoping for news on a Boom Boom Bungalow suspect but nothing doing.

The Sandpiper Nightclub was peaceful when he walked in. Band drinking at the bar before the first set. Some good-looking hippie girls with them. Beads and headbands and little oval sunglasses to hide their pupils. Canned Heat on the jukebox, that cool little number with the harmonica.

Verna sat at the other end of the bar, ignored him as he came over and sat down. He had to kind of squeeze onto the stool because Verna was big. She was a clerk in the county payroll office, did the Sheriff's, Fire, Ag Department, and Sanitation. Strawberry hair and an unhappy face that Andy could see the prettiness trying to get into. He always thought if Verna dropped fifty, threw on some makeup, and tried smiling, she'd be a stone fox. Though he wasn't sure how 'stone' got to be an adjective.

As it was, she had a crush on Andy that he'd never acknowledged. He let her buy his company with occasional payroll gossip. She pretended to be distrustful of phone conversations but Andy knew she was just lonely. She liked coming down to Laguna to see the cool people, rub up against the druggies and artists. A contact high. Andy enjoyed her company. Liked the way she disguised her fear with humor and hostility. Liked her insatiable lust for gossip, innuendo, insinuation. And her honesty.

'Orange juice and vodka,' she said.

'I love you, too.'

'You're such a huge liar.'

'I know.'

Andy ordered drinks. Glanced down the bar at the hippies. Clove cigarettes and sudden laughter. Glassed eyes. Slurred vowels. Wondered if he and Teresa sounded that way when they got loaded at night.

'Andy, what was it like, seeing her with her head cut off?'

'My heart sped up. It made my legs feel cold and weak.'

'Really?'

'It amazed me that someone would do that to someone else.'

Verna thought about this, said nothing as the drinks arrived and the barman went.

'Nick sees murder every day in homicide,' she said. 'And of course, Sharon every night in Orange.'

'The less you talk about that the better, Verna.'

'I've never told anyone but you.'

'Keep it that way.'

Andy disliked what Nick was doing and that it was known. Before, when he'd watched Nick and Katy together they made him believe that you could get married and stay in love. You could see them pass love back and forth. Like an invisible box, a big one, the size of a TV maybe, they'd always be handing it off or gathering it in. One of the few married couples he'd seen do that. Now they were just one more reason to skip the service. Maybe these dipshit hippies were right. Free love. Sure, why not? For Nick and Katy it was pretty pricey stuff.

And if a clerk in payroll knew, who didn't?

'Was it all bloody?'

'Less blood than you would think,' said Andy.

'I heard the Wolfman's beard had blood in it. Like he'd eaten part of her.'

'That's asinine, Verna.'

She shrugged.

'So, what's up?'

Verna rocked her glass. Nothing but ice and a red plastic straw. Andy waved the bartender for two more. Verna stared across at the liquor bottles. Kept staring at them until the drinks arrived and the barkeep was out of earshot.

'This is interesting,' she said. 'I do all those department payrolls, right? I get to see what everybody gets paid. Big deal. But I also cut special payment checks, too. You know, for subs or consultants, or emergencies. Stuff like that. The Sheriff's Department has an informant fund, for their snitches and spies and all. That money comes from us as "Discretionary, Informational" – one monthly sum based on the year's budget. That's the last we see of it. The department breaks it down division by division. And the divisions break it down for each detail. Homicide. Burg-Theft. Like that. Well, today I'm logging in the numbers on my ledger, making sure the amounts match the checks. Basic bookkeeping. And up comes Captain del Gado with a cardboard box full of Girl Scout cookies he'd sold to some of the people in payroll. He sets it on my desk, finds the order forms, and gets out the Thin Mints and Savannahs. Hands them to me, picks up the box, and goes. But guess what?'

'You ordered Shortbread.'

'No. There's a new sheet of paper on my desk. Came off the bottom of the box is all I can figure. Static electricity maybe. Anyhow, it's a typewritten disbursement log for narcotics detail. For inform-ants and drug buys, all that. Third from the bottom, in the amount of two hundred dollars?'

'Janelle Vonn.'

'Right.'

'On the Sheriff's payroll. I like this.'

Verna looked at him and nodded. Took a big drink. 'I thought you would.'

'Two hundred dollars,' mused Andy.

'So . . .'

'So you . . .'

'So, I've been hearing about Janelle Vonn all day, right? I mean the whole county building is buzzing with the beheaded beauty queen, so I discreetly visit my good friend—'

'Pam, in Assistant Sheriff Louden's office.'

'Right, and she tells me, in absolute strictest confidence, that Janelle Vonn has been on the payroll for *four years*.'

Andy clicked straight back to his conversation that morning with Craig, owner of Blue Beat records. Thought of the merry stoners he'd seen hanging around in the back of the store – Timothy Leary and Ronnie Joe Fowler and that Indian fakir with eyes like wet obsidian. The sweet smell of hashish. And Craig saying while he hung the black light behind the counter so the Cream poster would light up blue, *The thing about Janelle is she liked getting high, but she got it under control. Then she got into acid and really dug it. For her it was pure experience. Chick had a brain.*

But, thought Andy, to collect a paycheck she had to hang with the heads. Tell some tales. Deliver pay dirt, sooner or later. Try LSD and find out she really liked it.

Craig didn't know if Janelle had had a regular job or not.

Nick didn't, either, as of midnight Wednesday. He'd said all the pay stubs he'd found in her cottage were old.

Karl Vonn didn't know. Neither did Janelle's degenerate brothers.

Andy clicked back to another conversation. Five months ago, May. Ran into Janelle coming out of the White House bar with three locals he recognized. One was a big blond hippie guy who owned a local leather store. Cory somebody. One a hotshot movie director just back from making a surfing film in South Africa. And Jesse Black, the musician, scruffy and lost-looking as always.

Janelle had looked vibrant and self-conscious. Unforgettably lovely. A nominee on Oscar night. None of that hippie stuff. A tailored black leather jacket with silver on it and red accents. Black satin pants, leather boots. Dark waves of hair faceted by streetlight. Red lips and dimples. Skin pale in the fog.

The three men acted bored while Janelle stepped away to talk to Andy.

*Got my own pad here in town. I love Laguna. Everybody's so friendly.*

*You look good, Janelle.*

*I'm so sorry what happened to Clay. Call me some-time. Here. I'll write the number.*

Now Andy wondered if Janelle could have afforded a place of her own in Laguna on a snitch's salary. He made a note to ask Nick again if Janelle had had a job.

'What are you thinking about?' Verna asked.

He shrugged.

'Never *mind*,' she said.

What he was thinking about was the White House matchbook Janelle had written her phone number and address on. Tossed it in his change drawer. Never called because that night outside the White House his heart had fallen to the side-walk and bounced to Mars and back. Even though he was twenty-six and she was just a year out of high school. Even though he was with Teresa and intended to honor that. Even though he understood that Janelle Vonn was more valuable untouched by him.

So he'd kept the matchbook. Looked at it a few times. Saw her cottage from the beach a couple of times. But never called.

'I'll tell you what *I* was thinking about,' said Verna. 'I was wondering why the cops were paying a fifteen-year-old girl to risk her life.'

'Me, too.'

The band started off with 'Satisfaction,' ran off some Byrds and Dylan. Andy and Verna took a booth for themselves because there was hardly any crowd.

Teresa blew in around ten, glasses slightly askew and hair messed up by the breeze. Against the fashion of the moment, Teresa had recently cut her pretty auburn hair short. The night she did it she'd told Andy she wanted it businesslike but had left plenty of craven sex in it for him. Proven it, too.

One of her other reporters was with her, the guy who covered Newport Beach. Chas Birdwell. Andy disliked Chas's smug face and the degree he'd earned at Stanford as a classmate of Teresa's. She'd fired her former Newport Beach reporter, brought Chas down from San Francisco, and put him to work. Told jokes only they got. Knew all the same people. Stupid football games. Reunion every year, some rich kid's summer mansion up in Tahoe. All that shit you didn't get at Fullerton State, especially when you dropped out after two years.

As Teresa came across the empty dance floor toward him Andy had to smile. Something about her. Tall and slender. Cagey eyes in a pretty face, a wild laugh. Great brain. When she sat down and kissed his cheek he could smell the pot in her hair. And see the big black pupils in her gray eyes.

Chas offered Verna a dismissive little peace sign, Andy a nod, as he slid into the booth behind Teresa and sat down.

Five minutes later Jesse Black ambled in. Black had a guitar case in his hand, a worn peacoat. Then behind him, the leather store hippie in some cool black leather jacket like you'd figure. Cory. Black stayed by the stage. Cory headed straight for the bar. Cory must be six-five, thought Andy. Black stood with a forlorn expression, looking at the band.

'Uh-oh,' said Chas. 'Guitar boy thinks it's open mike night.'

'His name is Jesse Black and he's a better song-writer than you are a reporter,' said Andy.

'Whoa,' said Chas. 'I've been put in my place.'

'Cool it, Andy,' said Teresa.

Verna leaned toward them. 'He was—'

Andy found her knee under the table and squeezed it firmly.

'He was up in L.A.,' said Andy. 'Making a demo tape the last few months. Working the clubs.'

'Right,' said Verna, placing her hand over Andy's, still on her knee. 'That's about all I know about him.'

Chas nodded without interest. Shook the wave of thick blond hair off his forehead. Had one of those stiff imperialist mustaches. Like you should salute it.

Teresa looked at Andy oddly but he saw her curiosity melt into the high she was on. That's why she smoked it, he thought. For the way it dulled one part of her mind and sharpened another. Close one window. Open another. They said the LSD was best of all. Sandoz. Blotter. Windowpane. Orange Sunshine. Purple Haze. Wasn't sure if he had the balls to try it. Stories about people going permanently insane. Oops, wrong window. Didn't seem to have hurt Tim Leary any.

'So, what have you two been up to tonight?' Andy asked.

Teresa recounted her night so far with Chas: a Newport edition editorial/advertising meeting at six, quick bite at the Crab Cooker at seven, fund-raiser for the Charity League at the Newport Pavilion, you know how those things drag on forever.

Chas chuckled. Verna nodded. Andy watched Jesse Black as he propped his guitar case against the carpeted wall beside the stage and pulled out

140

a Martin with a pickup built over the sound hole.

The band finished 'Taxman' and the lead singer welcomed Jesse Black onstage.

Everyone clapped. Maybe eight people. The hippie girls with the clove cigarettes extra hard. They were checking out Cory at the bar.

Chas clapped stupidly loud, the wave of hair over his forehead jiggling.

Black slung on his guitar. Plugged in and strummed a chord. Made his way to the lead singer's mike, pulling his cord through the stands and monitors.

Little guy, young. Thin and pale. Dark stubble, dead eyes.

'Some songs for a girl I knew,' he said. Turned his back on the tiny audience and conferred with the lead guitarist.

'His high school sweetheart?' Chas whispered to Teresa. 'Died of a banana peel overdose?'

'That's dumb,' said Teresa.

'What do you expect from a spoiled moron?' asked Andy.

'Let's go outside,' said Chas.

'Piss on you.'

Teresa grabbed his ear and turned his face to hers. 'What's *wrong* with you?'

Andy jerked his head free. 'I'm sorry. No sleep. The Vonn thing has me wired and weird.'

'Go home and sleep. I'll be there later.'

'I'm writing tonight. First I want to hear some music.'

'Leave Chas alone. You don't get to abuse the personnel just because the boss is in love with you.'

'Good. Yeah. That's fair.'

For the next hour Jesse Black sang twelve of the prettiest songs Andy had ever heard. Sweet and smart. Passionate and humorful. Sexy, sad, beautiful. He was a good guitar player and his chords changed unexpectedly. His music sounded new and different in a way Andy couldn't put a finger on. The band knew most of the songs, you could tell. Filling in at the right time, backing off for the rest. Nice voice, too. Clear, a little high, something innocent and yearning in it.

The last one Jesse Black did alone. A song he'd finished about two hours ago, he said. 'Imagine You.' The band kept their places. Hung their heads and listened. Twenty-one-gun salute, thought Andy, rock and roll style. The drummer banged a stick on his high hat when he wiped his eyes, looked embarrassed.


A little while later Andy said goodbye to Teresa and walked Verna to her car. Kept walking up Coast Highway after she drove off. At St Ann's he went down the concrete stair steps to the sand. From the beach he could see Janelle Vonn's little cottage up on the rise. And the black ocean with a wobble of moonlight on it.

Should he have called her? Maybe learned what the inside of that cottage was like?

Would that have changed things? Changed what happened in the packinghouse?

He thought of Meredith in her red coat with the upturned collar and the falling stars. Married a dentist. Batch of kids already. Better that way. She deserved better than him.

Thought of Clay. That face of his. That grin. The confidence he had. His meanness that wasn't quite mean. The assumption that he was right and he would win and his cause was good. A sniper near Kontum. Hearts and minds. How many like him dead by now – seventeen, eighteen thousand? *Eighteen thousand!* For what? *It became necessary to destroy the village in order to save it.* He'd actually heard an army 'spokesman' quoted as saying that on TV the other night. The words had been haunting him ever since.

Andy also thought of himself. Standing right here on earth, this brief little man. Thought of Jesse Black's songs about Janelle and his own story about the Wolfman Terry Neemal and wondered at the difference between the two. He wanted to make something beautiful, like Jesse Black had made. Andy felt this thing inside that was Janelle but not only Janelle. Believed that a lot of people would want to have the same feeling if he could just give it to them.

Then he saw a light go on in Janelle Vonn's cottage. Saw a man move past a window behind the curtain. One of Nick's guys?

Nick himself?

Jesse Black?

Andy moved into the shadow of the bluff. Crunched along the ice plant until he made the stairs. Took them two at a time, trying to keep from slipping on the smooth sandy steps. Legs wobbly. Made the top and stayed with the shadow to the north wall of the house. Squatted down and leaned against it. Heart throbbing against his ribs so loud the world could hear it.

He could hear the man inside. Drawers quietly opening and closing. Closets. Cupboards. Hard shoes on wooden floors. Not urgent. Not covert, really. Methodical.

Ten minutes of that, then nothing. Andy's legs sore now, the circulation cut down. He moved closer to the north window, got his face up to the bottom corner of the weather-beaten frame.

The curtain didn't quite cover the pane so Andy got a peek in. Just a sliver but he made out the sofa and posters and part of a kitchen at the far end. A hallway leading back into the house.

Then the man coming from the hall toward him, into the kitchen. Just a split second of face in the light: white guy, late twenties, short dark hair. Suit and tie. He turned and came into the living room, sat on the sofa. Andy could see his profile. Dark eyes, looking up at the ceiling. Thoughtful. Considered. The guy sat there and stared for five minutes. Hardly blinked. Then he stood and went to the front door, locked it. Wiped the lock and knob with a white hankie and walked out.

Andy scrambled around the house, out of sight. Heard footsteps, a car door open and shut. The engine turn over.

When he heard tires moving on blacktop he peeked around the corner. A white four-door pulled up to Coast Highway and made a right. Got the California plate numbers.

He sat for a few minutes with his back against the yellow cottage. Wrote the numbers in his reporter's notebook. Then up to Coast Highway and the pay phone at the market. Took forever for this guy with a ponytail and earrings and eyes red as rubies to hang up. Pregnant woman on the other one, feeding in dimes like a slot machine.

Nick picked up on the fourth ring and Andy told him what he'd seen. Nick made him say everything at least twice. Taking notes, Andy could hear. He checked his watch when he hung up. It was almost one in the morning.

Back down to the sand. Then along the moon-silvered beach to Cress Street and his home with Teresa. She was still gone. Probably closing the 'Piper, thought Andy. If Chas wasn't such an asshole he'd be worried about her.

He sat in the living room for a while and thought. Nick hadn't ventured a guess as to who the guy might be. But Andy wasn't expecting one.

He poured a light drink and went into the little laundry room. His spot. Quiet with the door closed. Good light overhead. Typewriter on a rolling stand, a towel folded under the machine so it wouldn't bang and echo too much late at night and wake up Teresa. Smell of dryer lint and detergent in here, always liked it.

He took the manuscript out of the cabinet and looked it over. Three hundred and eighty-one pages. His third full novel. Two others too worthless to show, boxed right there in the cabinet side by side, like a couple of beds in an empty room. Proof of something, Andy believed. Stubbornness? Devotion? Vanity?

He looked down at the paper and thought about the scene. Where the smugglers heading from Mexico to Laguna drop the Orange Sunshine and trip all the way through Baja. Don't realize the *federales* are following them. Point where the adventure turns ugly.

*Strange Trippin'* by Andrew James Becker.

He stared at the blank page for a while, tried to let his mind fill up with the story.

But it wouldn't fill up. He couldn't even get interested. Couldn't think of anything but Janelle Vonn – *Baby, time will pass you by but you can catch up if you try* – in the packinghouse with her head ten feet away. And the guy in her house. And his unhappy brother trying to find out why.

Helluva first case. Now that was a story.

# 13

David set the ladder into the back of his work truck, then the two boxes of marquee letters. Drove slowly across the undulating parking lot.

His mind was troubled, his heart heavy. Janelle Vonn. He had no words for what had happened. Such a sweet girl. The limitless cruelty of man. He would have to address it in his message Sunday. Without a doubt. And that was the day after tomorrow. How?

He thought of the Wolfman Terry Neemal. And the chill that had shuddered through him when he first looked into Neemal's tan eyes from outside the protective custody cell at O.C. Jail. The man gave off waves of madness. But that was why David performed his jail ministry for the last eight years. To keep him in touch with the unfortunate and the misunderstood. Neemal didn't belong on the same planet as Janelle, thought David. An unholy thought. So wrong. All of it.

David looked out at the up-slanted parking

pads that had once allowed visitors to watch movies without straining their necks. Halfway across the parking lot he braked, put the truck into park, and looked back at the new chapel.

The building was simple and functional. To David it was magnificent. To grow in five quick years from a congregation of twenty-seven to nine hundred and fifty-two was a miracle. Literally. While Presbyterian Church (U.S.A.) attendance dropped almost 3 percent adjusted for the birthrate, the Grove Drive-In Church of God was flush with capital improvement and well on its way to paying off its loan.

The new chapel seated four hundred and thirty-eight, more with folding chairs on Easter and Christmas Eve. Stained glass in three directions. An epic triptych covering the Creation, the Life of Jesus, and the Resurrection. A handsome altar and pulpit. Wonderful sound system and acoustics. Gently curving maple pews to fit the gentle curve of the big room. Plenty of light, man-made and God-made. Dark green carpet with a pattern of small orange chevrons. Two Sunday worship services in the morning at eight-thirty and eleven. An evening service at dusk. Drive in. Walk in. Come as you are.

No more offering boxes to lug in from the exits. There was now a small offering box on every speaker stanchion. No rented organ and player. No more low snack bar ceilings or snack bar smells.

David turned away from the new chapel, thought back to the morning that Janelle had come to worship. Drugged and dirty. Debased. He thought of the distance she had traveled in the five years since. Her growth and maturity. Her intelligence and curiosity and beauty coming through. Blooming. No drugs or booze, for a while at least. Miss Tustin. The runs to Baja to help the poor. Then the *Playboy* scandal. Always sexually adventurous. Lord, what you put her through. Now this.

He looked out at the new speakers and parking spots that now made room for three hundred and fifty vehicles. And the new outside worship garden that seated fifty more worshipers during the clement months. And the playground for the kids.

All of this upon the newly laid asphalt parking surface painted a comforting shade of sky blue. David and one of his deacons cleaned the entire lot at sunrise every Sunday morning before services using two loud street sweepers donated by the City of Garden Grove. Those, and untold donated gallons of Orange Sunshine – a new asphalt cleaning product developed by Roger Stoltz's RoMar Industries. The product was actually made from the waste products of orange groves removed for development. It had a mild acidic action that cleaned asphalt beautifully without breaking it down. And a clean citrus smell. Orange County, then twenty-four other counties in eight other states, had contracted to purchase enough of it over the next four years to make Stoltz a comfortable man.

But it was difficult, thought David, to find much joy in sky blue asphalt, with the body of Janelle desecrated like that. How could he even approach that event in a sermon designed to be uplifting? Or at least cathartic?

David leaned his head on the steering wheel of the new Chevy. Prayed hard. For wisdom and understanding and words. *Give me the words, dear Lord. For my business and yours.*

Then he opened his eyes and looked up at the most impressive improvement that God had allowed him so far. The sole surviving movie screen was no longer a monstrous eyesore, but a hand-painted color panorama of the raising of Lazarus. Brilliant. Breathtaking. Awe-inspiring. David had commissioned the artists to enlarge and replicate the famous Rembrandt in every possible detail. The newspapers and TV had had a field day with it – three hundred and eleven days to complete. Four artists. Modern-day Michelangelo-Rembrandts hanging from scaffolds while they painted a twenty-foot Christ on a ninety-foot movie screen. Once-dead Lazarus with the breath of life blown back into him. Six months ago, early the first morning after the painting was complete, he'd taken pregnant Barbara and their two other children out to see *The Raising of Lazarus* in the clean light of dawn. The children had fidgeted. Barbara had noted the chill of the morning. David had slipped quietly to his knees and prayed.

David put the truck in gear and drove through the exit. He'd had a new marquee built just four months ago, a larger and brighter model. Purchased Roman-style letters, the most biblical-looking ones he could find. In black. They went beautifully with the neon Grove Drive-In Church of God sign above, an indigo blue cross draped by a garland of bright oranges with light green leaves.

He parked next to the marquee. Got out and looked up at the pithy slogan he displayed each week, just under the 'Sunday's Message' announcement. These short statements were often harder for him to come up with than an entire sermon. He subscribed to *Independent Ministries* magazine, which supplied dozens each month for ministers in a pinch. But this one was David's own:

*Offer the Lord what's right, not what's left*

Above it was the sermon title made irrelevant by the death of Janelle Vonn.

KEEPING YOUR HEART YOUNG THROUGH GOD'S LOVE

He set up the ladder, took down what letters he could reach. Moved the ladder and took down more. Stood there a minute when he was done and remembered all those years ago, how the marquee had bothered him so much. Because he feared it was just like his future: empty.

How silly that fear had been. His life was full. His ministry. His health. Barbara. Two children of their own and one adopted.

Emptiness is Janelle Vonn. No. Emptiness is who did that to her.

David got a Bible from the cab, then swung down the tailgate and sat. The morning was warm and clear, no breeze. He could see the cars out on busy Beach Boulevard, just one street over from the church.

He still had two days to write the message, but only one hour left to get its title onto the marquee. He turned to the Song of Solomon, looking for inspiration, comfort, and a title.


With great delight I sat in his shadow,
   and his fruit was sweet to my taste . . .
O that his left hand were under my head,
   and his right hand embraced me!


No, not that. He sighed, rubbed his temples, tried Psalms. Then Matthew, then Paul's first letter to the Corinthians.

All he needed was a title. So people would know his topic for this Sunday. What few words could do justice to a young woman, bright and lovely and troubled and murdered before she had had enough time to truly live a life?

Who had trusted him with her secrets as he had trusted her with his?

Then it came to him. First heard at the Sandpiper a few months ago, in the company of Janelle Vonn. From heaven through Jesse Black to David and his marquee:

Sunday's Message
A WAVE THAT NEVER MADE IT QUITE TO SHORE

Two days later David stood at the pulpit in his new chapel and looked out at his eight-thirty congregation. Face pale. Eyes burning in sadness. Not one empty seat, not even the folding chairs he'd set up because his heart told him that all three services would be full.

His parents were there. Nick and Katy and the kids. Andy and Teresa.

Karl Vonn and Ethan, out from Florida. Stone faces. Black hair slicked down. Somehow darker than the people around them.

Congressman Roger and Marie Stoltz in from Washington. Assemblyman Hennigan from Sacramento. The mayors of Tustin, Orange, and Anaheim.

Press all over the place and news crews from Los Angeles outside with video cameras and microphones.

David began by making the worshipers see that Janelle had been just like them. Beautiful and flawed and human. He told them how he had first met her in an orange grove back when he was just a boy and she a very little girl.

And how their families had become acquainted through the death of Janelle's mother. How the Vonns were the first family in need that he had ministered to as a young divinity student at San Anselmo's.

He told them about some of her troubles as a young teenager. The way she'd fought and changed and held on to what was good inside her.

He spent a long time on all of her good qualities, her humor and her creativity and her gentleness. Her generosity. How it pleased her to help people less fortunate than she was. How she'd always take the underdog. Some of this David knew from personal experience, some examples he had gotten from her family and friends.

So when he told them what had happened to her, even though every single person in the room knew already, the recognition issued through them all. Janelle was the wave that didn't make it quite to shore.

Then to the dangerous part of his message. The part that David believed but had trouble expressing.

He stated that what had happened to Janelle was a blessing for every person in this room. Maybe a miracle. Because *it did not happen to anyone else*. Because God had chosen Janelle for this work. Just as God had chosen Noah and Moses and Jesus, verily every one of us, for some special work on earth.

Throughout all this David sensed the doubt within the worshipers. Chosen? Me? For what? Not for something like that. He could see them recoil, each person just a fraction of an inch, but the inches became a communal mile of retreat. He looked out at them, said nothing. He let them think. Let them wonder what God would choose them for. He didn't tell them it would be for something glorious or grand, because not everything God did could be glorious and grand. Sometimes it was small and humble.

So when David suggested that for right now, for this specific moment, God had chosen for them to be here to worship Him and love one another, he could feel the relief wash through the room in one huge exhalation. The worshipers moved forward fractionally and the mile of retreat was reclaimed.

Then he moved into the heart of his message: that in God's hand a tragedy was a tool used to make a shape for love. The sculptor's chisel. The painter's brush.

'And we are the raw material,' he said. 'The rock and the canvas.'

He had never heard a more inspired rendition of 'Amazing Grace,' not an easy song for a congregation to sing.

'Let us bow our heads in prayer.'

When the prayer was over David heard the chorus of car horns from outside. The car worshipers were for the most part a younger and occasionally rowdy crowd. Sometimes the honking would last ten or fifteen seconds.

One minute later the last horn stopped.

David stood outside the chapel and shook hands with the worshipers.

'You healed my heart,' said a white-haired man.

'God healed your heart.'

'They hit us with mustard gas outside Calais and I saw half our men get cut to ribbons by machine guns. Now I know why they died and I didn't. I've been going to church and praying for sixty years. You healed my heart, Reverend Becker. *You* did.'

He took David's right hand in both of his, held tight and shook.

The woman next in line shook his hand and wiped a tear from her eye. 'Mine, too.'

Then hustled away.

The service drained him. They all did, but this one was almost exhausting. Took the spirit right out of him.

He was lying on the couch in his new office, rearranging his thoughts for the eleven o'clock worship, when Barbara knocked and cracked the door.

'Nick's here, honey.'

'Terrific,' he said softly. Sat up. Nick didn't look terrific at all. He looked tired and hungry. 'Come in, Nick. Where's Katy and the kids?'

'Outside at the playground.'

David stood and offered a tired smile to his wife as she softly pulled the door closed behind her.

'Sorry, David. But just one thing.'

'What's that?'

'Your sermon made my scalp crawl. It was that good.'

David smiled again, more energy this time. 'Hard to do, get a cop's scalp to crawl. How are you holding up, brother?'

'Fine. Katy's fine. Everything's fine. So, you know Jesse Black.'

'Janelle introduced us.'

'Yeah, he told me. I talked to him yesterday. Nice touch, using his lyric as a title.'

'I didn't think he'd mind.'

'Think he's got any violence in him?'

David plunked back down to the couch. 'None whatsoever.'

'When do you mail the worship programs?'

David turned to face his brother. 'Wednesday mornings. Why?'

'Janelle had today's program in her house on Thursday morning. But even if the U.S. mail got it there in twenty-four hours, she wasn't alive Wednesday to bring it in from the mailbox. So she got hers on Tuesday.'

David's heart shuddered but he lay back down on the sofa. 'Then she got an early copy. They print them up late on Tuesday afternoons.'

'Who picks them up?'

'Well, this last Tuesday it was Deacon Shaffner.'

'I have to talk to him.'

'I understand. You're trying to catch the bad guys. I'm trying to help the rest of us. Ask Barbara for his number. Better yet, here . . .'

David labored to his desk, consulted a book, and scribbled down a name and number.

'Rest up for round two, David. You were great.'

'Nick? You won't find a killer in my church.'

'How do you know?'

David studied his younger brother. Even in his own exhaustion David was alert enough to see the change in Nick. Janelle? The pressure to find who killed her? This was Nick's first case as lead. Scary.

'Are you okay?' David asked.

'Yeah, I'm perfect.'

David had the thought that Nick and Katy weren't right. With married men, it presented as dull anger. Married men became resentful in looking for something that had vanished. Looking for something they used to love but couldn't find anymore. Being married with children was hard. David knew that, all right. Sometimes it seemed like everything in the world conspired to make you lose the love for what you once loved most.

'You and Katy all right?'

'Same old.'

'I'll pray for you.'

'Thanks, brother.'

Nick walked out and David prayed. A short one for Nick and Katy. *Let them enjoy each other and find each other again in this busy* . . . but fell asleep halfway through it. Lurched awake six minutes later to rewrite the sermon just a little for the eleven o'clock.

# 14

Nick sat in Assistant Sheriff Gorman Harloff's office arranging his notes before he spoke. Monday morning. Clear and warm. Five days since the packinghouse.

Harloff was dark-lipped, silver-haired, and humorless. Sometimes referred to as Boris Karloff but never to his face. He had Crimes Against Persons and narcotics under him. CAP included homicide. He had a pen in hand and a legal pad on the desk.

Lobdell sat beside Nick staring down at his small, shiny shoes.

'Shoot,' said Harloff.

'Yes, sir,' said Nick. 'Janelle Vonn died of strangulation last Tuesday the first, sometime between noon and midnight. It looks like she was killed somewhere else but decapitated in the packinghouse. This, from the amount of blood we found. Our witness, Terry Neemal, says he saw a man go into the packinghouse late the night of the first. Neemal said the man was regular-sized and had something bulky over his shoulders.'

'Like a body?'

'That's possible, sir.'

'Strong guy. She weighed what?'

'One hundred and twelve pounds.'

'Pretty strong,' said Lobdell, lighting a cigarette. 'If he's wearing her like a mink stole.'

'But not a big man,' said Harloff.

Nick waited while Harloff wrote. 'Even with the tearing and trauma to her neck, Gershon found constriction marks. They're consistent with the shape of fingers and thumbs. None of the postmortem mutilation would account for them.'

'The sawing,' said Harloff.

'Correct. She was raped by a type A secretor. Gershon found semen inside her, genital bruising and abrasions. But here's a twist, sir – there was semen on her underwear also – type A non-secretor.'

'Two guys might have killed her?' asked Harloff.

'Maybe.'

'This Neemal, then?' asked Harloff. 'What's his ABO?'

'He's type A also,' said Lobdell.

Harloff made a note. 'Between the O and the A, that would include what, about eighty-five percent of the population?'

'Correct,' said Nick. 'We'd have better odds if neither was a secretor at all.'

'But don't forget,' said Lobdell, 'that Neemal is certifiably insane.'

'What does that mean?' asked Harloff. 'That he's more likely or less likely to have raped a woman and chopped her head off?'

'More, I'd say,' answered Lobdell. He blew one good ring, then a plume of Tareyton smoke toward the ceiling. 'Look, he's creeping around that night, says he saw this, says he saw that. Oh yeah? I think we should sweat him. See what comes out.'

Harloff looked at Nick. 'Any of Neemal's fingerprints at the scene?'

'None,' said Nick. 'He says he walked into the packinghouse, saw her, turned around, and walked back out. This was the next morning.'

Harloff wrote again. 'The building wasn't locked?'

'Neemal said he saw the guy slide open the main door. We found a padlock in the grove. Partial print on the lock. Not Neemal's.'

'Who does security?'

'Talon,' said Nick. 'They only patrol the SunBlesst site Thursday through Sunday. So their last check would have been two days earlier.'

Harloff wrote.

'Something's interesting, though,' said Lobdell. 'One of the Talon guards told us the older padlocks get hard to open. Rain and sun and they corrode. Won't take the key. Said you can line up the Schlage to look locked when it really isn't. You just get the links up inside the shackle and it looks locked. Then, you're making the rounds you just pull down and twist it open, pull it off, and you're done. Don't have to wrestle with a difficult lock and key. He wasn't the SunBlesst guard. Maybe just a blowhard, but that could have been what happened.'

Harloff considered. 'But none of the SunBlesst guards said the lock and key were bad?'

'Nope,' said Lobdell. 'Not that they would.'

Harloff wrote, frowned. Wrote some more. 'Go on.'

'She was approximately eight weeks pregnant,' said Nick. 'The zygote was apparently healthy at the time of her death.'

'Wish it could talk,' said Lobdell.

'I do, too,' said Nick. 'No drugs in her system. We believe she was an LSD user but there's no test for that. Blood alcohol was point-zero-eight, so she was drinking moderately. Except for the decapitation, she wasn't mutilated or tortured.'

'Pretty big exception,' said Lobdell.

'She defended herself. We got flesh and blood scrapings from under a thumbnail and three fingernails on her right hand. Type O. I had three fingers and a thumb amputated and frozen along with the scrapings.'

Nick saw the rise of Harloff's eyebrow but the assistant sheriff said nothing.

'She'd eaten Mexican food approximately four hours before she died,' said Nick. 'Gershon found it in her large intestine. I corroborated this with some take-out containers and a receipt in a wastebasket in her kitchen. Apparently she ate at home that night, with two men – "Red" and "Ho." Obviously they're key, but I haven't come up with them. Yet.'

'She have a date book?' asked Harloff.

'Yes, sir. It had the Red and Ho date, and lots more. And I found plenty of phone numbers and notes and scribbles in her house. Several pages torn from pay phone books, with names and numbers circled. Matchbooks. Business cards. She knew a lot of people. She had a wide range of friends and acquaintances.'

'Boyfriends?'

'At least one,' said Nick. 'A singer. Says he was up in Los Angeles that night. The names and numbers he gave me checked out. I'll talk to him again.'

Harloff nodded. 'I guess a fallen beauty queen might have as many boyfriends as she wanted.'

'We found some of her clothes thrown off toward one corner of the packinghouse,' Nick said. 'A black miniskirt and boots. No blood on them. No physiological fluids at all. So, he – or they – must have taken off those clothes before they used the saw.'

'What about that saw?' asked Harloff.

'A folding pruning saw with a ten-inch blade – 'Trim-Quick.' It's made by Garden Forge. Wooden handle, sells for around four dollars. It appears to be either new or very lightly used. The blade was ripped off where the bolt goes into the wood and we haven't come up with it. Yet. Maybe he took it with him. No prints on the handle but lots of blood. All samples we took off it were type B – Janelle's type. We're checking Tustin area nurseries and hardware stores that might carry them.'

'How long would it take?'

'What, sir?'

'To saw off her head.'

'Gershon said that depended on how hard he worked at it. Strong man, going fast, two or three minutes.'

Harloff made a note of this, too. 'Seems slow to me. Neemal see a car that night?'

'A large light-colored four-door,' said Nick. 'He didn't see it real well. He said maybe a Cadillac or a Lincoln or one of the big Chryslers. Late model.'

'His arm really have that much hair on it? The paper made him look like an ape.'

'There's a patch of it that thick, sir. A dermatologist in Santa Ana told me it's a type of birthmark. Rare. You see them on dark-skinned people. Neemal's mom was Haitian.'

'Find any of those hairs on Janelle?'

'No.'

'Wouldn't the papers love that?' Lobdell asked. 'Your brother could write Wolfman stories for weeks. Then a book and a movie.'

'My brother's story was good,' said Nick. 'He played down the Wolfman stuff.'

Lobdell shrugged. 'I had a birthmark like that, I might go crazy, too.'

'Neemal tried to kill his brother when he was just a child?' asked Harloff.

'Yes, sir. Set him on fire. The record is sealed but Neemal's old juvenile investigator works Burg-Theft here.'

'But the brother lived?'

'Third-degree burns over forty percent of his body. He died of cancer at twenty-five.'

Harloff wrote again. 'We've charged Neemal with the small stuff, so we can keep him?'

'Yes, sir,' said Nick. 'Vagrancy and trespassing. We could bump it to destruction of property and indecent exposure because he was crapping in the orange grove. Judge Miller came in high, as we asked. And Neemal has no money for a bond, anyway. So he's not going anywhere.'

'Should we work up a case for murder?'

'I don't think so,' said Nick. 'But I'll want to interview him some more. He's valuable as a witness. And if we cut him loose we might never see him again.'

Lobdell lit another smoke. 'Speaking of cuts, you left out the Wolfman's hands, Nicky.'

'Neemal has small cuts and abrasions,' said Nick.

'Consistent with defense wounds,' said Lobdell. 'According to the examiner.'

'But apparently a few days old,' said Nick.

'Look,' said Lobdell. 'In my opinion, if you have a dead beauty queen and an attempted murderer who finds her, doesn't tell anybody, then says some regular-sized Hercules lugged her into a packinghouse, and you got his semen on her and his hands are scratched up – guess what? You charge him. They'll just toss him back in the loony bin anyway.'

Harloff flipped a yellow page, wrote something, and underlined it twice. 'Nick?'

'I'm not ready to charge him.'

'His first case as lead,' said Lobdell. 'He's being careful. Everything by the book.'

Nick nodded, staring at Lobdell. He knew Harloff saw it but he didn't care.

'What are your conclusions so far, Nick?'

'The key is the dinner. Who are Red and Ho? They might have been the last people to see her alive. They might even be our A and O secretors. The wine and water glasses in Janelle's cottage were covered with prints. All we could get were smudges and overlaps. Bad luck. Just a mess.'

Harloff nodded. Nick knew that Harloff had worked Crimes Against Persons for most of his career. So Harloff understood that too many prints was almost as bad as none at all.

'The doorknobs gave us nothing but Janelle,' said Nick. He felt like he was making excuses. He wanted Harloff to know he was going to get this guy if it was the last thing he did.

'But we've got good descriptions, sir. The Pepito's hostess said Janelle came in with two men to pick up the order. Said they were both squares. Shirts and ties. Early thirties, both white. One was six foot one or so. Brown hair cut fairly short. Mustache. Good-looking but not overly so. Second was five-nine, short blond hair. Clean-shaven. The hostess is about Janelle's age. I asked her if there was anything threatening about the men. Anything odd or off or maybe dangerous. Nervous, agitated. She said no. Two "full-on squares" is what she said. One even wore a flag pin. Neither spoke to her. They took the food and talked to each other while Janelle paid for it. Maybe Red and Ho are unrelated to this. But I think whoever did this knew her. She'd been around the block enough to know what can happen. She wouldn't take off with just anybody. I know it's only speculation, but I think this guy hated her. Really hated her. The mutilation took time and it wasn't necessary. She knew him. The NCIC wasn't much help. They've got eight unsolved homicides with post-mortem decapitations in eight different states but some go back ten years. Most recent is Illinois – sixty-four and it was an elderly woman. Nothing reported in California. Nothing with a saw.'

'What about the associations?' asked Harloff.

Nick had already talked to the California Identifying Officers Association to see if any similar crimes had occurred in other California jurisdictions. A Humboldt County decapitation murder had been closed out earlier in the year when the son confessed to killing and mutilating his mother for 'mental cruelty.'

The California Homicide Officers Association had nothing but put him in touch with a half dozen other associations throughout the American West – Arizona, New Mexico, Nevada, Utah, Oregon, and Washington State. Nick had spent so much time on the phone over the three days his ear had swollen and his neck hurt. He'd come up with three current unsolved murders of young women with postmortem beheadings. It surprised him that they weren't reported to NCIC. But none of the mutilation killings had happened closer than four hundred miles away.

'Red and Ho,' said Harloff. 'Like "Better Dead Than Red"? Or like Ho Chi Minh?'

'I've gotten nothing political from this so far,' said Nick.

'Laguna's full of radicals,' said Lobdell. 'All kinds of political types. Marxists, Bolsheviks, anarchists, demonstrators, flag burners, atheists, God haters, peaceniks, hippies, yippies. Dopers and flower children. Fairies all over the place. That Leary nut from Harvard is still there with his LSD religion. You drive down Coast Highway on a hot night you can smell the marijuana in the air. The canyon there is full of dealers selling anything you can imagine. They call Woodland Street Dodge City because the law can't get in. Or so the hippies think.'

'I know,' said Harloff. 'I oversee narcotics.'

'I know you know,' said Lobdell. 'I'm just saying if Vonn was living in that mix down in Laguna, she could have had just about anybody over for Mexican takeout.'

'The two squares sound more like Mormons to me,' said Harloff. Then a rare smile. Dark lips, white teeth. 'Or insurance salesmen or FBI.'

Lobdell didn't answer.

'Interesting you should say that,' said Nick. 'One of my sources said a white male searched Janelle's cottage Thursday night. I tracked the car plates back to the FBI resident agency in Santa Ana.'

Harloff raised his eyebrows and tapped his pen on his desk. 'FBI? I know one of the agents there. I'll make a call and see what that was all about.'

'Appreciate it, sir.'

'Odd, though,' said Harloff, 'that they didn't contact us.'

In the silence Nick cleared his throat. Looked directly at Harloff. Time to play another one of Andy's tips. Thank God for little brothers who were also newspaper reporters.

'Sir,' Nick said. 'There's something else you can do to help us.'

'Shoot.'

'I heard that Janelle Vonn had been on the narcotics informant payroll for four years,' said Nick. 'If that's true, someone there knows her a lot better than we do, just coming in now. We need to talk.'

Harloff nodded curtly. 'Who told you that?'

'I'm not free to say.'

'Talk to del Gado.'

'Thank you, sir.'

Harloff studied him for a long time. Nick held his gaze for a beat, then looked away.

A few minutes later Frank del Gado, the narcotics captain, unhappily told Nick and Lobdell that he'd look into it.

When they got outside the building Nick stopped and looked at his partner. 'Hey, Lucky.'

'Yeah.'

'Fuck me again in front of my boss and you can find another partner. I don't care how it looks or who gets written up, I'm not working with a guy who won't stand by me.'

Lobdell eyed Nick. Almost smiled but didn't. Nodded instead. 'Good.'

# 15

They went to a late lunch at the new place, Lorenzo's, up in the Anaheim hills. Nick had found the Lorenzo's matchbook in Janelle Vonn's shoe box. And the Lorenzo's phone number written in three different places in the pile of papers by her phone.

He showed a five-by-seven black-and-white photograph of Janelle Vonn to the hostess. The hostess had long hair and a startlingly brief skirt. About Janelle's age. In Nick's opinion they shouldn't let girls dress that way, but he liked it when they did. Katherine would never be allowed to dress like that. The hostess had never seen Janelle.

The dining room was almost empty. A few people drinking in the bar. The steaks were pricey so Nick got the Ortega burger with a big wet chili on it. Lobdell went with the lunch special New York cut.

The waitress had seen Janelle Vonn here at

Lorenzo's about a week ago, she said.

And one time before that, maybe a month earlier. Both times large parties, thrown by the Lorenzo's owners.

'That's really a bummer what happened to her,' she said. 'She was younger than me.'

'What day of the week was she in?' asked Lobdell.

'Friday or Saturday. Super busy.'

'Are any of the owners in today?' asked Nick.

'Not today. They never tell us when they're coming. They just arrive. But let me get the manager.'

'We'll just knock on his door, say hello. Okay?' asked Nick.

'That's cool.'

The office was small, bright, and neat. Radio playing 'Soul Kitchen.' Smell of aftershave. Raquel Welch poster from *One Million Years B.C.* on the bathroom door. Fur bikini on a body like that, thought Nick. Unbelievable.

The manager didn't understand why he couldn't help the detectives but the owners of Lorenzo's could. Said he knew the operations up and down, knew personnel better than any of the investors, knew what was going on and what wasn't. He wore his hair short and a U.S. flag pin on his coat lapel. Nick thought it was odd that half the men in the country had hair like this and a flag pin while the other half had hair down to their backs and were loaded.

Nick showed him the picture.

'Oh,' he said quietly. 'Sure.'

'Sure what?' asked Nick.

'She's been in. Hard to forget a fox like her.'

The manager sat, flipped through a Rolodex file on his desk, and handed Nick a business card. Nick read it. Heart did a little hop. He handed the card to his partner.

'He'll put you in touch with the others,' said the manager. 'I think there's five investors total, maybe six. They're all *Journal* newspaper guys. Don't know anything about this business.'

'Enough to give you good reviews,' said Nick.

The manager smiled. 'Kind of biased, maybe.'

JONAS DESSINGER
*Associate Publisher*
*Orange County Journal*

'This the guy she was with?' asked Lobdell.

The manager shook his head and stood. 'Ask him.'

'I asked you.'

'Let's just ask Jonas,' said Nick.

They were near the *Journal* building in Costa Mesa at four. Lobdell had to stop at a convenience store pay phone on the way and call Shirley and talk to Kevin. Lucky's voice was always soft and serious when he talked to his wife. Then with his son it was loud and brusque. Nick bought a pack of cigarettes, stood under the overhang of a U-Totem market in Orange, and smoked one while he half eavesdropped on Lobdell barking at his son. Saved the rest of the pack for the Wolfman Neemal. Waste of thirty-four cents. Wondered what relation Jonas Dessinger was to Teresa, Andy's girlfriend. Hoped he and Lucky didn't have to walk through the newsroom, call attention to themselves, get Andy curious.

Nick watched the cars go up and down Tustin Avenue. Liked the new AMC Barracuda and the Mustang and the Dodge Dart convertible. Figured it would take a lot more overtime for a deputy with a wife and three to afford something like that on top of the Red Rocket, which they needed for the kids. Thought of his father and mother and how they drove the Studebaker until it quit. Right there on Holt Avenue, smoke billowing out of the grille like napalm is how Dad described it. Still waxed and polished, probably. What, hundred and fifty, two hundred thousand miles? Nick figured his mom and dad had plenty of miles left on them and that's what counted. Wondered at Max's obsession with the Communists, how he went crazy with it after Clay. Him and Roger Stoltz and their damned meetings and rallies. The booze. And Monika getting quieter and slower, like Max was stealing her energy. Part of her died when Clay did. A blind man could see that.

Lobdell walked from the phone booth, broad shoulders forward, head down in thought. Nick saw disappointment in Lucky's hard gray eyes as he shook his head and went to the car. Nick couldn't figure if Lucky was more pissed off or worried.

Jonas Dessinger kept them waiting for half an hour. Nice enough lobby but the receptionist had to give them badges and buzz open the door before they could come in and get on an elevator.

Third floor, office with views of Newport Boulevard and the tracts of Costa Mesa. Good-sized room, sparsely furnished. Framed *Journal* press club and CNPA awards on the walls. Funny leather and chrome furniture.

Dessinger was early thirties, dark-haired, gray-eyed. Thick mustache. Under six, slender. Tapered suit, a European look, not like those Botany 500s on TV. He had that funny hairstyle, covering the ear tops and a shock hanging down his forehead but short in back. No sideburns. Like he wanted it both ways, thought Nick. Half square, half hep. Like he'd wear half a flag pin.

Nick cast him as Red. Maybe. Pictured him balancing a full-grown woman over his shoulders while he pulled open a padlock, threw it into an orange grove, then slid open a two-hundred-pound door on rollers. Iffy. Maybe whoever it was put her down and picked her back up. Not easy, either.

Dessinger said that Janelle had been his guest at two dinner parties at Lorenzo's.

Jonas was a bachelor, by the way.

He and Janelle had been friends and lovers.

He had last seen her on the Saturday afternoon before she died, when she'd broken off their relationship after 'an almost unbelievable session of lovemaking.'

Jonas looked out a window, smiling privately. Then back to the detectives.

'How old are you?' asked Nick.

'Thirty-four.'

'She was nineteen,' said Nick.

'And that made us consenting adults.'

'Pathetic is what it makes you,' said Lobdell. 'Bet you didn't mention those dates in your fish-wrap newspaper social page, did you?'

'And the point of that would be . . .'

Nick felt the change then. The altered frequencies of the room as Lobdell's anger filled it. He could tell that Dessinger had no idea.

Lobdell stood and went to a window. Looked out. Just as well, thought Nick. Let him cool off.

'Where were you last Tuesday? Between noon and midnight, say.'

'Which is the approximate time of death?' asked Dessinger.

'Maybe,' said Nick.

Dessinger leaned forward and flipped back the pages of a desk calendar. 'Here in this building, noon to five, minus an hour-and-a-half lunch at the Ancient Mariner. Home to Newport by five-twenty. I live at the Bay Club.'

Of course he does, thought Nick.

'Nap, news, tennis, dinner. Drinks, drinks, drinks. Good nights around one A.M. There were four of us. I hate to drag them into this but—'

'Into what?' asked Nick.

'Janelle.'

'What, Saturday she's unbelievable but now she's something stuck to your shoe?' asked Lobdell.

'What does that mean?'

'He's referring to a certain callousness that comes off you, Jonas,' said Nick. 'He thinks you're an asshole. So do I.'

Dessinger looked at Lobdell, then Nick. Nick saw no worry at all in him.

'Moving right along, here are three numbers to call to corroborate my story.'

He took his time writing. Finally slid a sheet of typing paper across the desk to Nick. Capped his pen and returned it to the breast pocket of his tailored suit in one confident motion.

'Anything else, gentlemen? I've got an early dinner date tonight.'

'Poor girl,' said Lobdell.

'Good, then. It's been a pleasure.'

Dessinger rose and stood behind his desk. Offered a winning smile to Nick as he picked up the paper.

Lobdell shot a hand out with surprising speed, got hold of Dessinger's left ear, and forced his head to the desk. Dessinger yelped and bent at the middle to keep his ear on, spread his arms out, and chattered his feet like he was dancing a show tune. Lobdell walked him to the edge of the desk, then forced him down. Dessinger's legs collapsed and his chest hit the carpet with a huff. Lobdell knelt, ear still in one hand.

'What shall I do with him, Nicky?'

'I really don't know.'

'Take your time.'

'Here.'

Nick drew his ballpoint from his jacket pocket and wrote '19' on Dessinger's forehead. Blew on the numerals.

'It's a short editorial,' said Nick.

'Use Old Dutch cleanser and some steel wool,' said Lobdell. 'Get that ink right off before your date tonight.'

When they got in the elevator Nick looked at Lobdell's heavy face. Had to laugh. Lobdell did, too. Lit a cigarette.

'That was dumb,' said Nick.

'Yeah.'

'Harloff's going to kill us. I just got . . . pissed off.'

'Me, too,' said Lobdell. 'Look, Dessinger won't say anything. It'd ding his pride. Watch out for him, though.'

'How can you find out your lover was murdered and show absolutely no feeling?' asked Nick. 'There's people who didn't ever meet her who feel worse than that guy.'

'The shrinks got some name for it. Some kind of "path."'

179

'I've never seen anything like that.'

'Homicide gets you the winners,' said Lobdell. 'Wolfman. Newspaperman. You never know who's next.'

They stepped out of the building and into the crisp evening. Red leaves swaying on a box elder. Sky an unlimited blue. A new black Mustang flashed down the boulevard.

'Makes me hope his alibi is bullshit,' said Nick. 'Makes me want to bust him all the way to the chamber.'

'It's never the guys you want it to be,' said Lobdell. 'Usually some drunk little prick, loses his temper. Or thinks a gun makes him tough. Or some guy who's spent half his life in the slammer, doesn't care if he goes back or not. Dessinger couldn't hate anybody enough to do what we saw. Wouldn't mess up his clothes.'

Nick only just now worried that he'd done something to damage his brother. Andy had come up with good information – the FBI and the narc payroll – and he'd given them both to Nick. Pronto. In return Nick had helped mutilate Andy's boss. Maybe Dessinger hadn't been paying enough attention to connect Becker to Becker. Maybe Dessinger didn't have anything to do with the reporters. Better give Andy a heads-up either way.

Nick got Terry Neemal out of protective custody and into an interview room. Tossed the smokes on the table. The jailers had shaved his hair and beard for lice but left a gigantic mustache. The former Wolfman looked like a toy-breed dog trimmed for hot weather. They'd shaved down the wolfish arm hair, too. The skin was still almost black, like it was burned or paved. Terry rubbed it, frowning.

'They hacked me up.'

'It'll all grow back.'

Nick made small talk for a minute. Asked about the food and the exercise room and the other inmates. Neemal told him he'd met Nick's brother, the jail chaplain.

'Nice guy,' said Neemal.

'Let me see your hands again, Terry.'

Neemal held them out. Turned both over. Then turned one over, then the other, but flipped the first one back. Smiled at Nick like it was a magic trick.

'How'd you get the cuts and scrapes?'

'I told you. I don't know.'

'They were deep enough to bleed. To hurt and get infected and make scabs. But you don't know how you got them?'

'That's the truth. But I will say . . .'

Nick waited. On his first morning here, Neemal had been attacked by a trustee who said his sister had been a beauty queen. Hit Neemal across the shins with a broom handle. Deputies had over-whelmed the trustee but the incident seemed to have made Neemal feel important.

Since then, Neemal had kept a collection of newspaper clips about himself and allowed some deputies to photograph him, freakish arm prominently displayed. His posture was better. He was hurling back insults at the other inmates, who chided him whenever they could. *Wolfman. Head Chopper. Hairy Motherfucker Werewolf Man*. He ate every bit of his bad jail food and often asked for more.

Nick noticed that Neemal had developed a love of dramatic conversational pauses. He liked to set up his statements with the phrase 'But I will say . . .' He had changed minor details in his story several times. Nothing substantial. Nick had spent a half hour or so with Neemal every day since his arrest. Kept thinking the Wolfman would come up with something truly useful.

'What will you say, Terry?'

'That I saw the girl twice that night.'

Nick considered. 'Are you counting when she was on the man's back? The man who carried her into the packinghouse?'

'Actually not.'

Nick lit a smoke for Neemal and one for himself. 'Talk to me, Terry.'

Neemal crossed his arms and looked down at the table. Blew out smoke. 'I saw her once. Like I told you. Then I went back an hour later.'

This was new. 'Why?'

'I wanted to confirm what I thought I'd seen.'

'Confirm.'

'That means make sure.'

'I know what it means. And?'

'She was there all right. No head. Underpants.'

'And what did you do?'

'I don't remember anything until the police woke me up.'

'Not one thing?'

'No.'

'Not even walking out, sliding open that big heavy door, finding the way back to your lean-to in the dark?'

'No.'

'You went back and looked at her.'

'Correct.'

Nick stood there and watched Neemal smoke. 'You didn't take the saw blade?'

'No.'

'Kept it, put it somewhere for later?'

'Why would I do that?'

Nick shrugged. Had no idea why. 'What did the shrink say today?'

'Said I could have my old meds back if I wanted. I said no. I may see and hear stuff that isn't there but at least the reception is clear. With all the drugs from Atascadero it was like being underwater.'

'I'd like to know more about why you went back to see Janelle that second time.'

'So would I.'

Nick shook out another cigarette and handed it to Neemal. 'Did you kill her, Terry?'

Neemal looked down at the table again. 'I didn't kill her, I'm pretty sure. But I will say . . . that sometimes my memory falls behind, then jumps ahead and catches up.'

'Terry, after five days and everything we've been through, you tell me you're only pretty sure?'

'Uh-huh.'

'Next time, you tell me why you went back to see her.'

'Sure. Okay, Nick, I'll give it some thought. Thanks for the extra cigarettes. Would they put that in the paper?'

'Put what in?'

'If I had some reason why I went back and saw her.'

Nick looked into Neemal's mad tan eyes. Considered the possible answers. Then chose the one that would help him most. And would help Terry Neemal probably not at all.

'The newspapers would be interested in that. Yes.'

And I can get you an interview with the *Journal*'s best crime reporter, Nick thought.

'Good night, Terry. The deputy will be right in.'

By seven that night Nick had talked with Deacon Mike Shaffner, who said he'd picked up the worship programs at six o'clock last Tuesday night. No, he had not given one to Janelle Vonn or to anyone else. Hadn't seen Janelle.

Shaffner was very tall and thin, blond hair, gentle hands. Nick couldn't cast him as Red or Ho. Or anybody who would do the kind of violence he had seen.

Shaffner said he'd taken them home and put the mailing labels on, rubberbanded them into stacks, and set them in a paper Market Basket bag to take to the church in the morning for postage. There was a postage machine in the office, which saved him licking stamps. Though it still cost the same six cents for each one, which hit the Grove Drive-In Church pretty hard. He said he finally dropped them off at the post office in Orange Wednesday morning around ten.

Shaffner didn't know for sure, but he guessed the programs were printed by five o'clock. The job was done at the *Tustin Times* building, by a man named Gunnar.

'Nick Becker? I'm an old friend of Andy's,' said Gunnar.

He smiled a jagged smile at Nick. Held out a blackened hand. He was short, late sixties. Oddly tanned for this time of year. Sharp eyes and thin brown hair combed from one side of his head to the other.

'Oh, Andy was one of the best reporters we've had. I was glad to see him go. He needed to try bigger things. These little weeklies, you know, you stay too long and end up like me.'

'You seem all right,' said Nick.

Gunnar smiled. 'He likes the *Journal*?'

'I think so.'

'The Wolfman pictures were wonderful,' Gunnar said.

'It was good work.'

'He came by here a few months ago with the lady friend, Teresa. To say hi and for me to meet her. He likes me to know his women. I was pretty good friends with Meredith. I wished he could have stayed with her but it was impossible. You knew that Andy was going to go out and experience the world. But she has a family now. Like she wanted.'

Nick smelled the clinical scent of vodka. Looked around for the glass or bottle but saw neither. Noted the radio playing upstairs, oddly loud. Sounded like the big-band swing music his parents used to listen to on 78s.

Gunnar told him that the Grove Drive-In Church worship programs had been completely finished and boxed by 5:15 P.M. last Tuesday. He was sitting at his desk reading the blockbuster paperback *Valley of the Dolls* when Mike had come to pick them up. That was about six. Gunnar said he printed eleven hundred each week now. Used to be two hundred. The *Tustin Times* couldn't profit from such a small run, but Mae Overholt – J.J.'s widow – did it as a favor to God and David Becker. And *Valley of the Dolls* really wasn't as bad as some people said.

A side door opened and a handsome woman

came in, glanced at Gunnar and Nick with a pleasant smile. Mid-sixties, Nick figured. Had to be Mae. She waved in a way that promised no interruption. Just got something from a desk drawer and went back out. Looked like a roll of masking tape.

'Anyone else come by?' asked Nick. 'Maybe to check the print run, grab a few early copies?'

Nick heard a new song start upstairs. No doubt about this one – 'Smoke Gets in Your Eyes.' One of Max and Monika's favorites from when they were young. Danced to it in the living room. Boys hooting and fake throwing up.

'No,' said Gunnar with a sharp little smile. 'I've heard of people rushing the printer for an early copy of an important newspaper. But never in all my sixty-seven years have I had someone rush the printer for a worship program.'

'That's funny, isn't it?' asked Nick.

'It is.'

'Until you realize someone did exactly that. And gave a copy to a girl who was murdered a few hours later.'

Gunnar's already dark complexion went a shade darker. He took a deep breath, let it out. 'No, no. There is no humor at all in that.'

'Not much. Who could have gotten early copies without you knowing?'

Gunnar sighed. Looked down at the floor as if chastising himself. 'This is . . . no, this can't be what you mean.'

'Try me.'

'I spent forty-five minutes away from the presses that night. Between the time I finished the programs and six, when I was expecting Mike Shaffner.'

'Were those doors unlocked?'

'Yes.'

'Where were you?'

'Right upstairs. With Mae, having an aperitif and some conversation. We do that often now. Since Mr Overholt passed along. And I heard a car door shut. I didn't hear a car drive up, but I heard the door shut.'

'Because of the radio?'

'Yes. Mae and I were listening to the radio. I got up and looked out the window and saw Barbara Becker get out of a blue station wagon. I think it was a Kingswood Estate. The Chevy. A bunch of kids in the back.'

Nick frowned, tried to remember the exact words of his conversation with David. He hadn't said anything about Barbara and the flyers, had he?

'Did you go downstairs and talk to her?'

'By the time I got down there she was back in the car. I didn't run after her. I figured it was something to do with the flyers, and how important could that be?'

'She didn't take them?'

'No. Mike took them. Like I told you. Maybe fifteen minutes later.'

Mae came through the side door again. Another pleasant look for Nick. One a little sharper for Gunnar. She put a roll of tape back in the desk and left.

Nick called Sharon from a pay phone, said he wouldn't be over. She said fine, she was awful tired, too. They talked quietly a minute and hung up.

Then he called David and Barbara's house. Got Barbara because David was out. Made small talk, then asked about her picking up early copies of the worship flyer last Tuesday around quarter to six.

'I sure did,' said Barbara happily. 'Just a few for my youth group to send out. Nick, is everything okay?'

# 16

Andy Becker crunched along a gravel walkway toward one of the guesthouses behind Big Red in Bluebird Canyon.

Wednesday, a week after Janelle Vonn in the SunBlesst packinghouse. Light breeze, warm in the sun but cool in the shade. Seagulls crying over the beach. A hawk in the canyon pivoting just ahead of its own shadow, a flash of sun on its wings. Smell of ocean and sage and marijuana smoke.

The weather-beaten slat cottage sat at the far end of a mostly brown lawn. One of three, all similar. Wood silvered by the sun. Roof shingles warped. Stained-glass windows – hummingbirds and flowers. Small stands of plantain and giant bird-of-paradise for privacy. Beyond them rough hills sloping into the sharp blue Pacific.

Andy was about to knock when the cottage door slapped open. The window glass rattled. A young woman, batik sheet around her and nothing else, marched past, never looked at him. Bare feet on the gravel, orange hair flying, headed for the main house. Andy looked back at the girl and the big slouching home, barn red in the clear morning light. Big Red, all right. Paint peeling, blankets for curtains. Rain gutters askew.

Jesse Black stood in the cottage doorway. Hair a mess, jeans slung low and loose, a red plaid flannel shirt hanging out.

'I'm the writer,' said Andy. 'Thanks for meeting.'

'You were at the 'Piper last Thursday,' he said.

Andy offered his hand and Black lightly knocked his fist against it. Black looked past him toward Big Red, then back at Andy. His eyes were dark and lively. Dark stubble on a pale chin.

'Come on in.'

Andy stepped through the narrow door into a tiny living room with a small couch. Throw rugs and beanbags. To the left a galley-sized kitchen. Sink and refrigerator and small counter. Cupboards and a window. Down a very short hallway Andy could see another room and what looked like the foot of a bed.

But mostly what he saw were instruments. The well-used Martin with the pickup over the sound hole leaned in one corner. An old f-hole Epiphone and a small amplifier in another. A white Stratocaster sitting upright on the couch. Beside the couch a Sears Silvertone electric with the amp built into the case. A ukulele stood beneath a window facing north up the coast. Maracas. A tambourine. Two recorders and a harmonica on the kitchen counter next to a plastic bag half full of grass and rolling papers.

'Busted,' Jesse said without interest.

'I'm cool.'

'I didn't have that out when your brother was around. The whole compound was under FPA.'

Andy waited.

'Full Pig Alert,' said Jesse. Didn't smile but his eyes did.

'That's halfway funny,' said Andy. 'It's the cartoons of pigs dressed like cops getting shot and stabbed that bug me. Because he's my brother.'

'Yeah, it's all bullshit. One side against the other.'

Black motioned to the couch. Took the Strat and plunked himself onto a bright yellow bean-bag. 'I don't get why you want to talk to me. Your articles about her already came out.'

'I'm interested for myself,' said Andy.

'You mean for a book or screenplay?'

'No. For me. I liked her. I'd known her since I was twelve. I mean, never well, but still . . .'

Black strummed the electric. Unplugged, it made a distant sweet sound like it was under-water. 'She talked about you. You wrote the obit for her mother. She showed it to me. It was more than just an obituary, though. You got the mother's misery. But you knew the difference between pathos and tragedy. I grooved on it.'

'Thank you. Most people don't recognize the difference.'

'And you wrote that thing about her family. Now that was awesome. Got the stupid animal brothers and the innocence of Janelle and her sister. Changed the names and places, but you got the truth of it down. A lot of people knew it was her.'

'Not everybody,' said Andy. 'But, yeah. A lot of people.'

'People wanted to help her after that.'

Black strummed a change that Andy recognized from the Sandpiper set last Thursday night. 'Smoke?'

'Sure.'

Black set the guitar down and went to the kitchen counter. 'This *sinsemilla* is dynamite.'

'I've heard about it. You and Janelle smoke a lot?'

'No. She liked acid. Leary turned her on to a dose of genuine Sandoz and she took to it. Not every day. Maybe once a week. Liked a little tequila, too.'

Black rolled a joint in less than a minute. Tight, slender, and filled all the way to the ends. Torched it with a Bic. A sweet green smell and Andy felt the smoke fill his lungs and the instant tilt of his senses.

'Those were good songs at the Sandpiper,' said Andy. 'Even without knowing Janelle I would have liked them.'

'Outtasight.'

'"Imagine You" blew me away.'

'Came in a rush. Wrote it in a couple of days. Right after I heard.'

They passed the joint in silence. Finished half and let it go out. Jesse cranked open a hummingbird stained-glass window. Took the Stratocaster and sat back in the yellow beanbag.

Andy looked north out a clear window to Main Beach and the life-guard stand and the boardwalk. Waves lazy on the sand. A vulture shot across the sky startlingly close to the window. Could have reached out and touched him.

The door slammed open and the orange-haired girl swept in. Sheet still clinched around her with one hand and a beer in the other. Had to put down the beer to get the roach to her lips, the lighter to her sheet hand, and walk back out. Not a glance at either of them.

'Crystal,' said Jesse.

'Bummin'.'

Jesse shrugged. 'She's a good keyboardist. Kind of possessive, though.'

Andy could see the vulture, smaller now, framed in the window of sky. 'I saw her. Janelle. After it happened.'

'I'm glad I didn't.'

Andy felt his heartbeat echoing in his eardrums. Same thing every time, first few minutes of a high. The *sinsemilla* was stronger than any he'd ever had before.

'I'm not sure why I put myself through it,' said Andy.

'I've tried not to picture her that way,' said Black. 'It's bad enough to see that kind of thing in a book or something. But if it's someone you loved, almost impossible.'

'The first time I saw her was by that packinghouse. This was, man, fourteen years ago. Something like that.'

'The fight.'

'The rumble. After it was over her sister ran down the embankment with rocks in both hands and threw them at us 'cause we'd just wailed on her brothers. Then Janelle, she was maybe like four or five, she's got these two oranges and she's going to throw them but she changes her mind. Blue dress and cowboy boots. Looks at us, drops the oranges, says something about her brothers, and runs away.'

Jesse was picking now, a muted aquatic twang when he pushed the tremolo bar. 'First time I saw her was at the 'Piper. Playing a set on a dead Sunday evening. In she walks with some girlfriends. I played straight to her for the next hour. Directly to her. Forgot to take my break. Just her and me in that room. I sat with her and her friends after. They bought me drinks. I was freakin' in love with her by midnight. Still am.'

At the same time, Andy and Black both leaned over and pulled small beaten notebooks from their pant pockets.

Black saw what Andy had done, dropped the notebook in his lap, and picked the *Twilight Zone* intro on his high E string.

Andy smiled and made a note of Jesse forgetting his break the first time he played for Janelle. Pot made you pay attention to the small things. All immediately fascinating. Most pointless.

'What did you write?' Andy asked.

'I wrote *"in love with her by midnight."* It came with this A-minor riff. A lot of stuff I write in Laguna does. I think it has something to do with the ocean, or maybe the hawks. Or maybe this dope I get from Ronnie Joe. Listen.'

He strummed some chords and sang *'in love with her by midnight'* in a melody over them. Then again, but a different melody. Then another one. Andy was amazed anyone could do that, just invent three different melodies in thirty seconds. Black was full of music like Andy was full of words.

'What part of the song is it?' he asked.

'Who knows? Chorus, maybe. You know, hook line for the radio. Sing it loud enough to hear in a car. What did you write down?'

'You, forgetting your break when you first saw Janelle.'

'I wanted to sing my way right into her pants.'

'Guess you did.'

'Later, yeah.' Black played the A-minor riff again, looking through a stained-glass window back toward Big Red. 'I wasn't alone there. In her pants.'

'No?'

'No. I told her she was free. I meant it. She had a dude. She'd been hooked up with him awhile, and I think it was a long while. Hardly talked about him. Never told me his name. Never told me what he did or what he looked like or anything. The only time she even mentioned him was if she couldn't be with me. Once a week. Maybe twice. Then we'd be together three straight weeks and it was like there was no other guy. Then, well . . . she'd have to go.'

'Go for how long?'

'An evening,' said Black. 'Sometimes part of a weekend day. She'd come up here after she was done. She'd be quiet. Not unhappy, really. But subdued. Still.'

'Numb?'

'Maybe,' said Jesse. 'But not stoned. Not drunk. Just . . . calm.'

'You never saw him?'

'No. Never asked. Never followed her. Not my thing. People are free, you know? Free as they want to be.'

'Maybe she wanted to be less free,' said Andy.

'I don't think so. She had a thing with Cory, too. He's a bro. It was good karma for all of us. Least we thought it was.'

'She didn't want limits and rules and security?'

'Not Janelle.'

Jesse plucked the opening notes of 'Pretty Woman.'

'She was pregnant,' he said.

Andy's heart dropped and flipped. Damned pot was bad enough, but then this ton of information. 'Who was the father?'

'She didn't know,' Black said quietly. 'Maybe me. Maybe the mystery dude. Maybe Cory Bonnett. She was scheduled for an abortion on Friday afternoon. I was going to take her in.'

Andy's heart rushing in his ears again. He remembered Meredith and him at the clinic in Santa Ana. Dr Degaus Delineus. Suction. Over fast, but Meredith white and weak for hours. Dazed for days. Empty and distracted and tearful for weeks. So long to get over it. And he too foolish and young to understand what she was going through. What it meant to her body and her soul. What it meant that he hadn't asked her to marry him and have the child. Andy felt the spiraling descent of regret long avoided. Not that he should have married her. Not that she should have had the child. But that he should have *known*. Known what she was going through. Known what it meant. Known what it was like.

No, not what it was like – what it was.

He looked out the window. Felt like a small pale child being tossed back and forth by the gods through a dark and violent sky. The damned pot could clobber you with the past if you didn't look out. It would change your memories. Or change your version of them. Their shape. The revised history would slide right in and you'd think it had been true all along.

'She was going to have dinner with your brother the night she died,' said Jesse. 'Your other brother, the minister.'

'David? No way, man.'

'David and a friend of hers named Howard. I never met Howard. I talked to David a few times, though. He came to one of my gigs. He and Janelle were really tight. I don't know if it ever went off, the dinner. But that's what she told me she was going to do.'

'Were you invited?'

'No. After that, she was off to see the other guy. Mr Mystery Man. To tell him what was growing inside her and what she was going to do to it.'

Andy stood and went to the window. Drew in some cool sea air. Felt his nerves settle. Like the hackles of a dog going back down.

'What did Janelle do for money?' he asked.

'Modeling.'

'How often?'

'In the year I knew her I think she went out on one or two shoots,' said Jesse. 'Up in L.A. Gleason/Marx Agency.'

'You don't make a year's worth of food and rent in two shoots. She had a car?'

'Nice little VW. Powder blue. Just a year old.'

Powder blue, thought Andy. The marijuana plucked him out of the guest cottage and set him down in the packinghouse. Light slanting through the wallboards. Wind huffing outside, shaking the metal roof. Pigeons rustling in the smell of old wood and creosote.

Powder blue sweater.

Black-red around the empty neck.

Janelle's legs faint blue, too.

*Unholy shit.*

'She making payments on the car?' Andy asked absently. Hard to get his head back into this moment. Like a record skipping, taking him back, taking him back, taking him back . . .

'Free and clear,' said Jesse.

'How did she buy a new car?'

Jesse shrugged. 'She had cash coming in, but I don't know how or why. She didn't offer and I didn't press. She had some nice things. And she was generous. Bought me this. It was used, but it's a fine instrument.'

Jesse ran his fingers over the strings of the white Stratocaster.

Andy wondered at the shattered complexity of Janelle Vonn's life. Felt like every new thing he learned about her made her less understandable.

'You told my brother Nick all this, I take it.'

'Hell no,' said Jesse. 'Not the pregnancy or abortion. Not the dude she was with. Not the dinner with the reverend. None of that.'

'Well, why not?'

'I don't have a problem with the truth, but I do have a problem with who I tell it to. I don't dig the pigs. Sorry your bro is one of 'em, but I have my reasons. I didn't tell him, so I'm telling you.'

Then a light knock on the door and Jesse said, 'Come in.' A young blond woman put her head inside, smiled at Jesse. 'Hi, Jess.'

'Gail. Come on in.'

'You sure it's okay?'

'Sure I'm sure.'

She giggled and came in, still smiling. Denim jacket with a bright rainbow embroidered on a pocket flap. Flannel shirt and jeans with big holes in the knees. Suntanned kneecaps, bare feet. A toe ring. Round face, smooth straight hair past her shoulders. Skin like milk chocolate.

'This is Andy.'

'Peace, Andy,' she said. 'Hey, Jess, I got some knockout *sinsemilla* from Ronnie Joe.'

'Roll one up.'

'Already did. And Dr T. said there's a thousand hits of Orange Sunshine on their way to Laguna.'

'You might not want to talk about that right now,' said Jesse. A mildly amused glance at Andy. 'This guy here, he'll put it in the paper. Or worse.'

Gail lit the joint and offered it to Andy.

'No thanks. See you at the funeral, Jesse.'

'Later, bro.'

Janelle Vonn's casket was a deeply burnished Honduran mahogany with gold hardware. It was draped with one large arrangement of white roses. The coffin stand legs were solid with more white roses, as were the cross behind the pulpit, the altar, and the railing. Andy smelled the flowers the moment he walked inside the Grove Drive-In Church of God.

David eulogized Janelle to an overcapacity crowd. Even the folding chairs weren't enough. His words were brief and powerful.

Andy listened to his brother. Heard the radiant strength in David's voice. What a gift. Wondered if David had made it over to Janelle's for dinner with her and Howard. Not what David would want widely known. But it would be an interesting moment when he asked David that question. If he'd had dinner with Janelle that night, then David would certainly have told Nick already. It was probably old news. Would be nice to have been cc'd on that one, Andy thought. Not that he could do anything with it.

But Nick's mind would surely blow when he learned what Andy had learned. Mystery lover. Pregnant. Unless that was old news, too. The autopsy would reveal some of it.

Jesse Black performed 'Girl of the North Country' and 'Imagine You.' The music was dreamy and pure and you could hear the crowd breathing. Then sniffing back tears. The audience wasn't sure whether to clap, but when the applause began it mounted quickly and ran long. Black nodded once and walked out a front exit with wholesome Gail and orange-haired Crystal trailing behind him.

Andy sat with Teresa on his left and Nick on his right. As he looked around, what struck him most and hardest was how few of these people had even met her. She was a celebrity in death that she'd never been in life. An event. A symbol. An entertainment.

*Journal* stand sales had gone up 162 percent over the five days following her death, peaking with the Wolfman profile on Saturday. Subscriptions up, too. The *Journal* had capitalized. Janelle Vonn and related stories had run above the fold, right up there with Johnson and the war and the Russians and the space program. Display advertising orders had increased 26 percent, most of them for first-section placement, where the Janelle stories ran. The *Times* and the *Register* numbers were up, too, but not like the *Journal*'s.

So, they had given the people what they wanted. They'd kicked ass. Andy had kicked most of it himself. And here they were, all those people, asses kicked and showing up at a funeral for someone they never knew. Because of his words on a page. And a picture of a schizophrenic with a hairy hand.

But if he hadn't served up Janelle piping hot and fresh for them each day, someone else would have. Andy shook his head and looked down at his church shoes.

When it was over they joined the throng

moving outside to their cars for the short drive to Angel's Lawn and the grave.

Andy watched in numb silence as they lowered Janelle's coffin into the hole. Only later, while he stood alone by Clay's grave under a leafless sycamore, did the tears come heavy and hot.

The Becker family home stood pale against the trees in the cool October night. Andy parked next to David's blue Kingswood Estate station wagon. Behind Roger and Marie Stoltz's new white Cadillac. Nick wouldn't be there, which was fine with Andy.

It wasn't until after dinner that he got David alone in the study, closed the door. David was pale. He plopped into Max's big leather club chair. When David's strength left him it was like a house of cards collapsing. Andy poured a couple of ample scotches from Max's library bar, skipped the ice and water.

David mostly nodded his confirmation of Jesse Black's story. Yes, Janelle had a secret man. No, David had no idea who he was or what they did. Yes, she was pregnant and planning to abort. No, Janelle really didn't know who the father was.

Of course he'd told Nick all of this.

'Did you see her that last night?' asked Andy.

David sipped the drink. Looked at Andy with a level expression. 'We were going to have dinner,' he said. 'But Janelle changed her mind on Monday. Canceled.'

'Nick know about this?'

'If Jesse told you, he must have told Nick. I haven't.'

'Why?'

David looked down, scuffed the old wool rug with the toe of his wing tip. Drank again. 'I don't want it known, unless it would help in some way. I don't think it would put me in a good light.'

'Why?'

'Think hard, Andrew.'

'Proximity.'

'That's all it takes. In my . . . calling.'

'Was Barbara invited to the dinner, too?'

'Of course she was. See, Andy, that's what I mean. All I'm going to get from that broken dinner date is suspicion and innuendo. I don't need it.'

'Who's Howard?'

'Langton. Janelle's friend. She lived with his family after they busted her brothers and you wrote that article. And yes, just so you know, Howard's wife, Linda, was also on the invite list. In fact, the four of us had had dinner two or three times with Janelle and a date.'

'Why'd she cancel?'

'She didn't give a reason.' David leaned back. Closed his eyes. Twirled his drink glass, then set it on his thigh.

'What did she do for money?' asked Andy.

A faint shake of his head. 'I don't know, Andy. Am I supposed to know everything you need for an article? Come on.'

'Amazing,' said Andy.

'What?'

'That you could be her minister for so long and know so little about her. That I could write probably ten articles about her over the years and know so little about her. That Jesse Black could hang with her for almost a year and know so little about her.'

'She only gave what was asked for.'

'Why?'

'Because so much had been taken.'

'And there wasn't much left?'

'I think there was a great deal left. A great deal. She just hadn't learned yet that the more you give away the more you have.'

David pulled himself upright and walked out of the room. Andy poured another scotch. Could hear David saying his goodbyes.

His parents and the Stoltzes were in the darkened living room watching the late news. Andy sat on the sofa between Max and Monika. Noted that Roger and Marie Stoltz got the good recliners closer to the TV. His father's blue and his mother's white. And it wasn't just because Stoltz was a United States representative now. Andy remembered that Thanksgiving so long ago, the first night he'd made love with Meredith. The Stoltzes sat right where they are now, he thought, holding court.

The day's American casualties in Vietnam were

a reported twenty-two dead. Total for September was five hundred and thirty-nine. For the 'conflict' it was eighteen thousand four hundred and eight. Enemy dead today was twenty-six. President Johnson said American resolve would not waver and would never break. Two newscasters discussed the logic of destroying a village in order to save it. Then a commercial for new Oreos with creamier filling.

'Eighteen *thousand* four hundred and eight,' said Max. '*Americans*. Roger, you mean to tell me that a strategic nuclear bomb on Hanoi wouldn't end this war slick as a whistle?'

'Moscow would strike back.'

'Then bomb Moscow, too! It's Kalashnikovs that are killing our boys.'

'We all know that,' said Stoltz. 'And rhetorically that's an interesting stance. Practically, it will never happen.'

'You're right,' said Max. 'I thought Dick Nixon would run on that plank if anyone would. But no. He doesn't have the balls for it.'

'He's got to get into office first,' said Stoltz. 'Look what happened to Goldwater.'

'Dick will win it this time,' said Marie.

'Roger,' said Monika. 'I'm just glad you're our man in Washington now. Keep up the good fight.' She smiled. Big and beautiful. And a rarity, thought Andy.

Stoltz smiled, too. 'Business has never been better since Max and Marie started running it.'

Andy felt his anger rise at Stoltz. Automatic. Always had been. But it wasn't for anything he could ever put a finger on. Maybe his voice, his easy sincerity. His casually handsome face, the dumb/dashing aviator's mustache. Maybe something to do with the way Stoltz got Clay into the language institute, then the CIA, then killed. Or how he got David into Anaheim First Presbyterian right out of San Anselmo's, when there were so many extra ministers waiting. Or arranged the congratulations letter from Nixon when Nick graduated from the Sheriff's Academy. Or put Andy's disillusioned and heartbroken father to work at his goddamned chemical plant while *the representative* spent half his time swilling at the public trough in D.C.

And made his mother smile.

It annoyed Andy that Stoltz had infiltrated his family. Just like Stoltz brayed about the Commies infiltrating his government. The International Stoltz Conspiracy.

'I heard you got some more contracts for Orange Sunshine,' said Andy.

'That's right,' said Stoltz. 'Last month your father and Marie nailed down San Bernardino County. Thousands of miles of asphalt to clean. And they're paving thousands more.'

'That'll take a lot of rotten oranges.'

'More of those to come, too.'

'I liked it better when Orange County had orange trees instead of bulldozed groves,' said

Andy. 'When people like Max Becker had good work. When my mom used to smile.'

'Enough, Andy,' she said.

Stoltz nodded. 'He's right. I hate to see the groves go, too, Andy. But people need somewhere to live. And the Florida oranges are just as good for juice. At least we're using the last of the fruit.'

'*America will fall like overripe fruit into our hands,*' said Max.

'You watch, you'll see,' said Stoltz.

'Satan's hands,' said Monika.

'Every Soviet prediction since nineteen-seventeen has come true,' said Marie.

Andy stood, kissed his rigid mother, and ran a hand over his father's shoulder. Nodded to Marie. Shook Stoltz's hand, saw the scratches and a scab just below the thumb when he let go.

'You people are all crazy,' Andy said, and walked out.

# 17

David took two days off from work. Then
another. He'd never felt so drained. He couldn't
face another sermon or funeral or wedding or
baptism. Not one more witticism for the
marquee. Not another inmate who didn't do it.
Not one human being except for his immediate
family.

Barbara rewrote the sermon preempted by
Janelle. She was an excellent writer, adept at both
hermeneutics and homiletics. David invited her
to deliver the message on Sunday but Barbara
refused. He took a marquee adage from a magazine rather than compose one: *Exercise Daily – Walk
with the Lord*. Deacon Shaffner put it up and took
the old one down.

His doctor did an electrocardiograph. Normal.
Took blood for lab work, put a hurry-up on it,
and got results in a day. Normal. Did a thoracic
X ray to be safe. Normal again.

The doctor said he was in perfect health, that

God was taking care of David as well as David was taking care of God.

He took long walks on the beach in Newport with Barbara, Matthew, Rachel, and Wendy. Matthew was two now. Rachel almost one. Wendy was five. She was a Vietnamese girl David had arranged to be placed in an adoptive family that was part of his congregation. He had prayed long and hard for the well-being of the frail, frightened girl. One week later the entire family had been killed in a car accident caused by a speeding drunk driver. All of them except for Wendy, who at three years old was hurled cleanly from the open side window of the station wagon and caught in the blossom-heavy branches of a navel orange tree that grew beside the boulevard. Bruises, nicks, and a mild concussion. That was all.

David and Barbara brought her home from St Joseph Hospital, never a doubt that she belonged with them. And they were back in exactly one month for Barbara to give birth to Matthew.

Now, two years later, all three children were blessings to them. Rachel was peaceful and observant like her father. Matthew was mobile and fearless like his mother. Wendy was often delighted and took a helpful role with the younger ones. She had a large and selfless smile.

On the morning of his third day away from work, David was changing Matthew's diaper when Barbara put her head in the room.

'*Whew!* Special Agent Hambly? FBI?'

'Oh? On a Saturday.'

'Guess I'll finish this.'

They sat in the study of David's home, door closed, afternoon sun blunted by the shutters. Hambly was David's age, early thirties, with a compact face and body. Blue eyes, short dark hair, a deep dimple in the middle of his chin. His suit and shoes were brown. He moved the ottoman aside and lay his briefcase flat on it.

'I attended the memorial service,' said Hambly.

'Almost all the way back, on the left.'

'You were close, you and Janelle?'

'Yes.'

'It seemed like you'd known her a long time.'

'Fourteen years.'

'She liked LSD, didn't she?'

'I believe she tried it.'

'Tried it. Yeah. Liked Leary's Orange Sunshine, didn't she?'

'I'm not familiar with the different brands.'

'Brands,' said Hambly.

David sensed that Hambly was not interested in his own line of questioning.

'It's unusual for the FBI to investigate a murder,' said David.

'We're not. Did Janelle ever talk to you about political organizations?'

'Never. She had no interest in politics that I know of. Except she was against the war.'

'I'd call that politics.'

'As I just did, Mr Hambly.'

David still had the unbalancing feeling that Hambly wasn't asking questions he cared about. Until the next one, which Hambly delivered after moving to the edge of the sofa.

'What about the John Birch Society?'

'Janelle Vonn?'

Hambly said nothing. But he looked at David with a pugnacious blankness.

'Actually,' said David, 'she did mention the John Birch Society a few times. She asked me about them. What I knew. If they were legal. If they were good.'

'Legal?'

'She wasn't sure at first if they were a legitimate group,' said David, 'or perhaps an outlawed one.'

'What do you mean by *at first*?'

'When she first mentioned them.'

'Which was?' asked Hambly.

'Four, five years ago.'

'Did she know any members?'

'My father and mother are Birchers. Not that she knew them very well.'

'Give me the names of four of her friends,' said Hambly.

David nodded but didn't speak. He regarded the dimple and blue eyes of Special Agent Hambly. Saw that the dimple was too deep for a razor to safely negotiate. Little sprout of black whiskers dead center in the man's chin.

'No,' said David.

'Why not?'

'I don't like your attitude or your manners,' said David.

'Are you a friend of Roger Stoltz?'

'Yes.'

'Howard Langton?'

'Yes.'

'Good friends with them, Reverend Becker?'

'Not close.'

'Close enough to have dinner with Langton and Janelle the night she died?'

David's heart fluttered. 'That dinner date was canceled.'

Hambly squared the briefcase on the ottoman. The two latches burst upward with loud clicks and flashes of gold. Hambly slipped out a single 8½-by-11 black-and-white photograph. Pinching it with his forefinger and thumb, he held it up for David to see.

David remembered walking up to Janelle's door that evening. As in the picture.

Hambly held up another. David remembered sitting at the dinette in Janelle's cheerful little cottage with her and Howard Langton. All laughing. As in the picture. Who could possibly have taken these?

'There are more.'

'Why did you take them?'

'In conjunction with routine surveillance. And they turned out to be, well . . . useful.'

'What exactly is this about?' asked David. 'What exactly do you want?'

'First let me tell you what I don't want. I don't want to have to show these pictures to anybody. I really mean that.'

'And only I can prevent it.'

'Of course you can. Just tell me some stories.'

'About who?'

'Start with your father and Roger Stoltz. Tell me about their political activities and plans. Their personal opinions and relationships. Their faults and foibles. We know they're Birchers. We can handle the Birchers. And we know about the Klan. We can handle them, too. But we're hearing about this new thing down south, the National Volunteer Police. And we're hearing about it right here in Orange County. We're seeing "Support Your Local Police" bumper stickers given out at Max's meetings. We wonder if there might be a kind of bridge. A JBS bridge leading back to the Klan. Nobody heard Birchers crying when King got shot. President Johnson, being a Texan, is very concerned about white hate.'

'Sweet Jesus in heaven.'

'But our concerns don't stop with Mr Stoltz and Mr Becker. We're interested in everyone you know, Reverend. Nick is a terrific detective. You two must talk. And Andy's ingratiated himself with the Dessingers. I wonder at all he knows about this county. And look at your large and growing congregation. We'd love to know what certain of your believers are really doing and thinking. For instance the Robinsons, who are former members of the Socialist Workers Party. Or Dyson Krenek, who has a very *personal* relationship with a United States senator whose name I can't reveal. And there is the Martinez family, with blood ties to César Chávez. And poor Gina Ritter, with her husband a Democratic Party leader plugged into Hollywood and her son plugged into a heroin needle. Even the inmates you counsel at the jail, they must have some interesting stories to tell.'

'You're a pestilence.'

'Or Bob Washburn – Dr Robert Washburn – who teaches history and espouses Marxism out at the University of California at Irvine. How many students has he signed into membership in the American Communist Party?'

'None, that I know of.'

'But wouldn't it be good to really know for sure?'

David felt as if he'd been slugged in the stomach. He stood, took a deep breath, sat back down.

'And who really runs the RoMar Orange Sunshine plant?' asked the agent. 'Is it Max Becker or Marie Stoltz?'

'How would I know? Who cares?'

'We care. We are exactly who cares. Odd, isn't it? Orange Sunshine. Same name for LSD and for Stoltz's asphalt cleaner?'

David looked at Hambly but could hardly form thoughts, let alone answers.

'Reverend,' said Hambly, 'I'd be happy with information on just about anybody in your congregation. You have a lot of friends. I just want you to share once in a while. That's all. We don't have to meet. You never have to see me again. You just call me at a number I'll give you before I leave, and you say it's Judas. You just say, hello, Hambly, this is Judas. I thought of that code name just for you.'

'You are repugnant to me in every way possible,' said David.

'Back at you, Rev. I take it we have a deal. You want these?'

'Leave them on the sofa.'

'Tell me about your father and Stoltz,' said Hambly.

'Tell you what?'

'When they met. How they met. Are they faithful to their wives? What do they talk about at those long dinners? Are they really behind Nixon or isn't he tough enough on Communism for them? What do they really think of him? And Pat? What do they think of her? Mainly, what in hell's this National Volunteer Police? We don't think it's anything like a traditional volunteer service, where you get to dress up in a cute uniform and help out the local cops.'

'I can't do this right here, right now.'

'I understand, David. I really do. Here. Call me when you're ready to talk.'

He handed David an FBI card with a handwritten number on the back.

'Stoltz and Marie happy?'

'I really don't know,' said David.

'You've been their family minister for almost three years now. I use the word "family" loosely, since they don't have children.'

'We don't have those kinds of discussions.'

'Maybe you should.'

Hambly set the photographs on the sofa. Swung down the briefcase lid and snapped it shut.

'Well?' he asked. 'Anything else?'

'No.'

They stood and Hambly offered his hand.

'Get out of my house,' said David.

'Have a far-out and groovy afternoon, Rev.'


When Hambly had gone David called the FBI number on the card. A businesslike male voice answered, 'Good afternoon, Federal Bureau of Investigation,' so he hung up.

He slid to his knees and rested his forehead on the beige carpet. Arms around his middle. Prayed as hard as he'd ever prayed that news of his dinner with Janelle Vonn and what had happened after would never come out. Not to mention pictures.

*My God, my God, my God.*

His stomach ached and his heart ached and his head ached. He remembered something from an old San Anselmo's class called 'The Art of Prayer,' where Dr Rable showed them how during a prayer a rhetorical pause can be escalated to a potent dramatic caesura. You had to do it at the right time and have the courage to allow your listeners – or yourself – to go 'from restless to receptive.' So he just knelt there, head on the carpet and body revolting with worry, praying with silence. Not a word. Not a thought.

Waiting for an answer.

Waiting for a sign.

Waiting for a miracle.

Waiting.

David had tried this prayer of silence before. But as soon as the silence became ripe, Satan always came barreling into it, demanding to know if God really intervened in the affairs of men in the first place. Where was the proof? And if He didn't, then why spend a lifetime asking Him to? And Satan would remind David that God had not yet *conclusively* answered a single prayer of his. Not one that David could separate from mere coincidence. Not one that David could prove was an act of God. Satan said he knew plenty of ministers who were actually spoken to by God. It happened all the time. Maybe, said Lucifer, David was in the wrong calling.

So David held the silence as long as he could. Invited God into it. But it was the harpy voice of the devil that screeched into his mind in a whirlwind of dust and skidding boots like something from a cartoon. Less than a minute of peace was all David got.

And no answer.

A while later David dialed Nick but hung up

again, realizing he couldn't explain his situation without being revealed as a huge liar. And worse. The worship program he'd stupidly left at Janelle's was now the least of David's worries.

He thought of calling Andy and wondered what he'd say.

Ditto Mom and Dad.

Finally called Howard Langton and told him what had happened, to expect Hambly to come his way.

Langton, a high school civics teacher and football coach, was his usual bullish self, saying the bureau could kiss his ass before he'd rat on his friends. Though he had no desire to have it known that he'd dined without his wife at the home of a former student on the night of her murder.

By five that afternoon David finally had to get out of the house. He drove to Angel's Lawn and stood next to Clay's grave. He tried to do this once a week. Tried to pray for Clay's soul but couldn't concentrate.

So he drove the freeways. Got some motion. Steered and tried to pray and watched the exit signs blip past. Made him feel like he was progressing. Moving through time and space in a certain and purposeful way.

Then to Max and Monika's like he often did. Just to see them and share a few words. He loved them. And pitied them, too, because they'd overcome a lot in their lives but couldn't overcome

Clay. David had prayed on that a million times but sometimes even God couldn't heal a broken heart. Clay showed up in David's dreams all the time. Just like he had always been – brash and funny and confident. Like he didn't care he'd been killed outside a village few people in his own country could even name.

David parked in the driveway beside a black Lincoln four-door. Two men in dark suits by the Lincoln eyed him hard. David nodded and started up the walk and saw Dick Nixon coming from the house. Frown on his face, lips pursed. Gray suit and fresh haircut. Wing tips heavy on the concrete. Another Secret Service guy behind him.

Great, thought David. Like Hambly had conjured the meeting. Given him his first chance at betrayal.

Nixon smiled when he saw David, shook his hand. They made small talk there in the driveway for a minute. Nixon was interested in how the church was growing. He had that undistractable intensity that drew people, made them believe he was involved and concerned. Their man.

'Good luck in November, sir,' said David.

Nixon nodded solemnly. 'I hope for the best. But I do wish I could see more eye-to-eye with the JBS, David. I know your father and Roger Stoltz are disappointed. I am, too.'

'They'll support you.'

'It isn't that.'

221

David saw something dark pass across the former vice president's face. Dick had always seemed actively haunted.

'Good night, sir.'

'Regards to Barbara and the children.'

'And ours back to Pat.'

It was only six but Max appeared inebriated. Held a huge tumbler half full of gin and ice as evidence. Shot up from his blue recliner with a smile and his free hand extended. The old living room. So many memories. Cronkite and the body count for today: seventeen.

Monika smiled when she saw him come in. The same polite replica that had replaced her true smile the moment she'd heard about Clay. David leaned over, hugged her, and kissed her cheek. The bones in her back seemed large.

'Did you see Dick?' she asked.

'Said hi in the driveway.'

'He's going to win but he won't forget us,' she said. 'He's from Orange County. From good people. And he'll be a huge improvement over Johnson.'

David pulled up a dining room chair, sat between them.

Max told David all about his workday at RoMar Industries today. How Marie Stoltz *nominally* ran the operation but needed Max to get things accomplished. Shipped eight thousand barrels last week, lost a flatcar halfway across Texas, nobody hurt but four hundred thousand gallons of Orange

Sunshine wasted on tumbleweeds and armadillos, be the shiniest armadillos God ever saw.

'Drink, son?'

'No thanks, Dad.'

'Time for a refill.'

Max steered to the kitchen. Monika held David's hand, looking from him to the TV and back again. But mostly at the TV.

'How have you been, Mom?'

She patted his hand. 'Just so busy. You know.'

He really didn't know. Her children were grown and she didn't work. Max was gone forty hours a week at RoMar. She had no hobbies. And few interests except for the Birch Society meetings and publications.

Max lowered back into his chair, drink raised for balance.

'I'm working a few hours a week at the bookstore,' she said.

The American Opinion Bookstore, David knew. Official JBS propaganda outlet. Books on Communist takeovers and how the United Nations was a waste of time and money, how the Russians wanted America to fall. Until a couple of years ago the clerks would grouse about the tax when they rang up a sale. Because the California sales tax went to Governor Pat Brown, a Democrat. The clerks liked to say, If it's brown, flush it. David actually believed a lot of what the JBS said. Just didn't like the way they thought they were right and everybody else was stupid.

'Four hours, actually,' she said. 'But you know, son. One thing leads to another. Not enough hours in the day. You?'

David told them about Barbara's youth league and Matthew's language skills, Rachel's brave toddling, and Wendy's supernal calm as an older sister. For a few minutes he was able to appreciate his wife and children from a distance, in the telling of their virtues. And to forget Hambly and his pictures and the colossal stupidity of what he had done.

He drove away slowly, lost in thought. Prayed to get through this. Realized that you could drive across the entire continent never seeing farther than the beams of your headlights. Wondered if there might be a sermon in that metaphor.

Faith as your headlight.

That night in bed David lay trembling in Barbara's arms and told her what had happened with Special Agent Hambly. The breath caught in her throat when he said that Hambly had code-named him *Judas*. She used an oath that made the hair on the back of his neck stand up.

She made ferocious but tender love to him. She seemed to almost inhabit him at times like this. To feel what he was feeling.

After, she drew a warm bath and led him to it. She lit candles in the darkened bathroom. With her knees on a folded towel she leaned over the tub to work the shampoo into a lather, scrub the sponge up and down his back. And later to cup the handfuls of fresh water over his head.

'It may be time to settle on a partner,' she said.

'I want you to take over if anything happens.'

'No, David. We would lose the congregation. Properly prepared, they'll follow another man. But they won't stay with a woman.'

'I feel like giving up.'

'Of course you do,' she said. 'But in the morning you won't. You're a fighter and a warrior and a man of God. You have power in your heart. I've seen you down and you always get back up. Always.'

He felt the water running down his head. Heard the splash of it around him. Smelled the soap and conditioner and melting candle wax.

'I've narrowed down the candidates to two,' said Barbara. 'Either would be fine. Edmond has age and intelligence. Whitbrend has youth and ambition. They would both bring modest congregations. They're both amenable to the base agreement and incentive scale and escalators. They're both keenly aware that the way the congregation is growing, the sky is the limit, and that television will take us there. Literally. Look, David, here we are hardly moved into the new chapel and it's time to think about a larger one. The television ministry that you are so afraid of? It must happen, David. It will take your congregation from a thousand to millions. *Millions*. You are a very powerful and charismatic minister, Reverend

Becker. You have a responsibility to provide for your worshipers like you do for your family. As an employer would for his workers.'

'I know.'

She wiggled one of his earlobes. 'And you should benefit from your hard work like anyone else. God in heaven certainly does.'

'I don't presume to understand Him.'

'No. You're right. I won't, either.'

He sighed. Listened to the music of water hitting water.

'Call the younger one tomorrow morning,' he said quietly. 'Whitbrend. He had an interesting look in his eye.'

# 18

Janelle Vonn's pale blue Volkswagen Beetle sat in the shade of the impound yard. Hood up, engine compartment open, a layer of wind-blown dust on the windows. Nick and Lucky Lobdell looked down on it in the brisk fall morning.

It was Monday, October 14, thirteen days after the murder of Janelle Vonn. Nick could feel his case was cooling off. His evidence wasn't adding up. The clues still out there had scurried under rocks and were going to be harder and harder to find.

He was losing his momentum in this case and he knew it. Made his guts feel jerky and his head feel crowded.

And all of this after he was sure he'd caught the break he needed. When Red turned out to be the Reverend David and Ho turned out to be Janelle's benefactor Howard Langton. An absolute gift from heaven, delivered by his own brother, Andy.

227

But even that had dribbled off into uselessness. The date – David and Barbara, Howard and Linda, Janelle and whatever guy she might choose – had been canceled. No one knew why. The evening itself would have been nothing unusual. They had had dinner dates before.

So Nick couldn't escape the sinking feeling in his guts. First-case jinx? Maybe he wasn't ready for his own case? Maybe he was too careful?

Maybe he didn't have the experience to connect things or ask the right questions. Maybe he didn't have the stamina it took to miss your wife and kids and not sleep well and go over the same bits of evidence over and over and over. He thought of Sharon and his whole soul groaned. Because he missed her, too, and because he wished he'd never touched her.

And maybe it was just him, but Nick thought the captain was humoring him at the homicide detail wrap on Friday. And the assistant sheriff was subtly dismissing his efforts at the Crime Against Persons roll call on Thursday.

'What exactly are we doing?' asked Lobdell.

'I wanted to see this car again.'

Lobdell ran his finger across a back window. Left a dark streak in the dust.

'Your case,' said Lobdell.

'Yeah, I know.'

Nick stood by the driver's-side door and read again the responding officer's report on a suspicious vehicle. Filed five days after the murder.

Lemon Heights Sporting Goods owner made the call, said the car had been in the lot out front since the night in question. Hadn't moved. He had seen it come across the lot that night, late, maybe nine. Cute little Beetle. Shiny under the lights. Went to the far side of the parking lot where there weren't any cars. The owner looked out a few minutes later and saw the car still there and this girl standing beside a white Caddy talking to the driver. Got in the Caddy about ten minutes after nine and the car drove off.

Lemon Heights Sporting Goods was in a shopping center less than two hundred yards from the SunBlesst packinghouse.

The Beetle was only one year old. Nine thousand miles according to the impound report. No dents that Nick could see. Good tread on the tires. He checked the tread grooves for the odd bit of gravel or dirt that might be revealing. Found nothing.

Lobdell shook his head and sighed. 'I gotta call Shirley.'

Nick sat on the passenger side and looked at the fingerprint dust on the dash, door handles and window cranks, the shifter, hand brake, and steering wheel. The silver powder showed up best on the black plastic. All the prints had been processed. All were Janelle's.

Nick got down on his knees with a magnifier and tweezers and went over the floor mats. ID had done it once but he wanted to do it again.

Hair. Fiber. Small gravel. The bright red point of what looked like a liquidambar or maple leaf. October, he thought, right color for the time of year. He didn't collect, he just looked. Then the passenger's side and the back. Nothing unusual.

He sat in the front passenger seat. The glove compartment had a pair of sunglasses, a small pump bottle of Orange Sunshine air freshener, and a clear plastic makeup bag. Inside the bag Nick found base and blush, three lipsticks. Two brushes, two eyeliner pencils, and mascara.

He sprayed the air freshener toward the open door and whiffed. The smell was faint and familiar. Sprayed some on his fingertips and rubbed it with his thumb. Not strong, really. Just a hint of orange blossom. Sprayed and rubbed again. No, not like those late winter mornings when all of Tustin used to smell that way. Paradise would be like that. Nick had always thought if he could bottle that smell he could make a million. His mother used to say so. He and Clay had tried it one day, mashing up the blossoms and adding water. By the next morning, through some alchemical magic that bewildered them, the solution retained no smell whatsoever. But here in sixty-eight, thought Nick, somebody had finally captured a little of that smell.

He saw that Janelle had replaced her Blaupunkt radio with a Craig eight-track tape player/radio combination. Pretty nice one. Eighty, a hundred bucks installed. There was a shoe box of tapes on the passenger-side floor. Nick looked at the titles and set it down.

The side map pouches had more eight-tracks. A pencil and two pens. Two books of matches – Five Crowns from her job a year ago, and one from Bob's Big Boy. No maps.

The ashtray contained an alligator roach clip with a decorative thong of leather and three beads attached. The tray itself had a light dusting of ash.

Nick got out and lifted the front trunk door. Neat and practically empty. A spare tire, jumper cables, and a first-aid kit. The engine compartment was clean, no leaks or bad hoses that he could see. Nick looked at the tiny little motor. Air-cooled and practically powerless. A guy at his high school put radiator coolant in the oil reservoir, blew his engine. You could get a new VW for under two grand and they went forever on a tank of gas. But gas was cheap and there was no way to argue with V-8 power.

Nick got pliers and a flat-tip screwdriver from his kit and sat in the passenger seat. Pried off the door trim panel. Looked where the stoners liked to hide their stash. No stash, just the door latch assembly and the window crank with its toothed gear swabbed with grease.

He worked the trim panel back into place.

Lobdell ambled over from the yard office. 'They already looked there.'

'Get off my back, Lucky.'

'We got the last three saw stores to check.'

Nick drove. He could feel the tension coming off Lobdell, low-voltage but steady.

'What's up?' Nick asked.

'Kevin said some bad things to his mother. I won't tolerate it under my roof. Kid can say what he wants to me. But Shirley, shit. Shirley lives for that boy.'

In the first three days after the murder, Nick and Lobdell had found twenty-six Orange County stores that sold the Garden Forge Trim-Quick pruning saw. When they factored in south Los Angeles and north San Diego Counties, the number got up to almost a hundred. So far they had gotten through twenty-three. Three leads had proved fruitless. One still working. They had started with the stores closest to the Sun-Blesst packinghouse in Tustin. Now they were almost up to the Los Angeles County line, Nick increasingly pissed off that nothing was connecting up for him.

Nick drove and Lobdell looked out the window.

None of the clerks at Canning's Hardware in La Habra remembered selling a Trim-Quick recently.

The owner of a nursery in Fullerton sold one to a young mother with two children just last week.

A garden supplies manager at the Sears, Roebuck over by Knott's Berry Farm in Buena Park had sold one Trim-Quick to a man in shorts and a straw gardener's hat two Sundays ago. The Sunday before Janelle was murdered, thought Nick.

'I've seen him in here before,' said the manager. 'Always Sundays. Don't know his name. Nice fella. Brown hair, neat mustache, medium height and weight. Didn't see much of his face that day, because of the hat.'

Maybe that was the point, thought Nick. He remembered that two Sundays ago it was ninety degrees.

'Guess his age.'

'Thirty-five to forty. He also got snail bait, a flat of marigolds, potting soil, and a hand trowel. Paid cash, so don't ask me to find the check.'

'Maybe you'd call me if you see him in here again,' said Nick. He supplied a card and the manager put it in the pocket of his blue apron.

They were walking back out of the garden section of Sears when Nick saw the entire room tilt left, then right again. Like a ship. He stopped, braced himself. Lifted his arms for balance. Then lowered them to his side, embarrassed.

'What gives?' huffed Lobdell.

'Balance a little off.'

Like getting hit on the head by Ethan. Fourteen years ago and still not quite right. Never told anybody and maybe should have. To his irritation Nick watched a row of potted rhododendrons scoot forward, then move back. All six in unison. Like a dance step. Slick.

He breathed deeply, shook his head. Looked at Lobdell and felt better.

'I got conked when I was a kid,' he said. 'Every once in a while I just lose my balance for a second.'

'Great,' said Lobdell. 'Hope it doesn't happen when you're covering my butt with your forty-five.'

'I could only cover part of it anyway,' said Nick. He laughed but Lobdell didn't. 'Monkey Wards is next.'

By the time they finished striking out at Wards, Nick wasn't sure if he was really walking or not. The merchandise in the aisles was going past him but he wasn't aware of moving his legs or feet. The products advanced, reds and yellows and blues coming at high speed, then curlicuing upward like colored smoke and vanishing into the ceiling. A set of wrenches glided slowly through the room.

Outside the sunlight wavered in an orange mirage. Lobdell was talking as they made the car. Nick could hardly understand the words but he could see them wobbling through the air toward him like balloons filled with water.

'I don't feel right, Lucky.'

'You're acting wrong, Nick. The fuck'd you have for breakfast?'

'Katy made pancakes and eggs. Onions in the eggs.'

'I'll drive.'

'Thanks.'

\* \* \*

They made the 11:45 A.M. meeting with Captain Frank del Gado. Nick couldn't look him in the eye for more than a second or two. Del Gado's skin ran off like melting wax and Nick felt an urge to giggle. Even with the office door closed Nick heard things from the other side with startling volume and clarity. He felt that his ears had grown to huge proportion. Felt the bones in his face growing.

Lobdell had agreed to do the talking. 'We just wanted to follow up on this rumor about the beauty queen being on the narcotics payroll,' he said.

Del Gado was a sleek sixty, black hair combed straight back from a widow's peak. Goddamned Eddie Munster, thought Nick.

'Yeah,' said del Gado. 'So?'

'How long?' asked Lobdell.

'We worked with her during that thing with her brothers. We thought she might be helpful with where the pills and pot were coming from, and she was. All of her brothers were tied up with the Hessians. You get bikers, you get amphetamines. They make the damned things, zoom around the country distributing. Anyway, when the brother thing was over, we kept her on. You'd be amazed what people offered Miss Tustin, age eighteen.'

'Was she using?' Nick managed.

Del Gado's gaze seemed eternal. 'Enough to gain the confidence of certain people. Informants are free to do what they want. Within limits.'

'How high up the ladder was she?' asked Lobdell. 'Big boys, medium-sized, what?'

Del Gado tapped a Zippo on his desktop. Painfully loud. Nick jumped, rising from his chair to cover it and hoping the captain hadn't seen. He went to the window, looked out, then casually sat back down.

'Not big,' del Gado said, looking at Nick.

'What did you pay her?' asked Lobdell.

'It varied. Up to three hundred a month.'

'That's pretty good money for nothing big,' said Lobdell. Nick actually heard the words before they were spoken.

'Sometimes she was useful.'

'Sir,' said Nick. 'We need to talk to those drug people. Her connections and sources and friends. If one of them found out she was a snitch, that's a motive to kill her.' He lurched up and went to the window again, hoping he looked upset and serious. Took a deep breath, fighting the smile off his face.

'Talk to Troy Gant,' said del Gado. 'He's waiting outside.'

Gant was short and grubby. Stringy yellow hair, an attempted mustache, beat-up jeans and a loose sweatshirt with the sleeves cut out. He looked eighteen, maybe twenty. He looked at Lobdell with an openly hopeless expression. Turned his soft blue eyes on Nick and stared right through him.

'Come on,' he said. 'Let's motate.'

'Motate,' said Nick. 'Like "move" and "activate."'

'Right on, Sarge.'

Gant led them down a hallway past a water-cooler and a fire alarm box. Then into an empty conference room. A movie screen at one end, projector at the other. A tape recorder sat on one of the three horse-shoed tables.

Gant shut the door. 'You gotta be real careful here,' he said. 'Janelle was working with some people. I'm working with some of the same people. You want to talk to them, talk to them. They can't hurt her now. But you ask your questions just a little wrong, mix up something she could have told you for something only I could know and guess what, man – I'm seriously fuckin' blown. Let me tell you two guys something. Narcotics isn't about fun anymore. It isn't about young people experimenting anymore. It isn't about cosmic consciousness, no matter what the Brotherhood of Eternal Love says. It's about big dollars and strong dope. It's about permanently scrambled eggs and overdoses that stop your heart cold. It's about distribution and profit and getting product on the street so every man, woman, and child can fork over the cash and turn on. Laguna? Janelle's world? Bad people doing bad shit. Even del Gado underestimates it. Clear on that?'

'I think we can handle it,' said Lobdell.

'That's exactly what I'm afraid of,' said Gant.

'You thinking you can handle it because you're a big tough dude from homicide. You don't know piss about narco.'

Nick nodded.

Gant's eyes bore into Nick again. Silver fish leaping out of them, landing on the desk. Gant held up one finger and ran it up close across Nick's field of vision.

'With all respect, Investigator Becker, what the hell are you tripping on?' asked Gant.

'I don't know. I didn't know I was. I mean, I don't know what's going on. Del Gado's face melted and now there's fish all over the desk. And the tools at Sears—'

'Here.'

Gant took him by one arm – surprisingly strong for a little guy – and walked Nick back outside. Down the hall and into a bathroom. Ran some water in the sink, got Nick's face down close to it and splashed him good. Soaked some paper towels. Got his neck and hair. Walked Nick over to a stall and sat him down.

'What'd you take, Sarge?' he asked quietly.

'Eggs and—'

'Not food. Not breakfast. Something else.'

'Coffee in the cafeteria.'

'Something else. You smoke something funny, maybe?'

'I pretty much quit cigarettes two years ago.'

Nick tried to think of everything he'd put in his mouth since getting up.

'Tell me what you did this morning,' said Troy Gant.

Nick went through it. Detail by detail. Amazing to him that he could remember it. He was trying to explain the almost-orange-blossom smell of Janelle Vonn's air freshener when Gant sighed. He put a hand on Nick's shoulder.

Sitting on the toilet with a weird narc touching him sent a shiver of panic up Nick's backbone. Never claustrophobic but he felt that way now. Suffocating. Ugly thoughts and smells. He almost jumped up to run for it but the sinks behind Gant were breathing in and out, enlarging, then decreasing. Enlarging, then decreasing.

'You took a dose of Orange Sunshine LSD,' Troy said. 'Janelle got it from Tim Leary. Leary got it from Ronnie Joe Fowler. Fowler gets it from a lab up near San Francisco that nobody can find. What you got through your skin pores is pure LSD dissolved in distilled water. Instead of pills, the acid gurus are taking it orally. One spray in your mouth, you're flying in twenty minutes. On your hands, like happened to you – forty minutes. The air freshener label is their idea of being clever and funny. It actually fooled us for about a month because the label was so good.'

'Goddamn,' said Nick. 'I can't believe this stuff was legal until a couple of years ago.'

'Strong shit,' said Gant.

'He's been acting like a complete nutcase,' said Lobdell.

239

Gant helped Nick off the toilet. 'Get him down-stairs and drive him home. Nick, don't stop and rap with your buddies or the whole department's going to know. I'm going to give you Ronnie Joe Fowler's numbers. And a couple more people in Janelle's group. And some of the reports I wrote up, based on her information. But besides that I'm not going to tell you a single thing. I'm done. I don't exist for you. See me on the street, man – any street in the world – and just walk the other way.'

'Yes,' said Nick.

'I'll call you in a couple of hours,' said Gant.

'How long's this going to last?'

'One spray on your fingers about ten o'clock? And a whiff of another? You'll start coming down about five or six tonight. You'll still be high when you fall asleep, if you do.'

'Whopping hangover?'

'You'll feel fine,' said Gant. 'You'll remember all the cool stuff. You'll want to try it again some-time.'

'Wow. Not so sure about that.'

'See? That's what I mean. You may think homi-cide is tough, but narco is just plain scary. By the way, eat plenty. A couple of strong cocktails will help you come down. And one more thing – get the creep who killed her. She was a sweet girl.'

'Dad's home early!'
    'GIVE ME MY BATMOBILE!'

'QUIET! Honey, is everything okay?'

Nick stood blinking in the doorway. The orange wool carpet Katy had recently bought for the living room undulated like a field of windblown barley, stretching before him, out the sliding glass doors, across the backyard, over the flood control channel that ran behind their house, all the way to the horizon. Nick thought that he'd like to see the precise line where the orange carpet met the sky.

He turned and waved away Lobdell.

'Is everything okay, Nick?'

'Is everything okay, Dad?'

'Yes,' he said, stepping into the entryway. He knelt down and hugged Katherine and Stevie, both home with colds. Willie was at school.

'Do you feel okay, honey?' asked Katy.

He rose and smiled at her. She was huge and beautiful to him. Life rippled off her in visible vibrations, waves of shimmering purple and yellow.

'I see your beauty in a whole new way, Katy,' he said. She smiled guardedly. 'I'd started to think you were beautiful like a new truck or one of those big airliners they fly to New York. But you're not that at all. It's more to do with grace and blood. Not function, but . . . *form*.'

Katy's mouth fell open. He saw the hardness come to her eyes. The sudden worry.

'Katherine, Steven – go to your rooms.'

'But—'

'But—'

'*NOW!*'

'God, that's loud,' Nick said. Felt the sound waves pulverizing his eardrums.

'Come with me,' said Katy. She took his arm where Gant had taken it and led him back to the bedroom.

She closed the door and asked for his explanation.

After he told her she went out to check the children, came back in, locked the door, and stripped off his clothes. She made love to him three times that afternoon, in between lunch, laundry, getting Katherine and Steven down for naps, and picking up Willie at the bus stop.

By evening Nick felt like he'd been blasted through an entire universe of sex. Then pulled back through it to earth and his bed. Spent and empty. Whole body limp. Katy brought him dinner. And six fingers of scotch and ice with a little water in a giant red plastic tumbler.

Bloated with sensation, Nick curled up under the sheets naked and watched squadrons of identical purple tulips scroll down his inner vision. Then red Ford Country Squire station wagons with wood-look siding and 428s in them. Then blue fire hydrants. Then Janelle Vonn's disembodied head. She was alive and speaking but he couldn't hear what she was saying. A thousand Janelles. He tried to say something back but he couldn't move his mouth.

He slept for eleven hours. Woke up at six in time to pour Willie a bowl of Sugar Spangled Rice Krinkles.

Felt great.

# 19

He was on his way to headquarters by seven. A warm wind blew from the east off the desert, swaying the traffic lights on their cables and shivering the trees.

Nick thought about the things that had gone through his head the day before, frankly amazed that they could arrive so clear and strong, then vanish so completely. Like a Santa Ana wind had blown them into his brain and back out again.

And Katy. Incredible. It had been twenty-four days since they'd made love. And over seven years since they'd done anything like that when the sun was up. What had gotten into her?

The homicide room was empty. He made coffee and set the copies of Troy Gant's dossiers on his desk. There were four of them, all profiles of drug culture suspects apparently prepared from debriefings of Janelle. And from conversations, some covertly recorded by Janelle and others caught by telephone intercepts. Key excerpts had been transcribed and included in the files.

Timothy Leary.

Ronnie Joe Fowler.

Price Herald.

Cory Bonnett.

Nick read the synopsis that began each file:

TIMOTHY LEARY, 48, has been living in Laguna Beach since early April. He is 'spokesman' for the Brotherhood of Eternal Love, a 'church' recently founded there by approximately thirty members (see add'l file for RONNIE JOE FOWLER). LEARY is a charismatic former Harvard researcher who espouses widespread use of mind-altering drugs. He is very influential over young people and those uncertain in their beliefs and convictions. Because of his academic experience and notoriety he is accepted by the artistic and university community in Laguna Beach.

LEARY is not considered dangerous and is not known to carry weapons or resist arrest. He often smiles at law enforcement personnel. Many consider it a taunt. He is married to a former fashion model named ROSE-MARY and has a son, JACK. This is his third marriage. His first wife committed suicide.

Laguna Beach PD has LEARY under irregular surveillance. FBI has a dossier on

LEARY, little of which has been shared with us (see Orange County FBI Resident Agency, Special Agent Hambly).

It is known to law enforcement that LEARY'S Laguna Beach parties and 'happenings' encourage illegal drug use, permissive sexual behavior, and anti-American sentiments. LEARY was arrested for possession of marijuana in Laredo, Texas, last year. If convicted, he faces a thirty-year sentence.

Various Sheriff's Department informers supply firsthand information on Leary's activities. Of these, JANELLE VONN, through her personal relationship with LEARY, is our most productive. They met at a 'be-in' (drug party) in Laguna Beach in the summer of 1968. JANELLE accompanied JESSE BLACK, a young musician, to this party. BLACK and LEARY are friends. LEARY is forthcoming with JANELLE about his opinions and activities. He has made no threatening or sexual advances toward her. JANELLE admits to using LSD. Although JANELLE is nineteen years old, we feel that she is not in danger in her capacity as a paid and voluntary Sheriff's Department informant.

We also believe it possible that JANELLE has admitted her connection to us to LEARY and BLACK, and that any information she supplies is possibly misleading or false. Calls made to and from her phone and taped by JANELLE are likewise suspect.

EVERY EFFORT HAS BEEN MADE TO CORROBORATE JANELLE/LEARY INFORMATION WITH TWO (2) OTHER SOURCES.

Nick scanned the pages that followed.

There were encounters with Leary, as described by Janelle to del Gado and Gant. *He had joints in his pocket but no acid. I've never seen him carry the acid around. He's got a safe in his bedroom for it. He watches over it like it's gold. Which to him and some of his friends it is.*

Phone conversations – *Hello, Janelle dear. How do you like the sunshine today?*

*Groov-y!*

*Remember, Janelle, we are all God's flesh.*

Descriptions of Leary's home – *and lots of books of poetry, Ginsberg and Corso and Olson and . . .*

Be-ins. Happenings. Experiences. Parties and more parties.

Photographs, too, of Leary and Janelle and others on the beach in tai chi poses, Leary and Janelle smoking marijuana in a Laguna alleyway, Leary and two younger men outside a store called Mystic Arts World on Coast Highway.

Nick got another cup of coffee. Conjured up some of the hallucinogenic images from the day before. Most of them he couldn't remember. And the ones that he could remember had lost their power to dazzle or delight or disturb.

The next file was shorter:

RONNIE JOE FOWLER, 28, is one of the later members of the Brotherhood of Eternal Love.

The Brotherhood, as it is commonly called, encourages the use of LSD to induce mystical states. In the articles of incorporation of this alleged church, they say they're going to 'bring to the world a greater awareness of God through the teachings of Jesus Christ, Buddha, Ramakrishna, Babaji, Paramahansa Yogananda, Mahatma Gandhi,' etc. To support their 'religion' they opened a drug-paraphernalia store on Coast Highway in Laguna Beach called the Mystic Arts World.

However, in order to purchase land for the church, the Brotherhood has established international networks for smuggling illicit drugs into this country for sale. They are especially expert in the smuggling of hashish from Afghanistan. It is far more powerful than marijuana and reaps greater profits in the illegal marketplace.

FOWLER's role in the Brotherhood narcotics smuggling network is mainly in distribution of so-called Orange Sunshine lysergic acid diethylamide (LSD). It is alleged to be stronger and 'purer' than the laboratory-produced LSD made by Sandoz Laboratories of Switzerland. This dangerous hallucinogenic substance is believed to be manufactured in a secret Northern California drug lab. ANY INFORMATION RELATING TO THE EXISTENCE AND POSSIBLE LOCATION OF THIS LAB IS A HIGH PRIORITY OF NARCOTICS LAW ENFORCEMENT NATIONWIDE.

FOWLER is neither a gullible hippie nor a mystical shaman. He is a hardened criminal with ties to the Hell's Angels and Hessian motorcycle gangs. JANELLE VONN's brothers LENNY and CASEY are known Hessian members and convicted drug offenders. FOWLER has priors for assault with a deadly weapon (a knife) and grand theft. He was acquitted on forcible and statutory rape charges last year in Eugene, Oregon. He is known to have an engaging and outwardly friendly personality. He preys on females.

The file photographs showed a bull-necked man with lank black hair and a thick mustache. Balding on the top. Long sideburns and a hard jaw.

Nick sat back and wondered again if Lenny and Casey might have murdered their sister. She'd humiliated them semipublicly three years ago, with the drugs and sex testimony. Helped convict them. But their alibis held unless you figured Karl to lie for them.

No. The Vonn brothers had survived all that.

Gone back to their rat holes. It seemed a far stretch.

He read through the last two files. Price Herald was 'a flamboyant Laguna Beach antique dealer known to be supplying drugs of all kinds to the homosexual underground in Laguna Beach and Hollywood.' Two years ago Herald had been convicted of 'crimes against nature.' Not one of the public bathroom fairies, Nick saw, but a prosperous businessman who'd taken in a seventeen-year-old runaway. Later the boy had ratted out Herald in trade for a reduced marijuana charge. According to del Gado's narcotics detail, Herald was using the runaways to peddle dope and collect money.

Janelle had met him through a photographer who had shot her for *Orange County Illustrated* magazine when she was Miss Tustin.

According to JANELLE, HERALD claimed he was 'going to turn on every queer in Southern California and make some dough while I'm at it.' JANELLE has attended Herald's lavish and bizarre parties thrown in his Bluebird Canyon home. We consider HERALD an important drug culture figure, due to his influence in the large homosexual population in Southern California.

In his photograph, Herald looked overweight and affronted. He wore his hair in a ponytail and a paisley satin smoking jacket over a ruffled shirt.

The Pirate Queen look, thought Nick.

The last file was on Cory Bonnett. A sheet of paper stapled to the cover said that Bonnett had last been seen outside his home in Laguna Beach on October 3. The day after Janelle's body had been discovered, thought Nick.

*No outstanding warrants but approach with extreme caution.*

He opened and read:

BONNETT is a 22-year-old former water polo star at Santa Ana High School, where he was voted all-conference in 1964. He has adult convictions for assault and drunk in public. Mexican authorities in Michoacán believe he is responsible for the murders of two marijuana growers in that state. They were both shot execution style and their throats were cut. BONNETT is rumored to be in collusion with corrupt law enforcement officials in Tijuana and Ensenada, Mexico. According to JANELLE, BONNETT has referred to these murders but not stated his part in them to her.

BONNETT's juvenile record was sealed when he was eighteen, at the request of his parents. Offenses as a minor include arson, assault, receiving stolen property, and grand theft auto (see attached juvenile court transcripts). When sixteen, BONNETT beat his mother and father so badly that both were hospitalized.

BONNETT and his friends from Santa Ana High School have been trafficking marijuana and heroin across the border since 1965, according to witnesses, informants, and recordings. BONNETT is considered the source of up to one-quarter of the marijuana brought into the county from Mexico, and up to three-quarters of the heroin. BONNETT owns and flies a Cessna airplane between the United States and Mexico. The airplane is kept at Orange County Airport.

BONNETT owns Neck Deep Leather in Laguna Beach. They sell clothing and accessories made in Laguna Beach and Tijuana. We believe that BONNETT funnels drug profits through the shop, giving the money the appearance of legitimacy.

He is 6'4" tall and weighs 245 lbs. His Stanford-Binet IQ is 126. He is known to carry a gun in his waistband and a white-handled Mexican switchblade knife in his left front pant pocket. Although he lives in Laguna Beach, BONNETT is contemptuous of the Brotherhood of Eternal Love and disdainful of 'hippie' culture in general. He dislikes homosexuals. BONNETT appears to be motivated by money and by a taste for danger and violence. According to witnesses and informants, BONNETT does not use the contraband drugs he smuggles into this country.

Due to BONNETT's violent nature,

JANELLE and other OCSD informants are discouraged from initiating contact or being alone with him. JANELLE is aware of this man's behavior but shows no fear of him. JANELLE has joked about BONNETT being 'like a cool older brother' and that he 'watches out for me.' We have learned from JANELLE that she and BONNETT have a sexual relationship. They have traveled to Mexico together once and BONNETT has been to the yellow cottage several times.

DEPUTIES SHOULD CONSIDER BONNETT ARMED AND DANGEROUS AT ALL TIMES. According to several witnesses, including JANELLE, BONNETT has made numerous death threats against law enforcement, Brotherhood of Eternal Love members, and homosexuals. OCSD undercover narcotics deputy TROY GANT, who has established a relationship with BONNETT, believes that BONNETT is the most dangerous man in the county.

APPROACH WITH EXTREME CAUTION.

An IQ of 126, thought Nick. *A cool older brother*. Cut the growers' throats? Cut Janelle's? He remembered the initials *CB* from the scribbled numbers by her telephone – the guy who'd told him to kiss his ass on the phone. And Bonnett hadn't been seen since the day after her body was discovered.

Nick flipped through the juvenile court transcripts and looked at the photographs of Cory Bonnett. Good face. Big features, something offhand and hopeful in his expression. Chipped teeth, sun-bleached eyebrows, and a crooked nose. Blond wavy hair to his shoulders. The hippie affectation made him look more like a deranged Round Table knight than a love child. *He has been to the yellow cottage*. Nick didn't like the idea of tracking down a criminal with the same IQ as his own.

And he knew that none of these drug world contacts was the Sears, Roebuck customer who bought the Trim-Quick.

Though any of them could have bought or stolen one there or anywhere else.

And any of them could have been the one who raped and murdered Janelle and carried her into the SunBlesst packinghouse on his back.

He thought of large, violent Bonnett and Janelle flying down to Mexico. Being together in her little yellow cottage by the ocean.

*He has been to the yellow cottage*.

*The* yellow cottage, thought Nick. Not *her* yellow cottage. *The*.

An idea came to him. He went to Captain Frank del Gado's office. The captain was at his desk reading the *Journal*.

'Becker. What gives?'

'Did we rent Janelle Vonn's cottage for her?'

'More or less.'

'And we had a wiretap on the phone?' asked Nick.

'Sure. Court order. She knew. So.'

'Was the cottage miked for surveillance?'

'Yeah. So,' said del Gado.

'I want to hear the tapes.'

'We got hundreds of hours.'

'Good.'

Del Gado dropped the paper and looked at Nick. 'I'll have the dupes on your desk by end of day.'

Harloff came in a minute later, said he talked to Special Agent Hambly over at the bureau. FBI was interested in Janelle's friends Tim Leary and Roger Stoltz. Leary was high on President Johnson's new COINTELPRO New Left list. Stoltz was on Johnson's new COINTELPRO white hate list. Hambly wasn't working her murder at all.

A Fed working two counterintelligence programs, thought Nick. Glad we got to her place first.

'What's the Stoltz-Janelle connection?' asked Harloff.

'He helped her get straightened out after the molestations. Off the drugs.'

'Then these Laguna guys got her back on them.'

Nick spent an hour watching the ID fingerprint examiners trying to match the partial fingerprint from the packinghouse lock to those of Leary, Fowler, Herald, and Bonnett. The print was only big enough to contain one, maybe two, comparison points. California courts would accept ten points and nothing less.

But two good comparison points was a start. You couldn't bring them to court, but you could eliminate.

Nick looked at the lock print with his magnifying glass. A nice bifurcation. Clear and unambiguous. Almost certainly a thumb. The criminalists had done a good job on the lift.

Leary was a bust. He had the wrong basic pattern: a loop instead of a whorl. Leary the loop, thought Nick. It figured.

The ID examiner pointed out that Fowler's booking deputy had used a little too much ink. Some of the spaces were muddy and confused. Nick wondered why they'd let something like that pass. On Fowler's thumb, Nick couldn't really tell if he was looking at a ridge ending or a bifurcation or an ink bridge. It looked like a bifurcation more than an ink bridge. The pore pattern was totally obliterated.

Price Herald was a bust, too. A whorl, but a much tighter pattern than the lock print.

The examiner showed Nick that Bonnett had a similar bifurcation on his right thumb whorls, but Nick remembered that Bonnett was lefthanded. His left thumb, on the hand he'd logically use to pull off a lock, contained not a bi- but a *tri*-furcation. Still, they had found a comparison point. The distribution of sweat pores was similar but most examiners wouldn't bring the pore patterns into court.

So Bonnett, maybe. But he hadn't been seen since the day after Nick had stood in the SunBlesst packinghouse and looked down through the slanting sunlight at Janelle Vonn. Maybe the Laguna cops could give a hand finding him.

Nick had already eliminated the Talon Security guards, Terry Neemal, Jonas Dessinger – who'd been printed on a DUI arrest ten years ago, and brothers Casey and Lenny Vonn.

Jesse Black had never been fingerprinted but his alibi was good.

The trouble was, Janelle's killer may never have even touched that lock. Nick had no solid connection between the print and what happened that night. Someone could have pulled open that lock hours earlier. Days earlier. Someone with reasons unrelated to Janelle Vonn.

Nick sighed and sat back. Tapped the magnifying glass on the palm of one hand. Thought they should put all the prints on a big computer someday and let it match them up.

Two weeks into my first case, Nick thought. And no suspect.

# 20

'Two weeks and no suspect in the Vonn murder,' said sleek Jonas Dessinger. He touched his forehead. 'That's Thursday's lead story, all editions. And I want to know why our illustrious Sheriff's Department is holding the Wolfman Neemal but won't charge him in the murder.'

'You got it,' said Teresa Dessinger. 'Yours, Andy.'

Andy nodded. 'I'm interviewing Janelle's sister tonight. Lynette. If it goes well, I'll have that for Thursday, too. She told me on the phone she had some letters from Janelle.'

Letters she should have given to Nick when he interviewed her, thought Andy. He felt slightly guilty about keeping them a secret from Nick until he read them.

'Ask her how she feels about two weeks and no suspects,' said Jonas. 'And I also want a tough editorial on whether or not a homicide detail rookie is the right man to be heading up this case.

Laud the O.C. Sheriff's Department all you want, but isolate the dick and put the floodlights on him. All editions.'

'Wrongheaded,' said Andy. 'I won't touch it.'

Jonas chuckled and snugged his silk suit coat. Then sat back. 'Actually, Andy – you have to touch it. You're going to write it and you're going to sign it. It will mean something, coming from the *Journal's* best crime reporter.'

'And the dick's brother.'

'Exactly.'

You prick, Andy thought, but held his tongue. Jonas had been even more abrasive than usual since early last week, when Nick and Lobdell had written Janelle's age in black ink on the associate publisher's forehead. When Nick told him, Andy had laughed with grand satisfaction. Then seriously cussed out Nick for complicating his job. Nick had seemed more worried about it than he was. Around Jonas, Andy had played deaf and dumb.

'Jone,' said Teresa. 'Maybe Andy could write both but leave the editorial unsigned? No reason to set brother against brother like that. Nick gives Andy extra info. He's valuable to us.'

Jonas eyed his cousin with contempt. Then turned his gaze to Andy. Same gray eyes as Teresa, Andy thought. How could one pair be so brightly beautiful and the other so brutally stupid? He glanced at the associate publisher's forehead, then away. Wasn't there still some sign of abrasion, and the dark outline of 19? Almost biblical. Could ask David about it.

'I've made my decision, Teresa,' said Jonas. He fiddled with a gold cuff link. 'Andy's writing both and signing both and that's final. Now, onto "Nation," then the local editions . . .'

Andy sank down in his chair a little. Listened to Jonas and the editors and reporters argue whether to lead the 'Nation' page with Buzz's upcoming space walk or Cong artillery pounding Saigon. Watched Teresa take notes and make comments, puzzled that such a smart and organized woman could also be sexually qualmless and practically insatiable. Since they had worked the Oaxacan grass into the routine, their nightly sessions had gone from an hour to two, sometimes three hours. They were going through rubbers and ice cream at an astonishing pace. He was constantly sore and occasionally exhausted. He had begun to wonder if he was satisfying her. And she had said something yesterday evening on the phone to Chas Birdwell that was still bothering him. Something about 'Seven Seas time.' Seven Seas was a salad dressing. But the Seven Seas was also a motel in Newport not far from the *Journal* building. Andy pondered this as Teresa carried the vote for Cong artillery.

The Newport Beach edition decided to lead locally with a review of the opening of the French farce *Let's Get a Divorce* at South Coast Repertory theater.

Chas read his proposed lead:

'The South Coast Repertory production of *Let's Get a Divorce* opened yesterday, and though brightly performed, it can't compare with such diversions as playing poker or fighting with your wife.'

'Hmmm,' said Jonas.

'Change "wife" to "spouse,"' said Teresa. 'More than half our readers are female.'

'Do it,' said Jonas. 'Huntington Beach? What do you have?'

The Huntington Beach reporter read:

'You can move the oil derricks out of the small town but you can't move the oil, too.'

'Tight,' said Jonas. 'Becker?'

Andy sat up and tried to bring some force to his voice.

'A tough new city ordinance that jitterbugged into law last month will bounce the monkey, twist, frug, and mashed potato right off three Laguna nightclub stages.'

'Wordy,' said Jonas.

'I think it's bright and amusing,' said Teresa.

Huntington liked it; Newport didn't.

Andy stared at Chas.

'Tie goes to the runner,' said Jonas. 'We're done. Becker, stay here. I want to talk to you.'

When the others had filed out Jonas told Andy to close the door to the editorial conference room. Then he told him to sit down.

'You know what Nick did and his partner did to my forehead,' said Dessinger.

261

Andy nodded but said nothing.

'I won't forgive or forget that,' said Jonas. 'Ever.'

'I wouldn't, either.'

'Bet you two had a laugh over it, though. Didn't you?'

Andy nodded again. 'But I'm not writing a *Journal* editorial humiliating my brother.'

Jonas's smiling gaze went right through him. 'I thought about Nick. I made some inquiries. Made some more. Got what I needed. It wasn't hard.'

Andy saw it coming. Tried to look anticipatory and clueless.

'A lonely district attorney receptionist. A widow. Pretty eyes.'

'You lost me.'

'This will bring you back. *Sharon Santos*. You carried little friendly greetings back and forth between them in the beginning, remember? He's giving her more than greetings now. I've got witnesses at her apartment complex. I've got a statement she signed for my promise to keep it out of my paper.'

'Which you'll happily break.'

'I don't have to break it. I've got a better audience than the public.'

Then the sudden awareness of disaster, the first stomach-dropping loss of altitude. 'You'll just dump it all on Katy Becker.'

'Now you understand why you have to write the op-ed piece.'

Andy stood and Dessinger flinched. Then stood, too. He pulled his cuffs right.

'What do you want?' asked Andy. 'You want him off the case? Fired?'

Dessinger looked at Andy in what appeared to be genuine astonishment. 'I want him ruined.'

'You're not ruined. No one even knows. Nick did something stupid and felt bad. Forget about it.'

'I can't.'

Dessinger backed away from Andy, toward the door. 'You probably haven't noticed this because you're sleeping with my hot little cousin, but there hasn't been a Dessinger born on earth who possesses one grain of forgiveness in his heart. Or hers.'

'Be the first,' said Andy. 'Start a fad.'

'Have some fun with that editorial.'

'Look, Jonas, if you drop your bomb on Katy, Nick's going to drop you back on the *Times* and the *Register*. They'd love to know you were sleeping with Janelle Vonn.'

Dessinger frowned and shook his head. 'They've known it for months. I went out of my way to show her off. She was an absolute trophy, in every way. I can take that heat. I can use it to my advantage. I'm the single guy who dated the beauty queen that got her head sawed off. That makes me interesting. Nick has three children and a loyal wife and a widow girlfriend from work. That makes him rotten to the core.'

Andy considered his options. One came to mind. 'Not many people can make the hair stand up on the back of my neck like you can.'

Jonas cocked his head. 'That makes me proud. Let me know if you want some guidance on the article or the op-ed piece. And don't even think of going easy on Detective Becker.'

'What if I write a resignation letter instead?'

'I'll make someone else do them. And I'll get in touch with fat Katy. Your name on the articles is the only thing that's keeping me from doing that.'

Two hours later Andy had written both pieces. He had never written lies before and the words sat oddly on the paper. It left him tired, like the ribbon ink was blood that had come out of his body.

He put the originals and two sets of carbons in his briefcase, locked it, and headed out for Millie's.

Nick read them in the poor light of a red vinyl booth. He finished, rubbed his chin. 'It's these or Katy?'

Andy nodded.

'Oh man,' whispered Nick.

Andy placed the original articles in Jonas Dessinger's in-basket just after six that evening. Carbon number one went to his editor, Teresa. Carbon number two went into his top desk drawer.

Jonas called at 6:10 to say he loved the pieces.

He wanted to substitute the words 'bogged-down' and 'overmatched' for 'lengthy' and 'less experienced.'

Andy told him to take it up with Teresa.

Teresa called at 6:15 to say she couldn't believe her overbred cousin was putting him through this. She demanded to know what the cause of all this animosity was, but Andy wouldn't say. She thought 'overmatched' was speculative and untrue.

'Listen to what you wrote,' she said. '"After two agonizing weeks, we at the *Journal* have begun to wonder if the evidence that has stumped the rookie detective might be better evaluated by a more seasoned investigator."'

'Orders from your overbred cousin.'

'I can bad-mouth my family. You can't.'

'I have to bad-mouth my own.'

'Andy, what's going on?'

'Talk to the associate publisher. He's the psychopath fashion model on the third floor.'

'I'm going to.'

Andy called Verna and got a home number for Sharon Santos. It cost him drinks and maybe dinner. Sharon confirmed that she'd talked to a man identifying himself as Jonas Dessinger of the *Orange County Journal*. She had signed a 'kill statement' about her liaison with Nick Becker in order to prevent a story about it in the paper. She allowed that her neighbors had probably seen Nick more than once, and 'could possibly have heard some things.' Nick had helped this one neighbor jump her car, so she'd remember him, no problem. Sure, Nick knew all this. But Sharon was on his side all the way. She loved him and didn't want to ruin his marriage.

'Andy,' said Sharon, 'I'd kill myself before I'd hurt Nick.'

A chill shivered up Andy's back. 'Avoid both,' he said.

'All right.'

He left the building through the display advertising department back door. Couldn't face Teresa, whom he loved, or Jonas, whom he hated. Or the owlish copy editors or surly night-beat photogs.

Andy gunned his ice blue Corvair down Newport toward Coast Highway. Police band radio loud as always, top down, and the air cold on his face. Lynette's address in his reporter's notepad on the seat beside him.

He couldn't believe Jonas could make him screw over Nick like this. Make him screw himself over. Like a bad dream. All he ever wanted to do was write a decent book someday and stick by the people he loved. Not accomplishing either of those, he thought. Writing lies to hurt Nick was all he was doing. Either do that, or destroy Nick and Katy. He had the idea of getting Jonas off somewhere quiet to talk to him, maybe Jonas would get rational. Like maybe the end of the Newport Pier, and when they were done talking Andy could push him off.

# 21

Lynette Vonn lived up in Huntington Beach. She let Andy in without a smile. Straight black hair, early twenties, thin. Bell-bottoms made her look thinner. Barefoot. Yellow halter top with a work shirt over it. Big eyes. Andy saw in her none of her sister Janelle's casual radiance.

Lynette made them coffee and they sat in the den. Green shag carpet, a TV with rabbit ears, and a Magnavox hi-fi on a rolling stand with clear wheels. Andy smelled marijuana and incense. The house was a small craftsman cottage with a chain-link fence around the backyard and an oil pumper beyond the fence. Through the den window the pumper looked like a monstrous steel grasshopper gnawing away. The night was cool and the windows were open. Andy smelled ocean and crude oil. The neighbors had the radio on, 'Sunshine of Your Love' riding in with the smells.

Lynette told him she had left the Tustin home when she was fourteen. Run off with one of her brother Lenny's friends, Preach. Preach was twenty-five, drove a chopped black Harley with the words *God's Outlaw* painted on the tank in white. He could cook crank you wouldn't believe, clear as glass, keep you high for days and a tolerable crash. Taught other Hessians how to do it. Preach also had a religious streak, carried around a bag of rattlesnakes tied to the top of the sissy bar of his hog, and that bag would swing up against her back if they slowed down fast, a creepy feeling but she never got bit. Preach had devised this kind of religious service for Sunday mornings where you'd listen to him sermonize and take the snakes out of the bag and wave 'em around, but Preach had sewn their mouths shut with a big needle and dental floss and when they started starving he'd toss them out and get new ones. Which was easy when you're riding your Harley all around the desert giving lessons on crank production. But Preach had the other Hessians freaked out with those snakes and his own weird eyes – dark brown with blue around the edges. It was all rough sex, drugs, and fights until she ran out on him in Colusa, picked up a bus down to San Francisco, and moved in with a musician/heroin dealer. That lasted a year, coldest of her life, couldn't ever thaw out in that town.

'Wow,' said Andy.

Lynette shook her head and sighed. 'Pure crazy. I hitchhiked down here last year. Liked it and stayed. Had some money saved. I'm waitressing over at the Bear. I can't get you in free but I can get you good seats once you pay your way in.'

Andy had been to the Golden Bear a lot. Seen the Kingston Trio and Peter, Paul & Mary, and Pete Seeger and Dylan and all the folkies, but now they were doing almost all rock and roll, thank God.

'Did you and Janelle stay in touch?'

'It turned out that she wrote me a lot of letters but didn't know where to mail them. I pretty much dropped out. When I got this place and got clean I called her and she came over. Brought the letters in a box. It was kinda funny seeing her for the first time in six years. My sister was two years younger than me and we weren't very much alike.'

Andy looked at Lynette. *My sister*, he thought. 'Maybe you were more alike than you think.'

Lynette stared at Andy with her big brown eyes. 'What do you mean by that?'

'Well, you both had a talent for what most people would consider trouble.'

'No question it was trouble.'

'The same kind of hunger for something,' said Andy. 'But for what? To get to something better?'

'Just to get away, I think. Did you know her well?'

'No, not really. I admired her, though. Something about her.'

'She was pretty,' said Lynette.

'But more than pretty. Remember the guitar and tutu?'

'That tutu was mine.'

Andy looked out the window to the big oil pumper. It chomped away at the ground, drawing up the crude. He thought of Lynette throwing the rocks at them after the rumble by the packinghouse. And Janelle with the oranges she didn't throw. And Janelle on the porch of the Holt Avenue house, shaking her curls and rasping out that song. And Janelle coming out of the White House nightclub in Laguna that night. With Jesse Black and the surf movie guy and Cory Bonnett the leather store owner. The way the streetlight cast her face in the fog. *I'm so sorry what happened to Clay. Call me sometime.*

For the millionth time in his life, Andy's inner boot kicked his heart, hard, for never calling Janelle Vonn.

'Tough to explain,' he said.

'I'll get the letters.'

When Lynette came back into the room she had a cardboard box half full of letter envelopes. She tilted it so Andy could see. A hundred, he guessed. She set it on the floor at her feet and sat back down.

'You should have told Nick about these,' he said.

'I don't dig pigs.'

'Nick's not a pig. He helped Janelle way back when the trouble started.'

She stared at him. Andy felt sized up. 'I'm showing them to you,' she said. 'If there's something important, you tell him.'

Andy watched the oil pumper for a second. Heard the far-off hiss of cars out on Coast Highway. Then Hendrix on the radio.

'I never wrote back to my sister,' she said. She looked down at the box. Guided a strand of lank black hair behind her ear. 'Maybe that's why she wrote so much. It was kind of like she wrote and told me things because she knew I wouldn't judge. Like she was writing only for herself. But I did love her. She knew that, before the end.'

'When did she write the first one?'

'Early sixty-one. After Mom killed herself and I hooked up with Preach. She – my sister – was eleven. She knew what I'd done. Said in the letter she wanted us to come get her.'

*My sister.*

'Her brothers were molesting her by then.'

'Just starting. They'd done it to me, too. That was one of the reasons I split.'

'You were afraid to tell?'

Lynette turned her face from Andy. Looked out at the oil pump or the moon. 'Lenny'd hit you. Then Dad would hit Lenny A week later, the same thing all over again with Casey. It was scary. You blocked it out. Ethan was okay.'

Andy moved and sat on the couch with Lynette. He looked down into the box and picked up an envelope.

'That's an old one,' said Lynette. 'From her birthday in sixty-two.'

It was pale green and square. Andy ran his finger over the four-cent stamp with a rose on it. Lynette's name on the front but no address. He worked out a greeting card with a picture of a misty forest and the words *Love Speaks in Moments of Silence*.

He read out loud:

June 1, 1962
    Dear Lynette,
    Hey, sister, I turned thirteen today and graduate from seventh grade in two weeks! I'm still popular. I asked for makeup and a horse but don't think I'll get either. Dad still doesn't work much. Everything is crummy but the new Elvis album is really good. Over a year since you've been gone and I haven't got a note or phone call from you. That doesn't matter as long as you're okay. I love you anyway and I can visit you in my brain anytime I want!
    Love,
    J.

'My sister was optimistic then,' said Lynette.

Andy put the card in the envelope and the envelope back in the box. 'Can I see a more recent one?'

Lynette leaned forward. Held her hair back with one hand and worked the other through the

272

letters. She handed him a white legal-size envelope. It had Lynette's name and a five-cent stamp with Madonna and child, but that was all.

'Did she always put a stamp on?' asked Andy.

'Every one. For six years,' she said quietly. 'And always wrote the day's date, even though she never mailed one. Eighty-six letters and cards. She spent three dollars and ninety-eight cents on postage. Imagine what that would cost today.'

Andy nodded and looked into Lynette Vonn's earnest brown eyes.

He opened the letter, which was handwritten in black ink on a standard sheet of typing paper, and read out loud again:

August 11, 1967

Dear Sis,

They're taking my Miss Tustin title away because I got a cover on *Playboy*! Can you believe that? I showed less skin to *Playboy* than I did in the swimsuit competition! What hypocrites. Screw them. I've had enough.

I'm leaving Tustin. Think I'll go to Laguna Beach where it's beautiful and I don't know hardly anyone. I've got some financial backing and the Beetle from Roger to get me started. Maybe do more modeling because it pays well but you have to drive to L.A. and wait around for hours. Pretty much kicked the drugs and alky-hol but still like a little tequila now and then. You sip it, you don't slam it with lime and salt like those dumb college boys. Everybody's talking about LSD, how it makes you see things in a different way. They also say it's really strong. There's this guy in Laguna, Timothy Leary, and they say if you can experience LSD with him he'll get you into the right groove.

Jesse got an early tape of some new Hendrix music and duped one for me. There's this song called 'Little Wing' that speaks right into my heart. Really pretty words and guitar and Jimi's got a good voice. No Elvis, but you know what I mean. The guitar solo will totally blow your mind. $2.99 is a lot to pay for an album but it's worth the extra fifty cents for stereo instead of monaural. 'Course, you can't play a record when you're riding on the back of a hog!

I always think about you. You're like a myth to me now, this sister I had until she disappeared five lives ago. I mean years. I been through a lot and you've probably got some stories, too. Dad's pathetic but the boys are long gone so that's good. When I think of all the shit they put us through I'm surprised we didn't just shoot them one night in their sleep. Woulda been doing them a favor, not to mention us.

Anyway, I love you in my mind,

J.

'Roger Stoltz, the congressman?'

'Yeah.'

'I knew he helped her out when I wrote that article,' said Andy, 'but I didn't know he gave her money and a car.'

Lynette nodded. 'In one of the letters she said he went nuts for her.'

'*Nuts for her*,' said Andy. Felt a tingle in his fingertips.

'I can find the letter pretty easy.'

'Do that.'

Andy watched Lynette take a handful of envelopes, fan through them and then set them aside. She stopped midway through the second batch and handed him another legal-size white envelope.

'You've read them a lot,' he said.

'I didn't get them till late last year. Had some catching up to do. I can tell by the envelopes what's inside. The way she wrote my name, the kind of ink, the kind of envelope and stamp.'

'How many times have you read them?'

'Fifty, maybe.'

Andy opened the envelope. Lynette leaned over and read out loud with Andy:

November 19, 1965

    Hello Invisible Sis,

    How are ya? Had to write about this unbelievable deal that's happening to me.

    Did I tell you about Roger Stoltz? He's this

businessman and political guy who let me use his apartment in Newport Beach for a while and says he's going to get me a car next week. He's nuts for me and he's got the money. Married and old, don't know if you remember him or not. Marie his wife is really nice but has bad headaches. Roger is a real good guy and he's not bullshitting me, you know, he says he's going to do something, he does it. Had his dentist fix my cavities for free. Gave me five hundred bucks for some clothes and nice things. Says he'll give me a job when I'm eighteen. He invented a cleaner called Orange Sunshine that's mainly for driveways and streets. Roger doesn't want anything in return. It's just because he likes me. I don't believe that for one second, but hell, he wants to help.

Did you see the Beatles on Sullivan in September? I just love them so much. Saw Elvis too and still love him but I think he's getting sick of his own act. He's mostly sneering rather than smiling but I don't believe it. A guy that good-looking's got no reason to sneer.

Love,

J.


'Stoltz,' said Andy. He thought of the telegram Stoltz had sent from Washington when his first article about Janelle and the Wolfman had come out. He'd always thought there was something odd about it. No mention of Janelle, really. No acknowledgment of her death and what it might mean to Andy or anyone else. Even himself. Something brief and military, like: *Commendable article. Well done.*

'You're surprised,' said Lynette.

'A married man giving money and gifts to a girl who gets murdered? Yeah. I'm pretty damned surprised.'

'He rented her an apartment in Newport Beach. She wrote about going over there with him to see it. Big and sunny and right on the harbor. Expensive.'

Andy tried to shake the surprise out of his head so he could think straight. 'How long did she live there?'

'Not long. It was off and on. She only wrote one letter from that address. She wanted to live in Laguna. Get a place that was hers. Not someone else's.'

'That must have disappointed our Good Samaritan.'

'I can see right through him,' said Lynette. 'Even in the letters I can tell he wanted her for the same things any man would want her for. But she never did it with him. At least that's what she wrote, and I believe her.'

*Stoltz!*

'Did she keep writing after you moved here?'

Lynette shook her head. 'No. We spent plenty

of hours together, though. And on the phone.'

'Good times?'

'Yeah. She was in love with this singer. Jesse Black, down in Laguna.'

'Did she tell you she was pregnant?'

Lynette opened her mouth but didn't speak at first. Finally she shook her head. 'No. She died that way?'

'Eight weeks,' said Andy.

Lynette ran her long black hair behind her ears. Gathered the ponytail to one side and brought it forward over her left shoulder. Stared at the shag carpet. In this light her face looked Cherokee, like this girl he'd gone to high school with.

'Did you know that she was on the Sheriff's Department payroll?' asked Andy. 'As an informant?'

'She told me,' said Lynette. 'They were after the Laguna Beach acid heads, the Brotherhood of Eternal Love. And that Cory Bonnett cat. Guy that owns the leather store? I heard about him from some people at work one night. Bad dude. Not even the Hessians mess with him.'

Andy put the letter back in the envelope and dropped it into the box. Stood. 'I need to take these with me,' he said.

'No.'

'I need them,' he said. 'Nick needs them. This is evidence.'

She stood. 'I've got three guns hidden in this house, and I swear to God if you try, I'll use the nearest one. I shot Preach outside Tempe, Arizona. Just in the butt but it hurt like hell.'

Andy looked at her. Raised his empty hands like a bad guy and sat back down. 'Don't shoot. Can I just sit here and read awhile?'

'That would be fine. You want coffee, tea, or some hash?'

'Coffee is all.'

'It's good black Afghani. Brought in by the Brotherhood.'

'I tried some once and couldn't even type,' said Andy.

'That's pretty much the point. I got some dexies that'll cut the fog.'

'No. Thank you. I just want to read these letters.'

'Then stay and read them.'

'Why don't you say her name?'

Lynette's face reddened as she turned it away from him. She released the ponytail and a curtain of smooth black hair fell over her eyes. 'Because it hurts to hear it.'

Because you left her to your brothers, thought Andy. Yeah. That would hurt.

Andy read Janelle Vonn's letters while Lynette loaded up a small pipe with black crumbs and dabbed at them with a wooden match. She watched him silently as she smoked and Andy felt as if he were on display. It was usually him that made other people feel that way with all his questions. But no questions was worse. Lynette was trim and catlike with her bare feet tucked under her thighs and her eyes steady behind the hair. She finally set aside the pipe and melted into the couch.

Asleep by ten. Andy was maybe halfway through the letters. Some were four and five pages and he read them slowly. Bulletins from the great beyond.

Janelle was connected to everything. Neck deep in the Laguna LSD crowd. Neck deep with the Sheriff's Department narcs. Neck deep with David, and Jesse Black and even Representative (R) Roger goddamned Stoltz and his asphalt cleaner empire. Neck deep with Cory Bonnett, who owned a store called Neck Deep. Neck deep with football coach Howard Langton and all the Miss Tustin people until they kicked her out like a leper. But neck deep was a terrible modifier because it made Andy think of Janelle in her baby blue sweater with the empty turtle-neck. Up to her eyeballs . . . up to her elbows . . . up to her ears. He still couldn't get that horrific picture out of his mind.

He covered Lynette with a blanket from a closet, then boxed up all the letters and cards and snuck out the front door with them.

In the *Journal* building he ran copies of them on the big Xerox machine, light flashing under the cover with each slow pass. Called home and

Teresa said 'Come and get me.' Voice thick with smoke.

Almost an hour and a half later he was back on the road with the letters in the box beside him and the copies in his briefcase and the coastal fog making halos around the streetlights on Newport Boulevard.

Lynette was still asleep on the couch. Andy set the box of letters on the floor. She had bunched up the blanket around her throat with both hands. A small automatic pistol had fallen to the cushion by her head. Andy plucked it up with a nervous heart. In the kitchen he popped out the little magazine. Five .22 longs. Shit. One in the chamber, too. Set it on the counter by the toaster and the Cap'n Crunch.

He shook Lynette gently by the shoulders. Weird girl, he thought. Felt like she weighed under a hundred. Won't say her sister's name but she'd shoot you for the letters.

'I'm leaving,' he said.

'Stay.'

'I can't.'

'Get out.'

'Okay. The gun's by the cereal.'

Andy got home at two-thirty. Teresa was deep in sleep, didn't want to be touched. He set the stack of copies on his typewriter stand in the laundry room, sat down, and kept reading.

His eyes moved while his imagination created

scenes. He was not aware of the gentle sweet smell of the dryer or the insanely funny song of a mockingbird in the oleander bush outside. As he read, Janelle's voice came clearly to him and he could picture her.

*Roger showed me the apartment today.*

He saw Roger Stoltz holding open the door of a sunny apartment overlooking the bay in Newport. Saw the look on his face when she stepped in. Proud. Hopeful.

*Really a trippy place. Big window and the bay and sailboats all blue and white. Says it's a gift for as long as I want it. No strings attached.*

Saw Janelle take in the view, then turn and smile. Janelle trying to act happy. Trying to figure how she could let him down without breaking his soaring little heart. Without waking him from the dream that connected them.

Without making him furious.

Andy read it again and watched it again.

He heard the dialogue between Janelle and Stoltz. Not a lot of words. Almost formal. The age difference, he thought. Stoltz late thirties and Janelle sixteen. He saw Janelle's beauty and health, the shine of her hair and the sparkle in her eyes. He saw the fullness of her next to Stoltz's sparse, ascetic frame. How was it that her damage didn't show? He noted Stoltz's brisk mustache. The affected leather jacket. His eager eyes. Andy saw the blue ocean through the window behind them. The tide was ebbing and a pelican casually rode the onshore breeze.

A moment later Andy sat up. His arms were stiff and his temple was sore from where it had rested on his hands. Some of Janelle's letters had spilled onto the floor.

He looked out to the first light of morning. Wandered into the kitchen for more coffee. Called Nick. Nick picked up on the first ring, said he'd been up most of the night.

# 22

Nick walked into the Tustin Union High School varsity locker room before first period. A little woozy from lack of sleep. Like he was half dreaming. Three hours of del Gado's tapes the night before, to bed at 1 A.M. but slept lousy. Then up at five for two more hours of tapes. Hadn't said more than two words to Katy or the kids.

Nothing solid on the tapes. Janelle and Black. Janelle and Cory. Janelle and her sister, Lynette. Janelle and a bunch of other names Nick didn't recognize. Small talk. Party talk. Gossip. Nothing. But the sound of her voice made her seem alive and Nick kept picturing her at the Thanksgiving dinner all those years ago. And at David's church.

Lobdell had taken the morning off to take his son to the doctor. In addition to behaving badly, Kevin was never hungry and he was losing weight. Grades falling and he was sullen and mean and tired all the time. He'd dropped out of sports last year. Too bad because he could tackle anyone alive and hit a baseball a mile. Lucky said maybe there was a medical explanation for Kevin. And said he'd talk to Price Herald, the Laguna drug dealer, if he had the time.

The morning was cool and clear and the campus stirred Nick's memory in a good way.

The locker room hadn't changed much since he went all-CIF for the Tillers in fifty-five and fifty-six. Smell of soap and mildew and liniment, of old drains and sweat. It was quiet now, no lockers screeching open and banging shut. No coaches bellowing over towel fights and screaming students. Just the steady drip of the old showers and the echo of the drip.

Nick confirmed that the Tiller record board had been updated. His single-game rushing and season rushing records had both fallen just last year. He was still on the board for two second places, which made him proud in a modest way.

He found the locker he used for all three of his varsity years. The padlock looked exactly like the one he'd had, a black Master. He remembered the combination – 38-28-34 – because a classmate had once told him those were Marilyn Monroe's measurements. The locker room made him think of the playing field and the field made him think of the crowd and the crowd made him think of Katy. He'd played those games for the contest, but also for her. He imagined her bouncing around in the red, black, and white of the Tustin cheerleading squad. Saw her midair in an off-the-back jump, with the stadium lights beaming down and her hair flying up. Now it seemed like an old cliché. But then it was life itself.

Howard Langton, the offense coach, watched Nick approach through the safety window that separated the staff office from the lockers. Stood and swung open the door.

'Thanks for the time, Howard,' said Nick.

'You're welcome, Nick. Come in. It's been what, five or six years since that homecoming game?'

Langton's hand was as strong as the rest of him looked. Like he'd been carved out of something. Compact and handsome except for a bent nose. Not much neck. Monika would have called him a no-neck monster. Buzz cut, sweat shorts, white tennis shirt with an American flag pin.

Langton had gone all-Crestview League in fifty-three and all-CIF in fifty-four, leading the team during Nick's first varsity year. He was a QB with a slingshot arm and a love of blasting through linemen and taking the linebackers and defensive backs with him. Still on the board for QB rushing and total passing points in a season. Long Beach State turned him into a safety and he started three years. Too small for the pros.

They talked football for a few minutes. Tustin had a good team this year. Some excellent kids coming up, Howard said. Graves looked good at QB and Arnie Francis was ripping off heads as defensive end.

Nick caught the unusual parallel. Howard appeared not to.

Langton's eyes were green. Voice smooth and low. It was hard to imagine anyone hearing Coach Langton on the sideline, thought Nick. He remembered in the huddles years ago it was tough to hear Howard call the plays. And if Howard got pissed at the blockers he'd yank off his chin strap in the huddle and ping it hard off a lineman's helmet. About deafen you.

'So what's up, Nick?'

Nick nodded, slipped out his notebook and pen. 'Janelle. Mind?'

'No. Not at all.'

'You taught her civics, didn't you?'

'Yes. She was a good student. A good girl.'

'And she lived with you and your family from – let me check my notes here—'

'It was December of sixty-five through March of sixty-six. I can remember her and my girls playing the Beatles and Stones on that portable hi-fi Janelle had.'

'She loved music, didn't she?'

'Did she ever.'

Nick turned a page in his notebook. 'How did it go when she lived with you?'

'Fine. Easy girl to have around. Your brother suggested we take her in. This was after the drugs and the problems with her brothers, but she still needed some guidance. She never set foot in my home under the influence. That I knew about, anyway. My two girls were seven and nine and they really liked her. Like having a big sister. Linda – that's my wife – enjoyed her quite a bit. Janelle helped out with the girls. Never really had to ask her to.'

Nick nodded. 'Janelle had what looked like a dinner date on her calendar for the night she was murdered. It said "Red and Ho – seven." I had no idea who Red and Ho were until my little brother got to talking with David. I was lucky. David confirmed you three had a dinner date for that night but Janelle broke it.'

'True.'

'Tell me about that.'

Howard considered Nick with his peaceful green eyes. 'Janelle and Linda stayed in touch after Janelle left our home. I think Janelle looked up to Linda. To me, too. You know – people who managed to have a good marriage. So it was going to be Linda and me, David and Barbara, Janelle and her date. But she called that morning and said she couldn't do it. No reason. She just apologized and said we'd have to do it some other time.'

'Who was her date going to be?'

Howard shrugged, then reached into his desk drawer. He palmed a pack of smokes and an ashtray to the desktop. 'Linda didn't say.'

Nick made a note of the shrug and the smokes. 'Who took Janelle's cancellation call?'

'Linda, at home.'

'How did she sound?'

'Fine,' said Langton. He lit a cigarette and dropped the pack and matches back into the desk drawer. 'Linda had no reason to think anything was wrong.'

'Had you socialized with Janelle before?'

'Three dinners, since the time she was with us. Twice in restaurants. Once she cooked in an apartment in Newport. Spaghetti. Linda and I had never seen the Laguna place and we were looking forward to it.'

This pretty much matched what David had told him. Only one thing stuck out as odd. 'I didn't know she lived in Newport.'

'That was August of last year,' said Langton.

'Remember the address?'

'No, but Linda might. I'll ask her and call you.'

'I'd like to call her myself,' said Nick. 'Like to hear her version of things if you don't mind.'

Langton looked down at the desktop. 'Not at all,' he said quietly. 'She works part-time in the mornings, so afternoons are best.'

Nick set his notebook on the desk and looked around the staff office. Crowded little room. Two gray metal desks, two wheeled chairs. Linoleum floor. A dragster calendar, a Green Bay Packers poster, a Vince Lombardi poster. Two industrial lamps in the ceiling, the kind with the mesh to protect the bulb. Glass walls on two sides so they could keep an eye on the kids.

'Funny,' said Nick. 'I talked to the Pepito's

hostess. Janelle came in that night, with two guys. The description of the hostess fit you and David. I wondered if you two might have just fibbed a little. A married guy. A minister. A pretty ex-beauty queen who gets her head sawed off later the night you see her. Nobody wants a piece of that action.'

Langton's expression was compact and aggressive. 'I'm sure you asked your brother that.'

'Thought I'd ask you, too.'

'Janelle canceled us and went for dinner with some other guys. Pretty damned obvious, isn't it?'

'Guys who looked like you and David.'

'What's funny about that? There's a million early-thirties white guys in Orange County who look more or less like us.'

'Just checking, Howard.'

'Ugly things,' Howard said softly. 'I don't want to be associated with her. I'll admit that. Neither does David, I'm sure. Even though . . . I liked her. I really did.'

Nick sat back, looked around the office. Then at the locker room beyond the windows.

'What did you make of her and Roger Stoltz?'

Langton gave him a gloomy look. 'He set her up with a place. Gave her money. Janelle said they were friends.'

'Ever see them together?'

'No,' said Langton. 'She wasn't open about that relationship. I mean, David and Barbara knew – I think they may have introduced her to Stoltz in the first place. We knew Stoltz was a financial supporter of Janelle.'

'He paid for that Newport Beach apartment.' Nick remembered the excitement in Andy's voice a few hours ago. Five-thirty in the morning but Andy couldn't wait another minute to call. Lynette and her gun. Janelle's letters. Stoltz.

Howard Langton nodded but didn't meet Nick's eye.

'Do you know Cory Bonnett?' asked Nick.

'Bonnett? No.'

'Big guy. Long blond hair. Drugs and money, lives in Laguna.'

Langton shook his head. 'Laguna's full of guys like that.'

Nick looked out to the battered lockers. The old wall clock that still ran slow. The 'Fear Ye Who Enter Here' placard that went on to boast of the Tustin Tiller defense. They called themselves the Harpies.

'This looks like a good thing you have here,' said Nick. 'You play for the team, then a few years later you coach it.'

'It's what I always wanted to do,' said Langton. 'Now I'm thirty-three years old.'

Nick heard a door slam. Howard took a puff and ground out the cigarette. Stashed the ashtray and butt back in the desk drawer. Came up with a can, shot a half circle of room deodorant into the air and waved it with one hand. Not Orange Sunshine. A serviceman rolled past a dolly

291

loaded with white towels, bundled and tied.

'Now that I think about it,' said Howard, 'there's no reason for you to call Linda.'

Nick had seen this coming. Too much Linda this and Linda that and he was pretty sure he had the reason. 'Why's that?'

Langton looked down at the desk. 'Linda didn't talk to Janelle. I did. About the dinner, I mean.'

'How come?'

'Guess, Nick.'

'Because you were hoping to go without your wife.'

'Yeah.'

'Because you wanted to be alone with Janelle.'

Langton shrugged again. 'I don't have to respond to that,' he said.

Nick picked up his notepad, drew a large question mark on the open page. Flipped the cover down and slipped it into his pocket.

'You're not calling all the plays anymore, Howard. You're a schoolteacher and a coach. So the next time I ask you a question, tell me the truth.'

'Sorry, Nick. It's been difficult.'

'When was the last time you saw her?'

'She came nightclubbing up in Hollywood last month with me and some friends. Did the Whiskey and the Rainbow.'

'But I don't need to talk to Linda about that.'

'I told her it was an offensive coordinator's convention in Long Beach,' said Langton.

'What *did* you do that night? I'm talking about

October the first. That's the night Janelle was killed. Think about it if you have to because I want the truth the first time.'

Langton stood. 'Home. All night. If you don't believe it, call my wife.'

At eleven that morning Nick met Sharon Santos at Prentice Park in Santa Ana. It was a quiet little park down off First Street, not a place they'd see anyone they knew. They stood in front of the golden eagle cage, Sharon's hair up in a scarf and her eyes hidden by dark glasses.

Nick told her they'd have to break it off. She said she understood but would miss him. Said don't change your mind about this because I can't go off and on like a faucet.

Nick wanted to thank her for everything but it seemed like a lousy thing to say. Wanted to say he was sorry but that was worse.

He tried to kiss her goodbye but she turned away and walked back toward her car.

Just before lunch Nick stopped off at Representative Roger Stoltz's office in Tustin. It was less than a mile from the SunBlesst orange packinghouse. Nick knew from yesterday's paper that the congressman was in Washington. But Nick wanted his business card to be in Stoltz's secretary's hand when she called him on the phone to say that homicide detective Nick Becker had come to see him.

'May I tell him what this is about?' she asked.

'Janelle Vonn,' said Nick.

'Oh. Would you like to make an appointment? He'll be in this office Friday afternoon, day after tomorrow.'

'Let's do that.'

She swung open an appointment calendar, ran her pencil to the eighteenth.

Nick's eyes went straight to the box for Tuesday, October first. Couldn't make out the writing.

'How's four o'clock, Mr Becker?'

Nick sat with Terry Neemal while the former Wolfman ate his lunch. Green bean gravy and red gelatin caught in the big mustache. Neemal avoided looking at Nick for a long time. Then he fixed Nick with tan blankness.

'What if I did it?'

Nick shrugged.

'What if I confessed?'

'Well, then you could either ask for a trial or waive your right,' said Nick. 'If you waived the judge would sentence you. You'd probably get life. Maybe they'd commit you again. Talk to me, Terry.'

'Would I be a big story?'

'For the trial or sentencing, yeah. Then everybody would forget about you.'

'Seems reasonable.'

'You don't confess for attention, Terry.'

'Who said anything about that?'

'You did. Between the lines.'

Neemal turned his face back to the tray and didn't look up again for a long minute or two. 'Your brother says God will forgive me if I just ask.'

'Forgive you for what?'

'Whatever I've done,' said Neemal. 'Anything.'

'That's a good deal for you, then, Terry.'

'He's a fucked-up guy.'

'David or God?'

Neemal laughed. Tan eyes and teeth gleaming like a wet savanna, thought Nick.

'Your brother.'

'Oh yeah?'

Neemal nodded. 'He's close to God because he prays all the time. But you have to prove to me that that's good. You get too close to some things, it's bad. Fire. God.'

'Maybe being far away is worse.'

'God used to talk to me a lot,' said Neemal. 'Directly to me. I knew His voice. Told me to do things. Told me to walk across Arizona and I did. On the highways, I mean. Not the desert. That's a shitty way to live, God telling you what to do all the time. You're better off far away. Where you can have your own thoughts. Your brother listens to God too much. Got to stand on your own two feet.'

'Maybe there's some truth to that.'

'I masturbated on her. Whatever you found on her, that was mine.'

Nick said nothing for a beat. He lit two smokes, handed one to Neemal.

'Tell me about that,' said Nick.

'I just did.'

Nick studied him. 'It pisses me off when you hold out on me.'

Neemal nodded without looking at Nick. He explained that his sexual desires overwhelmed him. Hadn't happened since he was young. Had to do with the fires he set. Hoped Nick would forgive him for not bringing it up right away.

Nick listened. Remembered the half-burned pile of newspaper in the slanting packinghouse light. The smell of it. 'You want to get something off your conscience?'

'I'm going to hold for right now.'

'We're not playing blackjack. What happened to the saw blade?'

'No idea. I'm good for now. I'm done talking for now, Nick. Let me finish this Jell-O in privacy, will you?'

'Terry.'

'Yes, sir.'

'If you dick with me I can't help you.'

'I understand.'

'You'd better.'

Back at his desk Nick returned a call from Laguna Beach PD detective Don Rae. Rae said they still hadn't seen Bonnett, and one of his snitches was telling him Bonnett had split for Ensenada, down in Baja. Bonnett had a place down there. Rae had a friend on the Ensenada PD who was going to check it out. But another snitch said Bonnett was still around, looking to 'punish' whoever killed his friend Janelle. Rae told Nick to be careful with Bonnett – the gun, the knife, and the temper.

'Big guy,' said Rae. 'Just be careful.'

'Is his Cessna at Orange County?'

'No. And no flight plan filed, either.'

Nick thanked him and hung up. Wondered if he could handle a twenty-two-year-old six-foot-four-inch 245-pound ex-athlete bent on shooting, stabbing, or kicking the shit out of him. Nick had eight more years of wear and tear. He was four inches shorter. Got dizzy sometimes from the Vonns and that stupid rumble, what, fourteen years ago? And he was only twenty pounds over his high school playing weight of 175, which still left him *fifty* pounds short if it came to a fight. Some of it was flab, too, with the booze and lousy food and long hours. At least he'd pretty much quit the smokes. Getting old stank. And it still pissed him off that Bonnett's IQ was the same as his own. Like Bonnett had stolen it or something. Dumb to think that way, he knew. It didn't make sense.

Nick took a few minutes to compare Howard Langton's fingerprints with the partial print on the packinghouse lock. Langton's ten-set was on file with the California Department of Justice, along with those of every credentialed school-teacher in the state.

Nothing close enough to work with. Nick examined all ten prints but nothing popped.

He called Linda Langton. Said he was just making sure he had the facts right, checking some things that Howard had told him about the night Janelle was murdered. He lobbed her a few easy ones, then got to the only one that mattered.

She told him that her husband had been home all night. Why wouldn't he be? They had dinner and watched TV. Jerry Lewis and Red Skelton. Later a James Garner movie.

Her voice sounded hostile but she offered nothing at all about a canceled dinner date with Janelle Vonn.

Lobdell called a minute later, said he'd stopped off in Laguna to talk to Price Herald. Herald said he was at home with friends the night Janelle got it. The friends said the same thing. Scared but telling the truth, said Lobdell. All of them more worried about the Boom Boom Bungalow murder. Lobdell doubted that the sour old queen had raped, murdered, and mutilated a nineteen-year-old girl.

So did Nick. 'How's Kevin?'

'The doctor said he looked fine. Took some blood. On the way home I pulled the car over. Came down real hard on Kevin. I told him I didn't want him moping and sleeping all day on the weekends and looking at me like I'm dog puke. Cussing out his teachers and his mom. I told him if he doesn't shape up he's out of my house the day he turns eighteen. Get a job. Or he can do what I did. Join the service.'

'There's a war going on.'

'He knows that. I'm trying to get him to straighten up and fly right. Trying to motivate him. Shirley started crying, then telling me I was being completely unreasonable. Telling me I just make things worse.'

Nick thought about that scene. Glad he missed it.

'Nick, enjoy those kids of yours while they're young. They hit thirteen and everything changes. They don't love you anymore. Don't even like you. Makes you wonder where they went. You miss them and they're right there in front of you.'

# 23

Nick and Lobdell walked into Mystic Arts World in Laguna that evening around five. The flyers around town had said that Dr Timothy Leary would give a brief talk on 'Coming Together in the Psychedelic Age.'

The store was larger than it looked from the street. Two entrances and three long sections, and a meditation room in the back. Wild paintings on the walls. Drug paraphernalia, candles, incense and incense holders, brass gewgaws made in China and Turkey and India, odd percussion instruments, sandals and tie-dyed clothing, books on mysticism, psychopharmacology, Oriental religion, tantric and meditational texts, ancient Persian erotica, health foods, an endless selection of Turkish tobacco and clove cigarettes, eight-track tapes of 'mystical' music, some of which – a sitar, Nick was pretty sure – boinged and plinked from speakers mounted to the walls on either side of a poster that said 'Om Sweet Om.'

'It's like a Sears for heads,' said Nick.

'I got my sofa from Sears. Don't squirt any air freshener on yourself, Nicky.'

Nick inhaled the marvelously competing smells: clove and cinnamon, bay leaves and herbal teas, oils for the skin, genitals, hair. He picked up a comic book by R. Crumb. The characters looked harmlessly deranged. Then a book called the *I Ching*, not an autobiography of a person named Ching but a collection of oddly pithy sayings:

> Thus the superior man
> Takes thought of misfortune
> And arms himself against it in advance.

Then a copy of *The Egyptian Book of the Dead*. Nick fanned through the mysterious hieroglyphics and read a translation:

> I am pure, I am divine, I am might, I have a soul, I have become powerful, I am glorious, I have brought to you perfume [and] incense [and] natron.

Ronnie Joe Fowler took one look at them and said, 'Hey, everybody, the pigs are here.'

'Yeah, we came to talk about your rape charges in Oregon,' said Lobdell.

'Plenty of charges but no crime,' said Fowler. Stocky and strong. Black hair to his shoulders. 'Dismissed for lack of evidence.'

'We came for the program,' said Nick.

'Pigs aren't welcome,' said Fowler.

A man in a loose white shirt and pants stepped in front of Fowler. Offered his hand to Nick. 'And why not? It's all God's flesh. Hello, gentlemen, I'm Tim.'

Leary was tanned and handsome. Taller and older than Nick had expected. Sun-bleached hair, broad face. An engaging twinkle in his eyes.

Nick shook Leary's hand but Lobdell turned down the offer.

'We want to turn on, tune in, and drop out,' said Lobdell.

Leary looked at him and laughed. White teeth. Merry eyes. 'That's entirely up to you. You know, my yippie friends in the cities have changed that to "turn on, tune in, and kick ass."'

'I'm not raising my son to turn on,' said Lobdell. 'What kind of advice is that to give young people?'

'We don't give advice to children or anybody else,' said Fowler. 'We want people to think for themselves.'

'You're welcome to stay for the program,' said Leary. 'In spite of Ronnie's bad manners. Right, Ron?'

'Sure. Maybe they'll learn something.'

'We'd like to learn something about Janelle Vonn,' said Nick.

'I don't know shit about her,' said Fowler.

'I remember her very clearly,' said Leary. 'She

had a beauty like my wife, Rosemary. Janelle was so vibrant and alive. She was a piece of God walking on earth. Her energies were shaped like this—'

Leary raised both arms into a V, hands open and fingers spread. 'See? It's a bodily representation of the hexagram for peace, or tai. Receptive above, moving down. Creative below, moving up. It's the very first hexagram in the *I Ching* and I recognized it in Janelle immediately.'

'We found some of your LSD in her car,' said Nick.

'*My* LSD?'

'The Orange Sunshine air freshener.'

'Now, I've heard of such a thing,' said Leary. 'But I've never actually seen one.'

'Maybe you'll talk to us after the show tonight,' said Lobdell.

'I'll do anything I can to help you.'

'The pigs will stab you in the back, man,' said Fowler. 'Don't forget your pig friends in Texas.'

Lobdell looked down at Fowler. Nick felt the violence quotient spike inside Mystic Arts World. Unlike Jonas Dessinger, who was too naive to recognize danger, Ronnie Joe Fowler read it loud and clear.

'I'm cool,' he said, hands out and palms up, backing past a rack of Afghani clothing.

'We want to talk to you, too,' said Nick.

'Hey, I'm *cool*, man. I ain't going nowhere.' Fowler turned and headed for the back room.

'Pardon me, gentlemen,' said Leary. 'I have some consciousness to expand.'

The meditation room was big enough for forty standing people and it was almost full. Nick and Lobdell stayed in the back, their coats and ties freakish amid the robes and jeans and tie-dyes and batik prints and muslin. There was a narrow table at the front of the room. A brass holder and a smoking stick of incense sat on one end of it. Leary sat near the other.

'Shoulda worn my sandals,' said Lobdell. 'Cost Shirley eight and a half books of Green Stamps.'

Nick said nothing. He was studying the painting on the wall behind the table, a huge canvas shaped like a diamond with the evolution of life portrayed. It went from amoebas to God in an explosion of color and detail that challenged Nick's eyes. He didn't know anything about painting a picture, but it seemed like this must have taken a few thousand hours.

'Thing makes me dizzy,' said Lobdell.

'I kind of like it,' said Nick.

'Too much Orange Sunshine for you.'

A small woman with big hair looked at Nick and smiled. 'Far out,' she said. 'Even the cops are droppin'. I dropped last Monday and didn't come down till Wednesday.'

'Sure you're not still floating around up there?' asked Lobdell.

'No, I'm back to earth. It's always nice to come home.'

304

'I took it by accident,' said Nick. 'It was wild, but in the morning I felt pretty good.'

'Try smoking some dragon ball when you're tripping,' she said. 'The hash and opium mellow you out while the acid blows your mind.'

'I'll think about that,' said Nick.

The woman trailed him a smile as she moved closer to the front of the room. Nick and Lobdell stayed in the back, quarantined by wing tips and hidden guns.

A slender young man approached them. Hair in a ponytail, jeans and a loose woven shirt. Clear eyes, strong chin.

'I knew Janelle,' he said. 'I don't know anything about what happened but I'll help in any way I can.'

'Are you Brotherhood?' asked Nick.

'One of the original thirty. Richard Lucas. She was a very gentle girl. Terrific energy and curiosity. Used too much acid, if you ask me.'

'I thought that's what you guys did,' said Lobdell.

A neutral look from Lucas. He considered the crowd. Then Tim Leary making his way through it. 'We used to create space for light and vision. I'm not sure what we're doing now. You can contact me here anytime you want.'

'When did you see her last?' asked Nick.

'The day she died,' said Lucas. 'Late morning. She came into the store here and bought some incense. Patchouli.'

'Was she worried or anxious?'

Lucas smiled. Brightness in his eyes. 'She seemed calm and happy like she always did. The world is a slightly darker place without her in it. Excuse me. I'm needed up front. Come by again if you want to talk more. The Brotherhood is misunderstood. We do good things. We've helped a lot of people.'

Suddenly the room was buzzing with the syllable *om*. Leary now sat on the table cross-legged, fingers circled on his knees, smiling. 'I can't say *om* and smile, but I can't keep from smiling! I confess! I'm a hope fiend!'

After a few minutes the chanting subsided and Leary's voice took over the room. For the next twenty minutes he talked about the psychedelic experience opening the doors of perception and the psychopharmacologic evolution/revolution that was taking place in the world and how Ginsberg was right, *what the world needs is Johnson and Nikita and Mao and Ho and Kerouac and Burroughs and Mailer to all get together and drop heavy psychedelics and figure out a new holy apostolic method to strip the hate from the chromosomes of human experience and replace it with a little . . . illumination so the strings of the cosmos can vibrate in peace instead of madness!*

'And I thought my kids had imaginations,' whispered Nick.

*I don't sense that we are alone here. The quest for internal freedom, for the elixir of life, for the draft of*

*immortal revelation, isn't new. I believe we are unwit-*
*ting agents of a social process far too powerful for us to*
*control or more than dimly understand. A historical*
*movement that will inevitably change man at the very*
*center of his nature, his consciousness.*

'He's a lunatic with a big vocabulary,' Lobdell whispered.

'I don't think he's crazy,' Nick whispered back. 'It's belief. Fervor. Passion. He believes what he's saying.'

'You just like his air freshener.'

After half an hour of hopeful sermonizing, Leary invited everyone across the street to the beach for sunset and chanting.

They crossed Coast Highway at the signal and weaved down the sidewalk at Cleo Street. Nick and Lobdell brought up the rear. Up ahead Nick spotted Ronnie Joe Fowler and Troy Gant. They looked back at the same time, made the cops. Then both looked to their left and ahead, where Janelle Vonn's yellow cottage sat overlooking the ocean.

Nick felt the sand crunching under his shoes as he walked down the concrete steps to the beach. The sun burned down in an orange pool. Catalina Island sat in it like a black rock. Nick glanced straight up to a sky of weightless blue with one star already twinkling.

Fowler and Gant stood on a flat rock staring down at them. Fowler smiled and waved. Leary stood knee deep in the ocean, arms raised toward the setting sun. Some of the crowd joined him, others stayed on the wet bank of sand. More spread back into the sandstone and the seawall and Nick heard the communal syllable *om* again. A flock of seagulls cried overhead, dove through the air toward Leary, then straightened and glided out over the water by inches. A few minutes later the cool October night turned dark and Nick saw the flames of lighters and matches. The air around them filled with the sweet reek of clove and tobacco and marijuana.

'Like cocktail hour,' said Lobdell. 'Except you don't drink it, you smoke it.'

Later when the crowd drifted away they got Leary and Fowler off alone.

They walked north along the waterline. 'We – Rosemary and I – had Janelle to the house I think three times,' Leary said. 'Just casual get-togethers.'

'We heard they were be-ins,' said Nick.

'Exactly,' said Leary. 'Be-ins. Be in yourself. Be in the moment. Be in harmony with nature and those around you.'

'Clever,' said Lobdell. 'Janelle ever have any trouble at these orgies?'

'None,' said Leary. 'She was perfect.'

'She was nineteen is what she was,' said Nick.

'And there was very little if any orgiastic behavior at those gatherings,' said Leary.

'Did you give her drugs?' asked Lobdell.

'No. But I shared with her what I believe about LSD. How it will open the windows of the mind and the doors of perception. I think it's the most important chemical tool we have for helping society. I make no secret about what I believe, gentlemen. But I don't supply LSD to nineteen-year-old girls.'

'The air freshener acid was powerful,' said Nick. 'I got some on me by accident.'

'And what did you see?'

'More than was really there.'

'What you saw is *always* there, Detective Becker! It was *you* who arrived fresh and new!'

Leary had produced a flashlight. Nick watched the beam flicker along on the sand. To his right were the Laguna boardwalk and the old lifeguard tower. Beyond that Coast Highway and the Star Theater. They moved north away from the lights and into the darkness.

'You ever see anybody bothering her?' asked Nick.

'Men were attracted to her,' said Leary.

'What about Cory Bonnett?' asked Nick.

'Guy's a nutcase,' said Fowler. 'I can't even be in the same room with that creep.'

'He'd kick your fake hippie ass,' said Lobdell.

'Cory is a man headed for trouble,' said Leary.

The sand gave way to rocks. Leary and Fowler seemed to glide across them. Nick steadied himself, picking his way. In the faint moonlight it was hard to see the cracks and holes. The air had the tide-pool smell of ocean and of seaweed beginning to spoil.

'Janelle was working for the Sheriff's Department,' said Nick. 'As an informant. We didn't find that out until after she was murdered.'

'I never trusted her,' said Fowler. 'Didn't I tell you, Tim? Didn't I make her for a snitch right out?'

'Yes,' said Leary softly. He sounded genuinely disappointed. 'You did.'

'So,' said Nick. 'We thought if some genius like Fowler here figured that out, maybe that's a reason to shut her up. That's the kind of possibility that interests us.'

'I never touched her,' said Fowler. 'I got no interest in chicks that think they know everything. I crashed with some friends that night out in Dodge City. I'll give you numbers. You can ask them. I don't give a shit what you think.'

Leary stood on the rocks. White shirt and pants flapping in the stiff coast breeze. Nick felt the soles of his wing tips growing slick from the brine. Could use some sandals with tire-rubber soles like the hippies, he thought. A wave rushed across the rocks. Soaked him halfway up his calves.

'This world is full of experience,' said Leary. 'And the temptation of experience.'

'You and your drugs are temptation,' said Nick.

'But they're not my drugs and they haven't killed anyone.'

'There's that lady who jumped out of the skyscraper,' said Lobdell.

'She was under psychiatric treatment,' said Leary. 'LSD should probably not be prescribed for a potential suicide.'

'Your first wife killed herself,' said Lobdell.

'Yes. God bless her.'

Fowler had jumped up onto the rocks. Nimble for a thick strong man. Whispered something in Leary's ear, then laughed.

'Dr Leary, where were you on Tuesday night, October first?' asked Nick.

Leary looked at him but said nothing for a long moment. 'With my wife Rosemary and my son Jack. We ate at a Chinese restaurant downtown. That's a nasty insinuation you just made, if you're considering me a suspect.'

Leary aimed the flashlight at himself. The light turned his flesh pale red and cast shadows upward on his face. Weird guy, thought Nick. Figured Leary had spent more days frying on LSD than he had spent on the job as a homicide detective.

'Where I'm standing right now is called the Giggle Crack,' said Leary. He aimed the light down on the shiny black rocks. 'See the crack, where the water comes in and flows out? In daylight it's really quite beautiful. People like to see if they can get in, feel the tide swell around them. But there's a sharp edge they don't see and it snags their ankles and the water beats them terribly against the sharp rocks. The Giggle Crack has killed three people. Every ten years it claims a new victim. There it is again – the temptation of experience.'

'Someone raped and strangled Janelle,' said Nick. 'It wasn't temptation that did that.'

Leary shined the flashlight on Nick's face, then tilted it back at himself. 'Is this more to you than a case, Mr Becker?'

'I knew her when she was a little girl,' said Nick. 'She used to sing and dance.'

'I'm sure she was perfect in every way,' said Leary. 'I'm sorry I can't help you more. Goodbye. There's a trail to your right that leads up the bluff. It's easy to follow. There are feral cats in the brush. Their eyes glow faint yellow in the dark. They'll lead your way. Good night, gentlemen.'

Fowler handed Nick a piece of paper. 'My alibis. Check 'em all you want.'

They drifted away. Nick could see Leary's white clothes slowly vanish.

Nick and Lobdell climbed up the trail on the bluff, yellow cat eyes paired in the brush around them.

# 24

David walked the new chapel that morning with young Darren Whitbrend. David leaned slightly forward, half a step ahead of his prospective partner, hands locked behind the small of his back. He was finding it very difficult to shake the words that brother Andy had written about brother Nick in this morning's *Journal*. Max, their father, had called David just after 6 A.M., perplexed and fretful at the hostility between his sons.

'Is televangelism a word?' asked David.

'I heard it somewhere, sir,' said Whitbrend. 'And thought it was perfect.'

'Barbara tells me you're a televangelism guru,' said David.

'Guru was her word, sir,' said Whitbrend with a smile. Whitbrend was fair-complected and white-haired. Eyes small and quick. Round spectacles. He had a trim, wiry frame and a blunt face.

'I think televangelism is the future of ministry,' said Whitbrend. 'I think there will be a day, in

313

my lifetime, when churches become the studios for Christianity. Faith will surge across the airwaves. Entire networks will be dedicated to God's word. Empires built with satellites and antennas and closed-circuit broadcasts and pay-as-you-view events. A television set in every room and in every vehicle and in every public space. Screens so small they can fit in your pocket. Screens so big they're placed on the sides of build-ings. A staggering apparatus for transmitting faith and making money for God's purpose.'

David sighed and shook his head slightly.

'Is that distasteful to you, Reverend?'

'Grim shit,' David said.

'Why?'

Whitbrend was direct and comfortable with words. David wasn't sure how he felt about that.

'Like I said on the phone,' said David. 'I love my congregation. I don't want to lose them.'

'With respect, sir, if you don't televise, you'll surely lose them.'

'Preach to millions? How can one man minis-ter to millions? I can hardly keep Mrs Hartley's allergic papillon straight from Mrs *Harley's* aller-gic grandson.'

Whitbrend smiled. It was somehow transpar-ent and conspiratorial at the same time. It forced David to figure out which and he didn't appreci-ate the extra work. He noted that one of Whitbrend's neat front teeth was capped and slightly whiter than the others.

'Well, sir. As you and Mrs Becker and I understand, one man *can't* do everything. We see that it will take two. Two. You and whoever you choose for the astonishing journey you are making.'

David eyed the young minister. Whitbrend's résumé had billed him as a 'nondenominational, faith-based evangelist in the tradition of Billy Graham.' He was twenty-two. But it was difficult to see the spark in him. Billy Graham could light up like a Texas bonfire. You could feel the heat. Whitbrend, however, seemed only intelligent. And probably tenacious. David pictured him behind the pulpit here in the Grove Drive-In Church of God, unknowingly leading the congregation – *his* congregation – into bored resentment. Faith was joy. God was joy. Jesus was joy. Whitbrend was a Lutheran-trained mutineer without pizzazz.

Outside they toured the playground and storage buildings, the class-rooms and the extra drive-in stalls. David felt like a homeowner entertaining buyers he didn't want to sell to. They stood approximately two hundred feet back from the full-screen *Raising of Lazarus*, the optimal distance for taking it all in. The speaker-studded expanse of sky-blue asphalt stretched all around them.

'This is all well and good,' said Whitbrend. 'But your congregation deserves more. You want to inspire awe.'

David suspected he'd entirely misread Whit-brend. 'This inspires me every morning when I see it,' he said.

'With what? Not awe.'

David thought for a moment. 'Satisfaction. Every Saturday when the deacons and I run the street sweepers over it and dose it with Orange Sunshine. And the nice chapel we were just inside? And the painting up there? And the play-ground for the kids? This is a good thing, Whitbrend. I'm surprised you can't see that.'

'I see it, sir,' Whitbrend answered quietly. His face colored. 'And I agree with everything you just said. But it's quaint. You need majesty around you. Majesty a camera can capture and transmit. You need to broadcast your message from a place that looks like heaven. Sir, I understand that you are at a crossroads. You have a wonderful ministry here. But it's growing and you need a partner. My belief is that the only way to keep the traditional congre-gation is through television. That was my thesis at the seminary. I've given it some thought. May I entertain you with my vision of the Grove of God?'

'Go for it,' said David.

'Keep *The Raising of Lazarus*,' said the young minister. 'Erect three more screens at cardinal points, like they used to have here, and commis-sion equally impressive Christian paintings for them. These will serve as your franchise images. They will draw the curious to your services. Guided tours will be free. Postcards and T-shirts based on the paintings will be in demand. More importantly, the paintings will become the visual introduction to the televised 'Grove of God' worship hour, produced and distributed by the Grove of God in Orange.'

'This is the Grove *Drive-In* Church of God,' said David.

'Get rid of all of the drive-in stuff,' said Whitbrend. 'It's space-consuming, air-polluting, and it already – honestly – feels dated and over-stated. Like the giant rotating donuts and the huge plaster hot dogs you see in L.A.'

'Drive-in worship is the soul of my congrega-tion.'

'*Was*,' said Whitbrend. 'Bob Schuller started like this, then went on to much bigger and better things.'

David waved aside thoughts of Bob Schuller. 'The cars fill our lot every Sunday.'

'But believe me,' said Whitbrend, 'if they think that worshiping in their cars is convenient, they're going to love watching your sermons on televi-sion, at home, still in their jammies, with cereal and a cup of coffee.'

David pictured it. Family on the couch. Socks and slippers up on the coffee table. Milk dribbling on flannel. Kids with stuffed animals or plastic machine guns. Burps and farts and comments during his message. Not much different from inside the cars here on Sunday mornings, if you were honest about it.

'And do what with all this land?' asked David.

'Do you really want my opinion?'

'No, but I'm dying to hear it.'

Whitbrend smiled. '*Listen*. You tear out the car stalls. You tear down the outbuildings. Leave the playground. Convert the main chapel to a utility building, day school, study center, and business office.'

Whitbrend lifted an arm and pointed to the north. 'There, in what is now just asphalt and speakers, you build the Grove of God Chapel. It is magnificent without being showy. It is a true monument to God. You build it of mirrored glass that will magnify its dimensions when it appears on-screen, and will dazzle the viewer. Its look is neither modern nor old, but a . . . contemporary-Gothic synthesis that is both ancient and ageless. There is no asphalt around it, but a simple grove of orange trees – ten idyllic acres. The green leaves and bright fruit of the trees are caught in the reflective glass of the chapel. The chapel is the heart of the Grove of God. The center of Eden. The beginning of life. Through the beautiful trees winds a wide boulevard to and from the chapel. Not an asphalt boulevard. *Brick*. I think brick painted sky blue, like your asphalt, would be perfect. Inside, this is a chapel that God Himself would be honored to visit. Not just honored. He'd wipe His shoes before entering. And smile with pride. It is resplendent but controlled. It is internally wired for video and sound, of course. And from a pulpit of tasteful splendor you deliver the finest sermons of any televangelist in the country. *That* inspires me with awe.'

A ripple of fear and revelation shivered down David Becker's back. 'Are you an evangelist or a television marketer?'

Whitbrend blushed and looked away. 'I'm a minister by calling. But I've never delivered a sermon that can compare with one of yours. I'm not even in the same league. You have strength and authority. Your strength is wide and inclusive rather than focused and specific, which is what it takes to minister. I attend your church occasionally. When I can't, my wife attends on my behalf. In a white sixty-two Impala. She tape-records your sermons for me so I can learn from them. I'm probably the only minister on earth who hustles home from his Sunday duties so he can listen to another minister perform his. Incidentally, there's a nice aftermarket out there for tapes of your messages. I'm surprised you haven't tapped it yet.'

'Why flatter me? You've got twice the imagination and ambition that I do.'

'But you've got all the talent.'

David considered this twenty-two-year-old minister. 'What do you want?'

'To be a vehicle for God's power.'

'Does He speak to you?' asked David. More eagerness in the question than he had planned.

Whitbrend looked at David. His blush was gone

and his expression was grave. 'I feel that He guides me.'

'Have you ever actually heard His voice?'

'No,' said Whitbrend.

'Does that bother you?'

'It's the soil for my faith.'

'God's silence is the soil for your faith,' said David. 'That's good.'

Whitbrend shrugged. 'Have you? I mean, have you actually heard the Voice?'

'No. So I listen all the harder.'

'What more can anybody do?' asked Whitbrend.

An uncomfortable silence.

Then David looked out at *The Raising of Lazarus*. Saw the colors clear and rich in the morning sun. Tried to picture the Chapel of the Grove of God peaking toward the heavens. Imagined the glass flanks dotted with oranges. His own father could plant and tend the grove. David imagined his congregation inside. Imagined the sky bristling as the Word rode the airwaves to the corners of the universe. The Word the rider. His voice the horse.

'I'd like you to deliver the Sunday message,' said David. 'All three services. After that, we'll talk again.'

Whitbrend studied him with a tensile calm but a brightness in his eyes. Trying to keep his enthusiasm under control, thought David.

'Okay,' he said, breaking into a nervous smile.

David wondered how he'd broken the front

tooth. Why he didn't take the whiteness down a notch to match the others.

At ten that morning David counseled a young couple about their upcoming marriage. Ron and Diane. This was one of his favorite pastoral roles, because he got to experience the power and energy of love between human beings. The younger they were, the more pure and simple this love would be. David often believed he faltered in this capacity, because he failed to warn some young people strongly enough about all that can go wrong. The list was awfully damned long. Perils upon perils. So why not let them find out on their own? Maybe they'd be just fine. The divorce rate was soaring and this 'free love' thing seemed to have everyone under thirty heading for the sheets and everyone over thirty heading for the motel or the divorce court. But people were still getting married like there was no tomorrow. David tried to emphasize forgiveness, and giving your partner respect and liberty as well as love. Basically, with the young ones, he just sat across the desk from them while they held hands and nodded. Ron and Diane were very young and very much in love. Ron had gotten a medical exemption for flat feet from the draft board. Diane was going to put him through college. Ron was headed for IBM. Scrubbed, pink-faced, straight-toothed. They actually had pimples. Not severe acne, just the vestigial marks of youth. David noted that Ron hid an erection, which amused Diane. The young lovers made him smile.

Just before noon he ministered to a believer dying in a hospital. It wasn't easy to watch a person die. It challenged his belief in an afterlife when the present life so conspicuously and finally departed a body. And after such a long and tenacious fight. Life was the strongest thing he'd ever seen, but it was really kind of brief. It was there, then not. Really, totally, absolutely *not*. The dying person was a mother of three. Metastasized lung cancer, though she'd never smoked a cigarette in her life. Her children were too young to endure the scene, and the overwrought father was a blur of tears. He looked at David as if David's God – the one to whom he and his family had reported for duty every Sunday of their lives – had specifically chosen his wife for this unfair and painful end. Which David fully believed and was exactly what he'd said about Janelle Vonn in his sermon on her death. That God chose some people to endure so that others wouldn't have to. That we should love and respect these people.

The father looked at David like he wanted to kill someone.

When the children were ushered out David asked the young father if he would like to pray.

*I hate your fucking God,* he hissed, tears hitting the linoleum floor around him.

*Let's pray, anyway.*

That afternoon David sat in with the Grove

Drive-In Church youth league. It was Barbara's group, Tuesday and Thursdays. Social, spiritual, and philanthropic. They'd recently delivered another two thousand dollars' worth of new clothes to children in Tijuana. David sat at a table in the back of the meeting room, his presence simply to encourage them. Watched Barbara handle the details of a car-wash fundraiser. Thought back to an earlier voyage to Tijuana and the way Miss Tustin Janelle Vonn had been so beautiful and unself-conscious as she handed a new red sweater to a skinny wisp of a girl with dusty black hair and a smile bright as a lightbulb. The rain was pounding on a leaky sheet-metal roof and David clearly remembered what Janelle had said to the girl.

*Quiere a Dios con tu corazón, preciosa hermana. Pero lava tu pelo con tus manos.*

Love God with your heart, pretty sister. But wash your hair with your hands.

David looked down at the little stack of worship pamphlets on the table. Yellow this week. Leftovers from the Tuesday youth league meeting. Picked one up and read the title of his scheduled sermon, 'Integrity in a Relative World.' Had some nice moments in it, but not his best. A moot point, he thought, now that the Reverend Darren Whitbrend was set to take the stage. An acid test for the young minister. If Darren couldn't move the congregation, then there was no point in further discussion.

He thought again of Janelle and the towering foolishness he'd committed by bringing her an early copy of just such a worship pamphlet. On that of all nights. Night of nights. He closed his hands around the pamphlet and closed his eyes and thanked the Lord for the trust of a brother and the love of a wife and the loyalty of a friend. And prayed that the vile Hambly of the FBI had only been bluffing, trying to get something for nothing.

When David opened his eyes Nick was standing before him. He looked tired and unhappy. Exactly how he had looked every day since taking his first homicide case. But dark around the eyes now and heavier and somehow dangerous.

David set the curled worship program back on the table, stood, and led Nick outside.

'Terry Neemal wants to talk to you,' said Nick. 'I think he's going to confess.'

'He told me he didn't do it.'

'He's been changing his story. Better take your own car, David. If he's good for this, I might be there late.'

# 25

David followed Nick and Lobdell into the interview room. He'd never been in one before. He assumed the big mirror was really a window from the back. Like Whitbrend's chapel. And that it was wired for sound and maybe video, again like the chapel. A green metal table and four chairs were bolted to the floor. The tabletop was marked with scratches and what looked like cigarette burns. A black plastic ashtray. Bright light overhead. David wondered how many sins had been confessed in here. How many tears had fallen. How many hearts had finally cracked.

'I'm going to stand in that corner,' said Nick. 'Lucky's got the opposite. We might butt in. If things get hot, that's part of the deal. Stay cool. I'm taking off his cuffs. If he gets too close to you in a way I don't like, I'm going to move him away.'

'Usually the less you say the more you get,' said Lobdell.

David stood there awkwardly, unsure what to do. He watched Nick go to his corner, open a briefcase, and bring out a manila folder. Nick arranged three large black-and-white photographs from the packing-house on the table. Two of Janelle's body. One close-up of Janelle's face. All visible from wherever you sat or stood.

David stared down at them. Astonishing. Indescribable. He'd never seen anything like them before. It wasn't the death. It was the evil. The cruelty and obscenity. His throat tightened and his stomach dropped.

Then Nick set out three of the old SunBlesst orange crate labels with the girl who looked like Janelle. Also visible from anywhere in the room. He remembered them flying all around Tustin in the Santa Ana winds one fall. Where had he gotten those old things?

Then three childhood pictures of Janelle. Janelle sitting on a tree stump. Janelle holding a guitar. Petting a cat on a porch.

Then David watched Nick go again to his corner and come back with a child's stick horse. Happy little pony with a red felt tongue sticking out. Nick considered his tableau, then set the horse down diagonally amid the pictures.

'The horse was named Bobby,' said Nick. 'Used to be Janelle's. I'm trying to pry open Neemal's heart any way I can.'

'You never know what'll set them off,' said Lobdell.

'I've never seen pictures like these,' said David. He felt light-headed and nauseous. 'They're the most hideous things I've ever seen.'

'Maybe you should sit down, David,' said Nick.

'Where?'

'Put your back to the mirror,' said Nick.

'Yes. Of course.'

David worked his way into the unyielding metal chair. Took a deep breath against the sudden throbbing in his head. He folded his hands on his lap. Fixed his eyes on the doorknob across the room, well above the plain of horror and innocence laid out on the table in front of him.

Neemal seemed dwarflike in his baggy orange jumpsuit. The hair on his shaven head and face had grown back enough to cast shadows. The big mustache drooped. His tawny tan eyes settled on David as Nick took off the handcuffs. Neemal smiled at him. David saw the black mark on his hand and arm. Like a tract of burned land, he thought.

Rubbing one wrist, Neemal looked down and saw the photographs and labels and the stick horse. Stopped rubbing. Walked around the table, studying the pictures.

When he went behind David, David saw Nick ease in his direction. Heard the movement of Lobdell in the corner behind him.

Nick clicked on a tape recorder and spoke quickly. 'This is Investigator Nick Becker and Sergeant Al Lobdell, and the jail chaplain, the

Reverend David Becker. The suspect is Terry Neemal, who requested this interview and the presence of the Reverend David Becker. It's Thursday, October seventeenth, nineteen sixty-eight.'

David turned to see Lobdell leaning back in the corner, arms crossed and necktie crooked and his gut snugged into a wrinkled white shirt.

Neemal got back to where he started. 'I don't understand the horse.'

'Its name is Bobby,' said Nick. 'It was Janelle's.'

Neemal nodded, looking down at David. 'God forgives this?'

David had no idea whether God forgave this or not. Why should He?

'Yes,' said David, trusting in his God to lead him now.

'A person who does this can still go to heaven?' asked Neemal.

David felt his soul reverse and crawl back over itself. 'Yes.'

'How?' asked Neemal.

*Dear Father, speak through me now.*

'It is in His power,' said David.

'But what would the person have to do?'

*God help me.*

'Ask forgiveness. Lead a life of good acts from this moment forward. Be generous and honest and always help the people around you.'

*God will accept those puny acts for what these pictures show?*

Neemal stared at David for a long moment. Something new registered on his face but David wasn't sure what. Connivance? Subterfuge?

'I did it,' said Neemal.

David felt himself vanish. Because Terry Neemal's soul was in the hands of God, but his body was now owned by the People of California.

'Did what?' asked Nick, glancing hard at his brother.

'What you see in these pictures,' said Neemal.

'Which is what?' asked Nick.

'I killed her and chopped her head off. See?' Neemal nodded at the picture in front of him.

'Janelle Vonn was her name. You killed Janelle Vonn and chopped her head off?'

'Absolutely.'

Neemal started around the table again. Staring at the pictures. Stopped for a moment in front of each of the packinghouse shots. He had his blackened arm up, chin resting on his fist, elbow cradled in his other hand. When he went behind David again, Nick drifted toward them. Lobdell stepped forward, adjusted the tape recorder, stepped back.

'Terry,' said Nick. 'Of your own free will, you're saying you killed Janelle Vonn and chopped her head off?'

'Positively.'

'How did you do that?'

Neemal rounded David and stopped in front of the picture of Janelle's face. He looked down at David. 'I don't remember.'

'You remember that you killed her but you don't remember how you did it?' asked Nick.

'Precisely.'

'Tell me about that night, Terry,' said Nick. 'I want to know all about it.'

Neemal continued to stare down at David. Tan eyes, the big fan of mustache, his face beveled into light and shadow. 'Can I trust you?'

'Yes, Terry, but I—'

'And trust your God? Because the God that got inside my head for all those years was a real bad guy. Made me walk to Arizona.'

'Yes, you can trust Him but He—'

'I don't remember very much. Just that she was wearing a blue sweater. And boots and a short black skirt. I don't know what she was doing there. I was looking for something I lost. We talked.'

David looked to Nick, who nodded tightly.

David's voice was hardly more than a whisper. 'What did you say to her?'

'I don't remember very much. She had a very sweet voice.'

'Sit down now, Terry,' said Nick. 'Take the seat across from David. How about a cigarette and a cup of coffee?'

Neemal shuffled over, cuffs and sneakers flapping quietly on the floor. He slid into the metal chair opposite David. Nick took the seat to David's left. Lobdell stayed in his corner out of sight.

David kept his eyes on Terry Neemal's face. The images just below his line of sight wavered up into his awareness like bodies in a lake. Beyond them waited the tan eyes. A flame flickered into David's view and smoke rose from Neemal's cigarette.

'I was already in when she got there,' said Neemal. 'That night. Inside the packinghouse. Looking for some matches I lost.'

'How did you lose matches in the packing-house?' asked Nick.

'I lit a fire inside a few days before. I got cold. I left the matches there.'

David saw that Neemal was now staring at the coal of his cigarette.

'A book of paper matches, Terry?' asked Nick. 'Or a box of wooden ones?'

'Paper.'

'Plain, or some design or company name on the cover?' asked Nick.

David saw Neemal's brow furrow. Big thought lines across his forehead. He looked at the coal again, then brought the cigarette to his mouth and drew. 'Pep Boys. Manny, Moe, and Jack.'

Lobdell cleared his throat. Nick glanced back at his partner.

'Did you locate them again in the packing-house, Terry?' asked David.

Neemal shook his head. 'No. I did not. But I will say . . . that was when the girl came in.'

'Janelle?' asked David.

'Janelle *Vonn*,' said Neemal. *'Vonn.'*

'Then what happened?' asked David.

'She said, "Hello, how are you?" I said I was fine and what a lovely evening it was. After that, I remember nothing.'

'If you don't remember killing her, maybe you didn't,' said David.

'Maybe you're just making up a bunch of shit and wasting our time,' said Lobdell. Lobdell came around to the right of David. Stood behind the last open chair.

'Oh, I definitely did it,' said Neemal.

'Did you chop off her head before or after she was dead?' asked Nick.

'She was still alive.'

'What color was the handle of the machete you used to chop off her head?' asked Nick.

'Black.'

'How come you tossed the machete outside?' asked Lobdell.

'Well, obviously,' said Neemal, stubbing out his cigarette, 'so you wouldn't find it.'

'But we did. Where did you get it?' asked Nick. 'The machete?'

'Sav-On.'

'Terry,' said Lobdell. 'Are you ready to sign a confession?'

Neemal looked at David again. Took a deep breath. 'Yes. I am.'

'I'll write one up,' said Lobdell. 'You can read it and sign it and it will prove what Nick's other brother wrote about us in the paper this morning was shit.'

'I didn't agree with that article,' said Neemal. 'I think Nick is an excellent detective.'

'See?' said Lobdell, smiling. 'Just ask Wolfman.'

David felt half disgusted and half mystified by the proceedings. Man's law was not his area. But he felt obligated to speak. 'Is he competent to *sign* a confession?' he asked.

No one answered.

Lobdell straddled the bolted chair and huffed down into it. Pulled a pen and a notebook out of his coat pocket. Clicked the ballpoint with a meaty thumb, looked at Neemal with open disgust, and started writing.

David watched the pen wiggle above the notepad, heard the rapid scratch of point on paper.

Nick stood. David saw the darkness in his eyes, the bags under them. Nick glanced at him, then circled the table.

'Do you understand what it means to sign a confession?' asked Nick.

'I'm sane and I do,' said Neemal.

'The confession is going to say that you murdered Janelle Vonn in the packinghouse on October first of this year. It says you will cooperate with us by giving us details and information.'

David couldn't let this moment go unprotested, either. 'But if he's willing to sign a confession right now, then what's the hurry? Why can't you get the details and information first?'

'That's not how it works, Rev,' said Lobdell. 'With all respect, you got your church confessions, then you got your legal confessions. They're different. Here, Nick. This is ready for Mr Neemal to sign. He can use my pen. Then you can keep it for your grandkids or something – first murder confession you ever got, the actual pen. Terry, read this over and ask any questions you got. Then sign the bottom.'

Neemal took a deep breath. Arranged the notepad precisely. Read slowly and with apparent concentration.

Then he hung his head and began to cry.

'I'm sorry,' he whispered. 'I didn't kill her. I did what I said I did. About the . . . well, you remember, Nick. But I didn't kill her.'

'You saw the black skirt and the boots when you went back that second time, though,' said Nick.

Neemal nodded.

David had no idea what this 'second time' was all about. Neemal had never said anything about it to him.

'And you didn't find the Pep Boys matches because they were already in your pocket,' said Nick.

'That's true.' He sniffled.

'You used them to light the newspapers on fire before you masturbated.'

David's stomach dropped. What kind of a man

was this? And how could Nick understand him so thoroughly?

'Yes,' said Neemal.

'And you tossed the matches into the fire for an extra little burst.'

'I did do that, yes,' he said quietly.

'Because fire helps you climax.' Nick sighed.

David's imagination supplied an image of the Wolfman Neemal masturbating over Janelle's headless body as the newspapers burst into flames. An atrocious moment. David felt preyed upon by his own mind.

Neemal nodded again. He was no longer crying. But still looking down at the table. 'So I can't sign. I thought I could. I thought about it. I wanted to.'

'*Why*?' asked David.

'For the reporters. Then I could just kind of stay here and . . . you know, just stay here and have people write articles about me. But if I sign that they'll put me in the gas chamber.'

David couldn't formulate a meaningful reply.

'You disappoint me, Wolfie,' said Lobdell. 'I thought you might have had the presence of mind to pull off that murder. Had my money on you for a few days. I figured the crazy shit was just an act. But it isn't.'

Lobdell walked to the door and rapped on it. A deputy let him out.

In the silence David watched Neemal as he stared down at the table. 'Sorry, Nick. Guess I'll only get to stay in here a while longer.'

'Looks that way, Terry.'

'I'm sorry I couldn't confess. I . . . thought I could go through with it. Thought it would be best for everybody.'

'I understand,' said Nick.

Though David wasn't sure at all that he did.

'Thanks for your help, David,' said Nick.

'I helped no one.'

'I believed your God would forgive me,' said Neemal. 'It wasn't that, Reverend. You did your part.'

David didn't know what to say. This was like being trapped behind the looking glass. He couldn't wait to get outside and into some real air. Into a faintly logical world. He smelled dinner wafting in from the mess hall, which sickened him slightly.

'I'm hungry,' Neemal said. 'I want to go back to my cell and eat and get rested up for the *Register*. I got an interview tomorrow at nine.'

He stood and sighed and put his hands behind his back for Nick and the cuffs.


Ten minutes later David pulled into his driveway. Spent and stupefied. The white Ford that had been behind him since the jail slid under the big sycamore by the curb. His heart fell further.

David got out and lifted the garage door. He pulled Wendy's new bike out of the way, and Matthew's beloved Mickey Mouse guitar. Amazing what kids could leave in the sure path of a car.

He pulled the station wagon in. Got out and took a deep breath as he reached for the rope to pull down the door. Looked out at the darkening sky. Saw the kitchen light on at the Cranes' across the street. Looked at the Ford under the sycamore and knew he had to go face the music.

Hambly sat behind the wheel. Window down. News station on. Looked at David.

'Get in,' he said.

David went to the passenger side and got in.

'Five days,' said the agent.

'I've been thinking about your offer.'

'Offer? There's nothing to think about. You give me information or I send the pictures to the newspapers, your parents, brothers, wife, and key congregational members of the Grove Drive-In Church of God. I was very clear on that.'

David listened to the words but his mind jumped its track. He found himself understanding how people committed murder. And sympathizing with them.

'I'm not sure what to tell you,' he said.

'I'm sure you've thought about Stoltz and your father and the John Birch Society and the National Volunteer Police down south.'

'I actually haven't.'

'Too busy with God?'

'I don't see Stoltz,' said David. 'He's in Washington, where your bosses are.'

Hambly ignored the threat. 'What about Max

and his JBS chapter? Come on – I know you've attended meetings. I know you see *him*. I know you've heard things.'

'My father thinks the JBS is doing good work,' said David. 'Informing people about the Communist conspiracy. Some of their ideas seem a little . . . exaggerated. But they've never said one thing about shooting Negroes or whatever it is you're suggesting.'

'Not one thing?'

'Never. It's not a secret organization. They have bookstores and phone numbers you can call for information. They give away little red, white, and blue plastic pens with the number on them. They're dentists and engineers and lawyers and schoolteachers and—'

'I heard Dick Nixon was in town. Come by the old house last Saturday?'

David stared out the windshield. Saw Peg Crane at her kitchen window, looking out. Always there. Like she was washing dishes, but she was more like a DEW system for the block.

'Yes,' said David. 'We talked very briefly.'

'Finally,' said Hambly, as if hugely relieved.

David was aware of Hambly taking out a notebook and pen but he kept looking at Peg Crane. 'He asked about my church. He said he was sorry he couldn't see eye-to-eye with Dad and Stoltz.'

'Meaning what?'

'Whatever you want it to mean.'

'Go on.'

'I said I thought they'd support him in November.'

'How do you know that?' asked Hambly.

'It was just polite small talk.'

'Talking votes to a presidential candidate is small?'

'It was just my opinion,' David said.

'Was your father sorry, too, not seeing eye-to-eye with his old Yorba Linda buddy?'

'He didn't say, either way,' said David.

'Dick not quite aggressive enough for him? Won't destroy villages to save them? Not willing to drop the bomb on Moscow if they keep sending guns to the North Vietnamese?'

'Who cares what my father thinks of Richard Nixon?'

'Like I said before,' said Hambly, 'I care. I'm the one who cares.'

'That's all I'm going to say.'

David swung open the door, stepped out under the sycamore, and slammed it. Peg Crane hadn't moved. He sighed and looked back at the special agent.

Hambly grinned. 'Have you talked to that Marxist Washburn out at UCI? Figured out how many kids he's registered into the American Communist Party?'

'I have not.'

'Call anytime, Jude.'

David leaned in the open window. 'I will. I'll call you next time. Until then, stay off my block.

We have children and elderly people here. I don't want them in the presence of evil.'

'Evil,' said Hambly. 'Reverend, you crack me up. Hey, did you know your buddy Langton was questioned by the Laguna cops today? They wondered what he knew about the Boom Boom Bungalow killing.'

'I didn't know that.'

'They've got a witness who saw a guy running from the victim's room. Got into a car and sped away. Witness got the plates – for Howard's cute little Triumph convertible. Witness took his sweet time coming forward because he wasn't supposed to be boom-booming that night. But there it is.'

'That's not possible,' said David. 'Howard's wife will vouch for him.'

'Vouch or lie?'

David straightened, looked down at the grass. Breathed deeply. 'Lie. But—'

He couldn't continue. Thought of his Father in heaven but couldn't continue.

'But what, Rev?'

'Nothing. Nothing.'

David looked into the car. Hambly eyed him with the binary detachment of a rattlesnake. To strike or not to strike.

'My guess,' said Hambly, 'is the cops will smell something wrong unless Howard and his wife are both really talented liars. If they shake and break them, they'll put Howard in a lineup and see what the witness says. If the witness picks Howard, he'll have to use you as his alibi. This is a murder rap we're talking about. This is serious. Maybe you should be lining up your ducks, too.'

'What ducks?'

'If Howard tries to use you as an alibi, deny everything he says. Barbara would have to hang tough when she lies about being with you that night. But I'll bet she's tougher and cooler than you are.'

'Quite a bit,' he said quietly.

'And she does know about all this, right?'

'Yes,' he said, more quietly. He'd known it would end in disaster. All of it. Everything. Just a matter of when. The rest of his life blank and empty like that old marquee in front of the Grove Drive-In Theater.

'Janelle's not around to corroborate Howard's tale,' said Hambly. 'And I'm not going to. I really don't want to show those pictures. I'll just stay out of it.'

'Why would you do that?'

'You're no good to me if you lose your family, your congregation, and everything you've worked for. And you're a nice guy.'

'You're beyond evil.'

'Think about it, Judas. And imagine the alternative.'

# 26

It took Nick almost one hour to make the evening drive from Santa Ana to Los Angeles. Damned traffic. But nice to be driving the Red Rocket, which was usually for Katy and the kids. The 428 cc would really go if you stood on it. Too bad there were so many cars on the road right now, but on the way home he'd fly.

He used the time to wonder about Neemal and the odd kinks in some men's minds. Which was one of the reasons why Nick had wanted homicide detail. To understand the kinks. But why do that? To understand himself? Maybe. He had a theory that everyone had kinks. Different kinds. Different amounts. He turned on the news and watched the smog-stained peak of the Disneyland Matterhorn go by. A little red bobsled zoomed out of the mountain and back in.

The FBI 'Road School' was held at the sheriff's station downtown. Nick had heard about it from some friends in the Southern California chapter of the International Association for Identification. The FBI had this agent named Doug Teteni who could show you how to learn more from a murder scene. They said Teteni could make sense of things that didn't make sense at first. Teteni was especially good at what the FBI called 'stranger murders' – where men would kill people unknown to them, wait, then kill again. Teteni had worked on the infamous Gein case in Wisconsin, where the guy had made clothing and adorned furniture with the skin of his victims.

Nick sat in the back with a couple of guys he had met at the academy. Teteni was slender and neat, with rimless glasses and a crisp white shirt. He looked like a professor, Nick thought.

Teteni began talking about a New York City psychiatrist named Dr James Brussel, with whom Teteni had worked. It was Dr Brussel who was asked by the New York police in 1957 to help solve the Mad Bomber case. Nick remembered that. He'd been a freshman at Long Beach State when the arrest was made. The Mad Bomber had detonated thirty bombs in New York City since 1942. His targets had included Radio City Music Hall and Grand Central Station. He had sent angry, revealing letters to various newspapers. Dr Brussel was given crime scene photographs and copies of the letters and asked to describe the bomber for the police. Doug Teteni read the last few words of the description Brussel had given:

'Look for a heavy man. Middle-aged. Foreign-born. Roman Catholic. Single. Lives with a brother or sister. When you find him, chances are he'll be wearing a double-breasted suit. Buttoned.'

Teteni went on to say that when police arrested George Metesky for the bombings, he was heavy, single, middle-aged, foreign-born, Roman Catholic, and lived with not one sister but two. When Metesky was allowed to put on his jacket for the trip to the station, he put on a double-breasted suit coat and buttoned it.

A respectful murmur rose in the room. Nick was stunned and mystified by the details Brussel had come up with. Seemed like magic or witch-craft. He wondered for a second if he was in the wrong profession altogether. He would *never* have been able to do what Brussel did.

Teteni went on to say that, because of the letters, the Mad Bomber case had actually been fairly simple. Metesky had revealed a lot about himself in the letters he wrote. The buttoning of the coat was a small extrapolation Brussel had made based on the neatness and craft with which Metesky had constructed and concealed the bombs.

But Brussel would never have known so much about the suspect if he had not used *inductive* reasoning. Brussel and Teteni were encouraging homicide investigators across the nation to 'observe the singularities of a crime' and draw 'larger conclusions about the nature and motive of the criminal.' To understand who might be responsible for a crime, Teteni said, you had to 'read the murderer's book.' Teteni said that in order to catch certain killers, 'detectives should learn to *think* like them.'

Nick got the uneasy and thrilling feeling that he was just now beginning to comprehend something very important.

We need to learn to think like criminals, said Teteni, because of the 'changing nature' of murder in America. He said that traditionally, people were killed by people who knew them and lived close by. Now, said Teteni, with society becoming more mobile, opportunities were arising for a new kind of killer. This was the 'stranger killer,' who preyed upon unknown victims, often for sexual reasons. Teteni predicted that in the decades to come, greater mobility and less stability in the United States would create rising homicide rates and falling solution rates. That greater mobility and less stability, though often considered to be the mark of a free and prosperous society, would also lead to a weakening of traditions that kept our society in balance.

Nick thought of Ronnie Joe Fowler. Mobile. Sex attack in Oregon. Maybe one here? But his alibi was good. He'd been where he said he was on Tuesday, October first. Out on Woodland in Laguna Canyon. Dodge City. Not the SunBlesst packinghouse in Tustin.

Still, Nick agreed with Teteni. The changes that

were coming. Nick had never quite connected his gut feeling that his country was slipping somehow, with the mobility that Teteni talked about. But Nick had felt strongly for the last year or so that things were unraveling and would not be reraveled. Destroying to save. Mutual Assured Destruction. PCP to LSD. Kill the pigs. Burn down the village, your mind, your city, the world. He'd talked with David and Andy about these things not long ago. David was hopeful that meaningful, relevant Christian ministries such as his own would help maintain a balance. Andy thought the changes were good and America needed them. Nick didn't know what to think.

Next, Teteni talked about 'singularity,' in the sense that anything unique or unusual about a crime scene could be used to suggest what kind of person had committed the act. For instance, he said, a murder victim whose face was left covered by the killer with her own jacket was killed by someone with an active sense of right and wrong. He covers because he is ashamed of what he's done. Or a rapist who attacks suddenly from behind, with deadly force, is probably inexperienced and uncomfortable around women. He can't persuade her to go off with him to a safer place. The investigators will find him to be reclusive and physically unattractive. Teteni said that the more unique and unusual things were found in a crime scene, the better chances they had of solving the crime.

Nick tried to figure Janelle Vonn's head being cut off. A way to emphasize a need for silence? What could she know that would warrant murder and mutilation? Was it for something she had said, or even thought? How did this relate to the fact that she was raped? Could she have been the victim of one of these new 'stranger killers' who was not even in California anymore?

Last, Teteni then talked about sexual fantasy, control over helpless individuals and perpetrators who did not experience remorse. Perps who had once wanted to be policemen. Perps who took 'mementos.' Perps who went back to the crime scene. Perps who made him think that he was in the presence of evil, though that word was imprecise and out of fashion at the bureau now.

Teteni smiled weakly and wiped his forehead with a handkerchief. It looked to Nick like Teteni's job was taking a lot out of him. Reminded him of David.

After the class, Teteni sat at a table in the back of the room and examined the crime scene photographs from several case files brought by the detectives. Each detective told Teteni the basic facts of the case while the FBI special agent considered the photos. The detectives were told not to describe their prime suspects, if they had one.

Nick stood up close so he could see the pictures, too, and try to understand how Teteni was learning from them. Unlike Dr Brussel's dramatically detailed description, Teteni's speculations were more general but still practical.

When it was his turn, he handed Teteni the packinghouse photographs and described what they had discovered so far.

Teteni set the file on the table. Then opened it to the crime scene pictures. He listened and turned the pictures while Nick talked.

Nick saw that Teteni was patient and focused, but somehow methodical, too. He appeared to spend exactly the same amount of time on each photo. His hand ready to turn it over. Like an internal clock was ticking.

Finally he looked up at Nick.

'This packinghouse closed operations when?'

'Sixty-four.'

'It's hidden in the orange groves, or at least obscured by them?'

'Obscured.'

Teteni flipped to a packinghouse exterior. Nick could see the orange trees buffeted by the wind.

'You probably wouldn't know about it unless you had lived in the area?'

'Probably not.'

'Visible from any public road?'

'No.'

'Transients use it for sleeping, maybe young people for sex and drinking and drug use?'

'Yes.'

'She wasn't killed there?'

'No. We haven't found out where yet.'

'Vaginally raped?'

'Yes sir.'

Teteni turned to a picture of Janelle's severed head. Eyes open. Seeing nothing. 'I think it's a ruse.'

'Sir?'

'Call me Doug. This is not a stranger killing. This has nothing to do with transients. He knew her. He believes that she insulted and betrayed him in some way that is unspeakable to him. He killed her on impulse, by strangulation – no weapons and very little forethought. If he obtained the saw himself, it was likely *after* he'd killed her. More likely that he stumbled on it in some way, that it was already there, or already in his possession for other reasons. He removed her head to symbolically make sure she would never insult and betray him again. And to make himself appear insane. He placed her body here, in surroundings unrelated to her or to himself. I don't think he's done this kind of thing before and I don't think he'll do it again.'

'Why? What makes you say that?'

'No planning and unnecessary work. He took a great deal of risk and spent a good deal of time killing her in one place, then moving the body here for mutilation. Stranger killers are more organized. Age would be late thirties to late forties. Familiar with but no longer living in the area of the murder. I would say that he is either a professional of some kind or an artist

349

or craftsman. He has terrific pride in himself, or in his reputation or his creations, and that is what she insulted so badly to deserve this.'

Nick's heart was pounding. Then sinking as he watched Teteni close the file and hand it back to him.

'Would he take something from her as a reminder, like you talked about?'

'No. But unpracticed killers surprise us by what they remove from the scene simply to keep the police from finding it.'

'Does he want to be caught?' asked Nick.

'No,' said Teteni. 'He feels massive shame but even more massive fear of being caught. Did she have a large funeral or memorial service?'

'Several hundred.'

'He was probably there.'

Home movies, thought Nick. David always made Super 8 home movies of his Sunday services, so why not of the biggest funeral he'd ever done?

Nick's heart was beating strong and he believed that those movies would lead to something important. He believed for the first time in days that he was really going to crack this case. It had gotten into his head that if you never closed that first case, you could never call yourself good. You had to pass first grade. Make the cut.

'Someday I want to do what you do,' said Nick.

Some of the guys looked at him. He felt his face get red. Hadn't meant to blurt, but hadn't known what he wanted to do with the next thirty years of his life until right now. Talk about understanding the kinks.

'Give me your card, Nick,' said Teteni. He took out his handkerchief and wiped his forehead again. 'I'll call you if anything else comes to mind. Good luck. *Next?*'

Nick made David's home by eleven. Barbara was still up, got David out of bed. Then David took Nick to the Grove Drive-In to get the Super 8 film of Janelle's memorial service and funeral. There were four thirty-minute reels. David let him have the good projector but Nick had to promise to have it back by Saturday. David told him there was some crowd footage but not that much. Most of the movies showed, well, himself.

At home Nick moved the cars out of the garage and set the projector up on his big wheeled toolbox. Used the wall next to the Odd Box for a screen. Katy wandered out in her pj's and robe, kissed him dreamily, then wandered back into the house.

Nick watched all two hours and drank four beers without taking a leak.

It was just like he remembered. What, almost a thousand people? Vonns and Beckers and Langtons and Stoltzes and Dessingers. Jesse Black and Crystal and Gail and hundreds of Janelle's relatives and friends and neighbors he couldn't even identify. But the greatest numbers were the throng brought in by Janelle's momentary celebrity. The Headless Beauty Queen of Orange County. Everybody loves a pretty girl and a tragedy.

Nick hit pay dirt late in the fourth reel. Shot of the green slopes of the cemetery and the crowd. And there he was, squeezed into the people around him, looking down like he didn't want to be seen.

Hair pushed up under the hat. Black sunglasses. Trying to be small. But Cory Bonnett was unmistakable.

# 27

The next morning Andy stood on the porch of 1303 North Bayfront, Balboa Island, Newport Beach. He knocked again. The sliding door was open and a cool breeze lifted the curtains. He watched a stout Mexican woman lean a mop against a wall and come slowly toward him down a hallway.

Friday, October 18. Seventeen days after the murder.

Three days after reading Janelle Vonn's letters about Roger Stoltz.

Two days after his signed editorial in the *Orange County Journal* accused his older brother of incompetence. The deputies in the Sheriff's Department pressroom earlier this morning had ignored him. But carried on with the other reporters as usual. Andy had never been generally dismissed and didn't care for the feeling. It went without saying that his department sources had dried up.

Andy introduced himself in Spanish to the

cleaning lady. Said he was Mike Jones, one of Representative Stoltz's associates in the American Congress. Her name was Marci. He made small talk about the weather and maybe renting the place, because Mr Stoltz had told him what a nice apartment it was. She didn't know a Mr Stoltz. She knew Maid in America cleaning service because she'd been working for them for four years.

She smiled, incisors framed in gold. Stood aside. Andy said he'd be quick. She could keep on working and he'd be gone in just a few minutes.

Downstairs were the living room, kitchen, and two small bedrooms that shared a bath. Sparsely furnished. Nice maple floors. Throw rugs and prints of watercolors on the walls.

Andy pictured Janelle here. He unfolded the copy of the letter written in this apartment just over a year ago.


September 10, 1967

Dear Lynette,

Roger gave me the place in Newport fulltime. Practically made me move in. For now I guess it's okay. I don't like owing him even though he says I don't. His wife is sweet. Troy of the cops says I have some more money coming, but he's usually slow with it. Says his department might have an apartment in Laguna they could let me have awhile. I want MY place.

You can see the sailboats from the bedroom window. Roger thinks this is a healthier place for me to be than Laguna. He doesn't like all the drug things going on there. The long hair scares him. You know how old guys are.

I'm sitting on the bed upstairs while I write this letter. Hard to believe I'm eighteen already. Guess I should be happy but I'm not. I imagine me with a different face. And different hair. And a different name. And a different story behind me. I still love music. Went up to Laguna last night and met that LSD guy at a party. They offered me some and I said no, maybe some other time. Kinda scared of it. Lots of weird people around.

Upstairs Andy stepped into a big bedroom blasted with morning sunlight. Newport Harbor glittered beyond the picture window. Small sailboats rocked in the bright sunshine. The water was polished indigo with a V of white wake widening toward Andy.

White carpet. White walls. White curtains. Prints of flowers and cottages in white frames. Looked like something furnished for an older woman, thought Andy.

The single bed was neatly made. Pink quilt and matching pillowcases and a Raggedy Ann doll upright against one pillow. A low dresser with a mirror. A cane-back rocker. A few pairs of pants and some blouses in the closet. Price tags still on them. One pair of white sneakers with yellow psychedelic daisies on them. Andy turned one over. Never worn. Some T-shirts and tie-dyed stuff in the dresser. Brand new.

Andy opened the bathroom medicine cabinet: deodorant, a can of the same hairspray Meredith's mother had used. Brand-new bottle of aspirin.

And it hit him that someone had furnished the place the way they thought Janelle would like. But she didn't want a Raggedy Ann doll or old ladies' hairspray. Didn't want this place at all. Her letter to Lynette had said as much.

He found Marci downstairs and asked her how long she'd been cleaning the place.

'Since September, one year ago. Every week.'

'This was Janelle's apartment, right?'

'Yes. She was nice and spoke Spanish very well. I saw her only two times. Once when I first started. Then a few days before she died. I work here on Fridays.'

Andy nodded. Noted the dishless kitchen counters. The shining sink. The unblemished floor.

'You are not what you say you are,' said Marci. She shook her head but looked down.

Andy admitted he was a reporter. And a friend of Janelle's. This felt odd. He'd never considered himself a friend when she was living.

'Have you done the kitchen for today?'

'No.'

'Are there ever any dishes to do?'

'No.'

'What about the bed? Is it ever used?'

'Once,' she said. 'Friday after she died.'

'The landlord is Mr Stoltz?'

'I don't know his name. Slender with a mustache. Thirty-five years. Maybe more. He said nothing to me but hello and goodbye.'

'When?'

Marci looked up at the ceiling while she thought. 'Two Fridays ago.'

Two days after they found her in the packing-house, thought Andy. 'And the bed had been used?'

Marci blushed. 'Yes,' she said. 'It was not made. The sheets and pillowcases were gone. The bedspread and blanket were still here.'

He asked her what the landlord had done when he came here that day.

'He looked out the window upstairs. I was cleaning the bathroom and pretended I didn't see him. He wiped his eyes.'

Andy thought of the secret man Janelle kept from Jesse Black. Stoltz? Almost certainly. Thought of Janelle's letter to her sister. *Roger doesn't want anything in return except for me to be cool about it.*

Really.

His heart sped up a beat when he remembered the scratches and the scab on Roger Stoltz's hand that night at his parents' house. After the funeral.

Janelle, pregnant by Stoltz?

Threatening to keep the child and demanding money?

Offering an abortion for a price?

An argument? A fight?

Jesse Black had said that Janelle was scheduled for an abortion.

Had childless Stoltz wanted her to keep their baby, and she refused?

Andy asked Marci how she knew that Janelle had been murdered.

'Her picture was in the Spanish paper. They called her the Queen with No Head.'

Andy went through a door in the kitchen and into the garage. Small, for one car only. Dank and cool and he could smell the bay stronger. Noted that nobody could see him here if the big overhead garage door was shut. Tried to push it open with his foot but the outside latch was fastened. Found a light switch and turned it on.

Two red Schwinn ten-speeds hung end to end on brackets on one wall. Andy ran his finger along a crossbar. New paint shiny where the dust was gone. Below them a two-person Sears Whirlwind sailboat, tilted lengthwise. A sail-rigged mast hung above the bikes. Two orange life jackets hung from the pedals.

Toys, he thought. Toys for lovers. Never used and left behind.

He heard Lynette's words: *Even in the letters I can tell he wanted her for the same things any man would want her for. But she never did it with him. At least that's what she wrote, and I believe her.*

The concrete floor was clean. Old oil stains, faint and cut by bleach. Andy thought of Janelle's powder blue Volkswagen. Also provided, along with the apartment and other gifts, by humanitarian Roger Stoltz.

Who was an honored friend of his father.

Who could make his mother smile.

Who fixed David with a job out of seminary and Nick with a letter from Dick Nixon and Clay with a CIA scholarship to a language school the Beckers probably couldn't even afford and got Clay killed anyway.

Trouble was, Stoltz was in Washington, D.C., the night Janelle died. At least that's what Stoltz's congratulatory telegram on breaking the story had implied.

Back in the apartment Andy was surprised to find the telephone working. But why not, he wondered. Everything else was in running order. Even if the girl this was all for lived somewhere else entirely.

Representative Roger Stoltz's office in Tustin picked up on the second ring. Pleasant female voice.

'This is Andy Becker of the *Orange County Journal*. We're doing a story on Congressman Stoltz and need to confirm that he was here in Southern California on Tuesday, October the first, and attended a Republican Party fund-raiser hosted by John Wayne.'

'Oh. Let me see, Mr Becker. Just a moment.'

Andy stood there twirling the coiled phone cord. Heard paper rustling. Heard Marci running a vacuum upstairs. Then the woman came back on the line.

'No, Mr Becker. Roger was in Washington that day. The Un-American Activities House Committee had hearings and Roger is a member.'

'Right,' said Andy. 'The Commies.'

'Yes, Roger understands that the Communist threat is real. He has proof that there are still some American citizens working against their own government. Some are involved in espionage, others spew propaganda and dissent. By the way, I enjoy your articles very much.'

Andy went upstairs again. Looked out the picture window and heard Marci banging around in the bathroom.

He asked her if she'd ever seen Janelle and the landlord together here.

'No,' she said. 'I only saw her two times. Once was a year ago and once was three Fridays ago.'

'What was Janelle doing?'

'The first, she was putting some clothes in the dresser. Second time, she was sitting at the kitchen table downstairs with a man. He was very large and had long blond hair and a broken smile. He wore a bright shirt with palm trees on it and short pants and huaraches with car tires for a bottom. Like they make in Mexico.'

'What is a broken smile?'

'His teeth were broken. A little. Not all the way.'

Cory Bonnett, thought Andy. 'What was his name?'

'He didn't speak to me. She blushed when I came in and didn't look in my eyes. They looked like they were very . . . exhausted.'

'And this was when?'

'Friday. Before she died.'

Andy drove to the RoMar Industries headquarters in Tustin. It was across town from the SunBlesst packinghouse, part of a light commercial zone up by State 55.

Marie Stoltz led Andy through the offices, warehouse, and shipping/receiving.

'None of the manufacturing is done here,' she said. She was dark-haired and pretty in a delicate way. Very small. Made Andy think of a Japanese doll. 'The process is time-consuming and produces steam and noise. So we do the juicing, distilling, and blending up in Long Beach.'

'Interesting.'

'I'm happy that the *Journal* wants to do another story on us. Though I wonder why their crack crime reporter is writing it.'

She smiled sweetly.

Andy's father came bustling into the office from the warehouse. Sleeves up, brow furrowed, clipboard in hand. He still wore the Irish Setters Andy remembered from his childhood. Still had the straight-backed alertness and sharp eyes that had helped him be such a good shotgunner and fisherman.

His eyes widened when he saw Andy. 'Son, everything okay?'

'*Journal* wants another RoMar story,' said Andy. 'Focus this time is on Marie, running the company while her husband saves the world from Communism.'

Andy smiled. Got a small one from Marie and none from his father.

'The label machine's on the fritz again,' he said. 'Just in time for the late morning run.'

'Maybe Rollins can fix it,' said Marie.

'I think Rollins *broke* it,' said Max. 'I'll have to shut down, see what I can do with it. If I can't get it running right, we're calling Federated Label *again*. If they can't get here today this time, I'll line up someone else.'

'Thanks, Max. You know those machines drive me loony.'

Max nodded and pursed his lips. Shook Andy's hand. 'Duty calls,' he said. 'Nice seeing you, Andy. I'd like to talk to you about your piece on Nick when you have the time.'

Then he hustled back out, hailing Rollins before the door had even shut.

Andy watched him go. He had never realized until this moment how desperate his father was for distraction. Max wasn't that way before Clay. Before Clay, Max did what needed doing so he could do what his heart enjoyed. Hunting. Fishing. Reading. Banging around the kitchen with his wife. Playing some catch or basketball with his sons. But now, Andy saw, he'd do anything to keep from having to deal with what was inside him. He'd take some lousy job to prevent Marie from behaving like the business fool she almost certainly was. Keep the dollars rolling in for a patronizing friend like Stoltz. Pretend RoMar Industries and some label machine and a guy named Rollins were worth more than about thirty seconds of his life. Drink half a quart of gin a night and God knew how many beers.

'He's a good man,' said Marie.

'Thank you.'

'Five years since Clay.'

'Almost.'

'He's lucky to have you.'

'So,' said Andy, taking out his notebook. 'What prepared you to run a multimillion-dollar business?'

'Nothing,' she said. 'All I had was a home ec certificate from a junior college before I married Roger. Here, I just basically do what Roger says. Most of it's common sense. Building up a company like this, I couldn't do. I'm not smart or imaginative enough. But once it's up and running, well, it's just lots of hours and details and worry. I've gotten migraines all my life. But more now. So often, it seems.'

Through the cracked back door he could see his father standing by a large shiny machine.

Face-to-face with Rollins, no doubt. Hands on his hips. Leaning forward. Voice loud. Rollins shaking his head but not backing off.

Andy wanted to go flying through the air and spear Rollins like he'd speared Lenny Vonn.

Marie was watching, too. 'It probably looks like Max is here to prop me up. But I help him, also. That's why Roger set it up like this. It hurt him, what happened to your brother. And he sees what it did to Max and your mother. Excuse me. They'll stop acting like boys if I wander over.'

By the time Andy was halfway through his interview, Marie Stoltz was concussed by headache. She offered him a smile that made him wince. She tried to talk about the growing 'environmental movement,' which favored organic products like Orange Sunshine.

He thought she might vomit. He was going to ask some personal questions, such as her idea of trust in a marriage to a man who spent a lot of time three thousand miles from home. Maybe get her to corroborate that he was in Washington on that night. But he couldn't. He talked her into letting him just walk around on his own, get the feel of the place, snap a few pictures. She shut the office door when he went out.

Andy walked the labeling floor and the warehouse, the shipping and receiving docks. Chatted with the marketing people and the salespeople and the R & D people. Rollins looked like a

kicked dog. Max strode between the plant buildings in straight lines, clipboard tight, his steps
spaced for best distance and speed. He nodded
to his son.

Andy took some pictures but nothing the
*Journal* could really use. If he did manage to get
Teresa to approve a business-section puff piece on
RoMar Industries, it almost certainly wouldn't
require art. But it didn't hurt to have some file
shots, just in case something interesting were to
take place at RoMar.

It was a small miracle he'd even found the time
to come here, with all the extra work Jonas was
dumping on him. Since Nick's penmanship demo,
Dessinger was loading him up with the worst
assignments – soft features, society events, charity fund-raisers, the damned art museums. Teresa
tried to intervene but Jonas had rank.

He snapped the case back over his camera.
Squinted up at the midday sky. He had come here
for information but he had failed to find it. He'd
wanted to get closer to Roger Stoltz. To see if
Stoltz knew some things about the murder of the
girl he was supporting. To see what Marie knew.

Hell, he'd wanted to shove Representative (R)
Stoltz of California against a wall, grab his throat,
and make him confess that he had murdered his
mistress.

Even though he'd been three thousand miles
away the night she died.

Like he was right now.

So why do all this? Because Andy didn't like him? Because Stoltz was one of the few people who could make Monika smile? Because Stoltz had capitalized on the death of the orange groves, which had helped ruin Max, then employed him? Because he'd gotten Clay to join some heartless government agency that let him get killed in a worthless jungle? Because the good-looking, smooth-talking, vote-begging phony had had the balls to give Janelle Vonn money and a car and a place to live? Because Roger Stoltz had had the balls to offer her something real while he, Andrew James Becker, had been too timid and guilty to even call her when she'd asked him to?

Andy sighed and shook his head. Watched his father march from R & D to Admin.

Leave it to Nick now, he thought. He had given Nick everything he'd learned. Everything he'd seen. And read and heard and thought. From the fact that Janelle was a paid Sheriff's Department informant to the wound marks on Stoltz's hand. From Jesse Black's story of Janelle's pregnancy to the mystery man. From the guy with the FBI plates searching Janelle's cottage to the letters she'd written to Lynette. And now Andy could tell Nick about Stoltz and the bedsheets missing from the apartment Stoltz had offered to Janelle. An apartment in which Janelle didn't play house. Not with Stoltz, anyway. Where four days before she was murdered Janelle had sat at the kitchen table with a man suspected of two murders and who had beaten his own parents half to death. An apartment where, three days after she was murdered, Stoltz had stood at a window and wiped his eyes.

Three thousand miles away.

Too bad.

Andy told himself that he had tried. It had felt right. Maybe for the wrong reasons. Now Nick could have it all.

On his way out he knocked on the office door. His father told him to come in. Max was sitting in Marie's chair and tiny Marie was curled in his lap like a child. She cracked open one eye and gave Andy a wily, frightened look.

'Leave your visitor's badge in the box on the counter, son.'

He had just started up his ice-blue Corvair when he remembered something for the first time in eight years. Thanksgiving, 1960. David home from San Anselmo's, Clay with his smart friend Eileen. Nick and Katy. The Stoltzes and three Vonns. Meredith.

They were all in the family room for after-dinner drinks and conversation. Wine racing in his head and lust charging almost uncontrolled through him every time he looked at Meredith Thornton or brushed against her.

Roger and Marie Stoltz were seated in Max and Monika's blue and white recliners. Lynette and Janelle Vonn were brought to them like babes to Jesus.

What Andy remembered now, for the first time,

was the look on Roger Stoltz's face as he touched Janelle Vonn's pudgy eleven-year-old's arm and smiled down at her. An unmistakable expression, thought Andy. The same one his father had with Marie.

Pity.

# 28

'So yesterday, Shirley's doing the laundry and guess what she finds in Kevin's pants?' asked Lobdell. 'In a little ball of chewing gum foil?'

'Uppers,' said Nick.

'How did you know?'

'From his lipping off to his teachers and mom,' said Nick. 'And sleeping all weekend. You know, jacked up on the pills all week, then crashing. It came to me this morning when I was thinking about him and my third cup of coffee kicked in.'

Lucky fixed Nick with a look but said nothing while Nick turned off Laguna Canyon Road onto Stan Oaks. They were headed to Cory Bonnett's for a knock-and-talk. Bonnett looked good but not good enough for a search warrant. Nick figured their chances of catching him at home were small.

'I feel like a dumbass,' said Lobdell. 'Here I am a cop, I'm supposed to know these things. The signs.'

'Nobody figures their seventeen-year-old is taking pills.'

Lucky sighed. 'Shirley was upset. More than upset. Kevin made it worse, said he had no idea what the pills were, no idea how they got into his pants. I grounded him completely, for starters. I told Shirley I know a guy in narcotics detail – you know, Gant – who could come over and give Kevin a good shaking up. Really tell him what that shit can do to you. Kevin won't listen to me or his mom, so I figure maybe a young guy like Gant can scare him straight. But Shirley says if I call the cops on my own son she'll leave me and take Kevin with her. She's serious. She really means it. I wasn't going to have him arrested. That's not what I meant at all.'

Nick steered up the steep, winding road.

'Gets worse,' said Lobdell. 'Last night we sat Kevin down and asked him what was the reason for the pills. I mean, why was he taking that shit? And he says it's because he hates us, his mom and me. Can't wait to get out of the house. Hates the rules and the boredom and the homework and the chores and the teachers and me telling him what to do. Wants to be free. Says he's packing up the second he turns eighteen, going to goddamned Humboldt or some such thing. You know what they got there – rain and dope. Plenty of both. Know what I said?'

'I have an idea.'

'I said fine, son. Do it. A young man should be

free. I'll wish you all the luck in the world. I'll help you get a used car. They got a decent state college up there. I can send you off with my blessing and a little folding money. And Shirley—'

'Oh no.'

'Oh yeah. She hit the roof. Thinks I'm trying to kick him out. She's yelling at me and I'm yelling at Kevin again and Kevin's yelling at her and you know? That was the worst day of my life. I feel worse now than I did after hell week at the academy or that motorcycle wreck or the kidney stones back in sixty-four. I feel like I married a woman I don't even know and had a kid I don't even like.'

'I wish I had some advice.'

'That's the last thing I need. I just wanted to hear myself complain. But Nick?'

'Yeah.'

'Thanks for giving some thought to my son.'

Nick glanced across at his partner. 'You're welcome.'

'And look at that damned house.'

Nick stopped in the middle of the driveway. The big house loomed on the hillside above them. Redwood and smoked-glass windows and river rock. Like something you'd see in the Colorado mountains, thought Nick. Two stories high, three chimneys, and what looked like a pool house off to one side.

'That's another thing that pisses me off about these drug people,' said Lobdell, 'is all the money they make off of kids like Kevin. Look at the size of that thing. The guy's twenty-two years old.'

Nick drove slowly up the steep drive. There was another home a hundred yards off to the left and down. And one below it, almost out of view around the hillside. Besides that, just coastal scrub and prickly pear.

Bonnett's rock, wood, and glass castle dominated the hill. Above the roofline Nick saw only sky and a redtail hawk gliding on a thermal. Felt the temperature creep up as they climbed. Up closer Nick saw a big garage with all three of the doors open. Two vehicles inside. A blue and white pickup truck in the driveway.

Then a swimming pool. A weight-lifting bench loaded with a heavy barbell beside the clean blue water. A row of four green chaise longues. A pool house behind.

They parked and followed a walkway past the pool. It curved through a small stand of yellowing cottonwoods and brought them to a redwood stairway that led up to a deck and the big double front doors. Peepholes in both doors but no windows. Windows on either side of the doors but the blinds were drawn tight.

Nick rang the buzzer and waited. Lobdell knocked.

They followed the deck around the house. The windows all had blinds and the blinds were drawn. The north wall of the house was dark with stain. Moss between the slats. But on the sunny exposures the redwood had turned silver-gray in the sun. Lizards stuck to the warm boards of the west wall. Nick looked out to the blue Pacific wedged between the brown canyon hills. Smelled the sage and eucalyptus and just a hint of ocean blowing into the canyon from the sea.

They walked down to the pool house. The sliding glass door of the house was open. Curtains wafted in and out in the canyon breeze. Nick rapped on the glass with his knuckles, said 'O.C. sheriff's deputies.'

The voice came at him close and strong. 'Beat it.'

'We're here to see Cory,' said Nick. Hand to his auto. Hammer of the gun caught on the lining of his sport coat. Nudged it away with his fingers.

'Ain't here so beat it.'

Suddenly the curtains shot to the side. Big man right in front of Nick. Lobdell's arm came from behind him, .45 leading the way. Nick jumped back and drew cleanly.

Guy in the window put his hands up. Eyes big. Shaking his head. 'I don't have a gun,' he said.

'Step outside,' said Nick. '*Now.*' His heart pounded and his hands had gone cold.

'Don't shoot, man. I don't have a gun.'

'*Step outside,*' said Nick. 'Keep your hands where I can see them. Good. Easy. You can do it.'

Nick moved back and the man stepped from the pool house. Nick's age – thirty or so. He was big, naked except for a swimsuit. Skin dark. Long

black hair and a sharp little beard like a muske-
teer. Hands out but not up. A look on his face
like he'd done this before and could strangle
someone.

Lobdell turned him, looked him over, holstered
his Colt. 'Good way to get shot,' he said.

'I was asleep.'

'Middle of the day?' asked Lobdell. 'Must have
had a good night. What's your name?'

'Dirk George. No outstandings, not using, not
holding, not packing, not in the mood for cops.'

'I smell beer so at least you're drinking,' said
Lobdell.

'No law against that,' said Dirk.

'You house-sitting, Dirk?' asked Nick.

Dirk George looked at Nick. Still had the strangle look. 'What's it look like?'

'Answer the question,' said Nick.

'Cory's gone, man. I don't know where. I don't
care where. I'm staying in the pool house, watering the flowers. Keeping an eye out for the little
piggies.'

Nick's anger spiked. He looked at Lobdell, then
back at Dirk. Dirk was all invitation. The let's-
fight look. You saw it in jail when you were
young. Sometimes had to accept, just to make a
point.

'We want to ask Cory a few questions,' Nick
said.

'He isn't here. The big house is locked up and
nobody's home.'

Something moved behind the curtains. Nick saw bare feet below the swaying fabric. Red nails. A silver ring on the left middle toe.

'Come on out, miss,' he said.

The girl hesitated, then pushed through the curtain and onto the patio. Janelle's age, Nick guessed. Long blond hair. Beautiful suntanned skin. Blue eyes and freckles. A denim jacket with a rainbow embroidered on the pocket flap. Cutoff shorts.

Nick recognized her from Janelle's memorial service. One of the girls who'd come with Jesse Black. Andy had told him her name. Gail.

'Hi, guys,' she said.

'See, we're guys, not pigs,' said Nick. A flat stare at the man in the swimsuit.

She blushed and looked submissively at Dirk. Nick decided that if Dirk hurt her for what she said, he'd take it out of Dirk's suntanned hide somehow.

'Will you come with me, please?' Nick asked her.

She looked at him with a distrusting innocence.

'You don't have to, babe,' said Dirk.

'I saw you at Janelle's service,' said Nick. He took a couple of steps toward the big house.

Gail hesitated, then followed.

Nick walked into the stand of cottonwoods and stopped. Gail unrolled her coat sleeves against the chill in the shade.

'I'm sorry for all of that,' he said. 'I'm Nick Becker. Sheriff's investigator.'

'I'm Gail.'

'Dirk has a bad attitude.'

'He hates the fuzz.'

'That's up to him. We just had a few questions for Cory. Know where he is?'

She shook her head. 'He didn't tell me where he went. He asked me to stay here, keep an eye on things.'

'You, not Dirk.'

She nodded.

'Why are you hanging around with Mr George?'

'He's not so bad.'

'I mean, if it's just for dope, you can always buy your own.'

'Weird statement from a cop.'

'I don't dig guys like him and Cory with girls like you and Janelle. Cory and Dirk are creeps. Girls like Janelle and you are suckers. The creeps put up money or the dope and they get you.'

Gail said nothing. Shrugged.

'Were you and Janelle good friends?' asked Nick.

'No. We both liked Jesse. He liked her better than me. But we all got along.'

'See her that last night by any chance?'

She shook her head. 'No. I went to a concert.'

'What was Cory up to that night?'

'I don't know. Me and Cory had a thing a long time ago.'

'Couldn't have been that long,' said Nick.

She shrugged again. Straightened her back a little. Took a deep breath and stared through him.

'Look,' he said. 'We're not here to find anybody's stash. We're not here to hassle Dirk or you. We wanted to talk to Cory. So can we just look around a little?'

'You can't. That's why Cory asked me to stay here. You have no permission to search. That's what he told me to say.'

Nick nodded. Held her gaze for a moment. Had a feeling she wanted to help him. 'Are you okay?'

'What do you mean?'

Nick waited but she didn't offer anything.

'Creeps like Dirk can be hard on a girl,' he said.

'Anything beats home, Mr Detective.'

'Where's home?'

'Pacific Palisades.'

'Big dollars.'

'Plastic.'

'I grew up in Tustin,' he said. Then he took a chance. Figured it would open a door or not. 'Have you tried the Orange Sunshine air freshener?'

She smiled and colored. Prettiest skin Nick ever saw.

'I sprayed myself by accident,' said Nick. 'Tripped for a whole day and slept like a baby.'

'I stayed high for two days once,' she said.

'I found the bottle in Janelle's car.'

Gail shuddered inside her coat.

'What have you heard?' asked Nick.

'Heard?'

'About Janelle.'

'Everybody says it was someone from Tustin.'

'And?'

'Something to do with her old life there. Being Miss Tustin and the magazine picture and her brothers. Her mom committed suicide with rat poison.'

'When was the last time you saw her?'

Gail looked down at the walkway. Nick did, too. Two-by-sixes with alyssum and lobelia growing up through the spaces.

'I went to the Troubadour to hear Jesse play about a week before the murder. She was there. We sat together with some other people. Jesse took her home.'

Nick waited. Felt like Gail had something to say.

'You think Cory knows something about Janelle?' she asked.

'He's dangerous,' said Nick. 'She was hanging out with him. She liked the danger. See, she was helping us. Telling us things, for money. If Cory found out about that, he'd do something bad.'

'I didn't know that.'

'Keep it to yourself, Gail. I trust you.'

'The night she died, Cory and I were supposed to go see the Doors. He was going to pick me up at seven. He called me at quarter to and said he didn't feel good, was staying home. I said I'd come over and he said no. That meant he was with

378

someone else. He knew I knew. I figured, screw him. So I drove up to Hollywood myself and saw the band.'

'Was he with Janelle?'

Gail shrugged. 'Probably. She was his new thing.'

*New thing*, thought Nick.

'I knew Janelle when she was little,' said Nick. 'Just a girl. I need to find out who did this to her.'

'Was it really, actually, all the way cut off?'

Nick nodded. 'Completely off. You going to let me have a look around here, Gail? Or shall I just come back with a warrant?'

'You can't go in his house. It's got alarms and everything.'

'Then how about the grounds? The pool house and the garage and the property? Whatever's open and in plain sight?'

Gail nodded. 'Yes. Okay.'

Dirk cussed her when she told him they could look around. Lobdell cuffed him to a eucalyptus tree and told him to shut up or he'd arrest him for trespassing, assault, and disturbing the peace.

Dirk looked puzzled and pleased when Gail said she'd bring around a couple of chairs and beers and keep him company.

The pool house had a small living room, and a short hallway with two rooms in the back. A bar with stools. A dinette. Dishes piled in the sink.

Beer cans on the counters. Pretzels and canned nuts.

The fruit bowl on the little table contained two bananas, an orange, and a Smith & Wesson .357 magnum with a two-inch barrel. Nick used a tissue to pop the cylinder for a look at the serial number. Six magnum loads, six shiny primers looking at him. He balanced the gun on the fruit and wrote the numbers in his notebook.

'That'll blow a hole in you,' said Lobdell. 'There ought to be some way to keep creeps from having things like that.'

'Too many of both,' said Nick. Closed the cylinder.

They walked through the bedrooms but nothing looked unusual. Cory was big on stereos and televisions and posters from John Wayne westerns.

Back outside Lobdell smoked and Nick finished up his notes on what they'd seen in the pool house.

'The garage was open,' said Lobdell. He ground out the cigarette with his wing tip, kicked it under a cottonwood.

Nick stepped into the big garage and hit the lights. Two rows of good fluorescents flickered on. Shimmering into focus below were a white late-model Cadillac Coupe Deville and a new black Porsche 911S.

'Nice coupe,' said Lobdell.

Nick remembered what the Lemon Heights Sporting Goods owner had seen that night in the parking lot. And what Terry Neemal had seen later that same night outside the SunBlesst packinghouse.

'Maybe it met Janelle and her Beetle in the Sav-On parking lot,' said Nick. 'And left with her in it.'

'I like that idea.'

It had bothered Nick that Cory Bonnett disappeared two days after the murder. Now it bothered him more.

'That's *eight thousand* dollars' worth of German sports car,' said Lobdell. 'I had an uncle that marched into Auschwitz. I don't buy anything Kraut.'

Nick walked around the vehicles. One wall had shelves with boxes on them. The other had a long workbench with two vises, a table saw, a circular saw, a jigsaw, a band saw, a grinder, and two industrial sewing machines. There were a dozen leather punches hung from the peg-board behind the bench. Knives and scissors and handsaws, too. Ten different shapes and sizes, Nick saw. Gave him a weird feeling even though they were only tools.

No Trim-Quick, but plenty of other saws and shears and knives for cutting skin.

Nick still had the funny feeling inside as he looked at a stack of catalogues for leather apparel. And the little eight-shot .22 on top of them.

. . . *artist or craftsman . . . terrific pride . . . and that is what she insulted . . .*

An old wooden armoire sat open along the wall

beside the workbench. Nick saw the leather hanging inside. Black and brown and tan and red and blue. Scraps in boxes at the bottom. Good smell. A Winchester Model 12 leaning back in one corner behind the leather like it was trying to hide.

On the wall by the office closet was a calendar with a woman in a yellow bikini standing next to a small airplane. Beside it another calendar with a woman in a red bikini standing next to a black Porsche.

'Pretty girls, guns, and shiny machines,' said Lobdell. 'Fun hobbies. What kind of plane does he have?'

'Cessna,' said Nick. 'Out at Orange County Airport.'

'You wonder how a little plane like that can carry enough drugs into the country to pay for a place like this. For cars and pools.'

'He just flies down to Mexico to negotiate and buy,' said Nick. 'The drugs come north later. Some in cars. Some in bigger planes. They say Bonnett doesn't even look at what he imports. Disgusted by everything about it, except for the money.'

'These hippies, you watch,' said Lobdell. 'By the time they're my age they'll be carrying briefcases and wearing suits like their daddies. They'll all want to work for IBM again, drive overpriced German cars. They'll cut their hair for the dough. Tell their kids they never used dope or wore those dumbass clothes or called us pigs. You watch.'

Lobdell lit a cigarette. Nick smelled the butane, then the tobacco. Loved those smells. Liked the happy shear of metal on metal when the Zippo opened and closed. He missed the smokes. Just once in a while now. To bribe a subject, like Neemal. Build their trust in you and relax them.

Nick used his pen to prowl through the tools and containers on the workbench. Good stuff, well cared for. Some metal dust had mounded up on the grinder housing, but no clue as to what it had come from. Something for his plane? Nick thought of Bonnett's white-handled Mexican switchblade, wondered if he sharpened it here.

Why would a guy with leather-cutting tools use a garden pruner?

He stood before the shelves and read the white labels on the boxes: pots and pans, extra blankets, pictures, trophies, sports gear, lantern and stove, sleeping bags, tent. Max had always used stick-on labels, too.

Then something grabbed his eyes. The loose bundle of material on top of the tent box. One corner of it dangling down over the cardboard. Didn't fit with Cory Bonnett's garage at all. Like a fly in a glass of milk.

'I've been looking at that for the last thirty seconds, too,' said Lobdell. 'I've seen it before.'

White bedsheets with little pink roses.

'The curtains in Janelle's yellow cottage,' said Nick.

'Yep,' said Lobdell.

Nick stepped up closer, leaning in. 'I swear I'm looking at a bloodstain.'

Lobdell's big head lowered over Nick's shoulder. Nick smelled Old Spice aftershave and cigarette smoke. 'Looks like blood to me.'

Nick just stared at the sheets. And the small drop of what looked like blood. It most definitely looked like blood. For the first time since he'd left the packinghouse he believed he'd found something that truly mattered.

'This isn't the cleanest search here, Lucky. We could lose this stuff in court if we don't see a judge and get a warrant.'

'The sheets are in plain sight, Nick. The blood, too. We came here to question someone in connection with a murder. We got permission. The garage door was wide open so we looked around. How can Bonnett expect privacy in his garage with his door wide open and a bloody sheet in plain sight?'

'No. I want it right. Let's get a warrant.'

Nick couldn't take his eyes off the sheets and that little stain. Damn. It was like throwing in your line hour after hour, day after day. And you finally catch a big fish you only half believed was there.

'See?' asked Lobdell. 'My luck is rubbing off on you.'

'Yeah. But I still got a problem, Lucky.'

'I think I got it, too.'

'Say these are Janelle's sheets,' said Nick. 'Say she had two sets because she liked the pattern, got them on sale. Okay. I can believe that. One for the bed and one for the windows. But what are these doing *here*? What, Bonnett met her in Tustin, drove her back to Laguna to her place, killed her in her own bedroom, then changed the sheets and messed up the bed? Then drove back and dumped her at the packinghouse? Then brought evidence back to his own home?'

'That doesn't make any sense.'

'No kidding.'

*No planning and unnecessary work.*

'Except bringing back the evidence,' said Nick. 'I've been doing some reading. Heard this FBI guy up in L.A. And they got this new kind of killer out now. They're not dumb. They're more weird than dumb. They *like* doing what they do. And sometimes they'll take stuff from their victims, stuff that isn't worth anything. It helps them remember. Neemal likes fire. These guys like keepsakes of what they did. Maybe Bonnett's one of those. And the sheets turned him on.'

*Would he take something from her as a reminder, like you talked about?*

*No. But unpracticed killers surprise us by what they remove from the scene simply to keep the police from finding it.*

'Or maybe,' said Lobdell, 'he brought them back here to get rid of them. Panicked or forgot.'

Nick grasped for the logic in the sheets but

couldn't find it. No method to the madness. 'Let's get some paper and toss this place,' he said.

'I'll call deputies to seal it off,' said Lobdell. 'I'd hate to see Tarzan and Gidget clean this all up while we're gone.'

It took three hours to get the search warrant and back to Bonnett's home. Nick typed the supporting affidavit while Lobdell filled in the statutory page and dictated a 'hero paragraph' that made Nick sound like a seasoned murder investigator rather than the first-time lead detective he was. Lobdell kept harping on the 'training and experience' that led Nick to the 'strong opinion' that felony evidence would be found in Cory Bonnett's home. Lobdell said the secret was not to overstep the warrant once you were inside. If you had a doubt, like could you open a locked chest, or could you stick your head up into the attic, then you went back to the magistrate and got another warrant. That way, nothing got thrown out of court.

Just as Nick was ready to leave the homicide room his phone rang. It was Roger Stoltz, who said he was sorry that Nick had missed today's four o'clock appointment. He had been looking forward to talking with Nick. Was everything okay?

Nick apologized. Felt like a school kid without his homework. Told himself it's easy to forget appointments when evidence starts falling into your lap.

Stoltz asked him not to worry, said he was just in from D.C. a few hours ago and ready to go home.

'I'm looking forward to the weekend with Marie,' he said. 'Now Nick, look. My secretary here says you wanted to talk about Janelle. Anytime. Anywhere. I'll tell you what I know.'

'Thank you, sir.'

'Nick, do you have a suspect?'

'Possibly.'

Silence for a moment. A very deep sigh from the other end.

'I would still like to know about the Newport Beach apartment,' said Nick.

'Anytime and anywhere.'

'Thank you, sir.'

'Regards to Max and Monika. And to your brothers. We'll see David in church Sunday.'

'We'll be there, too,' said Nick.

By the time they got back to Cory Bonnett's house the afternoon had gone cool. A stiff breeze rattled yellow leaves off the cottonwoods. A raven tore across the sky with a mockingbird after him.

The blue and white pickup truck was gone. Two deputies stood near the garage, two more in a unit blocking the driveway.

'Good to have the troops,' said Lobdell. 'I had my hand in the cookie jar once, the guy comes home. I'm in the kitchen checking the cutlery box for a missing carving knife and he jumps me. Never heard him. Didn't see him. I got him under control, but he could have shot me or stabbed me easy.'

Superior court judge Wes Dickinson had thrown them a loose one, good for the main house, the pool house, the garage, and both vehicles in the garage. Even the trunks of the cars. It specified not only the bloodstained sheets but 'evidence of the subject's presence at the SunBlesst packinghouse on October 1 or 2 of this year; evidence of the subject as party to or having knowledge of the murder of Janelle Vonn; evidence that the subject had prior knowledge that this murder had been planned or would or was about to happen.'

'My kinda judge,' said Lobdell.

The Porsche was locked but the Cadillac wasn't. Nick used a flashlight and magnifying glass to examine the Coupe Deville's floorboard carpet and the red leather seats. Plenty of sand, dirt, fiber, bits of paper. Strands of what looked like human hair. Some light like Bonnett's and some dark like Janelle's. Probably latents all over this interior. Good stuff, he thought, but he'd get the ID boys on it later.

He popped the trunk. Saw the lid rise in the rearview. Heard Lobdell.

'Hmmm, Nick.'

Nick jumped out, walked back to Lobdell. Looked down into the spacious trunk. A small toolbox. A set of jumpers, some car wax, and rags in a box.

And a sleeping bag. Black plastic bottom outside for moisture. Yellow-and-black-checked flannel inside. Not rolled up. Not folded. Just crammed back in the far corner of the trunk.

Nick pulled it out and set it beside the box. Spread it out a little. Found the head end, began unzipping it. Big enough for two. Stubborn zipper and a musty smell.

Debris inside. Black stuff. Flecked and fragile. Like burned paper, thought Nick. Or soot. Some dark hairs. Easy to see on the yellow flannel. Blood. Crate label for SunBlesst packinghouse, pretty brunette with the orange again. Blood on that.

A saw blade. Swivel bolt still attached to a shard of wood. Blood all over them, too.

By four-thirty they'd tossed the house, too, but hadn't come up with much else.

By six-thirty they had a warrant for the arrest of Cory Bonnett.

By seven they'd talked to Don Rae of Laguna PD. Rae's source had confirmed that afternoon that Cory Bonnett was at his place near Ensenada. Kind of a compound, said Rae. People around him. Gringos and Mexicans. Unfriendly people. A compound in the hills.

Rae said he'd let Nick know the second Bonnett was headed stateside.

'Janelle Vonn,' said Rae. 'Incredible. No wonder he hit the road.'

Nick thanked him and hung up.

'Ensenada,' said Nick. 'A little out of our jurisdiction.'

'There's a way to bring him back here,' said Lobdell. 'You just gotta have the nerve for it.'

# 29

That Sunday David sat in the first row of the Grove Drive-In Church of God to watch Darren Whitbrend deliver his guest sermon.

The young minister looked fuller in his robes. More authoritative. David had noted Whitbrend's elevator shoes earlier in the vestry where they had enrobed. David could feel the worry coming off Whitbrend. Downcast eyes, tight jaw, few words.

Which was fine with David, who felt his own body on the verge of falling apart.

Barbara held one of his clammy hands. Wendy the other. Rachel lay on Barbara's lap wrapped in a blanket. Two-year-old Matthew sat beside his mother, frowning his way into a bowel movement.

David watched with envy. He hadn't had one since talking to Hambly, then Howard, on Thursday. Nothing would stay down long enough. He had drunk half a coffee mug of pink antacid earlier, trying to keep down his breakfast of white sandwich bread. Pretty much the same for dinner the night before. Almost no sleep. Hours of wide-awake worry that the cops would see through Linda Langton's words. That Howard would face a lineup and hang his final alibi on David. Then more hours of sweat and stomach pain, right on the cusp of sleep, as his conscience wriggled back into its deepest crannies to retrieve his most trivially shameful moments and present them to him for . . . what? These were things he hadn't even thought about for years. The time he slugged Clay for breaking a gallon mustard jar he wanted for butterflies. The time he told Lydia Maxwell she was the ugliest girl he'd ever seen. The time he purposefully overcooked Barbara's steak because she liked it rare and had called him a coward for not standing up to a drunk evangelist who had pawed her at a church mountain retreat two summers ago.

The pains in David's stomach were coming faster now, like contractions for birth.

He felt a drop of sweat roll off his nose but couldn't get a hand free in time to stop it. Watched it plop onto the leg of his Haggar knits.

Whitbrend began slowly and softly. His oratorical voice hardly stronger than his speaking voice. At first it seemed too low, so David found himself having to pay extra attention. Wondered why Whitbrend didn't just get a little closer to the mike. Then David realized the whole congregation was listening closely.

Whitbrend told about growing up in Oregon. In a godless family. No church, no prayer, no belief. He was a mean-tempered boy. Utterly self-ish. When he was seventeen he fell 'helplessly' in love with a girl. All he felt in his heart was love for her and for everything around him. Took her to the homecoming dance, the Sadie Hawkins dance, and the junior prom. On the way home from the prom a car ran a stop sign and crashed into them. He had lain trapped in the upturned car, caught in metal and vinyl under her bleed-ing, unmoving body, praying to the God he never knew to save her life. He told God he would do anything asked of him if He would spare her life.

Whitbrend looked down at the pulpit for a moment. It was so quiet David could hear the cars on faraway Beach Boulevard. Could hear the squirting and sloshing inside his own stomach.

Whitbrend stepped away from the pulpit, then back.

She was dead when the police got there, he said. They lifted her off him and took him to a hospital. He suffered a broken wrist and minor cuts. All that night he stayed in the hospital for observation, and he prayed to the God he never knew that when he awakened this would all be a bad dream. He squeezed his eyes and arched his back and trembled on his heels and he ground his teeth in prayer. Over and over and over. When he awakened his father was standing over the bed with a broken tooth in his hand.

The broken tooth, thought David. The cap just slightly whiter than the other teeth. A reminder of faith for anyone who had heard this story.

Brilliant.

Whitbrend looked down at the pulpit again. David admired this, too. What at first had seemed evasive now seemed humble. Darren Whitbrend was not asking the congregation to bear his burden. He was showing them how it was done. Alone. Through the making of scars. Through the capping of teeth broken by prayer.

The young minister looked out at the congregation.

He said that after the funeral he made the God he'd never known an offer.

'I offered my life and flesh and soul to Him,' said Whitbrend, 'if He would do one thing. That night I took the revolver from my father's drawer.'

He walked outside and down by the river. He popped the cylinder and removed all six cartridges. Threw one into the water. It didn't make a sound. Reloaded the other five and spun the cylinder hard, once. He closed it. And told the God he'd never known to save him only if he could know Him. And to take him if he could not. Then he sat down and pulled the trigger.

David heard the blood surging in his ears. Heard the dread and surprise ripple through his chapel, then the twitter of realization.

'And I ask all of you,' said Whitbrend, 'to let me share Him with you.'

Whitbrend opened his arms to the believers and smiled. David could see the cap from here. Almost took his breath away.

David's fever broke halfway through the closing prayer. While Whitbrend talked softly about peace beyond understanding, the tormented muscles of David's stomach relaxed and the ache departed from his bones. The demons in his mind were quiet. He felt his strength begin to return, the strength to love and care and offer. He knew he would soon have a partner to help him guide the future of this congregation. God would help him through this other thing. *Please, God, help me through this. It's the only thing I've ever asked that's all for me.*

The closing hymn was a thundering, joyful roar of the spirit.

That night they all had dinner at Max and Monika's home in the orange grove in Tustin. David and Barbara and the kids, Nick and Katy and theirs, Andy and Teresa.

David sat at one end of the long table, his father at the other. Everyone held hands while David said grace. He had never said a grace of more than one minute in his life but this night David took almost five. Wandered a little, because he hadn't thought about it ahead of time. Mentioned every person at the table. And Clay. Simple thanks, but so much to be thankful for.

When he opened his eyes David looked at every

person and thought a secret prayer that they would all be around this table, just like this, many times in the years ahead.

Nick listened to the grace. One hand in Katy's and one in Stevie's. Opened one eye and spied up and down the table. Been doing that since he was a kid, and wouldn't you know it, he caught Willie pulling the same stunt. Willie shut his eye and Nick almost smiled.

But he shared David's thankfulness and felt the grace of God hovering around them. It was a good family. Even without Clay it was still good. Everybody had their problems but that was human nature. That was life.

Nick paid extra attention at the 'watch over us' part. Really tried to make his heart open up and let God know he was needing something. He and Lobdell would be in Mexico by this time tomorrow. Katy's hand squeezed his hard. Her little brother had been beaten and robbed down there when Katy was nineteen and she'd never traveled there again. Hated the place. Hated that Nick had to go. But understood.

When he opened his eyes Nick looked again at every person and believed in his uneasy heart that this was the last time they would all be together.

Andy let David's words fall down on him like a warm rain. He didn't personally think that God heard or responded to prayers, but who really knew? It was nice to believe for a minute or two. He felt Teresa's hand and Wendy's hand. Both soft and warm, one grown and one growing. He thought of the way the years run through everyone like a big river. Of the way we hang on to our little crafts and try to get to wherever it is we think we're going. Sometimes flail and cough and spit up the river water, too. How some get a long journey and some get what Clay and Janelle got and some don't even get that much. Which meant the people still here, still on the river, really should be thankful for it.

When he opened his eyes Andy looked at every person at the table and knew he was lucky to be there among them.

# 30

Nick steered the red rocket south on I-5 while Lobdell smoked a cigarette and looked out at the new nuclear power plant at San Onofre.

The Country Squire had two surfboards strapped to the top and food and water and camping gear in the back. Nick and Lobdell had tried to dress more like surfers than cops but Nick figured they just looked like cops in sandals. They couldn't grow out their hair much in three days. Nick hadn't shaved and Lobdell said he hadn't used any Vitalis. Nick almost smiled when he first saw Lucky's small white feet.

'Look at that,' said Lobdell.

There was a Camp Pendleton Marine Corps helicopter low over the water on exercise, dangling a single soldier by a long rope, sea spray flying, blades flashing in the sun. *Eighteen thousand dead*, thought Nick. Clay killed near a village. Body at Angel's Lawn now but like he was never here. What bothered Nick wasn't that people died but that they were forgotten. Made him shudder if he thought about it so he didn't. But he still couldn't shake the feeling he'd had during David's prayer last night.

In San Ysidro they got Oscar Padilla car insurance and lunch. Lobdell wanted Sambo's for the last American food they'd get for a day or two. Maybe longer. Couldn't find one, though, so they settled on Denny's. Fine with Nick, who looked out the darkened windows at the bustling border town. Kept an eye on the Country Squire. Quite a load of valuables hidden down in it, under all the surf and camp gear. A short man bent by a shoulderload of serapes shuffled across the parking lot.

Once across Nick got into the TJ way of driving. Plenty of horn work and don't slow down or move over unless you have to. They honked and lurched through downtown, past the shop-windows of dresses and watches and jewelry and drawn chickens hanging with the feet still on. A taxi zoomed by on their right, almost picked off a guy jumping onto the curb. Nick watched an ancient Chevrolet pass with a rooftop loudspeaker blaring out the virtues of Fanta soft drink.

'Even smells different down here,' said Lobdell. Told Nick about this bar named the Blue Fox, had live donkey shows. Never been to one and had no interest but knew some guys who had.

Then up the grade out of Tijuana, past the

shantytowns in the hills, past the bullring and the hospitals for cancer cures to the coast road overlooking the brown rock cliffs and the deep roiling sea.

Nick looked out at the trash fires burning and the *'No Basura'* signs. A pack of skinny, big-eared dogs trotted along through the fires. Nick slowed for two Tijuana cop cars off to the right, lights flashing, four tan-uniformed cops standing over a body in the gutter. Around the bend a mountain of worn-out tires exhaled a tornado of black smoke that rose and spread out over the ocean in the faint offshore breeze.

'When the hippies complain about America, I tell 'em to come down here and look at this place,' said Lobdell.

Nick watched a big rig barrel down the highway toward them, hoped the guy's brakes were decent. Eased the Red Rocket as far to the right as he could but the truck kept drifting over. No shoulder. A cliff to the right. Nick felt the gravel under his right-side tires. His forearms locked and his car was swallowed by shadow, steel rushing past the windows, slam of wind and diesel roar, and Nick could feel how really light the Country Squire was, could feel it skittering on the gravel, wondered if the surfboards were about to tear off. Then a burst of blue sky and brown cliff as the curve of asphalt carried him into the next pass.

'Close,' said Lobdell.

'Still got my side mirror,' said Nick, hands shaking and stomach rock hard.

'Best country in the world for your car to break down,' said Lobdell. 'They can fix anything with anything.'

Mexico State Highway 1 led south through La Gloria and Costa Azul. Then Rosarito, Popotla, and Punta Descanso. El Morro and Santa Martha. Santini Las Gaviotas and Puerto Nuevo.

'Been there for lobster?' asked Lobdell.

'Katy won't come down here,' said Nick.

'Two-fifty for a full dinner. Shot of tequila, complimentary. Little place called Chela. You get to pick the lobster you want. Good bugs.'

They pulled over in La Fonda, just a few miles north of Ensenada.

'Cortazar said here, because there's tourists,' said Lobdell. 'But we're still away from Ensenada. He said park down by the hotel.'

Nick got out and stretched his legs. Imagined that truck bearing down on them again. Cooler here than in Orange County. Stiff breeze and the water crashing below. Vendors with pottery and silver and piñatas. Elvis and Rolling Stones and Beatles posters lacquered onto plywood. A boy selling small shellacked sand sharks on strings. Nick got two for Willie and Stevie. Seashell necklace for Katherine, really nice. Silver butterfly on a chain for Katy. Chiclets for everyone.

'Come on, tourist,' said Lobdell. 'Cortazar is here.'

They drove down a dirt road behind a dusty brown Chevy. Then up a hillside. Cortazar was an Ensenada cop Lobdell knew from years ago. They'd met working a car-theft ring in fifty-five. It was a two-country operation, real pros, but OCSD and Cortazar's state police busted the ring on its ass and everybody came out looking good. Lucky and Cortazar stayed in touch. Cortazar moved to Ensenada *policía municipal* and helped Lucky get a gringo rape fugitive back stateside in nineteen-sixty. Off-the-record kind of thing, because the United States–Mexico extradition treaty was tough to work with. Friends were the only way things got done down here and the Mexicans said the same thing about the *Estados Unidos*. Lucky had reciprocated two years later up in O.C. on a kidnap case. Later helped Cortazar's boy get a car wash job in Orange County, get good *papeles* and into a junior college. Kid was managing five car washes now, owned a home in Santa Ana.

The Chevy climbed a gentle rise, then took a sandy right turn and stopped. Nick followed and got out. Stood on the bluff top in the middle of the dead brown grass. Ocean across the highway, no clouds in the October sky. Burnt smell in the air.

Cortazar was dark and heavy. Mustache, nice smile, dark dome of head beaded with sweat. Big revolver on a thick belt, pants too big, cuffs dragging in the sand as he followed Lobdell to the back of the Red Rocket. His partner was Marcello. Young and thin and hardly spoke.

Nick swung open the door, flipped up the two small seats Willie and Stevie loved to use. Even with plenty of room up with Katherine, they'd sit back there and make faces at the motorists until Nick made them crawl back over and sit still and act like human beings. He missed the kids extra now, out here in the middle of this eternally burning nowhere.

Nick let Lobdell pull up the first burlap bag. Lobdell lifted it and looked around quickly. Cortazar chuckled but Marcello didn't. Lobdell untied the top, took the bottom and emptied it onto one of the little red vinyl seats. Two .22 automatic handguns, six .38 revolvers, two .357 magnum revolvers, and four .45 autos.

Cortazar whistled. Marcello stared.

Nick and Lobdell had gotten them out of the property room. It was a verbal transaction, 'approved' but deniable. The weapons had been confiscated from criminals. Not material to any pending cases. Not salable. Not useful. These would be listed as destroyed. One hundred seventy-four more where they came from and more coming every week. Most of them ended up in the ocean. Lobdell had said that these were destined for 'undersupplied Mexican law enforcement personnel' in return for 'information on an American beauty queen killer now residing out-of-country.' He told the property room sergeant they had enough on the guy to send him to the gas chamber twice. The property room sergeant had helped load them into Nick's take-home. The truth was the Mexican cops would keep most of them for themselves because the cops in Mexico had trouble getting permits for personal firearms. And they could always use a good throw-down gun. Made Nick think of the Mexico charity runs that David's church always made.

Nick had felt like a gunrunner bagging the weapons, then transferring the heavy, bulging bags into the family wagon under the bright lights of his garage last night. Katy had helped. And said for heaven's sake don't scratch my car and please be careful down there, there's no way I can raise these kids alone. It was late after the dinner at David and Barb's. The kids were asleep when Nick and Katy were done loading in the rifles and Katy switched off the garage light and pushed him onto the front seat of the Red Rocket and made love to him. Wouldn't let him up until she showed him how she felt. Cried when it was over, just a little. Said please be really careful down there 'cause if you don't come back I'll wanna die but won't be able to. Nick still couldn't figure what had gotten into Katy since the Orange Sunshine extravaganza but he liked it. Miraculous, like they were eighteen again.

The second bag contained ammunition. It was good factory stuff, new and boxed. Courtesy of

OCSD, said Lobdell as Cortazar smiled and nodded.

The rifles and shotguns were under the folded backseats. Nick pulled out the cases one at a time and handed them to Lucky. A Remington 12-gauge automatic, a Winchester 12-gauge pump, two Marlin .22 automatics, two old Springfields, and a nice bolt-action .30-06 with a custom stock and a good Weaver scope. And two surplus ammunition boxes, incredibly heavy as Nick yanked them up off the floorboards and carried them to the rear of the wagon.

'For ducks, coyotes, and deer,' said Lobdell.

'But of course,' said Cortazar with a chipper grin.

Marcello smiled slightly and Nick looked down into the rear bed of the Red Rocket and the twenty-one firearms and ammunition that lay there in the bright Baja sun.

'We can use these,' said Cortazar.

'You got them,' said Lobdell.

'We can use Bonnett,' said Nick.

'You'll get him,' said Cortazar. 'He will never remove another head.'

They backtracked to Rosarito and spent the night at the big hotel. They'd meet Cortazar the next morning and go get Bonnett. Cortazar didn't say exactly how. But he didn't want Bonnett's people making two gringo cops in Ensenada. At the hotel they just looked like a couple of surfers down for the waves.

Kind of, thought Nick. They ate in the hotel dining room. Quiet on a Monday in fall. Nice view of the long flat beach. Horses and riders up and down the sand. Waves small and no surfers out. A gang of vultures and a gang of seagulls battled over a large black lump that had washed up. Seagulls seemed to be winning until the incoming tide rolled it loose and pulled it away.

Lobdell went to his room and Nick stayed in the cantina. He sipped a couple of shots of good tequila recommended by the bartender. Nick thought about Katy and the kids, then Clay, then Sharon. Couldn't shake the feeling that the family would never be together again like the night before. Worried about David. Pale and quiet and peaceful like someone going into shock.

Neither Nick nor Lobdell could sleep long so they drank coffee, had breakfast, and waited for Cortazar. The Ensenada cop said there was no reason to do this early. In Mexico good things never happen early. No, go late and be relaxed.

Just before noon Cortazar's beaten Chevy appeared behind the cantina. Cortazar waved. Marcello sat beside him, thin as a switchblade. Behind the Chevy was a low-slung black Mercury with big rust spots and mismatched wheel covers. Four more men, staring straight ahead like you might overlook them. Nick looked at each face, notched them into memory.

He fell in behind the Mercury and picked up

Highway 1 south. Cortazar had explained that Bonnett would talk to him because the men in the Mercury had vouched for him. The men were not cops. They were marijuana businessmen from Nayarit. 'Friends' of Bonnett. Actually, they were cops, it was just that Bonnett didn't know this. The purpose of this meeting was for Cortazar to present himself to Bonnett as an agreeable Ensenada policeman eager to discuss a private airstrip owned by business-minded friends. Marcello was with him to establish Cortazar's 'seriousness.' Cortazar said that the six cops would control the situation and return to Nick and Lobdell with a handcuffed Señor Bonnett. Simple.

When Nick had asked him how many people were inside Bonnett's compound, Cortazar had shrugged and frowned as if Nick had missed a crucial point.

Cortazar's Chevy pulled off the highway at a signal, followed by the black Merc. Nick fell in behind and the caravan headed east. The road was dirt and wide and Nick clipped along at forty in a traveling cloud of dust. Saw a rock-pile memorial with plastic flowers faded by the sun. Then the road turned to washboard and Nick saw the camp gear jump into the air in the rearview and heard the shudder of shocks and the chatter of the dashboard like every nut and bolt was coming loose.

'Knock the fillings out of your teeth,' said

Lobdell. 'But they got good dentists down here. Cheap.'

Nick couldn't see much through the dust. Just scrub and brown grass hills. Some skinny cattle behind a fence of barbed wire and twisted branches. A post with a hubcap nailed on top to mark someone's driveway. A heavy old woman with her hair in a bun squinting at them as they went past.

The road got worse. A steep rocky rise. Then a long downslope carved by ruts left and right where the rain had funneled down over the years. Nick pulled down into first gear, had to get the wagon's tires to straddle some of the ruts but fit between others. Hit the brakes too hard and you slid and ended up in a ditch. He could barely see the red hood through the brown dust.

'Funny that Cortazar's boy ended up in the car-wash business,' said Lobdell. 'Must have had good training, growing up down here.'

A mile. Then two. Cortazar had told them they would stop three kilometers in. There, Nick was to turn left onto another dirt road and proceed five hundred meters, then turn around, pull off to the side, and wait. Turn off the engine. Nobody from Bonnett's compound would be able to see them. If someone did, they'd figure lost surfers. Nick and Lobdell were to stay in the car.

Another ten minutes and the taillights of the Mercury appeared like red eyes a mist. Nick slowed and turned left. Saw Cortazar wave, then his tires lift a fresh cloud as he accelerated toward Bonnett's compound. The driver of the Mercury looked back at Nick with sleepy disinterest, then the back end of the black car jerked and threw a rooster tail of dust back at them.

'Prick,' said Lobdell.

Nick drove a few hundred yards, made a four-point U-turn, pulled to the right, killed the engine. Let the dust settle, then rolled down the windows. The plan was to wait for Cortazar to come back with Bonnett. Then follow them north to La Fonda. There, they would transfer the prisoner to a green and white Ensenada PM cruiser with a good safety screen and head for the border crossing in TJ. They would use the commercial vehicle gate, where Cortazar had friends who were expecting them. It would go smoothly. They'd actually push Bonnett through a chain-link gate, into the waiting arms of Orange and San Diego County sheriff's deputies.

Happy ending, Cortazar had said.

Nick sat staring out at the dry hills. Warmer now, away from the beach. Lobdell smoked, flicked his butt into the middle of the road.

Then they heard the distant pop of gunfire. Fast and lots of it.

'What's your call, Nick?'

'I want Bonnett.'

'You can get hurt or killed,' said Lobdell. 'I can, too.'

'I can't just sit here, Luck.'

'Me, neither. Cortazar's a friend. Let's dig our guns out of the back.'

They followed the tire tracks for a bouncing, swerving mile. A sliding right, a left, then another fishtail of a right. Nick hoped they were following the right ones.

The compound lurched into view. A sprawling low casa. Two casitas toward the back. Three smaller outbuildings, all adobe. A big wooden barn behind. The wall around them was adobe, too, not high but lined on top with broken bottles. A practice bullring stood outside the wall to the east. On the west side was a strip of weed-sprouted asphalt and a faded wind sock. A shining Cessna prop plane waited at the far end, pointed south for takeoff, tie lines swaying in the breeze.

Fifty yards out Nick could see the compound gate was open. Saw Cortazar's Chevy and the black Mercury parked end to end, the Merc just inside the gate, doors open. Someone slumped from the driver's-side door. Someone lay on the ground near him. Another body in the dirt on the other side of the car.

He slid to a dusty stop and cut the engine. Heard the pop of it under the hood but no shots. Nothing else but his own heart beating in his chest.

Then, a man groaned. Pure pain. Like something from a distant hell.

Again. One long syllable, like he was trying to say something.

'*Ahhhhhhh . . .*'

'Let's get to the wall,' said Lobdell.

Nick threw open the door. Zigzagged a crazy pattern like they did at football workouts in high school. Breathing hard by the time he shouldered down against the adobe. Watched Lobdell lumbering across the brown earth with breathtaking slowness.

They lay in the hot dirt under the wall. Guns out, panting like dogs.

'*Ahhhhhhh . . .*'

'It's coming from behind the house,' said Nick.

'We can use the cars for cover going in,' said Lobdell. 'You first.'

Nick crawled along the wall. Bull thorns and broken glass. Came to the open gate and the back end of the black Mercury. Looked around the corner at the driver spilled half out of the car. Faceup, arms out, blood dripping from his mouth. The windshield was shot out. Safety glass glittering on the hood and in the dirt like tossed handfuls of diamonds. The man beside him was facedown, a revolver near one hand, patch of dark blood under his chest. Nick put his face to the ground and looked past the Merc's rear tires to the body on the other side. A big man, on his back, face toward Nick and the breeze moving his hair.

That left one from the Merc maybe still alive,

thought Nick. And maybe Cortazar and Marcello. And maybe this is just a bad dream.

He heard Lobdell brake. Came up and braced his piece on the adobe gate stanchion. The stanchion crumbled and his weapon slipped but Nick saw nothing over the sights and heard nothing but Lobdell heaving to a stop beside him.

'*Ahhhhhhh . . .*'

Out of his mind with pain, Nick thought.

'Get the door open but wait for me,' said Lobdell. 'Wait a second, get your wind.'

Nick took a deep breath. Got a good grip on the sweaty handle of the automatic. Hustled onto the driveway, jumped the dead man, and weaved his way to the shaded front porch of the casa. Made the portico steps in one leap, flattened himself against the cool adobe. Reached out and turned the knob and pushed it open.

Nick looked back toward Lucky. Lobdell charged up the driveway, stepped around the dead man and onto the porch.

'*Ahhhhhhh . . .*'

Nick swung his gun toward the nearest casita. Held steady on the front door but nothing moved. A bullet hole in the window glass, halo of blood around it. A curtain lilting.

Lobdell burst into the main house with his weapon up in both hands. Nick followed close behind him, scanning the dark interior. Big room. Big house. Smell of blood and gunpowder.

412

Marcello dead on the tile floor right under them, gun out. Looked like he'd been shot eight or ten times. Two guys dead across from him Nick didn't recognize. In the far end of the room Cortazar slouched dead on a big steerhide couch. Hands at his sides and no weapon out. Like he'd come in, sat on the couch, and been slaughtered. Another man on the kitchen floor Nick didn't recognize. Marcello had taken down three but not enough.

Nick put his fingers to Marcello's neck and got nothing. Lobdell tried Cortazar, then set his hand on Cortazar's shoulder like he was consoling him. In the silence Nick heard eternity.

'We're down to one,' he said.

'*Ahhhhhhh . . .*'

'Maybe that's him,' said Lobdell. 'Go careful now, Nick.'

They checked the rest of the house. Nothing moving but the hands of a clock in the bedroom.

Out a back door then, toward the moan. Nick first and down low, Lobdell behind. The first outbuilding was full of marijuana bricks wrapped in brown paper. Stacked high as Nick's head. A couple of industrial scales. Two small humidifiers misting away. Smell so strong Nick wondered if you could get high off it.

The second outbuilding was full of surfboards and wet suits, butane stoves, sleeping bags, tents. A rat scampered along the floor and whipped behind a surfboard.

The third building had a bloody drag mark on the front steps and an open front door. A revolver lay in the dirt. Nick could hear the fast breathing inside. He backed against the front wall.

'United States police! Come out.'

Again in Spanish.

*'Can't.'*

'Bonnett?'

*'Shot. Bad. Help. Ahhhhhhh . . .'*

Cory Bonnett lay on his back, head up against the wall. Arms and legs spread. Breathing rapid and shallow. Face white and bloody, eyes heavy. His left knee was shot through from the back. Bones flaring outward, splinters and gristle and blood. Right palm blown apart where he'd tried to block a bullet and his right shoulder oozing blood where it had gone through.

Nick held steady on him. 'You're under arrest for the murder of Janelle Vonn.'

*'I didn't do it. Water?'*

'I'll get it,' said Lobdell. 'If he jumps up all of a sudden, shoot him again.'

Nick saw Bonnett's blue eyes open wider to see who had spoken, then nearly close again. Breathing faster now.

*'Followed her to Tustin.'*

'Why?'

*'Worried.'*

'Followed her but didn't kill her?'

*'Yeah.'*

'Just looking out for her, like a big brother?'

Bonnett nodded and shivered.

'Stop talking, Cory, or you're going to die right here.'

Lobdell came back with a pot full of water. Nick knelt and steadied it for Bonnett to drink.

Bonnett shivered again. Nick heard a clicking sound – Bonnett's teeth on the pot rim. Then Bonnett jerked and drove a fist into Nick's stomach. Hard and low. When Nick looked down he saw the switchblade in him.

*'Fuck you, pig.'*

Nick jumped up and back. 'Lucky, this guy just stabbed me.'

Lucky kicked Bonnett in the face and pressed his gun against his forehead.

Nick couldn't figure what to do with the knife so he just stood there and looked at it. White handle. Just like the narco jacket said. Touched it. Pulled. It came out pretty easy. Didn't really hurt. Hardly any blood. Wasn't sure what to do with the thing now. Pushed the button, folded the blade in, put it in his pocket.

'Sit down, Nick,' said Lobdell. 'Sit down and breathe easy and apply pressure. I got this guy.'

Nick saw the violence in Lobdell's eyes and Nick thought for a second that he'd shoot. Instead he yanked Bonnett over by his hair and got the cuffs out.

*'Ahhhhhhh . . .'*

'Yeah.'

*'Ahhhhhhh . . .'*

'Yeah, yeah, yeah, go fuck yourself, you long-haired fairy.'

'*Ahhhhhh.*'

Nick looked down at the floor under him but didn't see any blood. It still didn't really hurt, either. Figured that was about the luckiest thing that had ever happened to him, the blade just hitting muscle. Was mostly muscle down there, anyway.

'If we take you to a hospital in Ensenada, we'll lose Bonnett to the Mexicans,' said Lobdell.

'Can he make it back to California?' asked Nick.

'I don't care one way or another. It's you I'm worried about.'

Nick looked down again and saw one drop of blood fall from his crotch to the floor.

'It's only an hour,' he said. 'I can make it.'

'I'm going to go get a car.'

'We'll need a trunk and a gag for Bonnett.'

'I understand that, Nick.'


They ended up in a blue Buick Electra that Lobdell had found in the barn. Cal plates, he said, helping Nick into the passenger seat, and a valid reg in the glove box. Bonnett's Baja car.

On the way to the highway Lucky stopped and stripped the plates and registration off the Country Squire. Took a couple of minutes to swap the plates with the Electra in case Bonnett's car was hot with customs. Grabbed some food and water just in case. Tossed the Buick plates in the bushes a mile down the road.

Then held a steady seventy miles an hour on Mexico State Highway I up past Ensenada and La Fonda and Puerto Nuevo and Santini Las Gaviotas.

Nick pushed the towel harder against his gut. Figured he had a nicked vessel down there after all because the blood wasn't stopping. Not fast, just steady. His throat was dry and he could feel the dust in his mouth. Looked down at his bloody, filthy hands.

'I can't believe this is happening, Lucky.'

'I'd trade it in for just about anything, Nick.'

'Cortazar and all those men,' said Nick.

'Nice wife. Her name is Ynez. I'll come back down and try to explain.'

'Fuck, man, I'm so sorry.'

'We're going to get you to a good American doctor. You're going to be okay and they're going to convict that shithead in the trunk if he lives. All we can do for Cortazar now is help his wife and family. Forget what happened. There's nothing we can do. Not one goddamned thing. You feeling okay, Nick?'

'It's been hurting good since La Fonda.'

'It ought to.'

'I'm going to need a blanket.'

*'You getting cold, Nick?'*

'Not that, just to hide this mess from customs.'

Nick felt the car accelerate.

'I threw some blankets and towels in the back,' said Lobdell. 'Don't worry, Nick. Your job right now is to close your eyes and think about Katy and the family and let me get us to TJ. Try to keep your pulse down.'

'I don't know if I can do that.'

'Try.'

Nick closed his eyes and let his head loll against the window. Road five feet from his head and vibration steady. Sun warm on his face. Thought of Katy and how she felt and knew she'd be furious at him for this but she'd forgive him so long as he lived through it. And Katherine and Willie and Stevie. What a really wonderful family.

'Think my dick nerve got cut?'

'Beats me,' said Lobdell. 'Eleven kliks to TJ.'

'Man, it hurts.'

Nick tried to ease off the pain by moving. Felt his butt slide on the vinyl seat. Felt the sticky wet on his hands. Held out the towel and shook his head. Goddamned thing was heavy.

'Toss it out the window when we get past this car,' said Lobdell.

Nick did.

Lobdell gave him a ghastly smile as he reached behind his seat and came up with a clean towel.

'Take it easy, Nick. Think of something good.'

Nick closed his eyes again, leaned his head against the warm glass. Thought of Katy leading cheers for the Tillers in fifty-five and fifty-six. Thought she was the prettiest girl in the world then until she came down the aisle on their wedding day, April sixth, a year later.

Remembered the class smartass telling him in the locker room back then that any guy who married right out of high school was gypping himself out of tons of good young pussy. Odd the way this had struck Nick. Probably truthful but a slap at Katy so Nick had grabbed the guy's hair and pulled his head into the toilet and given it a flush.

'Yeah, Luck. I just shoved his head in there and flushed it. I remember the way his voice echoed. Like he was gargling in a tunnel or something.'

'That's interesting, Nick. Quiet now.'

'Do you think there's really any truth at all to astrology?'

'You mean that age of Aquarius horseshit?'

'Or it could be not even related. In a direct way.'

'True. Close your eyes again, Nick. Don't talk so much. Just think about the first time Willie caught a fish.'

'Well—'

'Nicky, I don't want to hear about it, I just want you to be quiet.'

'It was at the county fair. He tossed a Ping-Pong ball in a little bowl with a fish in it. I got Stevie a turtle painted blue and Katherine a chameleon on a string. Kids sat in the back of the Red Rocket on the way home and watched it turn colors.'

'I like it when they're that age,' said Lobdell.

'Katy's gonna kill me for leaving that car down there. It cost us almost three thousand dollars.'

'Maybe we can get it back when we come down to see Ynez.'

Nick felt compelled to check his watch and did so. Immediately forgot the time and why he'd wanted it. Shifted again in the seat and felt the deep stab of pain in his guts. Moved the wadded towel and looked down. Seat not blue anymore. Running down the front and into the carpet now.

'I'm not gonna die.'

'There's the TJ bullring,' said Lobdell.

The border wait was long, though Nick had no way of knowing this. He was aware, then unaware, lucid one moment and nearly unconscious the next. Lucky had covered him with a blanket. Nick looked out through the window steamed by his own quickening breath, saw an old man in a white straw hat hold up a purple plaster Buddha bank, kept saying 'One dollar, one dollar,' turning it to show the slot where the coins would go. Saw a kid with a bunch of yellow paper flowers big as basketballs. Saw a Tarahumara woman with a weaving of a man running after a stag. Then he felt Lobdell putting something between the fingers of either his right hand or his left, heard Lobdell explaining he was going to light this just before they got up to the Mexican customs guy, and if Nick could take one puff on it and nod, that would really help them out. Didn't have to say anything or even open his eyes, just take a puff on this cigarette and maybe nod if he could and everything would be cool. Then, Lobdell said, they'd go about fifty yards and have to stop again for the American customs, but Lucky was just going to badge them, say his partner was sick and slide right through. If Nick could maybe open an eye or take a puff for the Americans, that would be patriotic, wouldn't it? Lobdell said Bay Hospital in Chula Vista was a good place, had a friend there once for tonsils. Just up the freeway. Then a minute later, maybe an hour, Nick was aware of a burning smell and he felt the cigarette between his fingers and heard Lobdell order him to take a puff. Nick brought the thing toward his head, got his lips around it. Drew in and nodded once and lowered his hand onto the blanket. He heard Lobdell saying something about his friend getting bad lobster in Puerto Nuevo last night. And maybe too much tequila at the Rosarito. Or not enough *menudo* this morning.

'Tequila,' Nick said softly. Took another puff.

'Hey, he's still alive,' said Lobdell.

*'What is in the trunk?'*

'Jumpers, a jack, and a spare.'

*'Visit Mexico again someday.'*

'Be back before you know it.'

Nick was aware of motion.

'One down, Nick,' said Lobdell. 'One to go. Swim hard, partner.'

Nick never experienced the brief stop at U.S.

Customs. The next thing he knew he was lying flat on his back looking up at the ceiling lights of an emergency room and someone was jabbing his arm and his stomach had burst into flames.

# 31

Andy got Katy and the kids to the hospital in Chula Vista first. Nick was in surgery and the waiting-room desk nurse said it might go long.

He took her aside.

'Is he going to be all right?' asked Andy.

'He's in surgery, Mr Becker. That's all we can say right now.'

'But what's his condition? This is a hospital, you must know what his condition is. If you don't, who does? Is he going to make it?'

'That's all we can say right now. Please sit down, or maybe take a walk.'

Andy started toward Nick's partner, Al Lobdell. Lobdell was standing with a group of what could only be plainclothes cops. He appeared to be explaining something very intense and complex, his hands out for emphasis, his big head forward.

Lobdell broke away and took Andy outside. Told him about the arrest warrant and the tip and waiting for Bonnett at the border. Pulling over his car in National City. Three guys with him. Bonnett making them, the foot chase, gunshots, the knife. Bonnett was critical, too. Shot up. Nick's car shot up, too, two blown-out windows. But Lobdell had brought Nick and Bonnett both right here to the same damned hospital in Nick's car, believe it or not. Faster than waiting for an ambulance.

When Andy had enough for a story he called it in to Teresa from a waiting-room phone, dictating from his notes.

'My God, Andy. Is he going to make it?'

'They won't tell me anything.'

'Are you okay? Are you coming home tonight?'

'It might be a couple of days. I'll call you later tonight.'

He sat with Katy on a yellow sofa. No expression on her big pretty face. Willie and Stevie on either side of her with their feet swinging back and forth. Katherine sat on the carpet finding the hidden pictures in a *Highlights* magazine.

Andy had never seen them this quiet.

David came into the waiting room half an hour later with Max and Monika.

Andy thought his brother looked pale and thin but somehow strong, too. Like rope. Like a man who had gone through bad things and survived.

His mother wore a hopeless expression. His

father stared at the other people in the waiting room as if daring them to give him bad news.

Just then a doctor pushed hurriedly through the back doors and waved the adults into a prayer room. He shut the door.

'I'm sorry but Nick has died.'

Andy felt his body tilting back into the earth. Sensed the deep black hole into which he was falling. Stared into the doctor's pained brown eyes, and opened his mouth but couldn't speak.

'I need to see him,' said David.

'You can't.'

'Of course I can. I'm his brother and an ordained minister. Take me to him immediately.'

Andy saw the strength gathered in his brother's eyes. The same strength Andy had always seen there, but it was focused now. It was narrow and intense. Not broad and radiant. Looked more like fury than love. Ferocious and irresistible.

The doctor nodded, turned, and led the way.

David's world tunneled down tighter with every step. He knew that his God and his faith and his brother would be salvaged or destroyed in the next minute.

He had never been in an operating room. The light was dim. He could sense that a fierce battle had just been lost here. Nick was under a bloody white blanket. A surgery nurse with her back to him was clanking implements from a stand into a stainless steel tray. The heart monitor showed a steady green horizontal line unbroken by life. A man in green scrubs and rubber gloves bloody to the wrists padded in, saw David, immediately turned and walked back out. The nurse folded back the blanket and revealed Nick's face. David's heart dropped and kept dropping. He touched his brother's forehead. Not warm, really, but not yet cool.

David closed his eyes. Felt nothing of his own body now except for his hand on Nick's head. Heard the clink of tools in the tray. Heard the human murmur outside the room. Heard the hum of lifesaving machines and waiting-room music sneaking through the ducts and airwaves. He silently told his God that now was the time to answer his prayer. Now was the time for God to reveal Himself in a visible and useful way. Now was the time to break the indifferent silence. A miracle was required. This modest miracle would be a declaration of His being and His caring. Simple gratitude, not to all mankind but to one man and his family. A way to acknowledge the bottomless love that David had always felt for Him, his God, who had remained reluctant and unavailable for so long.

Your humble servant, David.

Amen.

David heard the breath catch in the nurse's throat.

'Oh my God,' she whispered.

Opened his eyes and followed hers to the rhythm on the scope. Then the pulse within the rhythm.

# 32

Andy spent the night and half of the next day sitting with Nick. Watched the monitors and the rise and fall of his brother's chest. Thought about what David had done. Or God. Or a miracle of medicine.

When he couldn't sit and think one minute longer, Andy trudged to the waiting room. Bought coffee from the machine. Asked about the condition of Cory Bonnett. Critical. No change. No change. He wandered the floors and finally came to Bonnett's room, easily identified by the uniformed San Diego sheriff's deputies standing outside. They turned him away ten feet from the door and gave him no information whatsoever.

Back in the waiting-room lobby Andy poured dimes into the pay phone trying to get information on the car chase and the shoot-out. The more calls he made the less he understood what had happened.

He couldn't locate a single witness. He found

no reports except one – Lobdell's. Bonnett's friends had allegedly sped away in a stolen pickup truck, but Lobdell hadn't been able to get the plates. There were no stolen vehicle reports taken that night in National City. Nobody knew where Nick's 'shot-up' Country Squire wagon was. Or why he had driven his personal car to arrest an international fugitive at the border. Andy began to understand that Lobdell was lying.

National City Police were evasive. Chula Vista Police spent three hours 'confirming' his employment at the *Orange County Journal*. The San Diego Sheriff's public information line rang, then went dead over and over. The Orange County Sheriff's was just as cool and uninformative as they'd been since the day Andy had criticized his brother in print as ordered by Jonas Dessinger.

Nick drifted in and out of consciousness. Andy sat with Katy and the kids. Had lunch with them in the cafeteria. Max and Monika, too. Max tender with the grandchildren. Monika tense as a plucked guitar string.

After lunch Andy saw Sharon Santos crossing the lobby to the desk. Another miracle, Andy thought, that Katy and the kids were in with Nick right then. He headed Sharon off and told her Nick was going to make it. Told Sharon that if Katy saw her she'd put two and two together in about one second. Walked Sharon back to her car.

David had left the night before as if his mission was completed and his skills needed elsewhere.

He appeared stoic and unsurprised. Resigned. This mystified Andy, who had hoped to write with insight about the miraculous recovery of his brother. But there wasn't much to see into. All he had to go on was David's brief narrative of what had happened in the operating room after Nick had died.

*God brought him back to life.*

The doctors and nurses were as puzzled as Andy, but vibrantly pleased. All said this kind of thing happens. Some suggested that the heart monitor was somehow at fault.

No one answered David's office or home phones.

Just after two that afternoon Jonas Dessinger demanded by phone that Andy file a more detailed story than last night's 'prick teaser.' He wanted it by 5 P.M. for tomorrow. And he wanted to know why none of the San Diego County papers had run a story about the hero Nick Becker. Maybe the story from Lobdell was bull-shit. Maybe he was covering something up.

Dessinger ordered Andy to get Cory Bonnett's side of things if the suspect didn't croak first.

Teresa's secretary told him that she had gone home sick. Andy let the phone at their house ring for over a minute but nobody answered. She had sounded fine when he talked to her late last night. Although loaded. Kept asking him when he was coming home. Their wine-and-pot nights often left Andy wobbly in the morning, but Teresa usually popped right out of bed like an Olympian in training. Maybe she'd picked up a flu bug.

Andy had just hung up when he saw a red Country Squire station wagon roll past the smoked lobby windows. Thick layer of tan dust on it. A side window frame crusted with blown-out safety glass. Lobdell with one hand on the wheel and the other dangling a cigarette out the window.

Andy intercepted him halfway to the lobby.

'How is he?' asked Lobdell.

'Okay. Serious but the vitals all steady.'

'We gotta talk,' said Lobdell. Face and shirt and glasses caked with tan dust.

'I think so.'

'Let's sit in the wagon.'

Lobdell gave him the Mexico story just once. Wouldn't let Andy take notes. Wouldn't let him interrupt. Wouldn't let him ask questions. But Andy listened and the story held tight, made sense from the friend named Cortazar to the white-handled switchblade, and Andy knew the truth when he heard it.

'You can't print one word of it,' said Lobdell. He was sweating profusely and smelled bad. 'It'll ruin Nick and me. Make deep trouble for the sheriff, maybe even the U.S. government. Probably get Bonnett off. You gotta go with the story I told you last night. Play it down and let it go away. Stop pestering the cops and the deputies down here. They're with me for now, but any pressure and they can't cover. This isn't any of your business. Nick and I got our man. The public doesn't care so long as justice gets done. You stay out of it.'

'I understand.'

'You have to more than understand it, Andy.'

Andy stared down at the dusty dashboard of the Red Rocket. Noted the thin, sticky blood on the seat between his legs. Turned to see the two blown-out side windows. Looked out the smeared windshield at the bright October day.

He could lie for Nick. Probably get it past Dessinger if he created a source or two, manufactured a few quotes, maybe got Katy to say why Nick and Lobdell had taken down the family car. Bury Dessinger in details, invented or not. Yes, he could probably get away with it, for now. It would be an act of bravery. The same as the rumble by the packing-house when he was a kid, jumping Lenny Vonn. But Andy knew he wasn't a child anymore and this lie would not be a child's thing. It might cost him his career. It would surely lump him in with the politicians and police and businessmen and bureaucrats and thieves and hustlers and murderers he wrote about. With anyone who put what was practical ahead of what was true. It would finally make him a part of the corruption that had always stabbed his sense of right and wrong.

And what would happen to the truth? You couldn't treat it like that. It was too big to go away. Too strong. It would never stay down, no matter how high you piled the lies on top. It would bust loose someday, huge and furious, and it would bite off and spit out the heads of everyone who had tried to keep it down. And how would he explain why he had done such a thing? So a couple of cops could break the law they had sworn to uphold?

'You and Nick mess up and I've got to toss eight years of honest reporting to cover you.'

'It's a real pile of shit, Andy. There's eight dead men. Eight! How many widows and fatherless children does that make – thirty or forty? I don't even know.'

'You saved Nick.'

'He'd have done the same,' said Lobdell. 'It's just reflex. It doesn't mean anything.'

Andy wasn't sure he understood this. 'I'll go with your story,' he said.

'You're doing a good thing even if you don't see it.'

'I never thought lies were good,' said Andy.

'You change when you get older.'

'I feel older now. Feel like I learned something I don't want to know. I feel like hiding.'

'Same shit Adam went through before God kicked him out of paradise.'

'I feel thoroughly kicked out.'

'Me, too,' said Lobdell. 'I can't even remember what it looked like. How old are you?'

'Twenty-six.'

'Get married and have children. It'll distract you.'

Andy sighed and looked back again at the shattered windows, the layer of dust on the camping gear. 'I want some pictures of this car for the *Journal*.'

'Worth a thousand words.'

'You ditch the surfboards and shoot out the windows and spill some chicken blood before you drove it back?'

'Hamburger. Just for you.'

Andy made his desk by four and started writing. He was tired but his thoughts were clear and his fingers flew over the keys of the Selectric. He watched the whole chase and shoot-out unfold in his mind. Saw Bonnett swing the knife into Nick's body. Watched Lobdell struggle Nick and Bonnett into the Country Squire. Heard the big station wagon burning through the streets of Chula Vista on the way to Bay Hospital. Saw the monitor in Nick's hospital room start to blip. Saw the quiver of fresh life in his eyelid. Heard the catch of breath in the nurse's throat. Saw the stupefaction in David's face. He finished the story at 4:55. Triple-spaced, eighteen pages. Thrilling as a movie, he thought, and about as true.

Tried Teresa at home again but no answer. Noted that Chas Birdwell wasn't in his cubicle. Called the hospital and got an upgrade to 'serious condition' for Cory Bonnett.

Went into Jonas's office and said he had a totally bitchin' story. It had bullets, blood, and a hero who died and came back to life. A murder suspect in critical condition. It was even true. All he'd need was ten more minutes to double-check a few facts and corroborate an eyewitness account of the shoot-out in National City.

'It really went down like that?' asked Dessinger.

'Wait till you see my pictures of the car.'

Dessinger eyed him. Hard suspicion versus publishing a great story. Andy stared back with all the blankness he could muster.

'Sit down,' said Dessinger.

Andy sat but the associate publisher remained standing.

'Becker, the Laguna cops have a suspect in the Boom Boom Bungalow murder. They don't have enough to arrest him yet. But they're doing a lineup tomorrow for a witness who was there. Ten in the morning. Nobody knows this but the cops, the Sheriff's, and us. What I figured was, you could shoot the suspect coming into the jail. Hit him with some questions. It'll be our last chance if they arrest him after the lineup. I enjoy those pictures where the guy tries to squeeze through a doorway before the photog nails him. Or they hide behind a coat or briefcase.'

Andy felt a sudden childlike satisfaction in lying hugely to this man and getting away with it.

'You know where they bring them in and out for a lineup, don't you?' asked Dessinger.

435

'If they haven't arrested him, they'll bring him in through the professional visits entrance. Where the lawyers come and go.'

'Be there.'

'We don't usually do that, Jonas. We don't go public with a simple questioning. Not unless an arrest is made.'

Dessinger smiled. 'But I have a good feeling about this one.'

'Who's the suspect?'

'You'll love this. A Tustin High School football coach and history teacher. Howard Langton.'

Andy was always impressed that Jonas actually kept sources and got good information. Hard to believe anyone would trust him.

'I interviewed Langton a couple of weeks ago by phone,' Andy said. 'Janelle Vonn lived with him and his family back when she was in high school. He was her civics teacher.'

'I know.'

'What if Langton wasn't at the Boom Boom, Jonas?'

A trace of confusion crossed Dessinger's face, then passed. 'Hell, Becker, what if he was?'

As he walked back to his desk, a vague but unpleasant sensation spread inside Andy. A feeling that something horrible had just been brought closer to his understanding. Family man Howard Langton questioned in the murder of a man in a gay motel? On the same night a girl who used to live with him was decapitated? Going to put a nasty rash on Langton's reputation, even if the witness is wrong and Janelle was a coincidence. Stink sticks. *High School Football Coach Questioned in Boom Boom Bungalow Murder.*

Chas Birdwell's cubicle was still empty. One of the other reporters told him that Chas had called in sick that morning but had sounded pretty damned healthy.

Andy filed his story with Jonas and banged out a brief rewrite. Filed the rewrite, locked up his desk, and headed across the parking lot to his Corvair.

The evening was cool. Just a soft hiss from the palm trees along Newport Boulevard, almost lost in the louder hiss of car tires on the asphalt. Sleeplessness hit him like a drug.

But he mustered the energy to swing by the Seven Seas Motel in Newport. It was a sun-faded old place that advertised 'Free TV and Refrigeration.' He'd seen it a thousand times in his life, maybe more, on his hitchhiking trips from Tustin to Newport Beach as a boy. With its silhouette of a blue sailboat against a full white moon, it had once seemed romantic. Maybe that was why it stuck in his head a couple of weeks ago when Teresa joked about it with Chas on the phone. Her good buddy Chas, who couldn't do a rewrite correctly, let alone an original newspaper article.

Andy pulled into the Seven Seas parking lot

and followed it around back. Stopped and looked up. The window to 207 upstairs was open. Thin blue curtain puffing in and out. Teresa's new black Mustang directly below it and Chas Birdwell's restored yellow Porsche Speedster taking up two spaces in the far corner of the lot. The ocean breeze had blown Chas's car cover into a heap on the lee side of the Porsche.

Clever, thought Andy. Seven Seas time. Fooled me.

He drove home. Packed a few things. Loaded his manuscripts and typewriter into the Corvair trunk and locked it. Drained a large glass of scotch. Then another.

Called Lynette Vonn.

Andy's heart beat fast with the velocity of counterdumping Teresa. This was Mutual Assured Destruction. He'd never done anything like it.

'I thought I could take you to dinner tonight,' he said.

'I'm working the Bear. Jesse Black's playing. I can't get you in free but I can get you a good seat.'

'I don't want to get in *free*.'

Andy was surprised by his own tone of voice. By how damned mad he was.

'It's your scene, man,' said Lynette.

Andy slammed the front door and walked to the Corvair. Looked back at his and Teresa's place with the giant bird-of-paradise and plantain trees in front. Looked different now. Shabby, not cute.

438

She'd probably fire him. Save her cousin the trouble. Good. He'd go to the *Times* or the *Register*. Goddamned Chas Birdwell. IQ of what, fifty?

Andy got in. Rolled down the windows and lowered the top. Buttoned the boot. Tore down Cress, then up Coast Highway past Mystic Arts World and Janelle's yellow cottage and the old Laguna greeter with his wild gray hair waving at everyone like some demented St Peter at the gates of heaven on earth. Flogged the noisy little Corvair for Huntington Beach with the police band radio turned up loud.

He got a stool near the back. Lynette brought him a scotch and a beer, said she'd move him up for Jesse. She looked less stoned than when he'd last seen her. Hair up and shiny and a petite sleekness to her that he remembered. Miniskirt, nice legs.

A little man sat onstage with a guitar. Strummed away, not a bad voice. A folkie song about love and the end of the world. Made Andy's skin crawl.

'Who's this guy?'

'Charles something,' said Lynette. 'He's supposed to be cool.'

'I'll bet. Cowboy boots that tiny, you have to be cool.'

She looked at him with an expression that assumed the worst. Andy figured it was her go-to look, honed over twenty-one years as a molested girl, a biker, a junkie.

'You know,' she said, 'I really don't want any trouble.'

'You won't get any from me.'

She read his face and the circumstances like a headline. 'What, you broke up with your baby?'

'Kinda.'

'Don't get me in the middle of it.'

'I don't want you in the middle of it.'

'Then why are you sitting here in my night-club?'

Andy took a deep breath. Looked at Charles something. Long hair and scruffy beard.

'I'm trying to gain cruising altitude,' Andy said. 'I thought you were pretty.'

'My sister was pretty. I'm plain.'

'I disagree.'

'Is this about her or me? I want an answer *exactly* right now.'

Andy studied her. Could lie to her easy enough. Like he'd just lied to the *Journal*. But he knew the truth would come up and groin him sooner or later. Sooner, by the hard look on Lynette Vonn's face.

'Both.'

Something then issued behind her hardness. Pride in herself, as separate from her sister. And a pleased acknowledgment that Andy was good enough to sense her separate value.

'I'm better than a lie detector,' said Lynette. 'I

was bummed you wouldn't stay with me that night. I liked that you put the blanket on me.'

'And the gun by the Cap'n Crunch?'

'I don't usually do that. The gun, and that much hash. You'd made me a little nervous.'

Her smile tickled him in a minor way. He felt his anger inch over just a little, like a fat man making room on a bench.

'I'll move you up when Jesse plays.'

Ten minutes later the tiny man onstage stood and bowed. Hardly any applause. He stood there in the stage lights with a wild-eyed glare. Then he slung his guitar over one shoulder and flipped off the audience.

The overly chipper PA voice said, 'Let's hear it for Charles Manson, down from L.A. after recording with the Beach Boys!'

A couple of boos. People getting up, chairs scraping.

'Fuck Orange County!' called out the singer. 'You can smell the Birchers a hundred miles away.'

'Smell your BO,' someone called.

More boos then as the little man wrenched himself and his guitar backstage.

Five minutes later Charlie Manson leaned his guitar case on the bar and climbed into the stool next to Andy. Smelled like weed and beer. He curled his legs onto the cushion and sat on them to seem taller.

'You know Lynette?' asked Manson. 'I saw you talking to her.'

'She's a friend.'

'I'm going to get her to take me home tonight,' said Manson.

'I don't see how.' Andy figured he could provoke tiny Charlie but the singer just smiled.

'Don't get me wrong,' said Charlie. 'Nobody belongs to anybody. That's just middle-class bullshit. I know another Lynette and she's a fox, too. This here Lynette's sister was the beauty queen who got her head lifted. Weird and ugly shit, but life evolves through things like that. Darwin proved it. That's true about me and the Beach Boys, you know. Dennis Wilson's a good friend. I cowrote "Never Learn Not to Love" with him. I was going to do it as an encore but fuck these Republicans. You probably heard it on the radio.'

'Once.'

Manson stared at him. Theatrical eyes, glassy and penetrating. Almost made up for how short he was. 'You don't like music?'

'Some of it I do.'

'You like the Monkees? You know, that mod prefab crap they give you on TV?'

'I thought "I'm a Believer" was a good song.'

'A good song? I auditioned for that show. Producers told me I'd have had a part if I was a little younger. I said, Bob, Bert – I can change just about anything but my age. So they gave it to Micky Dolenz.'

'Was that the one with the cap?'

'No, no. That was Nesmith. What are you drinking? Looks expensive. Why don't you buy me one?'

Andy sensed a straight line to trouble. He had already vowed to prevent Lynette from taking this guy home.

'Sure.'

'Here, take one of these. Be worth something someday.'

Charlie dug into the pocket of his work shirt and handed Andy a guitar pick that said 'Charlie Manson' on it.

'I get 'em free from Dennis's friend.'

Lynette moved Andy and Charlie closer for the Jesse Black set. Put them at a front table full of girls who squirmed and squealed when Black came onstage. Andy recognized orange-haired Crystal from Black's crash cottage at Big Red. He nodded to her but her glazed eyes moved across him without registration.

'This guy's the real thing,' said Charlie. 'Gets more chicks than Ringo. He'll be a star if he can learn how to sing. Sounds like he's got toilet paper stuck in his throat sometimes.'

Black played four songs with just his guitar or piano, then brought out a band. Andy sensed less melancholy in the music than he had at the Sandpiper two nights after Janelle was murdered. Faster stuff now, driving and sexual and funny.

Songs about the road and the groupies and the loneliness you got used to.

They closed with a rocker called 'Hit the Highway,' and let the crowd call them back for a happily chaotic version of 'Louie, Louie' sung in Spanish. They waved and disappeared again but the crowd stood and yelled them out for one more.

This time it was just Black and his guitar for 'Imagine You.'

'Gives me goose bumps,' said Manson. 'It's about Lynette's sister.'

It gave Andy goose bumps, too. 'Don't take Lynette home tonight,' he said.

'Why not?'

'Because I'll kick the shit out of you if you try.'

'That's bourgeoisie bullshit, man.'

'It'll still hurt.'

Andy sat in the back at the bar for the second show. Had several more drinks than he should have. Saw the pay phones back by the rest rooms and thought about calling Teresa at home. She had probably noticed his things missing by now. Probably put them together with Seven Seas time. Probably hopped over to Chas's place to celebrate. Thought about calling Meredith but didn't do that, either.

He called Katy for a report on Nick. Nick was stable and talking. She'd brought the children home that afternoon. Katy went on at length about the miracle that the Lord had worked through David. A priest from a local parish had actually come by to view him. Nick, that is. Like he was a shroud or a bleeding crucifix or something. Andy listened to her and watched the room undulate. Saw dinky Charlie still up there with the Black girls, chattering away while they tried to ignore him.

He called Bay Hospital for a report on Bonnett. Stable and improving. He called Lobdell because he thought the detective would like to know that the elaborate lie he'd written for tomorrow's *Journal* was finished and filed.

Lobdell grunted. Said the sooner they could all forget about it the better, and hung up.

After the show Andy waited outside for Lynette. The crowd surged into the fresh air, bleary-eyed and rich with the smells of smoke and alcohol. It was almost midnight and a light fog had settled. The cars on Coast Highway looked to be in slow motion. Andy saw he could easily run out there. Dodge them like a matador and never get hit. Use his shirt for a *capa*. Beyond the sluggish cars he saw the pier vanishing into the mist. The lights receding out to sea. Only the alcohol and a waning lust for trouble kept him on his feet.

Charlie came out with Lynette and two of the Black fans. Strutted across the parking lot with a big smile on his face. Dwarfed by the women. Even his guitar case seemed unusually large.

'We're off to Lynette's for a party,' said Charlie. 'You ought to come with us.'

'I told you not to,' said Andy.

'Then out of my way, you dumb prick.'

It was like everything he hated happening at once: Clay and JFK, and how he'd treated Meredith, and Janelle in the packinghouse, and the thing Dessinger made him write about Nick, and the Stoltzes and their Orange Sunshine, and what was happening to his parents, and the eighteen thousand dead just like Clay and more dying every day, and destroying the village in order to save it, and the big Lobdell lie, and Seven Seas time. A convergence of everything he despised and wished he could change and knew he never could.

He grabbed Charlie by hair and crotch. Swung him around four times. The guitar case sailed out and crashed on a car. A woman screamed. Andy timed his release of Charlie to take him into the brick wall of the Golden Bear. Leaned back, bent his knees, and let go. Charlie hit hard, a bug on a windshield. Then crunched to the parking lot cursing quietly.

'Oh wow,' said one of the Black fans.

'Is he all right?' asked another.

Andy lost his balance when he let go of Manson. Next thing he knew Lynette had a hold of his arm and was pulling him across the parking lot. Cars wobbling around him. Faces in a swirl. Moon zigging and zagging with each step, stars flying like mosquitoes.

'That's a badass dude,' she said. 'He's done time and he's got friends.'

'Bring 'em *on.*'

'Oh man, there's the pigs. Andy, stand *up*! My car's right across the street.'

The last thing Andy remembered seeing that night was the green shag carpet of Lynette's living room rising up to meet him.

At quarter to ten the next morning he was standing outside the professional visits door at the Orange County jail. He stank and his clothes were wrinkled and he had the worst hangover of his life.

He fumbled a fresh roll of film into his Leica. Checked his watch. Felt the steady pounding in his head. Each throb capped with a high-pitched ping like a blacksmith's hammer ringing off an anvil. Couldn't believe Teresa. Couldn't believe he'd thrown a tiny folksinger against the wall of the Golden Bear. Relieved he hadn't slept with Lynette, though not exactly sure why he was relieved.

At ten sharp Howard Langton came walking up. It took Andy a second to make him. A baseball cap pulled down low and sunglasses and a big varsity jacket. Shoulders hunched up, head pointed straight ahead at the entrance.

Andy raised the Leica, dialed the coach into focus, and shot. The flash made Langton flinch. He stopped completely and his mouth opened.

Andy shot him again. Talked with the camera still to his face and his left hand keeping the focus good and his right finger clicking away.

'Coach Langton, were you at the Boom Boom Bungalow the night of the murder?'

'What the . . . *Andy?*'

'Andy Becker, *Orange County Journal*. Is it true that a witness has placed you at the Boom Boom murder scene?'

'I don't . . . there's no way . . . I can't talk to *you*. Don't take pictures! That's absolutely—'

'Coach Langton, were you at the Boom Boom Bungalow that night or weren't you?'

'I never even *saw* Adrian Stalling!'

'But were you there?'

'I was there but . . . that's missing the whole goddamned point!'

Langton came at him fast. Compact, muscular, balanced. Andy swung open the professional visits door, knowing the sign-in deputy would be there. Shot another picture of the coach as he saw the uniform just inside the door.

Langton stopped again. The deputy looked at him, then at Andy.

'Press isn't supposed to be here,' he said. 'Get out of here, Andy. They're expecting you, Mr Langton.'

Langton stood there, just a few feet shy of the open door. Like a guy stuck in a nightmare where he can't move, thought Andy. Only worse because this isn't a dream.

'Don't write about this until it's over,' said Langton.

'Why not?'

'It's all a big mistake. You just don't see it yet.'

'See what?'

'You don't understand. It's for your own good, Andy. Don't write. Don't run pictures. I'm telling you not to do it. For your family and yourself.'

'Got it,' said Andy.

'No, I can see you don't.'

Andy shot one more picture. Let go of the door and trotted back out to the parking lot. The Leica strap jerked with each step and Andy held the camera to ease the great percussions pulsing through his head. Made no difference at all.

He showered and shaved at the family house in Tustin. Monika made him a big lunch while he told her what had happened. His heart ached more now than in the Seven Seas parking lot. Monika said that things always happened for a reason.

Driving away, Andy thought of Meredith. Remembered that Thanksgiving with the Vonns. How absolutely he had loved her, then didn't. How he'd left her to see more of the world and write about it. Traded her for Seven Seas time. It pleased him that she had gotten what she wanted, the husband and the children and the house.

He turned up the radio and gunned the Corvair down Fourth Street.

He was at his desk at the *Journal* by noon. Three phone message slips that Teresa had called. He whisked them into his trash basket and called the Laguna cops.

Andy's buddy at the LBPD told him strictly off the record that Langton had been picked in the lineup. They were set to talk to him again this afternoon. They weren't in any hurry because Langton wasn't a flight risk. Family man fooling around at the Boom Boom, heh-heh.

Andy's former best Sheriff's Department source wouldn't tell him anything at all.

Next he called David. Asked him what he knew about Howard Langton and the Boom Boom Bungalow on the night Janelle was killed.

David told him what he'd said before. That he and Barbara and the Langtons had been invited to dinner by Janelle. Then the dinner had been postponed by Janelle for nonspecific reasons. David believed that the Langtons had stayed home that night, but wasn't sure because he'd been with Barbara and the children.

'A witness has put him at the Boom Boom Bungalow later that night,' said Andy. 'I saw Langton at the jail about forty minutes ago and guess what?'

'I'd rather not.'

'He admitted it.'

A silence.

'Did he say anything about it to you?' asked Andy.

'I just told you no. It was my belief he spent the evening at home with Linda.'

Teresa appeared in the entrance to his cubicle. He saw the tender fear in her eyes. Swung around in his chair, gave her his back.

'I have to lead with Langton's admission,' he said to his brother.

'Lead with what you have to, Andy. Did you take pictures of him, too?'

'Yep.'

'Heaven help Coach Howard,' David said softly. 'He's supposed to be innocent until proven guilty.'

'He is, David. And he also just admitted being at the scene of an unsolved murder. Maybe he could think about doing his civic duty and stepping forward with what he knows.'

'I guess he'll have to do just that.'

'Is Howard a homo?'

'Why would he be?'

'The Boom Boom Bungalow is a homo bar and motel.'

'I didn't know that. I do know Howard's got a wonderful family.'

Andy hung up and swung back to Teresa.

'We need to talk,' she said.

'I've got a story to write. Give me half an hour.'

'This can't wait.'

'Sure it can. Check-in time at the Seven Seas isn't until what, two o'clock?'

# 33

On Nick's first morning home he had breakfast with his family. He felt weak and disconnected. And grateful for every moment of life that buzzed around him.

He glanced at the Friday *Journal* while Willie and Katherine argued over the last of the Sugar Spangled Rice Krinkles. Katy lectured Stevie for prying the trim off the new Frigidaire again. Everyone tried to keep their voices down out of respect for Nick's scrape with death.

'I told you not to hang on the *refrigerator*, Stevie.'

'I was only trying to get the juice, *Mom*.'

Nick was surprised to read that Howard Langton had been questioned by Laguna PD in connection with the killing at the Boom Boom Bungalow. Andy's story and pictures. According to the article, Howard had admitted to the *Journal* being at the Boom Boom Bungalow that night. No comment from LBPD or OCSD. No comment from

Howard, except Andy's quoted 'I was, but . . .'

Nick remembered Howard's alibi and Linda's shaky corroboration. Thought it was bogus then. Knew it was bogus now, if Howard Langton was really fagging around at the Boom Boom Bungalow. Wouldn't that be something, to question a guy for one murder and he gets nailed for another? The picture made Howard look furtive and hapless, with the hat pulled down and the dark glasses.

Below the Howard Langton story Nick read that navy river patrol boats had wiped out a fleet of Vietcong junks and sampans on the My Tho but lost a minesweeper and suffered 'heavy losses.'

Just before eight Lobdell came by with a bag of Winchell's donuts for the kids and three coffees. The kids argued over frosting colors and sprinkles. Nick and Lobdell sat in the pleasant sunshine on the patio. Katy came out smiling and pulled over an extra chair for Nick's feet. Got a pad. With his legs up the pressure on his groin was less. Her smile had seemed extra beautiful to him ever since he had died. Radiant and rich and fulfilled.

She left them with the coffee and a lingering scent of Tabu perfume that Nick loved.

Nick waited then because he knew that Lobdell hadn't come over to bring donuts.

'The Sears garden-supplies guy called me yesterday,' said Lobdell. 'He saw Roger Stoltz on TV. Realized he was the guy who bought the

453

Trim-Quick pruning saw the Sunday before Janelle Vonn was killed.'

'He didn't recognize his own congressman when he sold him the saw?'

'He's not overly bright.'

Nick considered. 'Really. Stoltz.'

'Really.'

Nick tried to line it out like a prosecutor might. Even though it went against the evidence and what he knew to be true.

'Well, we know he gave her money and gifts, and the apartment in Newport. Kept it quiet as he could. We know Janelle died pregnant. According to Jesse Black, it was a mystery man's child. Say it was Stoltz. Say Janelle was going to shake him down for big dollars. Or ruin his career with a scandal. That's motive.'

Lobdell shrugged, sipped the coffee. 'But we got a witness who can put Janelle with Cory Bonnett, half a mile from where she died, on the *night* she died. They knew each other. On tape we've got them talking about humping, right? He's a violent SOB, too. And we've got a bloody saw blade from the trunk of Cory Bonnett's car trunk, sheets with her blood type on them, and a sleeping bag that's been dragged through the packinghouse where we found her. And Stoltz was in Washington, D.C., that night. Spending more public money to kill Commies in the jungle.'

'Yeah.'

'So Stoltz might have had some real paternity

problems shaping up, Nick. But Bonnett's our man.'

Nick nodded, watched a C-141 lowering toward the Santa Ana air station. An MP friend of his on base said they'd load off coffins fifty at a time. Always did it at night.

'That's a big coincidence he'd buy a Trim-Quick then. Right at that time.'

'Not if he had some trees to prune.'

'I'll talk to him.'

'Maybe I should do that. You rest.'

'Let me. He's a friend of the family.'

Lobdell drank more coffee. Looked up at the big plane.

'They transferred Bonnett from Bay Hospital to General last night,' he said. 'He's in good condition and he's hired Abbott Estle to defend him.'

Nick saw the transport plane disappear behind a liquidambar tree bright orange against the sky. Like the leaves had just pulled it in. Heard the high drone of the engines.

'Lucky?' he asked quietly. 'How are we going to handle Mexico?'

'We were never in Mexico.'

'Bonnett will use it. You know Estle will try to make it a bad arrest.'

'I don't know that at all. What, "My client was down in Mexico running drugs when these rotten deputies came and kidnapped him"? Nick, it's simple. It's one violent drug dealer against two honest cops. We got the stuff from his property with a good warrant. We picked him up at the border on a tip. Like Andy wrote. Read those articles again. Make sure you know exactly what they say we did. If Estle wants to get real involved and send a PI down to Baja, let him. The cops won't help them, I guarantee you that. And the bartenders always know when to shake their heads and act dumb. Nothing changes what Bonnett did to Janelle. We were never in Mexico, Nick.'

Nick had thought it through a thousand times and kept coming up with the same answer. 'Got it.'

'Don't worry.'

A long silence then. Nick watched a hummingbird zoom to a stop midair and stare at him. Throat shimmering in the sunlight like a wet ruby. Heard Katy inside hustling the kids out the door for the short walk to the bus stop. I'm alive to hear and see all this. Amazing. He pictured perjuring himself on a superior court witness stand in front of God and man. Thought a man given a new life might find something better to do with it than tell lies to save his own butt.

'Funny about Langton, isn't it?' asked Lobdell. 'He lies to us about one rap and they land on him for another.'

'His story smelled wrong.'

'But did you figure him for a fairy?'

'No.'

'Hard to tell sometimes.'

'I suppose you could be at the Boom Boom and not be a fairy,' said Nick.

Another silence. Nick felt tired and it wasn't even nine yet. Could still feel the sharp pain up inside him where the blade had cut muscle and bladder and bone. Doctors said they'd never seen a human live through that much blood loss and all the urine and gallbladder fluids backing up inside.

Nick had thought about that last hour over and over. Couldn't remember his last breath. The exact moment he had died. All he remembered were lights. And cold. And his powerful understanding that he was not going to live out the day.

Then nothing. Just a silent blackness that could have been three seconds or three centuries.

His awakening was like coming out of a long and troubled sleep. Except that he understood he had been given the perfect, intimate gift of life. Again.

*Twice.*

'You and Shirley and Kevin doing okay?'

Lobdell shrugged and shook his head. 'Kevin came into my room last night. Sat on the bed, made some small talk. Told me he didn't hate me. Just said it to be mean. To hurt something bigger than him. Said he felt stifled. Said he was taking the pills to feel happy but they made him mean later. I told him I understood how a young man needed to be free. I said Shirley and I might have tried too hard to control him because he was our only one and

457

we had him kind of late. I told him I loved him and I'd help him do what he wanted to do. He said that would be great, and walked out.'

Lobdell looked down at the patio. 'I respect what he's going through. It's not easy growing up. But I miss my boy. I really miss my little boy. Me and Shirley, we'll be okay.'

Nick worked his feet off the pad, straightened in his chair, leaned over and patted Lucky's shoulder.

Early that afternoon Nick drove his take-home car over to Roger Stoltz's house in Santa Ana. The day had gone dry and a warm breeze shivered the eucalyptus as Nick drove down Seventeenth Street.

Marie showed him into the den and helped him into a chair. Pushed an ottoman over. Roger sat at a desk with a look of concern. Necktie loose and a pencil in one hand and a pile of paper in front of him. Marie clicked on a lamp in one corner of the den and went out.

'You look better than I thought you would,' said Stoltz. 'That must have been an incredible ordeal.'

'I feel more than a little lucky to be here.'

'I took flak over Korea once. Missed my balls by about four inches but tore the bottom of my ass up pretty good. Scary feeling to know you're hurt but not know how bad.'

'I didn't know you were shot.'

'Chuck Newman got killed right next to me. Kenton, Ohio. I think about that day a lot.'

'I understand.'

Marie brought in two glasses of lemonade. Handed Nick the tall glass and a small yellow napkin. Roger watched and thanked her. Marie quietly shut the door.

'How can I help you?'

'Tell me about you and Janelle Vonn.'

Stoltz nodded. 'I tried my best to help her.'

'With the apartment and the money?'

'There was more than that.'

Stoltz dropped the pencil to the desktop and stood. Opened the blinds to let in more of the clean autumn light. He sat again and looked at Nick. Said he'd first met the Vonn family not long after Alma's suicide back in sixty. At Nick's house, actually. Remembered how dulled Karl Vonn had seemed. How damaged but proud the girls were. Both Janelle and Lynette, he said, didn't want their hurt to show. Stoltz said he understood in a flash that night, right there in the Becker house in Tustin, that the girls were undergoing some terrible experience. Stoltz had made discreet inquiries with law enforcement and through private sources but hadn't turned up anything solid. The brothers were bad, he said. But at that time no one knew how bad.

'I had the feeling that everyone just wished the Vonns would move on,' said Stoltz. 'Like bad weather. But they stayed.'

Stoltz said he saw Janelle again in the fall of sixty-five. She was sixteen by then. She was in a coffee shop with some older girlfriends. They were all loud and giggly and unkempt and obviously drunk or high. Manager came over to throw them out and Stoltz took him aside, then got the girls to straighten up so there wouldn't be a scene. He told Janelle to call him if there was anything she needed. Next day she did. Said she needed a place to stay. Said some people were after her. Roger checked with Marie and they offered Janelle the Newport apartment on Balboa Island. It was a summer rental for them and would have been empty most of that month anyway. They helped her move some things in. She'd just gotten her license and had a very old Dodge that smoked bad and smelled like wet dogs inside. Loaned her their Mercury, helped her sell off the Dodge. Got a hundred fifty for it. Paid for some dental work for Janelle. Bought her some clothes she needed and some books and records she might like.

'Marie and I weren't able to have children,' said Stoltz. 'So Marie and I got attached to Janelle very easily. Surrogate daughter to us. Marie was a country girl, always taking in strays. Big heart. Janelle was, well, pretty stray.'

Marie helped her furnish the apartment. Talked to her about things. They had her over for dinners. Goofed off together on the weekends sometimes, all three of them. They put Janelle to work part-time at RoMar – clerical. She was smart and competent.

Stoltz said that Janelle didn't like the apartment in Newport Beach. It was supposed to be temporary and she was soon back sleeping in the homes of her girlfriends. Drinking and using pills. Lost touch with her a little.

A month later David called him to say that he was trying to help her. Janelle had spoken highly of Marie and Roger. Would they be willing to encourage her to stop her drinking and pill taking and move in with friends of his – Linda and Howard Langton? Langton was a teacher and Christian and a fine man. Linda a good mother and very principled. Janelle moved in with them in December. Stayed until March. Then she began to split her time between the Newport apartment again and the Vonn place in Tustin.

'During those months, from December through March, that was when the community stepped up to help Janelle,' said Stoltz. 'Andy's article actually started it. She went to David's church, got involved with the youth group, did those Mexico things. Not too long after, she got interested in the Miss Tustin contest.'

Nick watched Stoltz pick up his pencil, tap the eraser on the desktop.

'With all respect, Congressman, were you sleeping with her?'

Stoltz colored deeply and shook his head. 'Jeez. With all respect back, Nick, no.'

'There was some speculation that she was your lover.'

'On whose part?'

'Jesse Black's.'

An injured gentleness settled into Roger Stoltz's eyes. 'That's too bad. It says something about human nature.'

'Why would Black believe that?'

'I don't know. He's a promiscuous and wasteful young man. Maybe he assumes the worst in people.'

'I've read Janelle's letters to Lynette. Janelle told her sister that she never went to bed with you.'

Stoltz looked up with a slight smile. 'Now I know I'm telling the truth.'

'Did you know she died pregnant?'

'I did not know that.'

Stoltz looked out the window, then back to Nick. 'I can't say I'm surprised. She told me about more than one lover. And she spoke of them in a careless way. She was very open to sexual encounters with men. Very open to alcohol for a time. Then pills. Then marijuana. Finally to LSD. They all seem to go together, the sex and the drugs and the music.'

'It's nineteen sixty-eight.'

'She deserved better, Nick. That's all I'll say in terms of judgment.'

'Who were the lovers?' asked Nick.

'Black, the singer. Jonas Dessinger at the

*Journal*. And of course the man who almost killed you, Cory Bonnett. There may have been others. It wasn't a subject I pursued with much interest.'

'Why?'

Stoltz's glance cut. 'Because I hated to think of those losers fucking over a girl that young and damaged.'

Nick nodded. 'Well said.'

A zip of pain issued from low and deep inside. He remembered his face against the warm window of Cory Bonnett's car down in Baja, thoughts about Katy pouring out of his imagination while his blood seeped onto the seat. He looked out the window to the Stoltz backyard garden.

'But she never told you she was pregnant?'

'She did not.'

'Is that an orange tree I see out there?'

Stoltz didn't turn to look through the blinds into his sun-blasted backyard. 'Yes. A navel. Why?'

'I'm wondering how you prune it.'

'With a pruning saw. This sounds like a line of trick questioning, Nick.'

'That's what was used on Janelle's head.'

Stoltz offered Nick a look of disappointment without surprise. Held Nick's gaze with his own but said nothing.

'Did you buy one recently, a pruning saw?'

Stoltz nodded. 'Yes. Sears, up by Knott's. Would have been . . .' He flipped backward through a desk calendar. Nick listened to the pages slap.

'Sunday, September twenty-nine. I'll show it to you if you want.'

'I'd like to see it.'

Nick felt another stab of pain when he pushed off the chair with both arms and came face-to-face with Stoltz.

'It's out in the potting shed, Nick.'

They walked to the living room, then out a sliding glass door. The brightness hit Nick hard. The breeze was warmer and stronger now. The backyard was big and surrounded by a six-foot grape stake fence long weathered to silver gray. There were raised beds for roses and flowers and a network of brick walkways. The navel tree was bright with fruit. So were a lemon, tangerine, and lime. The breeze shifted the leaves one way and then the other in a slow cadence. The potting shed was a rustic wood structure with a sun-faded fiberglass roof. The door was closed and latched but not locked.

'Marie does most of the gardening,' said Stoltz. 'I help with the heavy stuff. We have a gardener once a week for weeds.'

Stoltz pulled the latch away and swung open the wooden door. Held the door for Nick, let the breeze slap it all the way open behind them. Sun on fiberglass. Heat and light. Potting tables and the stacks of empty plastic pots, the watering cans hung on nails in the wall along with the trowels and hand rakes and weed stabbers.

'This was where I discovered the cleaning properties of fermenting citrus juice,' said Stoltz. 'I mixed my first few quarts of Orange Sunshine right here. First batch was an accident. I spilled it, wiped it up, and the wood floor came clean.'

Stoltz pointed out the Trim-Quick. Hanging between an old Rain Bird hose sprinkler and a pair of loppers. Blade folded shut.

'May I?'

'Whatever you need, Nick.'

Nick took it down. Noted the fresh shellac on the wooden handle. Unfolded the blade. Shiny and the bevels of the cutting edges still precise.

'Used once,' said Stoltz. 'On the acacia tree out front, not on a woman's neck.'

'The Sears clerk was just trying to help.'

'I understand,' said Stoltz.

'I am, too.'

'I understand that also. I wonder where Bonnett got his saw.'

'We're working on that,' said Nick. The heat was suddenly suffocating.

'The Santa Anas are kicking up again,' said Stoltz. 'More lemonade?'

'No thanks. I'll leave you to your Friday.'

'You okay, Nick?'

'I still feel like I have other people's blood in me.'

'Let's get back in where it's cool.'

\*    \*    \*

Late that afternoon the children took naps. Nick and Katy locked their bedroom door. Lay on top of their bedsheets and let the warm wind waft through the curtains and onto their skin. Nick rolled onto his side and ran his hand over the smooth capacious flank of his wife. She fondled him lightly for a while and they said nothing.

'Well, what do you know?' she whispered.

'It's working.'

'Working very well, so far.'

'I was worried about this, Katy.'

'I was, too. Guess what?'

'I give up.'

'We had that wild little LSD thingy on the four-teenth? Well, I was supposed to start on the twenty-first, the day you left for Mexico. I waited a few days 'cause of all the worry but snuck off to Doc Blair yesterday. He put a hurry-up on it for us. Nurse called while you were at Roger's.'

*'Kate, really?'*

'Really, Nick. Another bellowing, wailing, screaming, deafening, beautiful little person.'

# 34

That evening Andy stood off Laguna Canyon Road snapping pictures of the convertible and the huge tree. Convertible crushed like a stepped-on beer can. Tree trunk with just a gouge where the little car had accordioned into it, then sloughed off.

Based on early measurements and a witness who said that the Triumph driver never used his brakes, a CHP officer estimated the impact speed at almost one hundred miles an hour.

Andy had been less than five miles away, headed for the family home in Tustin, when the call came over the police band radio in his Corvair.

It wasn't until he brandished his press pass and eased closer to the body that he recognized the driver. Two sheriff's deputies were lowering him from the car to the stretcher. It looked to Andy as if every bone in Howard Langton's once magnificent body had been mashed to dust. Langton was flimsy and doll-like, only his clothes seeming to hold him together. He wore the same varsity jacket he'd worn to the jail the day before and in Andy's picture on the front page of the *Journal* that morning. Yellow leather arms drenched red now. An almost empty quart of vodka clinked into the dirt after him.

'I caused this,' said Andy.

'Out of the way, Becker.'

'I caused this.'

'Right. Out of the way.'

Andy watched them carry Langton past him and slide him into the coroner's van. Wind howling in the eucalyptus. A big red branch ripped away and crashed through the flashing silver leaves. Police radios crackled with news of fresh disaster elsewhere and scores of cars idled in the traffic jam. All eyes bolted to the catastrophe.

Andy found a place down by the lagoon. Sat down on the trunk of a fallen willow and cried.

# 35

On Sunday two of the major county dailies intimated that Howard Langton had killed Adrian Stalling in a lovers' quarrel, then driven his car with suicidal intent as the law closed in around him.

David read them at sunrise with an outraged sadness for his friend and disgust for the papers. Howard now a fag and a killer and a suicide.

Only Andy's *Journal* gave him half a chance. His article suggested that, based on an exclusive interview with Langton, he hadn't killed Stalling. Andy said that the Boom Boom witness could have been mistaken because witnesses faced with lineups often were. Or that Langton could in fact have been seen 'running' from the Boom Boom that night for reasons unrelated to the killing. After all, no one had seen the murder. Andy suggested that Langton was suicidal because he was homosexual and was about to be exposed.

David sat at his kitchen table. Wendy beside

him, with her usual observant quiet. She was an early riser like David, fond of silence and sunrise. The windows faced east and the morning sun spangled the walls with light. He closed his eyes and said another long prayer. Not for a miracle this time. Only for the proper words.

Two and a half hours later David took the pulpit looking gaunt but somehow vigorous. Thin and durable as a whip.

He talked about his friendship with Howard, beginning way back in high school. Talked about Howard's ferocious drive to win. His good sportsmanship. Remembered Howard sticking up for a new kid being picked on. Talked about going their separate ways after high school. Then renewing their friendship when Howard began attending the Grove Drive-In Church. David told of the youth group volunteer work Howard did. Told of the help Howard and Linda Langton had offered to Janelle Vonn. How Howard never had to be asked. He just saw what was needed and did it.

David stepped back from his pulpit. Bowed his head. Whitbrend's move. He saw that many of the congregation bowed their heads, too, but David didn't pray. Instead he stepped back up and sighed very loudly. The microphone picked up the alien sound. The speakers amplified it throughout the chapel. When David spoke again his voice was soft but clear.

'I will not let you remember Howard as a murderer,' he said. 'Let me tell you what happened that night at the Boom Boom Bungalow. I know because I was there with Howard.'

A moan of anxious revelation rose from the congregation. Then silence descended through it like a window slammed shut.

David looked out at his worshipers. Picked out special faces. Andy fifth row with his notebook already out and his mouth half open in disbelief. Max and Monika blank-faced and frozen, like defendants braced for the verdict. Nick and Katy with the three children between them. Nick's expression said that he had just misheard something and was ready for the correction. Katy had apparently missed it altogether, still scuffling with Katherine over a tithing envelope. Darren Whitbrend sat with his wife first row, Darren trim in his white robes and plainly flummoxed. David had told him before the service that Darren was free to join the people who would abandon the Grove Drive-In Church of God this morning. Darren had said he would never abandon David or the Grove. Said it uncertainly. Then twice more, with more emphasis, like he was talking himself into believing it. Denied it three times. From habit, David looked down at second row right, but Barbara had decided it would be best for everyone if she and the children missed this service.

*Dear God, help me move my lips.*

'We got takeout food from Pepito's,' he said.

'The three of us had eaten together before, several times, and we liked the Mexican food. Back in Janelle's cottage we prayed in thanks and ate. We drank wine. Around eight Janelle left with a friend of hers named Cory Bonnett.'

A firm murmur of recognition rippled through the audience, then ended.

*Dear God, help me tell my truth.*

'Howard and I stayed at Janelle's cottage for a couple of hours. Then we drove to the Boom Boom Bungalow to retrieve Howard's varsity jacket. He had left it there a week earlier and wanted to get it back.'

'My God,' someone said.

David felt something in him die as a family of five rose and made their way to an aisle. He wanted to chase them down. Make them sit and listen and understand. Make them forgive.

He heard the faint sound of car engines starting up outside.

'I drove Howard's convertible sports car to the Boom Boom Bungalow because he had had too much wine. I double-parked on Coast Highway by the entrance to the bar and lobby and waited with the passenger door open.'

'The hell with you!' someone shouted.

A mass grumble rose. For a moment David thought the protest was against the shouter.

But a family of six walked out.

Then two elderly couples.

And a family of four.

Tires screeched outside, rubber smoking on the sky blue asphalt.

The grumble stopped. A silence of anticipation, David thought. He heard the intake of his breath from the speakers.

'Less than one minute later,' he said, 'Howard came back. He trotted. He didn't run. The varsity jacket was over his shoulder. He was smiling. He had no time to kill someone. No reason to kill someone. He had never met Adrian Stalling. He had retrieved a jacket from the manager of the motel and come back to the car. That is all. Later I drove him back to Janelle's house and he was able to drive himself home. Howard Langton hurt no one. Do not remember him as a murderer. He was a gentle man who was born with certain faults and talents. As we all are.'

David watched a large clot of worshipers in the front rise and make quickly for the aisles. Then part of the middle section. Those in the back were closer to the main exits and many of them had already left the building. He felt disemboweled.

'Some of us can understand the terrible weight that Howard carried inside,' said David. 'And imagine what it's like to be different. To live in fear. To be hated if the truth is known. Howard asked for none of this. Howard was created by God. There is a place in God's world for imperfection. There must be, because we are all imperfect.'

By then, over half his congregation was gone.

David watched them bunching at the exits, the volume of their voices rising. He saw the anger and disgust on their turned faces.

Special Agent Hambly sat shaking his head. Looking up like David was the stupidest guy he'd ever seen.

Then David's pain began to change into something else. His agony dissolved and a magnificent peace overtook him. Even as his congregation deserted him, David understood that he had now accomplished two things he had always prayed for and wanted. God had worked a miracle through him. And God had given him the strength to speak the truth.

David watched his believers go.

'The service will continue now,' he said. 'For any of you who would like to stay.'

A loud clear voice answered him. 'God bless you, Reverend Becker. I'm staying. Please continue.'

David looked out at the speaker. An old man sitting almost alone now. The one whose platoon had been cut to ribbons by machine-gun fire outside Calais.

'I am an optimist,' said David. 'Our place of worship is half full and we have room for many more. Reverend Whitbrend, please come forward and lead us in prayer.'

Whitbrend swept up from the first row and took the steps to the proscenium two at a time.

\* \* \*

That evening at the family home in Tustin, David sat in the den with his parents and brothers. He'd never felt this self-conscious. Even at ordination at San Anselmo's, the first time he'd donned his robes and presumed to be a man of God. But beyond the self-consciousness was relief. And hanging over both of them like a slow-moving cold front was the dark power of losing someone you loved.

Max freshened David's drink, then his own. 'David,' he said. 'I don't know if anything more needs to be said right now. But that's never stopped me. Just know I love you and I'm sorry about what happened. All of it. I would imagine your career is ruined. But you told the truth and conducted yourself honorably today.'

'Thanks, Dad,' David managed.

'And I agree,' said Monika. 'What you did today was difficult.'

'It sure was.'

A fragile silence.

'I always wanted a queer preacher for a brother,' said Andy.

Shame punched through David like a bullet. He understood that this would be his cost for the truth. He looked down at the carpet and a small smile crossed his face.

'Me, too,' said Nick.

'My God, you boys are horrible,' said Monika.

'They're not so bad,' said David.

Then a long quiet. Ice clinking on glass. The

sounds of the children and TV in the living room. The exhale of the wind through the orange grove outside.

Max stood. 'Well, any other business before we have dinner?'

Andy stood, too. 'I enlisted in the United States Marine Corps yesterday. I'm reporting tomorrow. I want to know why Clay died and I want to write about it. Mom, I'm coming back alive. I promise you I'm coming back alive.'

David saw his father waver. Thought it was booze, then understood it was emotion that had rocked him.

Monika rose and hugged Andy so hard David could hear the joints cracking in her back.

Nick shook Andy's hand and said he was doing a good thing.

David wasn't sure if Andy wanted a hug from his queer preacher brother but he did ask everyone to bow their heads. He said a brief and elegant prayer.

When he was done Andy hugged him.

# 36

## *1970*

Orange County Superior Court, Department C-7.

'The defendant will rise.'

Cory Bonnett unfolded from the table and stood. Suit and tie. Hair cut short. Trim mustache. Judge Sewell had allowed him to be tried unmanacled until his first interruption or indiscretion. Six weeks later Bonnett's big freckled hands still hung free at his sides.

Nick sat second row behind the prosecutor's table. He had testified for three days in August, almost a month ago now. Then once last week during redirect. Had memorized Andy's articles and huddled with Lobdell. Lucky had called it 'synchronizing our watches.'

Abbott Estle couldn't catch them. Nick denied that he had ever gone to Mexico for any reason connected to Cory Bonnett. Lobdell corroborated him and he corroborated Lobdell. Estle's questions came to sound redundant, then badgering. His inferences unlikely. The People's objections were sustained. The harder Estle climbed, the faster he slid.

Bonnett stared at the floor during most of Nick's time on the stand. The few times their eyes met Nick saw contempt and hatred and arrogance. Nick held the look and gave them back.

Bonnett never testified and the evidence buried him.

*Janelle as informant. Bonnett as target. A sexual relationship. Janelle's disloyalty. Janelle's pregnancy by another man. Bonnett's jealousy. The witness who saw him follow her into the Sav-On parking lot and drive her away a few minutes later in his white Cadillac. Bonnett's disappearance. Bloody sheets – Janelle's blood type. The victim's three flesh-and-blood-packed fingernails – Bonnett's blood type. Bloody saw blade – Janelle's type once again, ladies and gentlemen, do you see a pattern emerging? Strangled in a Newport Beach apartment where the maid had seen them the Friday before she died. Dumped and decapitated in the SunBlesst orange packinghouse in Tustin. White Cadillac seen at packinghouse by witness Terry Neemal. Man seen carrying something body-sized into packinghouse by Terry Neemal. Yes, Terry Neemal is a transient. Transients lack homes, not eyes. Thank you, Mr Neemal. That will be all. No, Mr Neemal, thank you but you're finished. Yes, Mr Neemal, you're free to talk to the reporters.*

Nick could tell by the jurors' expressions that they believed. Sewell, too.

And they should, he thought. This, the part that matters, is all truth.

'Mr Bonnett, do you have anything to say before the verdict is read?'

Bonnett's voice was clear and strong. 'I didn't do it.'

'You were offered a chance to set us straight. Is that all you have to say, Mr Bonnett?'

'What else matters?'

'Noted. Foreman, have you filled out the verdict forms?'

'Yes, your honor.'

'Clerk, please read the verdicts.'

The clerk was a trim middle-aged woman with dark hair and frown lines around her mouth. She looked once at Bonnett. Once at Sewell. Then read:

'We the jury in the above-entitled action find the defendant, Cory Bonnett, guilty of murder in the second degree. On the charges of forcible rape we find the defendant guilty. On charges of assault with a deadly weapon upon a police officer we find the defendant guilty.'

The reporters bolted for the nearest telephones. Karl Vonn walked out with them.

'Bailiff,' said Sewell, 'please bind the prisoner for transport back to the jail. I'm going to set a sentencing date of September twenty-six. That's two weeks out. I've got some thinking to do and I want the time to do it. I would like to thank the jury again for their patience and insight. Court is adjourned.'

Nick shook hands with the prosecuting

attorneys. Shook hands with Lobdell and a couple of detectives. Sent one last long stare back at Cory Bonnett as the bailiff cuffed his hands behind his back.

'The defendant will rise.'

Nick watched the sentencing from a seat near the rear exit. Watched the reporters get ready to run for the phones. Funny to see that gaggle and no Andy. PFC Andrew Becker now stationed in Cu Chi province.

Nick watched the Honorable Edgar Sewell behold Cory Bonnett with hard unblinking eyes.

'Mr Bonnett, I've spent some hours thinking about you and what you did. I won't say I spent any sleepless nights wondering what your sentence should be. Though I spent a sleepless night or two after seeing the pictures of what you did to that girl. For the crime of murder in the second degree I sentence you to forty years in state prison. For the crime of forcible rape I sentence you to twelve years in state prison, to be served consecutively. For the assault with a deadly weapon upon a police officer I sentence you to five years in state prison, to be served consecutively.'

Nick heard the intake of breaths. Edgar Sewell continued to stare down at Bonnett.

'Mr Bonnett, the California penal code calls what you did a crime of passion. We know that passion can destroy just as surely as it can create.

This is a crime of jealousy and fury and waste the likes of which I hope never to hear about in my courtroom again. You will be eligible for parole in fifteen years should you demonstrate such fitness to the Board of Prison Terms. Use that time, Mr Bonnett, to reflect on the irrevocable damage and horror in what you have done, and upon the great potential you stole from young Janelle Vonn. Use that time to find your God and your soul and see if they can help *you* find a way back to your humanity again. Mr Bonnett, you have acted with what the law calls an abandoned and malignant heart. With what remains of your life see if there is anything you can do through which you can earn forgiveness and not just punishment. If not, Mr Bonnett, we'll see you in fifty-seven years. Some of us will. I'll be dead and you'll be eighty-one years old, which is even older than I am now.'

Nick took the stairs down to the first story. Heard the reporters storming out behind him. Saw Sharon marching toward the DA's office with an armful of files held to her chest.

He stepped out into the hot September afternoon. White thunderheads towered in the southeast. Up over Yuma, thought Nick. The rain will chase all the doves south. Thought of standing by a Yuma cotton field with his mom and dad and David and Clay and Andy, shotguns ready. And the way Max could spot those birds so far away. Just dots in the sky coming toward them.

The boys shaking with excitement and trying to find their safeties and Max chuckling while he swung and dropped a pair that landed right on the railroad tracks. Monika a good shot, too, but her heart wasn't really in it. David didn't like the killing. Clay the best shot of the four boys and didn't mind the killing at all. Andy involved but somehow outside himself, too, watching like he always did, like he'd be tested on it someday.

In Nick's mind the railroad tracks in Yuma became the railroad tracks running by the SunBlesst orange packinghouse. He knew they always would. Knew the packinghouse would connect to everything that would ever happen to him. As it had since he was sixteen.

He'd closed his first case.

Cost eight men their lives but he'd done it.

Caused immeasurable waves of sorrow and loss but he'd done it.

Cost him his own life but he'd done it.

For Janelle and for himself.

# 37

## *Here and Now*

'Listen to me, Nick. Everything we thought about Janelle Vonn was wrong.'

'Explain yourself,' I said.

Andy cocked his head to the side a little. Leaned closer to me. Vietnam had wrecked his hearing. A bomb in a tunnel, Cu Chi province. Enough earth between the bomb and Andy that he didn't get any frag, but the pressure blew his eardrums. Got bad hearing and a Purple Heart for it.

'I don't think Bonnett killed her, Nick.'

So there it was. Thirty-six years. Fast as an eye blink back to Janelle.

'You'll have a hard time proving that to me,' I said. 'That was a good case, Andy. We nailed it. The jury deliberated, what, two hours? We might have worked around the arrest a little, but that's it.'

'I'm not talking about the arrest.'

I heard the pigeons cooing and saw the sunshine coming through the slats of the packinghouse. Felt

483

the hot Santa Ana wind blowing in the orange trees outside. Saw Andy standing there with his camera and the terrible thing that lay between us. Clear as the day it happened.

Andy shook his head and looked at me with some irritation. 'Maybe we should take a drive, Nick. Kind of hard for me to hear with those waves crashing out there.'

The young couple at the next table were looking over at us. Probably never heard of Janelle Vonn. Just these two old farts with menus at arm's length talking about the past. Sixty-two and sixty-six. One hard-of-hearing, the other still sometimes got light-headed from a rumble in an orange grove fifty-something years ago.

We took Andy's convertible. He put the top down, so I knew the bit about the waves was BS. He didn't want anyone hearing this. Andy can't sit still anyhow. Always eager about the next thing. Sixty-two years old and still strong and skinny. Was always wound tight but he came back from Nam with this weird energy he can't turn off. Went there to understand what happened to Clay, to bring something of Clay back to us. Made him more like Clay. Faster than before. A little reckless. A little mean. He's a big-time writer now. Makes a ton. Lives in Laguna on the beach. Novels and screenplays and articles in magazines that smell like cologne. Been married to Lynette for thirty-something years now. Six kids.

'I was in Washington last week doing some

interviews with Homeland Security,' he said. 'Stoltz was having a party so he invited me. I'm no fan of Stoltz and I don't like Georgetown parties, but Lynette *does* like parties, so I figure what the hell? Plus, Stoltz is one of the reps on the Homeland oversight committee, so I figure maybe I'll learn something interesting. It's a boring Georgetown party. Not even Lynette can find anyone fun to talk to. Then I get to talking with this lady. A little younger than me. Sixty-ish. Turns out she's Stoltz's secretary from way back in sixty-eight. I remember her – Martha. She's worked for him for thirty-six years. She started out as his Washington office receptionist.'

I had a hazy memory of having talked to someone named Martha in Stoltz's Washington office back in October of sixty-eight.

Andy steered through the cute San Clemente streets. Picked up I-5 heading south and gunned it. His fancy new German car has one of those transmissions right on the steering wheel. Screams through the gears and you never even take your hands off it.

'So Martha and I are talking and she says – this comes right out of nowhere, Nick – she says that she wrote the telegram to me on the Janelle murder story. Now, I always thought it was an odd telegram. Kind of formal and stiff, and you know how Roger is, he's a pol. He can always say the right thing. She said she thought about that telegram a lot because she was so young at the time, and she'd known when she wrote it that it didn't sound right. Didn't sound like a man who had just had a friend murdered. She said that over the years she wrote more than a few telegrams for Roger. Common for busy congressional reps. The routine stuff, like condolences, congratulations, birthdays, whatever. The pols all know that an official Washington, D.C., telegram makes people outside the beltway feel important. Makes them think their elected officials are paying attention. But this was the first one she'd ever been asked to write. She was twenty-four. Said she worked on it for over an hour but knew it came out stilted and wrong. So, after thirty-six years Martha apologized to me for a poorly written telegram.'

Andy zoomed south past the nuclear plant at San Onofre. He still had a shortwave radio mounted in the car to track the law enforcement chatter. Hadn't turned it on.

'Okay, Andy,' I said. 'Martha wrote you a telegram because Stoltz didn't have time to do it himself.'

Andy looked at me, then back at the road. 'She was so unhappy with it she actually called him to get some help with it. Laughed when she told me that. Stoltz was home in California by then. This is two days after the murder, right? Well, Marie answered and said Roger was sleeping. He was exhausted. He'd flown between LAX and Dulles three times in three days. Being a representative was the hardest work Roger had ever done. Made running a business look easy. Marie said the telegram was okay. Send it. If Roger was ever unhappy about it, she'd take the blame.'

'Okay.'

'Nick, I thought about that off and on for the next five days. I'm trying to do my Homeland interviews but my mind keeps wandering back to what Martha said. Why does a congressman fly across the country three times in three days? Why not just stay put one place or the other? So I called a friend with United Airlines security. He can't go back that far with records. So I talk to some people in the Congressional Travel Office, since they pay work-related travel. They tell me Stoltz was in Washington, D.C., the day Janelle was killed.'

'We know that.'

Andy gunned it. Campgrounds and railroad tracks flashing by at a hundred miles per hour.

'But he was in California *that night*.'

'I'm listening now.'

'I checked the House of Representatives Detailed Statement of Disbursements for July through December of sixty-eight. On October first Stoltz attended the House Committee meeting, like his Tustin secretary said he did. What she didn't say is that Stoltz flew home on a noon flight that put him back in California at four P.M. Why not? Because she had no idea. Martha didn't, either. She told us way back then that Roger was

487

in Washington that day. She *still* thinks he was. He flew out. It's right there in the disbursement log. Public record.'

I nodded. 'Okay, so Stoltz wanted to wow you with a personal message from the nation's capital when he was really in California taking a nap. He fibbed. So what?'

'It puts everything in a new light, Nick. Stoltz and Janelle. Everything he bought her. She being pregnant. The scratches I saw on his hand later that week. The fact that Roger Stoltz and Cory Bonnett both drove white late-model Caddies. Damn, Nick – he'd bought a Trim-Quick two days before someone cut off her head with one. Now I find out he was right here in California that night.'

I remembered what Bonnett had said to me that day down in Baja. While he lay in anguish on the floor with his knee shot out and the switchblade palmed in one hand.

*Followed her to Tustin.*

*Why?*

*Worried.*

*Followed her but didn't kill her?*

*Yeah.*

*Just looking out for her, like a big brother?*

'Andy,' I said. 'None of that dents the case against Bonnett.'

'This might.'

Andy reached across me, pulled a wadded-up plastic supermarket bag out of his glove compartment. Got it open and dangled a clear plastic bag with a black and yellow disposable razor and a couple of balled tissues in it. Smiled.

'Goddammit, Andy.'

'Remember the flesh underneath Janelle's nails?'

'Type A. Same as Bonnett's.'

Andy looked at me again. Hooked those blue eyes into me. 'Nick, forty percent of the population has type A. That was big forensic news in sixty-eight. Today it's a joke because we can type the DNA. Right, Mr Former Homicide Detective and FBI Man?'

I put it together.

'You took a leak in Stoltz's Georgetown bathroom and stole a razor. To type against the flesh under Janelle's nails.'

Andy shook his head. 'Worse. I wasn't thinking fast enough in Georgetown. So I stole a whole trash can off his curb in Tustin at five-thirty yesterday morning. Trash day. Stunk up my Yukon but I got what I wanted.'

'Goddamn, Andy.'

'Roger will be damned if I'm right about this. You know how it is the last time you shave with a disposable? You have no reason to rinse it out very well. You're not using it again. You're tossing it. There's gunk in there, Nick. Could see it with my own two eyes. And I found some pink disposables, too, so I don't think this was Marie's.'

We pulled off at a vista point and watched people throw bread to the seagulls. Cooler and windy out there on the point with the Pacific surging blue below and the gulls crying and diving for the food. I started to get a feeling like I had that day in the Chula Vista hospital thirty-six years ago. When I knew I was going to die and there was nothing I could do about it. The feeling that something's already happened and you're just there to see it through.

What if I'd gotten the wrong guy?

'So you're asking me to get it reopened,' I said.

'I'm giving you first crack at it. If you don't want to, I understand. But it would be a good thing, Nick, if you put the wrong guy away but managed to get him back out. And also a good thing if you nailed the man who really did it.'

'Thirty-six years later.'

'I know you took her fingers, Nick. Gershon told me the day after the autopsy. I know the Sheriff keeps that kind of stuff frozen for murder cases. I did an article once on the "felony freezer" and all the oddities you guys kept in there. I didn't write about the fingers. Anyway, I can petition the county for them and the sample scrapings. If they say no to me, I'll hire a defense lawyer for Bonnett and he'll get his hands on that stuff. Either way, I can hire a private lab to cook the DNA and compare it to what's between those razor blades. If Janelle's fingernail flesh comes up Bonnett, fine. I was wrong. But if it matches the razor, I'll have a helluva story on my hands. Young cop. First case. Girl he knew. Wrong guy in prison for thirty-six years and counting. Congressman with a young girl's blood on his soul while he takes care of Homeland Security. Old cop finally gets his man. I admit I could never stand Roger Stoltz. But I couldn't make up a better story if I wanted to, Nick.'

Andy dropped me off back at the Fisherman's.

'I'll think about this,' I said.

'I bet you will, brother. Love to Katy and all.'

'Back to Lynette and yours.'

I couldn't pass up the obvious question. 'Andy, have you told Lynette?'

'Yeah. She said you'd get it reopened.'

'Why did she think that?'

'She said you'd do the right thing.'

But I didn't think about it long. I thought about it for a lot less time than I spent on the witness stand perjuring myself in nineteen sixty-eight.

I was on good enough terms with the new sheriff to get the fingers and scrapings out of one of the felony freezers. Homicide evidence is kept permanently for occasions exactly like this one. It took some paperwork that few people would ever see. An after-hours thing. Finally boiled down to just me and a deputy and the freezer. I hadn't walked those halls for thirty years and they made me think of Sharon and that day I went on the acid trip and Lucky Lobdell. Lenny, Casey, and Ethan Vonn. Janelle. All of it came blowing back like it was driven by high wind.

I arranged the thumbs and fingers and scrapings on the light table. They had all turned black with age. Strange to choose from among them like they were jewels to be set. I took off one glove to touch one of Janelle Vonn's fingers with my own. Just to actually touch her skin with my skin. Nothing I had seen as a homicide detective or later, as an FBI special agent working on VICAP or behavioral science, stilled my soul like those black thumbs and fingers. My heart was in my throat and there were tears in my eyes.

Using tweezers, I chose one finger with a shred of what I knew to be human flesh still lodged under the nail. And one separately bagged piece of frozen skin.

I packaged my two samples. Got the Trim-Quick and blade out of Property, too. What memories those brought back.

I arranged the cold things in my cooler for the trip down to Regentech Laboratories in San Diego. I know the director there, Cristin Russim. She testified for the bureau a few times and she's the best forensic DNA scientist I know. Even better, I knew I could trust her to keep this one quiet. Which was why I paid for the job myself. Didn't want the Sheriff's Department involved yet. They'd retest it, anyway, if I found what I thought I'd find. I told Cristin absolutely nothing about the case. Just dropped off the black finger and flesh and used tissues and the disposable razor and asked her to tell me who was who.

Left the rest to her.

* * *

Katy and I stayed the week in San Diego. Did Sea World and the Wild Animal Park and the Embarcadero. Saw a play and went to a concert. Shopped. Wrote postcards to the children and grandchildren. Looked forward to getting back to Newport Beach. We got a cozy little place there ten years ago when the bureau finally sent me back to Orange County. Small and only one place to park but right on the sand at Eighteenth Street.

Cristin called me that Thursday evening. Said the DNA from under the fingernails was the same as in the razor. Same as in the tissues. Same human being. Good markers, easy ID. She'd say so in court if legendary crime fighter Nick Becker asked her to.

'Might take you up on that,' I said jauntily.

I told her I'd be right over to pick up the report and the finger. She said she'd frozen the finger quickly after testing and it was good as new.

'You're white,' said Katy.

'It was Stoltz.'

'There's got to be some mistake, honey.'

'There was. I made it.'

'What are you going to do now?'

'I don't know.'

# 38

The next evening I drove up to the Stoltzes' house in the Tustin hills. Nice place, most of it behind a wall but no gate. You can drive right in.

Tustin's different now. Orange trees long gone. Even out in Bryan and Myford and Irvine not a grove left. Houses packed in tight. Car dealerships and franchised everything, one big shopping opportunity. Doesn't have a smell anymore, not like oranges anyway. Used to be a sign on the Fourth Street freeway exit that said 'Welcome to Tustin – the Beverly Hills of Orange County.' Not really sure who came up with that one, or when they took it down.

Roger and Marie were in the front yard. Big straw hats and baggy nylon pants. U.S. Representative Roger Stoltz closing in on seventy-seven years, serving out his last term. Marie even older than that. Millionaires fifty times over from Orange Sunshine cleanser but still lived where they'd always lived. Bigger place is all.

They stared at me as I pulled up. Waved when I got out. Marie went into the house and I heard a screen door rattle shut.

'Hello, Nick Becker,' said Roger. 'What brings you to these parts?'

I shook his hand. Strong, warm, and dry. 'That's a hard one to answer.'

'Is that a fact?' He looked at my briefcase. Frowned.

'Maybe you and I should talk in private, Roger.'

'Whatever you say. But Marie went to get lemonade for us so don't hurt her feelings. Here, sit in the shade a minute and be social.'

I set my briefcase down next to a round redwood picnic table under a magnolia. Four little curved benches. Fresh lacquer on the wood and the magnolia heavy with big white flowers.

Stoltz sat and stared toward the wall. Still had the crisp mustache. His black hair had gone white and waxy but it was still there. Sharp eyes, no glasses. Little U.S. flag pin on his shirt pocket. You see those a lot these days. I thought of Terry Neemal's description of the man he saw that night. Walking up the steps of the SunBlesst packinghouse with something bulky slung over his shoulder. *Regular-sized.*

We didn't elicit that testimony because Cory Bonnett was six-four. Abbott Estle found it but the People argued that it was night. Neemal was a hundred and fifty feet away. What's the difference in inches between six-four and 'regular-sized'? Two inches? Four? In the dark with something big over the shoulders?

'Janelle again?' asked Stoltz.

'Yes. Janelle.'

Marie came from the house. A stocky Latino walked behind her with a tray and three tall lemonades. Marie was hunched and very small. Took her forever to get to the little table. The helper set out the drinks and napkins. Glanced at me. Headed back up the walk. Marie took one long look at Roger and a short look at me and said, 'I'll be in the house if you need me.'

'Thanks, darling.' He raised his cheek to her and she kissed it. Barely had to stoop. Labored back up the walkway to the porch.

'So,' said Stoltz. He was still staring at the wall. 'I saw Andy and Lynette last week. My party in Georgetown.'

'He told me.'

'He had quite a little talk with Martha,' said Stoltz.

'She told him about writing your telegram.'

Stoltz smiled. His teeth were small and even and surprisingly white. 'I remember that. Poor girl so worried about everything. Best staffer I ever had for running an office. And she really understood the Communist threat. Kept her thirty-six years, which tells you something.'

'She told Andy about trying to call you for help with that telegram. The telegram about Janelle.'

He looked at me again. 'Yes, I remember that.'

'And Martha mentioned you coming and going three times in three days, couldn't find you. Andy thought that was odd. Andy talked to the Congressional Travel Office. Checked the House disbursements statements for October sixty-eight and found out you flew back to California about four P.M. the day Janelle was killed.'

'Really?'

'Really.'

'I've forgotten.'

'Everyone told us you were in D.C. that night, sir.'

'Are you sure about this plane flight?'

'I'm sure.'

Stoltz considered me. Forgot about the wall. Turned to face me squarely. 'I'm failing to see the point. This proves nothing, Nick.'

I opened my briefcase, which turns on the tape recorder. Set a small plastic first-aid box on the lacquered redwood tabletop. Popped it open. Inside there were no scissors or tape or disinfectant. Just dry ice and a small plastic bag with something black in it.

I set the bag on the table. Stoltz looked at it, then up at me, then down at the finger again.

'This proves something,' I said. I set one of the Regentech reports on the table. Put the bagged finger on top of it. Black on white. 'I had a private lab cook up the DNA from the flesh under Janelle's fingernail. That finger right there.'

Stoltz stared at me with a cagey glitter in his

eyes. 'What, some amateurish laboratory in San Diego?'

'One of the best. The flesh is yours.'

Stoltz looked at me like he was intrigued. 'Okay. Just *say* that's true for the sake of argument. Say that flesh is mine. Even say I killed the girl. What would you do?'

'Get Bonnett out.'

'Why?'

'Why?'

'Yes, why? He killed at least two men in Mexico, you know. Beat his parents. Sold God knows how many pounds of dope to this country's youth. To young people like Janelle. Nick, justice has been done.'

'Not with you sitting in your front yard it hasn't.'

'Would you ruin your own career over a nothing like Cory Bonnett?'

I shrugged. Pushed the lab report and finger closer to him. Made sure the finger was pointing right at him. Crude, but at the bureau we learned this kind of thing really works. Hit the guy with something physical. I'd wrapped the bloody old Trim-Quick in a clean pillowcase. Took it out of my briefcase and set it beside the report. If the SunBlesst packinghouse were still standing I'd have taken him back there for this conversation.

Stoltz looked at these things. Frowned. Still a little detached.

'A reputation is all a man really has, Nick.'

'Touch the finger if you want,' I said. 'Take it out of the bag if you want to.'

Stoltz stared down at it. Touched it through the plastic. Looked back at me. He had a very different expression on his face by then. The look of acceptance.

I pictured myself as a small red sailboat beginning to circle Roger Stoltz's drain. Circling the current of his logic and his despair. Closing in on the center. The black suckhole of corrupted reason that justifies a horrible act. I've spent a lifetime learning what these drains look like. How to enter and exit them without drowning. Everyone's got one. Some are small and easy to find. For small lies and small secrets. But some are enormous and cunningly concealed. Like an underground river. They can carry anything you can imagine. And sometimes much more.

Stoltz was seventy-six years old. He'd been waiting thirty-six years for this.

So I let go and began to circle.

'Sure, Roger,' I said. 'A man's reputation is important. But some people have a conscience, too. You do. I've known it for sixty-something years. You've done nothing but good things for me and my family.'

'Yes. And I did think very highly of Janelle.'

'I know you did. And I understand why you had to do it, Roger. I understand what it must have been like.'

A gray tiger cat jumped into Stoltz's lap. Skinny,

green eyes. Could hear his motor from where I sat. Stoltz ran a gnarled hand down its back and tried to fix me with his tough old eyes. But he blinked.

'I loved her,' he said. 'Really, genuinely, truly loved her. I offered her everything I had. The material things were the least of it.'

Stoltz's forehead wrinkled with sad sincerity. 'I offered to divorce Marie and marry Janelle. To provide her with a fine home and travel and an education and the means to raise her child. She didn't even know who the father was! Do you know what it feels like, Mr Becker, to offer *everything* and be refused?'

I studied the intensity on Stoltz's face. I couldn't find even a trace of doubt in it. He believed. And I knew then, from a lifetime of hearing confessions, that Stoltz would tell me everything. It's always the guys who think they were right who tell you everything.

'The tragedy of Janelle and me, Mr Becker, were the drugs and the men who gave her the drugs. Starting with her brothers. The drugs ate her away from inside. You saw her beauty. I know you did. My *God*, when she was crowned Miss Tustin! But you never saw inside her, did you? Let me tell you, she was empty. Black. Janelle was a wasteland of everything this life can offer. A wasteland of life itself. Of all my love and all my plans. Of her own potential. And I was supposed to let that one small but tremendous hope slip down an abortionist's drain? It would have been monstrous. I had to do something.'

Destroy the village in order to save it.

Destroy the woman in order to save her.

Destroy a life in order to save it.

'I do understand your logic, Roger.'

Stoltz looked at me then as a man of faith. A man who wanted to share that faith. Have it believed by someone other than just himself.

The cat hopped onto the table. Nosed Stoltz's lemonade glass.

'She came to Tustin that night and I met her in the Sav-On parking lot. Took my Caddy to the Newport apartment. A pretty blue sweater and a black miniskirt. Boots. Hair so fresh and dark and sweet. My God, she was beautiful. She told me she didn't want to see me again. Wanted to completely break off our friendship. She told me I'd become too forceful and demanding. I wanted too much from her. She had bought me a St Christopher pendant to protect me on my "travels" away from her. She put it around my neck. And I don't know what happened at that point, Mr Becker, but I suddenly became more forceful and demanding than I had ever been. More than I had ever imagined I could be. It was more than just sexual. More than just anger. I was compelled. I was possessed. It was the first and only time I did that to her. She resisted. It was an unbearable pleasure to overpower her. And I'll admit, Mr Becker, I made a mistake. I overreacted. I panicked. When I put her in the trunk I saw the new pruning saw that had fallen out of its bag. The packinghouse seemed like a good place to take her. I don't know what I'd have done if the lock had been locked. Threw her purse in the grove. And it seemed to me, Mr Becker . . . it seemed to me—'

Stoltz paused and fixed me with his dark eyes again. The cat put its nose to the finger, sniffed twice. Then to the saw, sniffed twice. Curled away in minor fear and hopped off the table.

'It seemed to me that the best way to protect myself was to do something hateful to her. Do something that only a man who hated her could do. So, the saw. Because it was not something that a man who loved her would ever do.'

'That's reasonable.'

'The blade came off and I took it. I had no idea what to do with it but I knew I might use it. An hour later I had showered at the Motel 6 on Tustin Avenue and I sat on the bed and looked at the blank TV screen and figured I'd blame it on Cory Bonnett. I had to do something. I'd already had a private eye investigate him for me. I wanted to know who Janelle was seeing. About bankrupted me, there were so many. Cory seemed most believable as a murderer. As soon as he heard about her he left the country. He knew the police would suspect him. Which made it easy to get in and out of his garage. Good luck for me that we drove similar cars. Very good.'

'Where did you get the saw you showed me back in sixty-eight, in your potting shed?'

'Bought it out in McLean, Virginia, a few days after Janelle. Checked it through in my suitcase. It came in handy, didn't it? More lemonade?'

'Sure.'

'Marie!' Stoltz's eyes were glassy with tears and his voice cracked so he had to call her again.

'So now what, Becker?'

'I'll talk to the DA. If you'll sign a confession it will make things easy for everyone. If not, you'll be arrested and tried.'

'On the basis of what?'

'Andy's conversations with Martha and the ticket purchases. The DA will order another DNA comparison and the flesh under Janelle's nails will be shown to be yours. The tape recording I just made might not get into evidence but it will sure get the DA investigators pointed in the right direction.'

The screen door slammed. Marie came slowly toward us. The man behind her had a tray with a pitcher on it. I put the finger and saw and report back into my briefcase in plenty of time.

When she was done pouring the lemonade Marie smiled at me. Kissed her husband again and began the long journey back to the house.

'I'll need a few days to get things in order around here,' said Stoltz.

'No. We're going now. It took me thirty-six years and I'm not waiting one more hour.'

'Afraid I'll run?'

'Or kill Marie and yourself.'

That glint in his eyes again. 'Let me take a leak. Put on some decent clothes. Get a lawyer to meet us down there.'

'Okay.'

I followed Roger in. He walked slowly. Looked around like he might not ever see any of it again. Which he wouldn't. Nice home. Cool and roomy. Old furniture. Funny wallpaper. Marie sitting in the big living room all alone with the TV on. The hired man doing something in the kitchen.

Marie eyed us as we walked toward the bedroom.

I watched Roger get a shirt and pants from the closet. Lay them over one shoulder. Socks, underpants, and what-have-you from a chest of drawers.

I followed him toward the bathroom.

'Be right out,' he said.

I stepped forward quickly. Quick for an old guy. Took the revolver from him. Socks and underpants falling to the floor.

'Don't do that to Marie,' I said. Slid the .38 into my waistband. Bent over and picked up the socks and underpants. Back stiff and knees sore.

'She'll fall apart with me in jail,' said Stoltz.

'She'll live to be a hundred trying to help you. Leave the bathroom door open, Roger.'


I waited until we were in my car to cuff him to the clothes hanger in back. Went back in and explained things to Marie. Made sure the hired man would be there that night in case Marie had a hard time of it.

'Drive past the packinghouse,' said Roger.

'They tore it down thirty years ago.'

'Really.'

'They put a street in and named it Packers Circle.'

Roger pursed his lips. 'I never had the . . . courage to go back there. Drive over, anyway, would you?'

'Sure.'

I parked on Packers Circle. We looked at the stores. Nice young families buying things. Not a trace of what had been there before or what had happened. Maybe that's good. Let people get on with life.

We sat there for a long time. Didn't say one word.

# 39

Three days later I was guest of honor at the Sheriff's Department press conference. They wanted someone accountable and no longer with the department. I was perfect.

Cory Bonnett and a public defender sat stage right at a table behind the podium. District Attorney Rick Doss and I sat stage left. A big county seal on the wall behind us and a roomful of reporters and cameras and tape recorders in front.

Sheriff Walt Wallen took the mike. Tall and slow-moving, wears glasses to read. Was a senior at Garden Grove High School when we brought Bonnett across the border in the trunk of his own car.

Wallen played it like the pro he is. Said we got fooled by a cold-blooded killer. Nobody's perfect, not even us. Put a little sympathy into his voice. All that wasted time for Mr Bonnett. County had worked up a voluntary onetime

$75,000 restitution to help Mr Bonnett get back on his feet. Wouldn't go higher because the County wasn't at fault.

Bonnett himself looked healthy and dazed. Was always a big man but plenty of prison food and endless hours on the iron pile had made him heavy with muscle. Blond hair long again. A Vandyke like the young men are wearing now. A blue aloha shirt with surfboards printed on it. Arms thick and freckled and dusted with hair that shone gold in the light. Eyes small and blue. Same IQ as me, I thought. One hundred twenty-six. Wondered why that always bothered me. Bonnett was fifty-eight. Twenty-two when we took him down for a crime he didn't commit.

When the sheriff was done the DA said a few words.

Then Bonnett limped to the podium and bent the mike up to his height.

'I told you thirty-six years ago I didn't do it and nobody would believe me.'

His voice shook. A murder trial and conviction and thirty-four years in the big house, but a press conference was making him nervous.

'My lawyer wouldn't let me get up there and say so. The cops had all this evidence that some-body put in my garage in Laguna. You ruined a big part of my life. It's great to be getting out. But thanks for nothing. Fuck off and die.'

The reporters exploded with questions but Bonnett made the back door in a stiff-legged trot.

Blond hair trailing and aloha shirt rippling surfboards through the air. A deputy let him out.

When I got to the podium for questions it was a mud bath. The Stoltz story had been broken the day before but details of the frame were few. So the reporters wanted to know if I'd planted evidence. I said no. Then they went to inexperience, job stress, and a gung-ho first-year detective's mistakes. I said maybe. They kept wanting to know if I'd ever doubted Bonnett's guilt. I said no. How I'd *felt* when I learned I was wrong. I said surprised. How I *felt* about *taking away thirty-six years of a man's life*. I said all the evidence we had pointed directly at him and the jury deliberated for one hour and fifty-two minutes. They wanted to know if my family's friendship with Stoltz gave him an advantage. I said no, what gave Stoltz an advantage was fury, desperation, and luck. I gave a full law enforcement performance. I didn't apologize. I'd bleed over this the rest of my life but wasn't going to share it with anybody. Except for Katy. Maybe my brothers. You know – save the worst for the people you care about most.

After the press conference I went down to David's chapel in Laguna. He was up on a ladder washing the windows. It's a converted house on Woodland, out in the canyon. Dodge City. Where Bonnett and Leary and Fowler and the Brotherhood of Eternal Love were experiencing all their psychedelic fun back in nineteen sixty-eight. Janelle, too. The neighborhood is still funky and genuine. Surfboards leaning on fences. Unfinished oil paintings on easels in the shade. Little plastic swimming pools so the kids can beat the heat.

'Doesn't look like a safe place for an old man,' I said.

'The Lord will knock me off when He wants to.'

'Ain't that the truth.'

'Press conference go well?' David asked.

'Not bad.'

We sat in the cool of the chapel. Side by side in folding chairs.

The Canyon Chapel of God isn't anything like the Grove used to be. Just a gutted three-bedroom canyon cottage. Good windows. Kitchen still there because refreshments are important. Bathroom in back. The rest just one open room. Shiny ash floors. No pews. There are stacks of folding chairs against the rear wall, and when you come in to worship you take one. Put it back when the service is over. Nothing fancy for the preacher. A podium like at the news conference. Instead of a county seal there's a clear acrylic cross on the wall behind that lights up sky blue when you turn it on.

'Good you let Bonnett go,' said David. 'Interesting that Andy's dislike of Stoltz led him to the truth. Maybe I could build a sermon around that idea.'

'He's going to write a book about it.'

'Be a fat one,' said David.

'He's got more energy than a two-peckered goat.'

'You're in a house of God, Nick.'

'Sorry, David. How are you?'

'Fine. Fine. Thanks for asking.'

Within a year of David's coming-out confession sermon in October of sixty-eight he sold the Grove Drive-In Chapel of God. Darren Whitbrend and a consortium of investors forked over almost a million five. David sold the land, the buildings, the name, everything. Took his family around the world. They lived in Jerusalem for a year. Dar es Salaam a year. Quito, Ecuador, until Barbara had a seizure and they came back to San Francisco for surgery. Brain tumor the size of a golf ball but benign. Doing fine.

David bought a building in Newport and started a new church but it never caught on. Struggled for a few years. Most of the congregation was Laguna gays so David sold the Newport site and bought this cottage here in the canyon. Had a hundred in his congregation before you knew it. Then the eighties and over half of them died of AIDS. Fifty-three. Church helped pay for treatment and hospice and lawyers and burials. Close to bankrupted it. David doing funerals for guys he knew. Two in a week once. Called me that week and said he wasn't sure if he could preach anymore.

Things turned around and now he's up to almost two hundred. Barbara stuck with him. She travels a lot without him. They've always had an understanding though I'm not sure exactly how it works. Their kids are grown and fine. Whitbrend's doing okay for himself over at the Grove from what I hear. Haven't set foot in there since David left. Turned out Adrian Stalling was stabbed to death by a jealous lover that night at the Boom Boom Bungalow. The killer looked enough like Howard Langton you could mistake him in a lineup. The witness took two weeks to come forward because he was afraid. Trying to keep the same secret David and Howard were trying to keep.

David got the disease, too. They say it's under control but he's been losing weight the last few months. Ears look bigger. Makes me worry.

'Really,' he said. 'I'm fine.'

I watched dust specks rise in a shaft of sunlight. 'I was thinking you'd say a prayer for me.'

David leaned back and examined me. 'You've never asked for that before. Even when you were dying.'

'Ask God to forgive me for what I did to Cory Bonnett. I could have done better.'

'It's better if it comes from you.'

'I've said a thousand of them. I want one from you.'

'Well. Let's pray, Nick.'

\*     \*     \*

Lobdell died ten years ago. He was seventy-nine, retired up in Lake Arrowhead. Hung around with a bunch of old cops who had places up there. Fish the lake, tell lies. I'd go up a couple of times a year to see him and Shirley. We'd always end up talking Baja. How I puffed the cigarette and said 'tequila' for Mexican customs. Waved at the U.S. guys and didn't wake up until we hit the hospital. Kevin went off at eighteen, knocked around the country some. Became a park ranger in Yellowstone, married a Montana girl, and made Lucky a granddad.

My father went next. Heart attack in the garage while he was repairing a leaf blower. Eighty-four. After the death of Clay and the paving over of the orange groves that had needed him, Max replaced enjoyment with busy-ness. Just wanted to be useful. Never saw that the people who loved him wanted his company, not his know-how. Silenced him when the Soviet Union fell apart. He'd liked fighting the enemy much more than winning. Nobody left to tangle with. We'd had a nice hour the week before he died. Katy and Mom in the kitchen. Dad in the blue recliner and me in the white recliner with the news on low. Can't remember what we talked about but it was pleasant.

Mom made ninety and died last year. She'd finally gotten past Clay somehow. Accommodated it. Saw his name on the memorial wall in Washington and something inside her let go. Better after that, found things to do away from

Dad. Learned to swim at the Y in Santa Ana and did it almost every day. Group of ladies got tight. Volunteer work at St Joseph's. Wrote a long history of the Beckers, from Germany and Ireland and England to the pepper fields of Anaheim. Hours of research and it came out well. Bound in leather. Spent her last two years with David and Barbara. The grandkids drove her around. Pool in the backyard and they found her at the bottom of it on a hot summer day. Embolism.

Katy and I are doing just fine. Willie is a newscaster for KNX radio up in L.A. Put that strong voice of his to good use. Katherine sells newspaper advertising and raised three kids. Stevie is offense coach at Tustin High School. Took Howard's old job. I go to all the games. Sometimes I'll drive out to catch a practice, see how the team is looking. Listen to Stevie bellow at the players. Put that strong voice to good use, too, I can tell you. Our little Paul died a few hours after he was born. I wasn't sure Katy and I would make it through that. There's no sadness like it.

I still stay up late but don't drink as much. Quit that after Baja. Walk the neighborhood with Katy in the evening. Prowl the house after she's asleep. No good reason. Once a cop, always on duty. Mostly just sit and read and think. Sometimes go to the garage and pull open the Odd Box and touch the things I've collected. Still there, all of it. From the Mercury launch rock to the switchblade with the white handle to Charlie Manson's guitar pick. Andy about flipped that day in sixty-nine when he realized who the little folksinger was. Gave me the guitar pick for a birthday present. The night before they let Bonnett out I held the slat I'd ripped off the packinghouse floor. Nails still in it. Funny smell. Hard to imagine it had taken thirty-six years to cancel that case. Sometimes I touch the tiny cap they'd put on little Paul's head when he was born. Light blue. Girls got pink. Something wrong with his heart. Maybe the air freshener I used. Maybe what I did with Sharon. I don't know.

I miss being young. I miss being young and strong. Young and fast. Young and in love. Nothing like it. Old love is good, too. But you get the feeling that the world mainly just wants you out of the way.

A couple of days ago I went down to a surfing break called Rockpile in Laguna. Heard Cory Bonnett was there in the evenings. Andy told me this. One evening they surfed and Andy got Bonnet telling stories. Andy will do anything to hear a good story, even hang out with the guy who killed his brother. Lynette and one of Bonnett's girlfriends came down later and they hit a Laguna restaurant and drank late. Andy says the women were on Bonnett like you wouldn't believe. Innocent studmuffin, soulful blue eyes, his girl murdered, all that.

I sat on a flat rock at low tide and watched him ride the waves. He had a stiff leg from the gunshot. Gave him a jerky kind of motion getting onto the board. Once he was up he couldn't really bend it too well so he stood up tall. Made him look casual in the big waves. Plus he was a pretty huge guy. People got right out of his way.

I went back to Rockpile again yesterday. Had worked on my speech half the night before but still wasn't sure what to say.

Bonnett surfed until it was almost dark. Last guy out. I sat on the same rock and watched the sky go from blue to orange to indigo. Catalina black on the horizon. He finally came in. Limped south toward the hotel. Board under one arm, backpack over the other shoulder.

I caught up with him. He turned and stopped and looked down at me. Had me by four inches and sixty or eighty pounds. And thirty-six years of rage.

'I'm sorry it happened,' I said. 'I got fooled.'

'That's all?'

'We didn't plant anything. I wanted you to know that.'

'All that little prick Stoltz?'

'All.'

'And now I'm supposed to what?' asked Bonnett.

'Up to you. Is there anything I can do for you?'

'Give me back thirty-six years.'

'Would if I could.'

'Then just get out of my sight.'

I walked north to the Giggle Crack. Watched the water surge in and shoot up. Some kids out on it, barefoot on the sharp rocks, leaning forward to see in. I ran them off and heard something about 'old fart, mind your own business.'

My own business.

Farther up the beach I did something I'd always wanted to do. Shucked off everything but my boxers and wedding ring and waded in. Cold. Fell in face first and let the waves pull me out and push me in. Flipped onto my back and watched the stars glide back and forth. Imagined one of those crate labels with the pretty girl and the orange blowing in the Tustin wind. Don't know why. Everything connects. Closed my eyes for a second and remembered that blackness at the hospital. How it could have gone on forever and almost did.

Sometimes at night I'll start to fall asleep and catch myself. Jerk away from that big black forever. I want to stay on this side of it.

So I opened my eyes again and felt my hands on the sand below me, my body sliding toward the beach. Stood up and shook off and hustled over to my things. Old man in his underpants on a public beach. Not a pretty sight but you only get one life, two at the most.

Got to live a little.

# The Blue Hour

## Jefferson Parker

'A superior thriller'                               *Mail on Sunday*

He takes the women from shopping malls. They are beautiful, sophisticated, but he treats them like animals, and when he's done he leaves only his grisly signature to taunt the Orange County police – a purse full of entrails. Where are the bodies? How can these women disappear so completely? Whatever the Purse Snatcher has done to them, it surely cannot be worse than the imaginings of a shock-hardened police force . . . but they don't know the sick mind they're dealing with.

Detective Hess has given his life to the police, but now illness is looking to claim him. Merci Rayborn is at the beginning of her career and she's determined to get to the top, whatever it takes. Assigned to the case by a boss with a hidden agenda, Hess and Merci at first agree on just one thing: they want to catch the Purse Snatcher and see him fry. But as another woman disappears, and then another, they become united through their obsession with a case that will change both their lives forever.

'The crimes are sickening, the killer is a monster and the gadgets of destruction are truly bizarre. It must be another insanely imaginative thriller from Jefferson Parker'
*New York Times*

ISBN: 0 00 651369 7

# Black Water

## Jefferson Parker

A promising young cop shot, apparently by his own hand. His beautiful wife found dead in their home. It looks tragic but straightforward – murder-suicide, just one of those things.

Well, *attempted* murder-suicide. Because Archie Wildcraft isn't dead. In fact he's running around with a bullet in his head, trying to find his wife's killers. Or – if he's guilty – just running. And because of the head wound, not even he's sure what happened that night.

It's detective Merci Rayborn's job to be sure – and to catch Archie. But she can't decide if her doubts about his guilt are real, or a hang-over from screwing up another case, a mistake that lost her a lot of friends. But if Archie didn't kill his wife, who did? And why?

'An expertly plotted thriller … Parker gets better and better'                              *Literary Review*

'Insanely imaginative'                              *Washington Post*

ISBN: 0 00 712219 5